Praise for *The Wildlings*

". . . Fast-paced and exciting . . . if you like quick, enjoyable reads, then this book is for you. . . . Scott Ciencin is someone to watch out for . . . give him a chance and I'm sure he'll go far. Recommended."

—Mike Baker, *Cemetery Dance*

"Ciencin has created a different type of vampire novel. These vampires are believable in their struggle for power among themselves. . . . I love this vampire society he has created and await the conclusion in *Parliament of Blood*. . . ."

—Gary Roen, *New Orleans Times-Picayune*

Praise for *The Vampire Odyssey*

"The ultimate art of the novel is the art of storytelling, and there are too few writers today who can weave a tale the reader simply cannot put down. Scott Ciencin is such a storyteller. Read this book. You will not only be delighted, you will also be enchanted."

—Stuart M. Kaminsky, Egar-Award-Winning author of *Death of a Russian Priest*

". . . A dark stew of mystery, horror, and suspense. Darkly erotic and breathtakingly tense, the book takes the reader on a wild tour of some of the darkest, fear-filled landscapes of L.A. . . . read it, and enjoy the ride!"

—Rick Hautala, author of *Dark Silence* and *Cold Whisper*

D1052706

The non-stop thrills of *Parliament of Blood*
can also be found in Scott Ciencin's other Zebra releases . . .

On the stands now:
The Vampire Odyssey
Beneath the glitter of Beverly Hills chic, pulsed a world driven
by dark powers, wild desires, and an unrelenting hunger . . . A
vampire pack swarms over Beverly Hills and the wild nightclubs
of L.A., searching not only for prey, but also for those who carry
vampire blood in their veins—Initiates who must learn the rites
and secrets of their ancient heritage in order to be turned fully
and forever . . .

The Wildlings
On the glistening, blood-soaked streets of Los Angeles, the
world of vampires branded them *Wildlings*—vampires who killed
their own kind. For them, there was only one punishment, and
the vampire cabal, lurking beneath the glitzy world of show business, vowed to find these Wildlings and annihilate them. Their
war was just beginning . . .

PARLIAMENT OF BLOOD

SCOTT CIENCIN

ZEBRA BOOKS
KENSINGTON PUBLISHING CORP.

ZEBRA BOOKS

are published by

Kensington Publishing Corp.
475 Park Avenue South
New York, NY 10016

Copyright © 1992 by Scott Ciencin

All rights reserved. No part of this book may be repro-
duced in any form or by any means without the prior written consent of the Publisher, excepting brief quotes used in
reviews.

Zebra and the Z logo are trademarks of Kensington Publishing Corp.

If you purchased this book without a cover you should be
aware that this book is stolen property. It was reported as
"unsold and destroyed" to the Publisher and neither the
Author nor the Publisher has received any payment for this
"stripped book."

First Printing: December, 1992

Printed in the United States of America

DEDICATION

This book is dedicated with undying love and boundless admiration to Denise Resko, my collaborator, partner, and true companion in all things. Her presence and influence can be felt throughout this novel, and her generous contributions helped to heal the soul of this work, and its author.

Special thanks to Annie Olsen, Mike Murray, and Amy Boule of Lifeguard One and the University Hospital in Albuquerque, Bob Johnson, and Sally Tyree.

Come lay thy head upon my breast,
And I will kiss thee into rest.

— Byron, *The Bride of Abydos,* Canto I, Stanza 11

Every murderer is probably somebody's old friend.

— Agatha Christie

Part One

When The Masks Fall Away

reservations, and merchants from the city would of-

Prologue

Evan Thomas could not believe what was happening. It felt like a dream, a fantasy. The saleswoman was staring at him and he felt certain that she wanted him as much as he wanted her. He had come to the exclusive men's clothing store on impulse. It would have been foolish to actually buy anything here, though he could easily afford it on what he had been skimming off the top from his employer, that bastard De Santo, for the past three months.

He had worked for the tall, elegantly groomed Spaniard for five years, handling the shit work for dozens of his smaller holdings. He was the one who handled the complaints and made decisions that helped each of the smaller businesses turn a profit year after year. Evan had waited patiently for the day to come when his efforts would be recognized. Instead, he had been passed over for a promotion in favor of a man with minimal experience whom De Santo had hired off the street. That was when Evan had begun to subtly adjust the profit margins of a few of his companies, siphoning off money into separate accounts, playing a shell game with figures until the overall numbers tallied exactly correct, even though he was now the CEO of his own "private investment firm" away from the offices of De Santo and Du Prey.

He was certain no one would notice any discrepancies. He had gotten away with it and would continue to do so as long as he was smart. If he had started to live beyond the means of his salary, he might draw attention, and he didn't want to do that until he was well away from the company.

Evan was thirty-one, with wavy brown hair, a strong jawline, and sharp features. He wore gray Dockers and a white short-sleeve shirt. He was trim, and would have liked a better-defined physique, but his efforts to build one generally faltered after several weeks of intense workouts. He would miss a day, a weekend, a full week, and soon it would be a month or more since he had picked up his hand weights or gone to the gym, and soon thereafter his membership in the gym would elapse.

He was attractive, though he didn't think so, and his lack of confidence often served to push away the women he sought to attract. In his lifetime, he had only slept with two women: his first real girlfriend, in college, and Kelly, the bookstore manager he had married after graduation. Kelly had found someone else, and they had been granted a divorce on his thirty-first birthday, six months ago. It had been almost eleven months since he had made love with a woman, and a part of him truly believed that he would never be with anyone again.

Then he had walked into Giantoni's Fine Men's Fashions ten minutes before closing, and had immediately caught the attention of a beautiful saleswoman. Unless there was someone else in the back, she was working alone. There were two other customers, one she had been waiting on and another who had been there before Evan. In her sensual, throaty voice, she had told Evan that she would be with him in a moment, and had winked before turning away.

At first he thought he was imagining her interest. Things like this didn't happen to him. Hell, they didn't really happen to anyone, so far as he could tell, except to the characters created by the writers of the *Penthouse* and *Gallery* letter columns. But the last time he'd looked in her direction, he'd seen her smile invitingly. A few minutes ago, she had even brushed past him. The sweet, delicate fragrance of her perfume had stayed with him, making his heart race.

He had turned and watched her tall, shapely body. The contours of her flesh overpowered the restraints of her skirt, which seemed to be molded to her flesh. Her clothes were as much a slave to her as he would have liked to have been. She wore a pure white waist-length jacket that was completely open in front. She had bent over once, and he had strained to see as much of her body as he could. Her breasts were held in a lacy blue bra that barely reached above her nipples.

She was magnificent.

Her skirt and shoes were white, her legs incredibly long and smooth. She wore lacy blue gloves, and occasionally sucked one or two of her fingers. He'd caught her doing this and she'd grinned, allowing the finger to slide from her lips and trace the hollow between her collarbones as she smiled. The woman's dark eyes seemed to sparkle with crimson, but he was certain that was just a reflection, a trick of the light. Her soft features and full red lips were framed by a wild mane of platinum-blond hair cascading past her shoulders.

The two other customers left the store. She spent a few moments at the door with the last man, laughing and nodding, before she closed the door behind him. Evan's heart nearly exploded in his chest when he realized that he was alone in the shop with the beautiful blonde.

"Hi," she said as she touched his arm lightly. A blazing current was sent through his entire body as her lace-enshrouded fingers grazed the bare flesh of his arm.

Evan didn't have the first idea what to say to this goddess. He felt the muscles in his stomach tighten, and he knew that the erection hidden by his slacks would sag in a moment. What in the hell had he been thinking, believing that a woman like this could be at all interested in him? She was just doing her job. Being friendly.

11

Turning the customers on a little bit to make sure they'd buy something, or at least go into the changing room and have the fantasy that she would follow them in. That was all.

"I'm not exactly sure what I'm looking for. I guess I'm just looking around." He swallowed hard and shrugged. "I mean, it's late, isn't it? You're probably already closed, aren't you? Or, I mean, supposed to be closed."

"That's right," she said, running her hand up his arm. "I locked the door so no one else will wander in."

God, he was hard. He wanted this woman more than he had wanted any woman in his entire life. He shuddered. "But I really don't know what I want."

"I think you do," she said, reaching down to take his hand in hers. "You seem to appreciate nice things. *Beautiful* things. Am I wrong?"

"You're not wrong." He was trying not to look down the open front of her jacket, at her breasts, but what he saw in her eyes made him wonder if she might like that.

"There are things I can show you," she said, bringing his hand up and easing it under her jacket, on her firm, heavy breast. Her erect nipple fit into the palm of his hand.

Evan began to sweat. He couldn't believe this was happening. The woman leaned in and kissed his neck. He fondled her breast lightly and quaked as she plunged her tongue in his ear.

She withdrew her tongue, pressed her body against his, and whispered, "I can show you some very hot things. Wet things. Tight things. Would you like that?"

"Yes," he said, thinking all the while, this is impossible. This is not happening. This *cannot* be happening.

Her breast felt so perfect in his hand, and he did not resist as she eased one of her powerful legs over his, suddenly pressing her crotch against him. She angled her face toward the changing room.

"Do you know how many guys want to take me in there?" she asked, panting slightly as she ground herself

12

upon him. He caressed her firm, perfect ass with his free hand, too overcome with desire to resist.

"Probably all of them," he whispered.

"Do you know how many have ever gotten me in there?"

"No."

She kissed him hard, plunging her tongue between his lips. When he tried to match her, she sucked his tongue into her mouth, making him wonder if she was going to suck it right down her throat. He pictured her doing the same thing with his cock.

"You'll be the first," she moaned, tearing herself away from him. She walked to the doorway of the changing room and he followed her inside without hesitation. The room had dark oak walls and a long shelf jutting from the far wall. Plush lavender cushions were layered on the seat. The saleswoman sat upon the cushions and stripped off her white jacket. Evan knelt before her and he kissed her greedily. He took her breasts into his hands, alternately sucking each nipple through the fabric of her bra as she moaned and ran her fingers through his hair. His hands went down to the edge of her skirt and she raised her hips to allow him to shove it back. Her blue lace panties matched her gloves. He ran his hand over the surface of the lace and was stunned when he felt the hot, wet lips of her sex. The panties had a slit in the front.

"You were looking for something, weren't you?" he asked.

"I want to get fucked."

Her hand closed over his crotch and he cried, "Oh, *Jesus!*"

"You like that?"

"Yes." He shuddered as she unzipped his pants and took out his throbbing member. His gaze was fixed upon her hands as she worked the flesh of his cock expertly, moving it up and down in her gloved hand. "Don't you want it in your mouth?"

"Eventually," she said, stroking him harder and

faster. "When you're ready to come. You're not ready to come yet, are you?"

"No."

"Anything you want to do first?"

"I want to fuck you."

"Good," she said, smiling. "Then we can both get what we want."

She eased back on the small shelf and he knelt before her, thankful that the shelf was at just the right height. He rubbed himself over the lips of her sex, then poised himself at the entrance, prepared to go in slowly, a little bit at a time, giving her a chance to expand around him, to get used to accommodating his length. Without warning, she hooked her ankles around the small of his back and drove him forward. She was so wet that he slid all the way into her on the first stroke. Her eyes shot open wide and she gasped. He knew that he should have been thinking about protection—he didn't even know this girl's name, he had only seen her for the first time a few minutes ago and suddenly he was making love to her—but he couldn't bring himself to care. All that mattered to him were the sensations, the sheer excitement of having this woman, this stranger. The feel of her open-slit lace panties against his skin was amazing.

He had entered her and had been driven up as far as he could go, and had remained there, reveling in the hot wet channel which gripped him harder than he had ever been gripped before.

"Do it," she said. "Come on. I need it. Please."

"Please what?"

"You know."

"Say it."

She bit her lip. "Please, fuck me."

"Yes," he said, easing himself back until he was almost outside of her, then slamming himself into her depths. She brought her ankles back around him and offered encouragement, helping to drive him in harder and deeper. He gripped her hips and dragged her onto him, slamming into her with lightning-fast motions as she bucked against him, moaning and screaming for him to fuck her and never stop.

When he felt the sensations building within him and knew that he would not be able to forestall his orgasm, he felt an instant of regret. He had wanted to make love to her in a variety of positions. Perhaps she would let him cover her sex with his mouth after he had come, bringing her to the brink while he had a chance to recover, get hard again, and fuck her some more.

"What's your name?" he asked, recalling her earlier promise to take him in her mouth when he was ready to explode. He wanted to tell her to do that, but he wanted to call her by name when he did.

She threw her head back, grinding the top of her skull against the wall as she wailed, "God, oh, Christ, don't stop, keep going, I'm going to come."

"What's your name?" he repeated, smiling broadly at the power he had over this woman. She said something, but it was in a hard, guttural voice, a sharp gasp of sound that might have been an answer to his question, or simply another cry of ecstasy. Then he saw her long hair moving in a different direction than her face, and couldn't quite comprehend what he was seeing.

"What?" he asked dreamily, the sensations reaching their apex. There was no way he could pull out of her now. It panicked him for an instant; then his desire overcame his reason once more. But her hair, why was her hair like that, what was he seeing?

Suddenly she unleashed a pure, animal cry of pleasure, and he not only heard it with his ears, it seemed to drive itself directly in his mind, echoing there as she gripped his arm with her left hand and hauled herself up. Thank God, he thought. He wanted to see her face as she came.

Her hair remained behind. "What?" he asked again, suddenly staring at the spiky platinum mass of sweat-drenched hair that had sprung from under the wig she had worn. But that was the least disturbing part of what he had seen. Her eyes—her dark, beautiful, hypnotic

15

eyes — were bathed in crimson. The woman's mouth was open wide in a twisted, perverse smile, no longer revealing the perfectly shaped white teeth he had seen only instants earlier. Her mouth was filled with razor-sharp canines, and he had a brief glimpse of her hands from the periphery of his vision. The nails had burst from the tips of the lacy gloves and had extended into bone-white talons.

"What — " he began again, the only word that would come to his mind. Then he felt a rush of air and registered something impossible. The room was spinning in a full three-sixty and he could no longer feel anything below his neck. He saw the woman's monstrous face recede, caught sight of the floor, the light in the ceiling, then his own headless body with blood spouting in a torrent, reaching up to the ceiling as the woman leaned forward.

He wanted to say "what" one more time, and might have even moved his lips. He couldn't be sure. After that, Evan Thomas saw and felt nothing at all.

The vampire had felt her victim come inside her the moment she had torn his head from his shoulders. The hot, wet spray had been exactly what she had needed to push her over the brink, and she opened her mouth to collect the gouts of blood that were erupting from his savaged neck. A seething orgasm tore through her as she gripped the headless corpse with her legs, keeping the still-hard cock in her as she fed and came.

When the sensations became too much for her, she released the corpse of her victim and lay back, gasping and panting, her face and hair covered in blood. Her dress was soaked through. When she felt that she could move again, her legs no longer completely watery, she stripped off her clothes and reached down to cover her hands with his blood, smearing it over her breasts. The final sensual blast of sensations moved through her. The vampire knelt before the severed head and licked at its lips for a moment.

16

"Too bad you had to die, Evan," she said, brushing his wavy hair into place. It had fallen into his eyes. "You really were a pretty good fuck. We could have had some fun."

She got up and stripped off her clothes, then pulled a pair of slippers and a towel from the underside of the bench, where she had taped them earlier, and cleaned herself off. When she was no longer running the risk of dripping blood on the carpet outside the dressing room, she put on the slippers and went to the back, where she changed into black leather boots, pants, and a jacket, which she zipped up only part of the way. She returned to the changing room with a body bag, loaded Evan's corpse into it, stuffing his head at the wrong end, and zipped it up before she dragged it out of the changing room, to the back. She brought separate large black plastic trash bags into the changing room for the lavender cushions and collected them, sealing the bags tight. The last thing she wanted was for them to leak outside of this room. Then she tore the rug from the floor, rolled it up, and bagged it with the wig and the clothes she had been wearing. Once these items were in the back, she returned to the changing room with a mop, towels, and a pail. The vampire sighed as she looked at how much blood had struck the ceiling and light fixture.

She *hated* this domestic shit, but she had chosen to be extravagant and make the mess, so there was no point in complaining. Besides, this killing was an audition, a chance to demonstrate her skills. One skill she had never before attempted to master was the ability to follow orders. That would have to change if she was to get anywhere in this world. She had been on her own for two years, ever since her family had been killed. The vampire had convinced herself that she was going to leave the pack anyway, that their deaths had only served to free her to follow whatever bliss entered her mind, to be her own master. But she had become lonely after a time, and needed to feel like a part of something once

17

more. Getting into another pack would have been difficult, and even if she had achieved it, she would have been no better off than she had been before, the junior member of the group, the last one in, the first one out. If she was going to make a change, she wanted it to really matter.

She had been ordered to kill this man as a test, but the man who had given her the order had added a surprising stipulation:

"I want you to do something *pleasant* for him first. His thieving was really of little consequence, and I'd allow him to live if I were the only one who knew about it. But I have a board of directors and a partner who would never let me live it down. It would be unwise for me to let it get around that you can steal from me and not pay for it."

"Something pleasant for him," she had repeated dully, as if she had been unable to understand the concept of pleasantries, or why it pertained to this murder. It also wasn't her place to ask. Her curiosity, however, must have been plainly visible, because he'd offered an explanation:

"I would have advanced him, but he's one of *them,* and he's quite dependable in his position. I like him. He's what you might call 'a good kid.' But this is business and it must be done. So do something pleasant for him before you fulfill the contract. You'll have my gratitude . . ."

The vampire had done what had been asked of her. She had followed Evan Thomas, spent time in his mind, and culled a particular fantasy he had read about in a dirty magazine and particularly loved. Then she had made him forget about his erotic daydream so that it would seem fresh and new when he actually experienced it. She had placed the compulsion in his head to come to the clothing shop, and spent a day making preparations.

A half hour later, after she had wiped the room clean, placed a new patch of matching carpet in the dressing

18

room, secured it in place with the nail gun she had stolen, and placed new cushions on the wooden shelf, the vampire went to the woman whose shift she had taken over. The woman sat in a corner of a back room, reading a paperback romance.

"You'd be amazed at the sales I got for you, sweetie," the vampire said, projecting into the woman's mind the dull events of the last hour before the prey arrived. The creature had used her powers to rack up several sales, and to feed off the immense desire she provoked in the clientele.

The saleswoman nodded, barely looking up. The vampire had programmed her well. The human would go home and remember nothing more than a typical evening on the job. The vampire would have liked to have made the woman handle the cleanup, but the events might have been traumatic enough to shatter the walls that had been erected in her mind. No matter, it was done. The only true pain in the ass tonight had been wearing the wig. She hadn't felt like expending the effort in projecting a false appearance when there was so much succulent desire and heavenly fear to be used. Besides, it wouldn't have worked. There were too many mirrors in the store. She laughed. So many of the strutting macho peacocks she encountered were nothing more than little boys who were terrified of women and needed to dominate them to feel secure with themselves.

It was funny. The vampire had almost come to understand why her employer had asked her to be especially sweet to this one. He was a far superior lover — and probably a better man — than most of the steroid-sucking, muscle-rippling hair fags that had managed to get their own weekly television shows in this town. She'd actually liked him.

That touch of fondness didn't stop her from loading his remains and the other evidence into the trunk of her stolen black Toyota, which had been parked behind the store.

The vampire drove to an abandoned construction site

where she moved freely among the homeless, who sensed that she should be left alone. She burned the rugs, the cushions, and the wig. Driving on to the rendezvous, the vampire stopped a block before the creek where she was meant to deposit the body.

"Shit, shit, shit!" she hissed, realizing that she had forgotten something. The vampire pulled off the road, anxiously cutting glances ahead to see if her employer was already there, waiting. It was unlikely. She was early. Nevertheless, her hands trembled slightly as she opened the trunk and unzipped the body bag. This meant so fucking much to her and here she was right on the edge of screwing it all up. She reached in, found Evan's severed head, and pulled the pair of handcuffs from her jacket pocket. The vampire raised one of the corpse's wrists and closed the first bracelet around it. Then she transformed her hand into a talon and drove two holes through the flesh of the head, so that she could fit the handcuff through. A Wildling had started to leave its kills in this condition in San Diego over a year ago, and since then, it had become the prescribed method among their kind of leaving a message after an execution:

Fuck with me, this is what you get.

The vampire stuffed the body into the bag once more, wiped the sweat from her brow, and closed the trunk.

"Forget something?" a voice asked behind her.

The vampire nearly cried out as she spun around to face the beautiful sight of Christian De Santo, her employer. He was wearing an expensive Armani original, a stylish charcoal suit with a red power tie. His shiny black hair was slicked back and gathered in a ponytail, and his teal eyes gleamed catlike in the darkness. De Santo was unbearably handsome, with thick eyebrows, elegantly sculpted cheekbones, a strong nose, square jaw, and lips that were full and moist. His body was perfectly defined, meaty, but not grotesquely so. She had seen pictures of him when he had posed for *Playgirl,* and had wondered what kind of a lover he would be. That had been one of her many reasons for seeking him out.

But only one.

"Everything went well?" De Santo asked.

"Yes. Perfectly."

He lowered his gaze and said, "Good." She was caught unprepared as his hand lunged out and grabbed the back of her head. De Santo dragged her up from her feet, and lashed out with his own power, reaching deeply into her mind. The vampire immediately dropped her walls of resistance, well aware that they would do little good against someone of De Santo's age and abilities. Though he looked thirty, she knew he was at least seven hundred years old. He might have even crossed a millennium, according to her sources.

De Santo probed her memories quickly and efficiently, then released his hold on her body and her mind.

"Very good," he said amiably.

The vampire relaxed. If it had been anyone else, she would have fought, perhaps to her own death, to keep herself from being violated in the manner De Santo had just used. He had warned, however, that he would want first-hand confirmation. She simply hadn't expected him to be so fast. He'd moved like a slick, black cat, ruthless and dangerous. In his position, she might have done the same. Had he asked permission, or announced his intentions, she might have erected false memories to hide her failings. This way, he had seen everything.

The vampire wondered if De Santo had sensed how aroused she had become. He could have her if that interested him, of course. But that didn't seem to be the case.

"You want to work for me," he said in a slightly tired voice.

"I want to learn from you. I want to help you. You're an important man. You used to be a member of the Parliament."

21

"That's your goal, is it?"

"The blood of the Ancients," she said. "Yeah. I want it."

"You know there are others of our kind who think it should be theirs for the taking. They shouldn't have to earn it. There are thousands of them. Why come to me, instead of them?"

"Because the underground can't possibly win. They're idiots. The blood of the Ancients is a gift, freely given. Even if they were to kill the Three, it wouldn't mean they would—"

"All right," he said, turning from her dismissively. "I've heard too much of this lately."

The vampire walked with De Santo for a moment, waiting for him to speak.

"Why did you choose me?" he asked. I'm a *former* member of the Parliament. I had good reason to leave."

"You can't leave," the vampire said. "Not when the blood of the Ancients is inside you. You can walk in the light. You can do anything. The Parliament might let you walk away, but they never let you leave. It's like that old song by the Eagles. You're in for life. You're connected."

"How many of them did you try to approach?"

The vampire flinched. She hesitated, then said, "Only one."

"Which one?"

"Marchester. The one they call Dark Angel."

"Why him?"

The vampire shrugged. She ran her hand through her spiky platinum-blond hair and said, "I guess I liked the name."

"He rebuked you? Wanted no part of you?"

"That's right."

"It's amazing you got to him directly."

"I got to you, didn't I?" she asked in a seductive voice, unzipping the front of her jacket to show her breasts. He glanced at her, frowned, and looked away. She zipped herself back up and felt like an idiot.

22

"To put it in your terms, if all you want is to get *fucked,* then keep going the way you're going. You're going to get *fucked,* but not the way you mean."

The words were difficult, but she spoke them anyway: "I apologize."

They approached the bridge leading over the small creek and De Santo placed both of his hands on the rail. "Do you understand how I conduct my interviews?"

She recalled his invasion of her thoughts a few moments ago. "I think so. Yes."

"If you try to resist me, if you hold anything back, I will tear you to pieces. Is that understood?"

"Yes," she said, slightly confused. A moment ago he'd seized her thoughts. Now he was asking permission.

His reply was to lash out with his mind, slipping inside her without preamble. The action was so savage, his power so furious and overwhelming, that the vampire blacked out under the assault.

When she woke, the air was cooler, and the first streaks of sunlight were piercing the horizon. She was still standing next to De Santo. Neither had moved. She looked at the light and started to panic.

"Turn and walk slowly to my car," De Santo said. "You've won the position."

"The light . . ."

"My driver understands what to do. The glass is black. It will hold out the light."

"The body. Evan."

"It will be taken care of. Go."

The vampire swallowed hard, wondering where in the hell De Santo had parked. He pointed toward the other edge of the bridge. This was another test. He was always calm. Panic seemed to disgust him. She had to show that she was worthy of the honor he was bestowing upon her.

With a grin, the vampire turned and said, "Why?"

"Pardon?" De Santo did not look up.

"Why are you giving me this position?"

23

De Santo shook his head. "You've made certain associations that might prove useful."

"To whom? To you?"

"To both of us, perhaps."

The vampire did not move. He finally looked up at her, glanced back to the sunlight that would soon be sweeping over the horizon, and gave her a fleeting smile. "You're making a new start. Do you prefer to go back to your formal name, Angelique Marie Olander? Or do you wish to go by the other name?"

"You've been in my thoughts."

"Yes."

"You know everything that's happened to me. Everything that's made me into what's standing in front of you today. Do you really need to ask that question?"

De Santo shrugged elegantly. "It was a simple question. Answer it."

"Angel," the vampire said as she felt the light begin to burn her flesh. She turned and walked slowly away from Christian De Santo, determined to walk at this steady pace until she reached the car waiting at the other side of the bridge.

"Call me Angel."

his veins and his frightened subconscious was fighting

Chapter One

*She had promised to never again perform miracles.
The promise had been an easy one to make, and she
had understood her mother's reasons for making her
commit to this sacrifice: Miracles were dangerous;
they drew attention. For six months she had honored
that promise, using her wild talents only in subtle
ways.*

Then she encountered the shattered boy.

Danielle Walthers gazed at the horrifying sights
laid out before her, and suddenly desired nothing
more than to wake from the nightmare that had engulfed her life for the past three years. Surrounding
her was the wreckage of a Desert Way airliner that
had gone down south of Albuquerque and north of
the Mescalero Apache reservation. She stood near a
chopper whose lightning-quick blades were only now
beginning to slow and become visible. The words
"Lifeguard One" were painted on the craft. The helicopter was red and white with turquoise trim.

She was one half of the air ambulance's medical
crew. Her partner, Max Collins, was a large man with
thinning blond hair, a cherubic grin, sparking blue
eyes, and a compassionate manner. He looked like a
woodsman or a camp counselor, and had in fact
worked in both capacities while putting himself
through college. Dani was the flight nurse, Max the
flight paramedic. They shared their duties equally.

They had been dispatched from the University of New Mexico trauma center in Albuquerque, the only facility in the state with airlift capabilities. The hospital also had a fixed-wing, but that would do them little good, under the circumstances. The land before her was rolling volcanic rock and all but a few areas were inaccessible to terrain vehicles. A fixed-wing would find it impossible to land here.

From the periphery of her vision, she could see pine trees, bushes, cactus, and patches of shrub brush that were on fire. The steaming black surface beneath her feet reflected the blazing desert heat. Given time, the rubber soles of her shoes would melt on the rocks; the heat could easily wear out a pair of boots in a one-day hike. Her feet were already sore and she was covered in sweat.

Ahead, upon the smoldering ground, lay the remains of the aircraft. Dani recalled the sulfurous black cloud that had been visible from a distance as their pilot had flown them to the crash site. She had expected to find no survivors, and had been shocked as they had closed in on the downed airplane and saw victims crawling from the wreckage.

They had known the latitude and longitude of the plane's resting place from the pilot's final transmissions. The pilot and copilot would be dead, of course. Judging from the twisted wreckage, those closest to the nose of the aircraft would have been crushed to death, their bodies having suffered the most horribly. Dani had flown on a similar craft and knew the plane's setup: A single seat was located on either side of the center aisle. The pilot's and copilot's chairs were clearly visible to the passengers. About twenty people would be on board during a good flight. Dani judged that about half that number were dead, the other half in desperate need of help.

She tried to picture the crash. The fuel was kept in the wings of the aircraft, and they had apparently broken off and exploded on impact, sending the body of the plane forward like a bullet. If the ground had been soft, the craft might have burrowed into the earth and disintegrated. Instead, it had skittered over the hard black rock like a stone skipping over a still pond until it had come to a stop.

"Elizabeth," a voice said behind her. "Are you all right?"

Dani turned at the mention of her assumed name and saw the grim face of Freddy Aimes, their carrot-topped, acne-ridden twenty-four-year-old pilot. Freddy had a firm but wiry build and only two expressions that Dani had ever seen: blithe indifference or grave seriousness.

"Elizabeth?" he repeated.

Dani's right hand absently went to her I.D. tag. It bore the name and photograph of a young Native American who had died far from the reservation. People believed Dani to be the woman in the photograph. When they looked at her, it was not a statuesque brunette with golden eyes and fiery red lips they saw, it was a shorter woman with black hair, gray eyes, and swarthy skin. Her inhuman power ensured this. The deception had been necessitated by her actions in California before she had fled: To protect her mother and the child Samantha Walthers was carrying, Dani had killed others of her monstrous race, and was now in hiding from their avengers.

"I'm fine," Dani said, but that had been a lie. She could not look at the carnage before her without feeling the old hungers and desires rise up within her. The fear and agony of the survivors snaked into her mind and elicited a near-sexual longing within her.

"Look at the wings back there," Freddy said, pointing at the flaming, detached objects. "They used JP-4 fuel. Someone told me once you could put a cigarette out in JP-4. Course, I asked if he had done it and he said no. The point is, they must have hit goddamn hard for the wings to break off and go up like that. Maybe there was a vapor, or they were on fire. I didn't hear how this happened."

"No, me neither," Dani said, turning away from the young pilot. The chopper was leased from Rocky Mountain Helicopter and Freddy was an employee of that company. He was an extra pair of hands with a good and willing heart, but he was not a trained medical technician and could not treat trauma victims. That left Dani and Max with the sole responsibility of tending to the survivors of the crash.

She wondered how she could go near the wounded when the need inside her refused to be suppressed. The bloodhunger had begun as a gnawing deep in her soul, the sensation of a thousand tiny sets of teeth ripping apart the defensive walls she had painstakingly erected. Her body tingled and her every nerve was alive. She fought the inner seduction, the knowledge that pleasure so far beyond human sensation could be hers if she stopped fighting what was inside her and let it go. The desire sweeping through her was something she had fought many times in the past. It was a part of her and would remain as such until she died. For almost a year her need had been under control. She knew that in a way she had been teasing it, challenging it to overtake her by placing herself in situations exactly like this one, but she had always remained its master.

What was different this time? she wondered. Not that it mattered. She would triumph against it now, just as she had before. Driving the demons down was always difficult, and it required her to focus her thoughts elsewhere, even though Freddy was waiting for her and Max had already begun to assist the wounded. She knew there was a job to be done, lives to be saved, and her hesitation could prove deadly, but she had to be in full control of herself before she went near those who had been hurt.

Fingering the fake I.D. clipped to her breast pocket, Dani thought of Elizabeth Altsoba, the woman in the photograph. The young woman had

28

been with her boyfriend, who was drunk, and they had driven off the road and crashed into the base of a hard, craggy hillside. Dani and her adopted mother had seen smoke from the road and had gone to investigate. Dani had been worried to have her pregnant mother go along, but Samantha Walthers would not be dissuaded.

The boyfriend was dead, and the young woman had lived long enough for Dani to learn her secrets before she died. The steering column of the old Ford had gutted her, and all Dani could do for her was take her from her place of agony and make her death painless, merciful. On a primal level, Elizabeth had understood that Dani had been born with powers that could be used either to heal or destroy. Dani had been one of the few members of her race to choose the ways of the healer, but her life had been destroyed and she could not follow her dream of one day becoming a physician. Elizabeth had gone through years of training to become a R.N., and she had coupled her desire to help others with her love of flight — something else she shared with Dani.

Elizabeth allowed Dani to take all the knowledge she had spent her adult life accumulating. After Elizabeth had died, Dani had assumed the woman's life. Taking the woman's identity had been easy. Securing proper medical attention for her mother during her delivery had been a difficult task, even with her godlike abilities, but Dani had ultimately succeeded.

For a long time, she had been unafraid of using her powers; her control over her inhuman blood and the ravenous need that would never fully leave her had been under control. But now, as she felt the succulent fear and desire for release that flooded from the dozens of survivors of the plane crash, and smelled the hot, pumping blood of the wounded, Dani struggled to retain that control.

Forcing herself into action, Dani walked forward into hell. The pilot followed, carrying a set of supplies identical to those Max had grabbed as he hurried from the chopper. They immediately encountered the body of a naked man. He had been thrown from his clothes. Dani knew that he would be dead, but she checked for a pulse anyway. Pulling herself away from the dead man, Dani went to the crumpled body of the airplane. It had been ripped open where the wings had been, and those openings had widened considerably. Clothing and personal belongings covered the ground. The luggage compartments beneath the passengers' feet had opened and suitcases had exploded along the final path of the plane. Parts of chairs and lengths of ruptured metal were strewn everywhere.

A few people were on their feet, wandering among their now-communal belongings, ignoring Max's pleas for them to remain still. One of them, a woman, tripped on a pile of debris and cried out as she hit the red-hot ground. The fallen woman cried out that there was a snake near her and Freddy ran to help. He called out that everything was fine a moment later. They all knew that the area was a rattlesnake haven. Dani would not have been surprised to find several of the creatures among the wreckage, but fortunately, they had not yet arrived.

Max called to Dani as she approached. "It looks like all cat-twos and cat-threes."

She nodded. Their first duty had been to create a triage, separating those who had been hurt according to their injuries. Category-three trauma victims were the walking wounded, those who were hurt but could be seen in the emergency room. The category-two cases were more seriously injured, but not critically; they could wait a few hours. It was the category-one situations that required immediate attention.

The interior of the plane was strewn with items that had burst from the overhead luggage racks. Files strewn from ripped-open briefcases cluttered the walkways. A handful of shattered cameras with rolls of exposed film lay on the torn-open rubber and metal floor. Some people had remained in their chairs, unwilling or unable to move.

Dani waded through the victims, trying not to look at their eyes. She didn't want to hear their cries of pain or feel the emotions that rushed from them in pounding waves. Several spit angry words in her face, as each person wanted her full attention, and that was something she could not give. Dani had learned that the victims who had enough strength and will to scream and curse were generally the ones who were least in need of attention. The quiet ones were another matter. They could be in shock, or in the final stages of death.

Dani withdrew her microcasette and began by checking the ABCs, ensuring that each person had an open airway and was breathing properly. Next she checked for shock, and made each person recite their names.

The flight crew's primary on-scene duties were to assess the situation, initiate treatment, and communicate with the hospital. The University of New Mexico medical center hosted several hospitals and was a level-one trauma center. They were in the process of assuming a make-ready position to put their full disaster plan into play when Lifeguard One had departed.

"Broken femur, not a compound," Dani recited into the recorder as she examined a woman in her forties who constantly complained and refused to stay still. She catalogued the woman's other injuries, cautioned her to lay quietly, then moved on to another victim.

"I'm gonna sue!" the woman shouted. "I'm gonna sue every last one of you worthless shits! Do you know who I am? Do you have any fucking idea who I am!?"

Deep inside, Dani's bloodneed throbbed and she felt the sudden urge to go back and rip the woman's

31

throat out. She blotted out the woman's screams and recited the visible injuries of a man in his late sixties. He seemed alert and appreciative, and he did not interrupt her.

Good, Dani. Concentrate on the facts. Detach out. Maybe we can get through this.

She worked closely with Max. Freddy assisted. Those with burn injuries were given IV fluid, their wounds cleaned, tended, and packed. Several people had multiple lacerations, which was not surprising considering the amount of Plexiglas and metal flying all over during the crash. Their heads, arms, and backs had been cut up badly.

Under normal circumstances, Dani would have used her abilities to release endorphins inside the victims, helping to anesthetize them, or she might have altered their perceptions to make them unable to register their pain. She could not understand why her hunger had chosen this time to resurface so powerfully; she had seen worse suffering in her brief career with the hospital, and had always been able to force her inhuman desires under control.

Venturing deeper into the body of the airplane, they found two people with fractured spines. These victims had been curious to see what was going on just before impact and had not maintained the crash positions. A man they might have mistaken for dead lay with tears welling in his eyes. He was paralyzed, the victim of a broken neck.

Dani and Max worked to stabilize him. Freddy was with them, offering reassurance to the man as the medical team performed their duties. Suddenly, Dani felt a lancing pain in her skull that was so intense it made her cry out and withdraw from the wounded man. She shuddered as the pain came again and Freddy grabbed her arm.

"Elizabeth, what is it?" Freddy asked. Max looked up with concern.

"Nothing, I . . ." Dani stopped, the pain returning

with enough force to drive her to her knees. She heard Freddy draw a sharp breath, and wondered if the illusion she was projecting had momentarily faltered.

"Freddy, get her out of here," Max said gently. "We're almost done with Mr. Warren. I can finish alone."

"No!" Dani cried, resisting Freddy's attempts to move her. She turned and rose on watery legs, taking a few steps closer to the ruined front end of the airplane. The pain grew more intense, but Dani was prepared for it now and she was able to create buffers in her mind to force the sensations away. Beneath the agony assailing her had been a steady torrent of incredible fear. For a single, shameful moment, she had been unable to resist the urge to consume the powerful wave of emotions that had washed over her. The pleasure she received forced away the pain she had sensed.

But whose pain had it been? she wondered. It wasn't her own. It was coming to her from outside. She had been close to almost all of the survivors and had not suffered such a reaction. Walking to the twisted metal shapes which had been ground into a blood-streaked wall looming ahead, Dani placed her hand on what had once been a headrest and gasped as the waves of fear and agony crashed over her again.

"What in the hell!?" whispered Max behind her. She knew that this time the visage of Elizabeth had faltered and she lowered her head, keeping her back turned to her co-workers. It was dark enough within the hull of the plane for them to doubt what they were seeing and wonder if the heat was getting to them. From their vantage points directly behind her, only her hair would have changed, flickering between straight and wavy.

The sensations were coming from somewhere close. Dani looked at the wreckage before her and wondered if it was possible that someone was alive in there;

trapped, but alive. It seemed like the only plausible explanation. Dani reached out with her power, which she focused into a bright, silver thread, and recoiled the instant she made contact with the victim trapped in the crushed forward section of the plane.

"Jesus," she whispered, shaking as she attempted to force away the delirious surge of panic which had rushed into her at the brief touch of her power to the victim's pain-wracked mind. The fear she had encountered was the most pure — perhaps the most potent — she had ever tasted. No wonder her power was attempting to spiral out of control.

Dani wasn't sure what to do. She knew from her fleeting contact with the victim that it was a boy, a young teenager whose first name was Bobby. The mental picture she received of him was blurred by his pain. She considered reaching across the physical distance separating them with her power and plunging the boy into unconsciousness. If Dani could make him unable to register his pain and fear, she wouldn't have to worry about falling victim to her hunger, which had been reawakened by the child's pain. But there could be serious repercussions if he was already in shock. His perception of the pain might have been the only thing that was keeping him going, giving him the will to live. If Dani took that away, he might not survive long enough for her to get to him.

"Elizabeth!" Max said behind her. "What are you doing? Are you all right?"

Dani closed her eyes and forced herself to concentrate on the boy who needed her.

"If you're not all right, then get out of here!"

"I can't do that," she said, feeling her power well up inside her. She knew that she would have to use her wild talent to convince Freddy and Max to help her. Fearfully reaching out with her power, she once again made contact with the agony-ridden teenager, but this time she acted as a conductor, sending his pain through her own fevered brain to reach the consciousnesses of the men behind her. Freddy and Max gasped in unison. Dani knew that they would register the cries of anguish she had heard in her mind as physical screams.

"Shit," Freddy said. "Someone's alive in all that." Beside him, Max blanched. "How in the hell are we going to get to him?"

Dani understood the problem. They had no heavy extraction equipment, no jaws of life. If the rescue team had been able to reach the crash site, they would have been prepared for this. The tools the medical crew had with them included scissors that could cut metal, and Max dispatched Freddy to get them from the chopper. What they really needed was a hydraulic spreader that would puncture the skin of the twisted metal wall and create a pathway in much the same manner as a can opener.

Her strength was much greater than that of a human. The only choice was to reveal herself, using her power to doctor the perceptions and memories of her partner and the pilot. Unfortunately, that would have to wait until after Bobby had been treated. The boy's constant stream of fear would make it difficult to use her psychic talents with any degree of accuracy, or any true finesse.

Dani brushed past Max, who had moved behind her, and gripped one end of a curved metal support beam. The beam had been sticking out of the gap made by the torn-off wing. Before her partner could say anything, Dani tore it loose. The effort made her shoulders ache. In her hands lay what appeared to be a two-by-four made of steel. She aimed it high at the wall before her and drove it forward like a battering ram. The muscles in her arms and chest burned. Her jaws had slammed together with enough force that Dani wouldn't have been surprised if several of her teeth ended up chipped or broken.

"Elizabeth," Max whispered, unable to believe what he was witnessing. Dani hoped he would write it off

to one of those miraculous explosions of strength humans sometimes displayed under stress. She was an Initiate, the offspring of a human mother and an Immortal, as those of her race chose to call themselves.

There was another name for them:

Vampires.

Dani drove the steel support forward three more times before the steadily deepening dent she had been making imploded and allowed the metal to be driven through. Dani had a horrible image of the boy's head being wedged close to the point she had chosen as her entry point, but she quickly chased it away. She had burst through fairly high, at eye level, and his screams had not abated.

From the periphery of her vision, Dani saw Max staring at her in shock. The anguished cries of the trapped boy had not abated, and his fear had fully awakened the demon in Dani's blood. She had unleashed her hunger to give her the animal strength necessary to reach the boy. All that remained of Danielle Walthers was focused on the imminent task of harnessing the demon once the boy had been reached.

The illusion of "Elizabeth" had fallen away and Max had seen it go. He was staring at her blazing, golden eyes, his own fear and the screams of the crash victims who had also seen Dani change providing a tempting alternative to the prey that was so difficult to reach. But she knew she had to get to the boy. His fear had drawn the demon out; only his fear and perhaps his blood would satisfy them.

Yanking the beam out of the opening she had created, Dani allowed the metal to fall, then began to tear at the opening with her hands. Gripping the metal tightly, Dani pulled with all her strength. She felt the opening give. The metal screamed in protest as she dragged it forward, tearing it until she had created a narrow passage. She was breathing hard, sweat matting her hair to her face. Any exertion was dangerous in the sweltering desert heat, particularly in the confined space of the wrecked airplane, but Dani did not stop. Taking another section of the thick metal in her hands, Dani brought the wall down, creating two large drooping slabs of metal that looked like the petals of a twisted steel rose.

The agony she had felt from the boy rushed at her like a blast from a furnace. Dani faltered and Max steadied her. His hands were trembling and he clearly did not comprehend what was happening, but he was willing to help. For that, the part of her that was still Dani felt intense gratitude. She did not have the strength to place him under a compulsion.

"I've got to get in there," she whispered hungrily.

Silently, Max helped to lift her up to the opening. Dani felt the jagged edges and wished she had been thinking a little more clearly. It would have been less dangerous to go through the opening if the metal had been forced inward and away from her. She gripped the edges of the passageway and hauled herself through with the aid of her partner. The jagged metal tore several rivulets in her stomach, but she ignored the flaring pain and crawled into the labyrinthian wreckage. Max handed her a bag filled with supplies and she took it without thinking. There were spaces between the debris, corridors she could move through for a few feet before she had to break through yet another pile of metal.

The corpses she encountered in the forward section were horrifying. She found two people who had assumed the crash positions and had their heads driven against the seats before them with such impact that their skulls had popped open like eggs; blood and brains were everywhere. Others had been decapitated. The slick floor was a dark crimson. One man had literally disintegrated. The area was littered with the scattered, bloody fragments of human beings.

Deep inside the wreckage, she found the shattered boy. A hollow had been formed by the falling metal, a tiny space for the curled-up teenager to fit inside.

Supports had fallen into place, holding back the crushing walls of debris. The boy appeared to be about sixteen, with chestnut-brown hair matted to his bloody forehead. His features were Spanish. A long, thin support beam had been driven through his side, pinning him in place. Both of his legs and his right arm were broken, manipulated by the crash into strange, unnatural positions.

Dani felt the demon within her shudder with delight. Left on its own, her monstrous need would have caused her to descend upon the boy, slowly torturing him to death, savoring his moans and cries. Dani attempted to fight down her lust for the child's pain, focusing her will on the very reasons she had become a healer. She recalled the first lives she had saved with her powers, and the hundreds which had followed. The boy's agony thundered and pulsed within her, but she refused it, using every bit of her strength to force away her hungers. She felt her mind clearing, and bent down to examine the child more closely.

His eyes flashed open.

Forcing herself to smile, Dani said, "Don't be scared, you're going to be . . ."

Dani was unable to finish. Something clawed at the veil of her consciousness. It was alive, whatever it was, a dark, repellent thing that wanted to settle into her mind. Focusing her power into a sharp, bright silver thread that was as lean and deadly as a whip, Dani lashed out, repelling the invader. She felt it retreat and stared into the face of the boy.

"Jesus," she whispered as understanding swept over her.

He was an Initiate, another of her kind.

Chapter Two

Isleta. New Mexico.

The burned woman was making her weekly delivery.

Thomas Begay, a gentle elderly man with soft blue eyes and a paunch, looked forward to her visits. He ran the Trading Post, the only general store that did business with the burned woman, and was known as the hardest negotiator living on the pueblo. His reputation had suffered because of the woman, whom he paid exorbitant amounts for her rich, delicious bread.

His wife had told him that the bread was not that special; in fact, it was not even as good as many of the loaves baked by other women on the res. That did not stop him from buying every loaf the burned woman made, and gorging himself on it as if it were a rare delicacy. He didn't care that only the tourists bought her bread, the locals shunning it because they said they knew better. He spoke in good conscience when he testified to the nature of the burned woman's product, and few had ever seen him so enthusiastic over any subject. Though his belief in what he said could not be argued, very few living on the pueblo would ever agree with him. That was surprising, because his business sense was near-legendary in the community.

Cigarettes, potato chips, bread, and sodas were often sold from trailers. There was no sales tax on the reservations, and merchants from the city would often arrive to take advantage of this. Tourists were wary of such operations, and Thomas Begay had specialized in making outsiders feel welcome. There were very few successful businesses within the village, other than the spattering of bars and the opulent Bingo Palace, where there was no limit to prizes. More than a million dollars' worth of prizes was given away each year at the gambling hall. But the Vegas-style flashing lights of the Bingo Palace were seen a mile or two *outside* the village. It was a given that Thomas Begay knew what he was doing, and if he wanted to risk his good money and reputation by boldly displaying the burned woman's worthless bread, that was his choice.

The burned woman knew nothing of the controversy surrounding her homemade bread. She was an outsider to most, not having been born in the community. Elizabeth Altsoba had vouched for the woman, claiming that she was a relative on her father's side. Everyone knew the story of Elizabeth Altsoba's parents: Her mother had been a resident of Isleta, her father a Spaniard from south of the border. Immigration had deported her father and Elizabeth's mother had gone with him. Elizabeth was seven when they were both killed in what was rumored to be a drug-related slaughter. The child was sent back to the res, where she had lived ever since.

The burned woman's name was Paloma. In Spanish, her name meant "Dove." Many of the people found this amusing, as the burned woman was anything but an object of beauty. Her face was covered most of the time by scarfs. Only her eyes, part of her forehead, and her hands were ever exposed, and they were ugly masses of scar tissue and repulsive, sallow, bulbous flesh. The woman's eyes, the only part of her that were not hideously deformed, were very dark and knowing. Some had even found them beautiful, particularly as they were set in stark contrast to the wom-

40

an's ruined flesh.

Thomas Begay had found Paloma's eyes to be devastating. He could not look away from them, even when the burned woman was not paying him the slightest bit of attention. Thomas's wife, Sarah, moved behind the counter, intentionally jostling her husband. Her wide, dark face was set in a frown.

In hushed tones, Thomas said to his wife, "What is it?"

Sarah looked in the direction of the burned woman. "I don't like her coming in here."

"Why?"

"She is not one of us."

"Elizabeth says she is family. The only family she has outside the pueblo."

"She doesn't need family outside the pueblo. We raised her. And if that evil one were part of her family, why did she not come forward years ago when the courts petitioned for a living relative to care for Elizabeth?"

"Paloma didn't know. Her brother was not close to her. It wasn't until recently that Elizabeth and Paloma found each other. You know that. Or would you call the child a liar?"

"No. But Paloma has magic. She may have worked it on the child. She has certainly worked it on *you*."

"Ridiculous."

"Her bread is gritty, it tastes as if her secret ingredient comes from her sticking her finger down her throat. It sits in the stomach for most of the day, making anyone but you feel as if a spirit were playing games with their insides."

"Then don't eat it. To me, it is delicious."

"She has magic. Soon she will bid you to come to her hogan at night and pleasure her. You will see how understanding I am if you find her wretched body as sweet as her terrible bread."

Thomas Begay shook his head. He considered telling his wife that no woman could taste so sweet as

41

she. Before he met his beloved, he had lain with half a dozen women and could not bear to put his mouth upon them. Since his marriage, he had come to live for the times when he had her thighs pressed against his ears. He would say it in a whisper, of course, and he would touch her buttocks ever so gently. Sarah would forget about the burned woman very quickly after that.

He was about to speak when he looked up and saw Paloma standing only a few feet away. Her beautiful eyes were brimming with tears. Thomas Begay felt his heart sink as he asked, "Paloma, what is wrong?"

The burned woman looked away. She had been carrying an oversized satchel loaded with loaves of her fresh-made bread, direct from her *orno*. Every week she proudly went on about her secret ingredients and how she diligently swept out the hot coals before putting her precious loaves in the outdoor oven. Thomas Begay knew from the woman's sad eyes that he would never hear her excitedly go on about her homemade bread ever again. Sarah's disparaging words had been overheard by the burned woman. The pain in Paloma's eyes made Thomas feel like striking his wife, a barbaric act he had never before contemplated in his life.

The burned woman said nothing. She turned and walked away.

Thomas rushed around the counter, following her, and called out, "Paloma, wait! I will still buy your bread!"

She froze and hung her head. Her body was shaking. The need in his voice had penetrated her apparent resolve to storm out of the general store and never come back. Paloma emptied the contents of her satchel on a nearby counter.

"I will not sell it to you," she said, her lips trembling, "but you may have it, as a gift."

His hands ran over the loaves tentatively. He could not face the idea of living without her weekly deliveries. "And when these are gone?"

The burned woman looked past him, to his wife, who was wearing a stern but frightened expression. Paloma touched Thomas's chest and said, "You may come to my hogan and perhaps I will bake you some more."

She turned, and her hand was on the door when he asked her to wait once again. Paloma walked out of the store, into the street, where Thomas followed her.

"I have something for you. Proof that I am not the only one who finds your bread so—so *sumptuous*."

She lowered her head. "Thomas, please. You are very kind, but this is not necessary."

Frantically, the older man patted down his pockets until he found a sealed white envelope and handed it to Paloma. "Take this. You must."

Trembling, Paloma reached out with her gnarled, burned hand and took the letter.

"Open it."

"Not now," she said, and turned from him a final time. He watched as she walked to the corner, rounded it, and vanished from view. Suddenly, he felt something twist within his chest. He feared that he was having an attack of some kind. Something was tearing away from him, a strange tension of which he had not been aware fell away, and he heard the voice of Elizabeth Altsoba whisper something in his mind. He could only understand a part of it.

—so long as she sells her fresh-made bread to you, you will be a slave, you will need—

The voice disappeared, and several seconds later, when Thomas Begay tried to bring it back, he found that he could not. A few seconds after that, the meaning of the words he had just listened to became muddy. Then he could no longer remember hearing them at all. Confusion washed over him as he reentered his store and went to the loaves Paloma had left behind.

Was it possible that Sarah was right? he wondered.

Could Paloma have been some kind of witch?

"Thomas, what's wrong?" Sarah asked sharply from behind the counter.

He could not answer her. The man felt an unexplainable compulsion to taste Paloma's bread.

"Thomas, what are you doing?" Sarah came to him, placing her hand on his arm as he stood before the loaves and ripped the first apart with his hands, jamming a chunk into his mouth as if he were an animal.

The older man chewed on the bread for a few moments, then turned and spat it out on the floor, shocked to learn that it *was* as truly awful as everyone had been saying from the beginning.

The burned woman kept her head low as she hurried home. She was thankful for the scarfs obscuring her face, and for the searing light of midday, which further cloaked her face in shadows. Only a handful of people greeted her as she walked briskly through the dirt roads, which were set in no particular pattern. The houses were built first and the roads were made to accommodate people getting to their houses.

Stray dogs sometimes approached her, smelling the crumbs from the loaves she had baked. A pair of particularly brave or desperate black dogs, their ribs poking from their flesh, stopped before her, whining piteously. She felt an odd weight in her satchel, checked it, and found one last loaf that had been wedged down close to the bottom. The woman pulled it out, tore it open, and threw it to the dogs. They went after it with incredible enthusiasm.

The pain in the burned woman's heart was lifted slightly. At least *they* liked it. She had been worried that even the dogs would turn away from her bread. She passed a small group of children playing, studying their faces. They were happy, but they wouldn't stay happy for long. Not in this place. They would

44

come to understand what they were missing, and the bitterness would set in. Their bright eyes would become dark.

Stop it, she told herself. *You have no right to judge these people.* It was true. She was angry and hurt, lashing out at the villagers because she didn't want to be angry at the one person who deserved her rage. During the last year, she had seen amazing things. The Native Americans had kept alive the practice of the extended family. The children were raised by aunts, uncles, and grandparents, while the parents went to the city and worked. In this manner, the children learned the old ways from their elders.

Their schooling was hardly neglected. Isleta had strong Spanish roots, though it had been run by a tribal government since 1947. The Catholic Church was predominant, and near the church, at the center of the village, was the Plaza, which covered perhaps two acres, including a spattering of houses. The governor was based at the Plaza, where the counselors met to decide policy. Reading programs for the children were heavily endorsed, and the welfare of the young was a paramount concern.

The slow process of assimilation between traditional and so-called "modern" ways could be seen at the offices of the community health representatives and the EMTs with their equipment and land vehicles, which coexisted at the Plaza with medicine men blessed with healing powers.

The people understood that something as severe as cancer would not be cured by a visit to the local healer, but many other minor sicknesses were often treated successfully. The burned woman had gone there with her infant, and had seen the healer performing such varied tasks as setting bones or offering emotional help. They performed prayers involving a great deal of touching, but there was no singing, as she had expected. That was preserved for ceremonial *ways*. Much of the medicine men's powers came to them from faith, which was always freely given.

When the medical facilities at the res and the powers of the healers were not enough, there was a public health facility in Albuquerque. Many Isleta people were professionals there, working as dieticians, diabetic specialists, record clerks, and practical nurses.

Nevertheless, she always felt as if she were walking through a perfectly preserved monument to a far worse time. So many of the houses looked the same. Practically every house had round outdoor ovens called *ornos*.

When the burned woman had first arrived at the res, she had wanted to work, and needed to understand all she could of the community, and so she had studied the procedures that went into the construction of houses in Isleta.

The houses were made of adobe and plastered with mud and straw. Adobe was a mixture of dough and clay that was put in forms about twelve by eight inches wide, and four to six inches deep. They were dried out in the sun and put in a mold that generally accommodated two or three bricks. Later, they were turned over on a flat surface and allowed to dry, after which they were flipped a final time and stacked on their sides. There was another method of construction using adobe. The workers would cut directly from the ground a natural mud, root, and straw mixture that was found near the riverbed on the Rio Grande. This was stacked near the river and hauled to the construction site.

The burned woman looked more closely at the houses, attempting to calm herself and drive away the hurt she was feeling over her rejection by concentrating on the facts she had learned about her adopted home. The community was racially integrated, with many residents who were varying mixtures of Native Americans, Spaniards, blacks, Orientals, or Anglos. Housing was being built outside the village, the first signs of urban development already visible. Cable might take another decade to arrive in the village, but there were a few satellite dishes and antennas in the outlying areas.

Within the village, however, the housing methods had changed little over the years. Ladders rose up to the tops of the houses, and occasionally she saw racks outside, near the *ornos*. The racks had four cedar posts with a platform on the top. They generally sat eight feet off the ground, taking up a ten-by-ten-foot square. Most of these were used for the drying and storage of wood for the winter. The burned woman used hers to dry clothes.

She arrived outside her home, contemplating what she would see when she walked in the door. She was dying to take a shower, but most of the pueblos did not have running water within the village property. To clean herself, she would have to bathe in the round tin tub, two feet in diameter and a foot deep, after heating the water on her wood stove. She had a fireplace that had been a great comfort during the winter. Her wood stove looked like an antique, with four knobby legs. She had a water tank, a heater, two beds, a television, an old VCR, and a host of books that had been purchased in used bookstores in Albuquerque.

The thought depressed her. She didn't want to go back inside. Her eyes were still wet with her tears, and she thought about what had happened. Her bread had been rejected, that was all. How had she become so fragile? she wondered. Why had this come to mean so much to her?

She knew the answers, of course. The bread had been important to her because she could no longer work in her chosen profession. The baking gave her something to do, something that gave her a measure of self-worth. That was foolish, she knew. She had something else that was much more valuable: She had a son and he was amazing, a constant source of discovery and pride.

Even his miraculous existence did not erase the simple truth that for twenty years she had earned a living, and she missed that sense of independence. Making the bread had been such a small thing, but it had come to mean very much to her. Now she realized that all she had accomplished was a lie. Thomas Begay had been *forced* to believe that he enjoyed her baking. His perceptions had been altered, his mind programmed like that of a computer to respond in ways the burned woman would find pleasing and flattering.

The burned woman suddenly found herself raising the white envelope Thomas had handed to her and tearing it open. She didn't want to look inside. Thomas had probably written the letter himself — or composed it and had someone else write it out for him and sign a false name, so that she wouldn't recognize the handwriting. It might have been another part of his conditioning.

Or the author might have been someone who truly enjoyed what she had done. She read the note and began to shake once more.

"Oh, Jesus," she whispered. "Oh, Heavenly Mother of Christ."

The few words written in bold block letters on the page struck her with all the force and intensity of a bullet to her skull. This was not possible. It couldn't be real. It couldn't be happening. She read the note again:

I know the truth, Sam. You have nothing to fear. Trust me. I love you.

It was unsigned.

Samantha Walthers looked at her front door and saw that the hair she had placed in the jamb had been broken. Someone was inside her house, waiting for her. Presumably, the same person who had left the note. Michael had been left with Dorothea, down the street. Samantha tore away the scarf, revealing the

48

smooth skin of her lower face. The burn makeup only extended midway down her nose. She was forty, and the hard living of the last year had toughened her flesh, pulling her skin tighter on the bones. But she was still beautiful, with curling, brunette hair that had been cropped short and hidden by another scarf, elegantly sculpted features, and a finely honed physique which she kept hidden under her layered dress. She glanced around to see if there would be any witnesses to the miraculous transformation that was about to take place. Not that it would matter, if what she suspected was true.

She looked around, feeling ludicrous. But that was all right; picturing herself as a female version of Clark Kent about to strip off his clothing and become the Man of Steel was better than allowing her terror to become her entire world. In a way, she almost felt relieved. She had been waiting for this moment, and could have spent her entire life never knowing if it would one day arrive or not. Now that it was upon her, all she wanted to do was get it over with.

There was no one else on the street. Sam whipped off the baggy dress and revealed that she was wearing black running shorts extending to mid-thigh, a spandex top, and a set of holsters, one over each hip, carrying silver-plated 9-mm Berettas.

Bet you can't carry just one, *girls . . .*

She had been worried that her footprints would give away that she was armed if she had only carried one gun. An observant lawman would have seen that one footprint went deeper than the other. She decided that if she was going to have a counterweight, it might as well have been the Beretta's twin.

Sitting beneath the false bottom in her satchel was a portable flamethrower that looked like a can of Raid with a lawn-mower attachment, but was actually an experimental government-issue model that Dani had stolen. She took it out, put her hand in the molded black grip, then leaned down and placed a heavy stone in the satchel. Drawing a deep breath, Sam closed her eyes and felt another twinge of annoyance at her daughter, Dani. Not only had the girl known how terrible a cook her mother was, and taken steps to ensure the woman's happiness by playing with Thomas Begay's mind, she had also brought home the videotape of *Butch Cassidy and the Sundance Kid* one day last week. The final scenes played out in Sam's head as she spun around the door and hurled her satchel up over the wall of her house. As she heard it strike the roof, Sam kicked in her own door and barreled inside, weapon drawn, prepared to fire at the first thing that moved.

Chapter Three

Dani had been overwhelmed by the boy's pain because he was literally broadcasting it, and the demons within his blood were calling to her own. Easing her power forward, she brushed the perimeter of his consciousness and was relieved to find no true malice. He was desperate and afraid. She guessed that his powers had only recently manifested, perhaps in the wake of the crash. But he was a male Initiate. That meant it was very likely that his true father had raised him, or had been involved in his development. She thought of Richard Sterling, the bastard Immortal who had raped her mother, and Bill Yoshino, the man who had taken her virginity and turned her into a god, if only for a short time. This boy could be turned, and if he were, he might become something worse than either of them.

What does that matter? she asked herself, fighting off her bloodhunger. *Are you going to let him die because of what might happen, what he could turn into later? Right now he's just a frightened kid. People might say that it would be wonderful to go back in time and kill the worst monsters in history when they were children, but this is different. You have a baby brother who's no more guilty than this child. Should Michael die because of what he* might *become?*

She considered some of what she had done in the

past, and realized that many would not have believed her worthy of existence either had they known the acts she'd been fated to perform. There really was no choice. She had dedicated her life to healing, and that was not a commitment she would willingly abandon.

"I'm going to help you," she whispered. "You're different. You know that, don't you?"

The boy said nothing. His eyes were glistening with tears and he was trembling, his flesh pale. He might have been going into shock.

"I'm going to do things. They're meant to help you. If you fight me, we could both end up getting hurt. Do you understand?"

The boy seemed unable to focus on her. The cooperation she had hoped to achieve was no longer a likely prospect. She was going to have to burrow past the wall of pain surrounding him. Dani drew a sharp breath and uncoiled her silver thread, slicing through the red-hot surface of the boy's thoughts. His agony threatened to consume her, but she held on and searched to find a single image that might provide the boy with the sense of purpose he would need to fight along with her for his life. The teenager's thoughts were a chaotic swirl, but from the madness brought about by his pain and fear she found what she had desired:

Before her loomed the beautiful face of a dark-haired woman who was reaching out to her, smiling lovingly, and caressing the side of her face. Dani could see the woman's features reflected in those of the teenager.

"I love you, Bobby," his mother said. "You're my whole world. I live for you. Only for you."

The woman began to cry. "I'll never let them have you," she said. "So long as I live, I'll find a way to keep you safe. Believe me, Bobby. I will. . . ."

Dani could feel the outpouring of love this woman held for the boy and felt a cascade of relief. She focused the boy's perceptions on this single image, drawing his attention away from the pain. His panic subsided and the incredible waves of fear radiating from him dissipated.

The boy had been displaying the common signs of shock — an elevated pulse, low blood pressure, fast breathing, incredible anxiety. She eased her power deeper into his brain, provoking chemical reactions that helped to stabilize his blood pressure. She administered IV fluids but it wasn't enough. She needed blood that she could force into him. His blood pressure *had* to be maintained.

Internally, the boy was bleeding severely. She caused his system to collect the blood leaking from his ruptured organs and force it back into the body cavity, but it was only a temporary solution. There was a separate hole in his spleen that might not rupture right away, but could rupture on the flight back. Blood was already leaking out of the spleen to collect in the sac. The boy would have to be moved, and there was no way she could get him back to the rear of the plane through the same route she had taken. Any movements would have to be slow and methodical, and the metal rod which had impaled his side could easily shift and cause even more damage.

He was not having a problem breathing. The rod had not punctured his lung, though it might have if it had fallen a few inches the other way. Carefully reaching under him, Dani felt for the other end of the metal rod. It protruded from his back, but was not lodged deeply into the debris. Dani held the rod, dragging it loose as she slowly brought the boy forward, twisting his body so that she could apply pressure to the exit wound and bandage the torn, bloody flesh. Allowing him to settle back, she did the same for the entry wound. Her grip on the metal had kept it from rubbing against the already pierced muscles and chipped bone within the boy. It had moved with him. Carefully sizing up the consistency of the metal rod, Dani was relieved to find that it was fairly brittle.

Bobby, you've got to be very still, Dani whispered in the confines of his thoughts. She could easily have seized complete control of his body and forced him to remain still, but his fear might have returned. Dani could not risk feeling the intense sensations he had been broadcasting with his power.

When she felt his body become perfectly motionless she gripped the end of the metal rod jutting from his body, holding it in place, and snapped off the two feet of metal jutting from above his wound. Bobby did not flinch.

That was wonderful, she said. *You're very brave.*

Dani worked for several minutes setting the boy's legs and arm, using her power to block the signals the pain receptors were sending to his brain. She felt them instead, and bit down on her lips with the agony, drawing blood. For an instant she felt something rise up and approach her mind. She was certain that the boy's power had manifested and licked at her pain, but it had withdrawn so quickly that it had presented no real threat.

He was fighting his own bloodneed, she realized, and the knowledge pleased her. She looked around, hoping to find some way to get him out of here. Her instinct had been to attack the wall of debris behind the shattered boy. That would be the quickest way to access the outside. But the wreckage was perched precariously around the boy and there was a chance that her efforts might bring it all down on him. She had no other option but to try and move forward.

I'm not leaving you, Bobby. But I've got to find a way out for us.

The boy gave no reply, but something that approximated understanding gleamed in his eyes. Dani tore herself away from him, crawling forward through a bloody field of severed heads and hands, across a small area that was slick with blood. She maintained her mental link to the boy, though she shielded him from the horrors she witnessed. Dani felt her knees slide and she tumbled forward, reaching out to grasp any object to steady her. Her hand closed over something hard and wet. When she looked up, she saw that it was a bone jutting from a corpse wearing a uniform.

"Christ," she whispered, pulling away.

The way ahead of her was blocked, but she recalled the upward tilt of the plane's twisted nose and began to pound at the metal floor beneath her. A section broke free of its rivets beneath her assault and she grabbed at its edges, peeling it upward. The maze of fused metal beneath her offered no hope. She crawled back to the shattered boy and took his hand.

There was only one avenue open to her. She would have to use her power to control Freddy and Max, sending them back to the hospital with instructions to get extraction tools airlifted in. The military base might have to get involved. The press would certainly be ready for it. She had used her power to avoid photographers and television cameramen from her first day. Her psychic talents meant nothing to a camera. It would take the image of Danielle Walthers, not her assumed identity. That had been one of her mother's primary concerns over Dani taking the job: The press liked nothing more than to swarm over disasters. Once she had been careless and her image had been recorded by an amateur videographer. She recalled his look of confusion as he gazed at her through the viewfinder and saw something completely different from what his unaided eyes perceived. Dani had followed him, nearly losing him twice, and had taken first the tape and then his memories.

Dani looked at Bobby, unable to see anything other than her baby brother Michael at this boy's age. There was really no choice. She would have to release her hold on Bobby long enough to locate the minds of Max and Freddy, and direct them to perform the tasks she required.

Bobby, she whispered soothingly in his mind, *I*

*don't want you to be afraid. I'm going to be apart
from you for a little while, but I promise, I won't go
far.*

She was about to withdraw when suddenly, she felt
his entire body seize up. For the first time, she heard
his voice within her mind:

Don't leave!

He clawed at her shoulder with his one good arm
and strained against her, moving the metal shaft still
imbedded in his side. Screaming in pain, the boy fell
back, doing even more damage to himself. Dani
hadn't expected him to panic like this. She had left
him physically to explore the rest of the aircraft and
he had been perfectly calm.

"Bobby, don't!" she cried, but it was too late, he
was spasming, going into convulsions, and his movements were causing the metal fragment within him to
scissor back and forth, sawing at him from the inside.
She felt the intense pain that snaked through his body
as the metal tore into his lung. He gasped and shuddered, and soon blood would appear from his lips.

She was losing him and her best efforts to take control of him were failing. The demons within his blood
were taking command of him, and they did not realize that they were killing him.

Dani gathered her power and unleashed it against
the boy, snuffing out his conscious mind. His body
relaxed, but as she had feared, a trickle of blood
escaped his lips. Her own fears threatened to overtake her and she forced them down. She didn't
have the equipment necessary to save him, and her
power was limited to provoking responses within
his own physiology, helping to speed up his own
natural healing.

Bobby was hemorrhaging internally. Despite her efforts to manipulate his body chemistry, he was descending rapidly into shock. If he had been a human,
she could have forced his body to respond to her
commands, but the blood of Immortals also ran in

his veins and his frightened subconscious was fighting her. His blood pressure was dropping and the blood was leaking out of his body cavity.

Dani looked down to see that the bandages she had placed on his wounds were soaked red with blood. By the time she was able to get back to the opening she had made in the midsection of the plane and return with the equipment she would need for the boy, he would be dead.

Anger welled up inside her and she turned her attention to the wall of twisted metal behind the child. Beyond that wall lay the outside, where Max and Freddy could help her work on the teenager utilizing the full battery of equipment with which the air ambulance had been outfitted. A metal shell had been formed around Bobby, several beams having fallen to create support struts. Dani did not want to think about what would happen if those supports were to fall. It was possible that they had performed their task, holding back the collapse of the hull which would have crushed Bobby to death, and that now they were unnecessary; it was also possible that they were keeping a cloud of debris from raining down on the boy.

Dani positioned herself over the teenager, gently pulling him close to her, and reached down for a large chunk of metal that had fallen nearby. She rammed the foot-and-a-half-long slab of metal into the wall behind them with enough force to create a spark. A lancing pain bit through her shoulder, but she did not stop. Relentlessly, Dani struck with the metal slab, beating it against the tangled mass that had once been the hull of the aircraft until she found a weak spot. She heard a groan and saw one of the support beams bend slightly. Above her, the dented and cracked mass of plastic and steel sagged. Dani struck at the wall again, concentrating on the weakened area, and tried to convince herself that she was doing the right thing. She was terrified of dying here, and she had a respon-

57

sibility to her mother, and to Michael. If the Immortals ever found them, Dani would be their best weapon against them. Without her, they would have almost no chance. Nevertheless, she could not let this boy die.

She struck out, and did not stop until she felt a beam fly outward and a stream of harsh white light flooded in. Dani threw herself against the opening, screaming for her partner to find her. From above, she heard a scraping, a deep, throaty growl, and cried out as the roof collapsed.

The debris crashed down on her back and she struggled to hold herself in place, shielding Bobby. She felt a heavy object strike the back of her head, and an iron support beam raked across her shoulders and back like a talon. A deadweight dropped onto her back and she heard a snap, then felt an outpouring of liquid in her knees. But she did not collapse under the onslaught. She continued to pound away at the opening beside her, widening it with her efforts, even as more debris fell upon her. Glaring light struck her from the side, and she felt as if she were in a bad Hammer movie from the sixties, walled up in a dungeon, attempting to break out. The heroes and heroines never escaped from their confinement in those films. They might get close, but then it would all come down upon them and they would die screaming. Dani tried to avert her thoughts from death scenes, but she could not completely erase the images she had of a single metal beam slamming down and impaling her, or a slab of metal falling down on her head and cracking open her skull, spilling her brains to the floor. So long as she allowed her fear to wash over her, it drove the hunger and madness of her blood from her. She needed her blood right now; she needed its strength in her frenzy to survive.

The rain of metal ceased, though Dani had not lessened her motions. She drove at the opening she created, looking at it from the periphery of her vision, wondering if it would be possible to ease Bobby's slender form through the opening. Perhaps not, but the equipment she needed to save his life would pass through. She coiled her power and sent her silver thread into Max, who brought blood and other supplies she needed. Dani worked frantically, ignoring her own pain, her injuries, concentrating on saving the teenager's life. She screamed with pleasure and relief when Bobby's condition finally stabilized, then remained with him as Max and Freddy took several of the wounded back to the trauma center and returned with the spreaders they would need to widen the hole Dani had made in the hull of the shattered airliner. She had been in their minds, programming them to believe that the sudden shifting of weight from above had caused the metal to tear open beside her, making them forget that they had seen her true face, and the face of her undiluted hunger. They were only too happy to forget, making her task much easier. When they were gone, she turned her power on each of the survivors left behind, editing their memories. Then she turned her full attention on Bobby, using her powers to speed up his body's unnatural healing abilities, repairing what damage she could before the others returned.

When she was finally able to move again, after the hole she had created in the plane's hull had been widened to accommodate passage and they had both been taken out, Dani felt as if she had no right to be alive after her ordeal, much less to feel the euphoria that was rushing through her. Sitting in the chopper, massaging her cramped muscles, feeling the chill of the various salves that had been packed tightly against her own wounds, Dani was unable to keep herself from smiling as the helicopter lifted into the air, heading back for civilization. Once again she had cheated her blood. She had forced her dark, inhuman nature under her control, bending its powers and twisting her murderous needs to a use that might have

59

sickened another of her kind. The boy had been saved.

Once again, she had gambled with the evil inside her, and she had *won*.

Chapter Four

Nothing moved.

In the center of the room, a man stood in the metal bath basin, hands raised. Chairs had been stacked and a drape had been hung to hide the man's identity. The window was behind him, and he was silhouetted by the harsh blue-white light.

"You've got to be fucking kidding me," Sam said as she checked her safety zone, looked all around the room, and kicked the door shut behind her. "Don't move."

"I had no intention of moving," a deep, rich voice said.

Sam recognized the voice. None of this made any sense. She went to the curtain and yanked it away, revealing a handsome Native American in his late thirties or early forties. His eyes were gray and black. A scar ran along his entire skull, starting somewhere near the base, continuing around to cut into his forehead, sink between his eyes, and end in the hollow beneath his right cheekbone. The man's features were thick and proud, and he had an incongruous set of Cupid's lips. His graying hair was cropped short. The middle finger of his right hand was missing.

"Peter Red Cloud," Sam said. Peter ran the small video store on the other side of the pueblo. Sam was a regular customer, but the conversations she had with the man had been limited at best. They barely knew each other. Without allowing her aim to waver, Sam flickered her gaze in the direction of his blood-engorged cock. "What the hell is *that* for?"

"I was, ah—thinking of you."

She leveled the muzzle of her gun at the center of Peter's forehead. "Think about something else then. I want you in the sunlight."

He looked down at his nude, soaking-wet body. "Like this?"

"Yeah. Stand by the window."

"If that's what you want."

She didn't have to repeat her order. Her cold eyes made it clear that she would shoot him if he did not follow her every command. Peter stepped out of the basin and walked to the window. "I want the sunlight touching you," she said.

He moved so that the rays were falling directly upon his flesh, bathing his back and neck. A yellow-white aura framed his broad, deeply tanned shoulders. Sam didn't know what this would prove. She had seen him in the sunlight many times. Images flashed into her mind. She saw the vampire Alyana and her assistants standing in direct sunlight while Marissa, the young woman they had hunted, screamed as her flesh was melted away under the sun's burning rays. Alyana and her assistants had been Parliament. They had power beyond what any of the other vampires had displayed. But even Alyana could not stay in the light forever.

She waited for Peter to display some sign of pain or discomfort. They stood together, in silence, for close to an hour. Other than his sex shriveling up due to his apparent embarrassment or fear, or simply lack of attention, he was unmoving. Sam's arm was sore from keeping her weapon raised. Alyana could not have withstood this punishment, but she was not the most powerful of their kind. Red Cloud could still prove to be a vampire. Sam had seen Dani with Peter many times, but he could have been powerful enough to

62

shield his true nature from the girl's inhuman senses.

When she had read the note, she had believed that it had been from her pursuers, another of their nasty tricks. The vampires were rarely direct. They preferred to play games. For all Sam knew, everything she was experiencing at the moment might have only existed in her mind. She might have already been captured. They might have taken her son, Michael. He was the one they really wanted anyway.

Sam had briefly contemplated going to Dorothea's place and checking on her son, but she knew that if the vampires were making their move against her, and knew this much about her secret life, he was already in their hands. Her only chance of seeing him again would be to play out the scenario the vampires were creating for her and see where it took her.

She looked at the man before her. He might well be Peter. Or he might be a vampire, one more powerful than she had ever conceived of, masquerading as Peter. If the former was the case, was he working for them? Had he been one of their operatives all along? If the latter was the case, nothing she could do would make the slightest bit of difference.

"I'm wondering," Sam said quietly.

"Yes," Peter said, his voice becoming slightly throaty. His mouth was dry. He was afraid.

"I only have two options, so far as I can see."

"Is that so?"

"Yes. If I don't want to stand here for the rest of my life, I'm either going to have to trust you or kill you."

Peter frowned and furrowed his brow. In a pleasant tone he asked, "Does the decision have to be made right now?"

"I'm getting awfully tired."

"I understand." A slight smile broke on his face. "You could always try talking to me. If that doesn't work, there's always time to blow my head off."

She nodded, wondering if killing him would even

be possible. If he was a vampire, he could make her think that she had killed him. Or he could seize control of her body and make it impossible for her to squeeze the trigger. This was as bad as the Salem witch trials. The only way to prove his innocence was to murder him.

"So sit down," Sam said.

He began to move forward.

"No. Sit right there. I want you to stay in the light."

"I understand," he said pleasantly.

Sam sat in the corner, her back against the wall. "Why did they send you?"

"No one sent me."

Another possibility occurred to her. Peter might have been programmed by the vampires, just as Thomas Begay had been by Dani. The man might not be aware of his condition. But what purpose would any of this serve? she wondered.

"Did you write the note?" Sam asked.

"Yes."

"Why did you write the note?"

He shrugged. "Because I'm in love with you."

"Bullshit."

"It's true. I love you."

"Shut up."

"All right."

Sam stared into his cool gray eyes. "How did you find out about me?"

He nodded. This was the question for which he had been waiting. "Do you remember that movie you wanted? *Bread and Chocolate?*"

"Uh-huh."

"I was able to get a copy. It's not released, but I knew it would make you happy, and I managed to buy a black-market bootleg. It cost a fortune and the quality's poor, but—"

"This isn't about your video store."

"Yes, Sam. It is. That's where I fell in love with you."

"I suppose it would have to be. That's the only place we've ever met."

"It's not the only place I've ever seen you, though. The tape came in and I decided to come here with it."

Sam felt a slight chill. She wondered if Peter was cold. That didn't matter. He was lucky he wasn't dead. "When was this?"

"A few weeks ago. I came to the door and was about to knock. But something stopped me."

It was finally beginning to make sense to Sam. She bit her lip and said, "Go on."

"I could hear the splash of water. I knew you were taking a bath. I'm not really proud of what I did, but I was feeling things that I hadn't felt in fifteen years." He tapped his chest. "I was in love with you. I *am* in love with you."

"Stop saying that."

"I was feeling crazy. I walked around the outside of your house and looked through the window."

"Jesus."

"Do you want to know why I fell in love with you?"

"Sure, okay. Christ."

"It was because of the way you held yourself. As Paloma, a deformed, burned woman, people would shun you and you didn't care. You had a pride that could not be mistaken, and you were at peace here, in your heart." He touched his chest once again. "When we talked, I looked into your eyes and I saw my future."

"What movie is that from?" Sam asked angrily.

"I don't know. I think I made it up."

"I doubt it. Go on."

"I had never seen what you really looked like. I told myself I didn't care about the burns. I would love you no matter what."

"This is fucking ridiculous," Sam said. "You don't know me. Whatever you thought you were in love with, it didn't have anything to do with me."

"I don't agree."

"No," she said, gesturing with her Beretta, "and look where it's gotten you." She shook her head and finally released her grip on the hand-held flame unit. Her fingers were cramping up.

He pointed at her hand and said, "I could massage your hand . . ." Sam rose to one knee and leveled her weapon at Peter.

"Move and I'll blow your balls off."

"I'm pretty comfortable here."

"Good. So you decided that you loved me and you couldn't pass up this opportunity to give your dick a workout while you watched me in the bath."

"No. It wasn't like that."

"Then how was it?"

"I believed that you were burnt. I didn't care. But I am only human, and I was afraid that if I waited until I was making love to you to see your body for the first time, I might have a reaction that would hurt you. I told myself that if I could see it before, I wouldn't react badly."

"And then you saw me without the makeup."

"Yes."

"But what made you put my face to my name? You couldn't have seen me for long. Even if you had, how did you know who I was?"

"At the store?"

"Yeah?"

"In the john?"

"Right."

"There's a couple of old magazines sitting in there. *People* magazines. I must have glanced at those magazines a million times. Too lazy to buy new ones. One of them had a write-up on you, after the Hellfire Incident."

"Shit," Sam said, lowering the weapon. This was real. The vampires had nothing to do with this. She set the weapon down. "Peter, I don't know anything about you. I don't *feel* anything for you."

"That's what time is for."

66

"Time," she said. "Don't give me that shit. I was married once. I was hurt in ways that took me twenty years to get over. It was that long before I let myself open up all the way again with a man."

"This man. He was Michael's father?"

"Yes."

"You regret it."

"I don't regret that I have Michael."

"No, of course not. But you wish you hadn't given yourself to this man."

"He was a bastard."

"What happened to him?"

"He died." She neglected to mention that he was a vampire whom she had set on fire and shot seven times in the head.

"Was it what he deserved for the way he mistreated you?"

"As a matter of fact, it was."

"Then it's good that he died."

"Yes." She swallowed hard, wondering exactly where he had placed his clothes. She asked him and he told her. Sam gathered them up and threw them at Peter. "Get dressed."

He stood and slipped into his jeans, buttoned up his white shirt, and eased his feet into his boots. His hair was still damp.

"What was with the bath?" Sam asked, realizing that she had made a decision. What was she thinking? She couldn't let him go. He knew too much. There was a third option beyond killing the man or trusting him. She could have Dani enter his mind and make him forget what he had learned.

She thought of what Richard Sterling had done to her. He had used her worst nightmares against her, controlling her body and her mind. Planted his child within her.

Worst of all, he had made her trust him.

"I felt you should be given the opportunity to see what you would be getting."

"Christ. That's such arrogant, male bullshit that I'm tempted to blow your dick off just on basic principles."

"Does this mean you've decided to trust me, rather than kill me?"

"You're crazy and you scare the shit out of me."

"I'm sorry. That's not what I want to do at all. I love you."

"You're not going to stop, are you?"

"I can't."

Sam regarded him warily. He had not asked what she was running from, and that had startled her. It would have been the first question most people would ask. "Aren't you at all curious?"

"In time, you'll tell me everything. We have the rest of our lives."

"You're a fucking basket case, you know that?"

"Yes."

She stared at his face. "All right. Then you tell me something. How did you get the scar?"

He looked away, contemplating the floor in embarrassment, then said, "I was a soldier. I served two hitches in the 'Nam. Volunteered. I saw people die every day, but I was never touched. Didn't get so much as a scratch. Then the Bush Administration called me up during the Gulf crisis."

"Were you in the city? Was it the bombing?"

"Actually, it was a defective power tool that flew out of control. Caught me here"—he gestured at the base of his skull—"went all the way around, fell off here, by my cheek. I'm still getting checks."

"Amazing."

"Usually, people wish to know about the missing finger."

"I didn't think I'd get a straight answer."

Peter walked to the door and hesitated. "You can trust me, Sam. You must know that. Will you give me a chance?"

"If your hand reaches the knob and I haven't shot you, you have some kind of an answer."

Nodding, he opened the door and went outside. She slammed the door shut, realizing that her hand had started to shake once more.

It was over. They would have to move on. She couldn't take the chance that Peter would stay quiet. He occasionally wrote video review columns for a few of the smaller papers in Albuquerque. That meant he had newspaper contacts. He could expose her easily.

Sam thought about what she had seen in his eyes. He didn't actually appear to be insane. If anything, he seemed totally sincere. But the same could have been said for Richard Sterling. She had too many responsibilities; she could not risk her family's future by putting it in the hands of someone like Peter Red Cloud.

Sam set her weapon back in its holster and went to her upright closet, where she began the arduous task of reassembling her disguise before she could go to Dorothea's and pick up her son.

When she was ready, she went outside and found a note tacked to her front door. It was from Peter. She read it and nearly smiled.

Marry me and I will eat every loaf of bread you make.

She shook her head, crumpled up the note, and threw it on the grass.

Chapter Five

Darkness had come many times for the boy since the crash. Darkness and unbridled fury. He had been unable to express his anger, unable to show how deeply he had been seething with rage over all that had happened.

Bobby De Santo lay on the operating table, struggling to maintain his reason despite the drugs which had been pumped into him. He could not tell if he had been there for minutes or for hours. At the moment, he could not move. Breathing was difficult; he was being assisted by a machine. If he had been a human being, rather than the offspring of a human female and a vampire, he would have been unable to hold onto his anger and stay conscious, using his power to force the human operating staff to believe that he was completely under the anesthesia.

He thought of the woman who had saved his life and the perception she had of him. As far as she knew, he had been incoherent, driven mad by the pain, but in truth, he had been aware of everything that had been happening to him. He had given himself over to the agony of his wounds for a purpose: Danielle Walthers, that filthy Wildling *slut,* would never have been so willing to help him had she known what was truly in his heart. She might have even helped him to die. The woman had been close to penetrating the psychic walls he had painstakingly erected to shut her out; she had glimpsed images from his past and had thankfully misinterpreted them. The tearful outpouring of love she had witnessed had indeed come from his birth mother, the whore Mia Valeska. He could picture the scene perfectly and saw the woman's worn face rise up before him.

"I love you, Bobby," Valeska had whispered only weeks earlier. "You are my whole world. I live for you. Only for you."

The Walthers bitch had not seen Bobby's reaction to his mother's tearful cry. He had struck the woman hard in the face, enjoying the shock and fear that rolled off her in shimmering waves coupled with her pain. Danielle Walthers had no idea that Bobby might have beaten Mia Valeska to death if his father had not appeared and stopped him. Bobby considered the woman a tramp and hated her for a multitude of reasons, chiefly because she had refused to marry his father and had damned him to life as a bastard.

His father, Christian De Santo, was a powerful, highly respected man. He was also an Immortal, and a former member of the Parliament. The blood of the Ancients ran in his veins. If Bobby's legitimacy had been important to his father, the man could have easily forced Valeska to marry him. They could have divorced afterwards or the bitch could have been killed. Bobby wouldn't have cared, so long as he had been born with full claim on his father's legacy.

Christian De Santo had made a decision: He had chosen to honor the wishes of the human. Bobby knew that he could live a thousand lifetimes and never understand why his father had chosen to put the needs of a slut like Mia Valeska before those of his firstborn, his *male heir*. His father could have broken the woman's will, but he had chosen to leave her whole.

After Bobby's birth, De Santo had made it very

71

clear that she could leave his home at any time and no harm would come to her. The boy, however, would remain behind. Out of love for her son—or perhaps hatred of De Santo—Mia Valeska had remained.

Bobby had not been told any of this by his parents. He had believed himself to be legitimate. A birth certificate that appeared legal was in his father's possessions and it listed his mother as Vanessa De Santo. According to what he had been raised to believe, his father had married Vanessa three months before Bobby's conception and she had died in childbirth. Mia Valeska was a servant, nothing more. Documents existed to prove all of this. But documents could be forged.

In the past two and a half years, from the day Bobby's powers as an Initiate had begun to manifest, the sons of Christian De Santo's business associates had suddenly befriended Bobby. It had been from Clint and Jeremy Tyler that he had learned the truth. At first he had not believed it possible. His father could not have lied to him. He'd obsessed over what he had been told for months, and finally, in one of his father's rare, unguarded moments, Bobby had used his power to leap beyond the man's defenses and learn the truth.

They had argued, practically attacked one another, but ultimately the boy had backed down. Christian had instructed Bobby to accept Mia Valeska. Bobby De Santo had great plans for his future, and he would not achieve them if he were unable to rely on his father's fortune. For almost two years he had been forced to suffer the loving attentions of his true mother, until one night he had been unable to take any more.

Think about something else, he warned himself. But his thoughts were consumed by hatred, and as Mia Valeska was not here for him to vent his rage upon, he thought about Danielle Walthers instead. Bobby knew what his father would say about the events of the last few hours: Christian De Santo would tell him that he owed a debt of honor to Walthers for saving his life. If she had been a man, he might have agreed. But he had allowed his fear of death to overwhelm his reason, and he had placed his life in the hands of a fallen Immortal. That she was a *female* made it even more intolerable.

Bobby and his friends often had clandestine discussions about the old ways, the teachings of Antonius and the Ancients. They knew it was better to die than to face life beholden to a woman. The humiliation would follow them throughout eternity, and the shame would hold them back from ever being considered for a position in the Parliament.

He thought again of the last time he had seen his true mother, Mia Valeska, alive. Bobby had felt nothing for her but loathing and he had projected his feelings into her mind, his hatred assailing her thoughts with the same vigor he'd used to attack her body.

That night, Mia Valeska had taken her own life. The note she had left behind had been addressed to Bobby and had simply read:

You are your father's son.

That had been the worst insult. He was nothing like his father. For all the man's power, for all his ruthlessness, Christian De Santo was weak. He had allowed a *human woman* to triumph over him. And his son had given ultimate power over his life to a female Initiate, a Wildling who had slain two members of the Parliament and had somehow escaped their vengeance.

Perhaps Mia Valeska was right after all.

No, he could not accept that. Danielle Walthers had saved his life, and it followed that she had power over him, but he was not totally without recourse. Bobby thought of the time after the crash, when he had miraculously found himself alive. He lay there in the worst pain of his life, attempting to think of anything except his torments. He recalled the last fight with his father. Then Bobby had been sent away to spend time in Albuquerque with an old friend of Christian De Santo, a man who might yet have a "civilizing influence" on the boy. Bobby had gone willingly. He had known that he had gone too far with his father. His feelings of triumph over Mia Valeska's suicide—though he had not used his power to bring it about—had made De Santo fly into a murderous rage. In time, he would send for his son.

The crash had been Bobby's fault. He had been bored and had begun to play games, feeding on the fear of the passengers, driving many of them into a frenzy. His power had reached the crew, and one flight attendant in particular. The attendant had attacked the pilot and copilot, smashing at the controls until the plane had begun a descent from which there had been no going back. Bobby had been certain that he would die—by all rights, he should have died—but he was spared. He had lain in exquisite agony until the helicopter bearing the Wildling arrived.

Walthers had put herself at risk for him; she had used her powers in ways he would never have thought to use his own, performing tasks that were both dangerous and heartrending. But in those brief moments when she had been unaware that the blood of Immortals also ran within him, the time when she had first become aware that someone was trapped in the shattered forward section of the plane, Walthers had suffered his agony for him, and he had delved into her mind, keeping her thoroughly unaware of his actions and his true nature. He had learned of her fight with the Parliament, and of the child her adoptive mother, Samantha Walthers, had carried.

A male child.

Danielle and her mother planned to raise the boy as Bobby's human mother would have raised him, had she been given the chance: as a human boy, completely ordinary. But a day would come when his powers would manifest. He wondered how Mia Valeska would have handled Bobby then. His father had been honest with him. Valeska would have made him feel like a freak, and would have trained him to hold down his true nature at any cost.

Samantha Walthers might do the same with her child. He would learn of his powers, feel the inhuman lusts rise up within him, and be taught — what? That he could be a healer, like his older sister? Maybe they would get him to become a *psychologist*. Bobby had been to psychologists — two were Initiates, another a full Immortal. They had helped him to adjust to his strange new powers and his inhuman needs.

Whatever the case, the Walthers women would do whatever they could to keep Samantha's son away from others of their kind. The doctrines of Antonius, the centurion who drank the blood of Christ and died, only to be resurrected three days later to become the firstborn immortal son of Lucifer — these teachings would come to him bastardized, if they reached him at all.

Males of their kind were precious. They were born very rarely, the most prevalent offspring being the female. But a woman of their race could not reproduce, and so the baby girls were considered without value and generally killed or discarded. If Bobby were able to deliver the murderers of two members of the Parliament and sweeten the deal with a male child, his apparent cowardice would seem like heroism. He could tell the others that he had suffered the ministrations of the Walthers woman only so that he could live to bring her to justice.

It would be easier, of course, and the risk would be considerably lessened if he were to have the women quietly killed and the infant taken. But that would not be an easy task. Others had tried, others more powerful than himself or anyone he could enlist to perform the task, and they had all failed.

There was one last option: He could forget all of it and get on with his life. Walthers was not the type to call in a debt such as the one he owed her. She probably wouldn't consider that he owed her anything at all. The woman was attempting to spend her life in hiding from her own kind; she was certainly not about to seek out another Immortal and gloat over the shame she had caused Bobby De Santo.

But what if she were found and brought to justice? Her memories would be splayed by her attackers, and they might learn that he was once within her mind and he had allowed her to go free. They would say that he had paid his debt and they would not come after him. He would also never rise within their ranks.

There was only one viable option. Bobby reached out with his power and snaked within the mind of the closest female, a short, strawberry-blond nurse named Ronna Kaye. Though she was nothing but a lowly human female, even *she* should be able to perform the simple task he was easing into her mind.

He had placed people under compulsions before, and although he had never been this weak when he had attempted it in the past, he was convinced that he could count on her to make the phone call he was unable to make. She would recite the message he was implanting in her brain, and would forget all of it and return to her duties the moment she was finished.

There. It was done. He withdrew his power and settled back.

Now, at last, he could sleep.

Ronna Kaye stopped in the middle of the procedure as Bobby De Santo's words bore into her skull. Her hazel eyes became dull. Her crow's-feet and the slight age lines around her mouth softened as her attractive face slackened. Her petite, five-foot-three-inch body relaxed fully. She had entered the nursing field out of a genuine desire to help others. It was this desire that Bobby De Santo's power had targeted, amplifying it until her need to assist him consumed her. Suddenly nothing was more important to her than fulfilling Bobby's wish that she deliver his message.

Bobby had been unaware that he had made a mistake.

He had perceived Ronna Kaye only as a nurse. At her core, she had always seen herself as a helper. That had been enough for Bobby. He had not bothered to look further. If he had, he would have known that she had left the nursing field and entered medical school a decade earlier.

Ronna Kaye was the surgeon performing the operation.

The loss of a nurse during the procedure might have thrown the operating room into chaos, but the situation could have been brought under control. Ronna's frightening and sudden disconnection from reality startled the other members of the team. When she stiffened and dropped her scalpel into the splayed-open chest of the patient, fear erupted from the remaining members of the team. Ronna turned and walked away as the others screamed at her and tried to stabilize the boy.

Bobby's vital signs had been fluctuating as he strained to see his wishes fulfilled. The power coursing within his blood should have been allowed to follow its normal course, helping to speed up his healing. Instead, Bobby's will, driven by his hatred, had been so great that his power had been directed away from this task and his system had been thrown into chaos. Despite the chemicals being pumped into his body, and the efforts of the machines and the medical team, Bobby's blood pressure rose, his body spasmed, and his limbs violently flailed. The teenager's conscious mind had retreated and the animalistic *thing* that existed within his blood had taken command, lashing out in fear and pain. All it knew were primal emotions.

The operating staff was thrown into a panic by Bobby's power. They each crumpled to the floor, drawing themselves up into fetal positions as they pleaded and begged for the fear that had become their world to somehow vanish. Only Ronna had been unaffected. Bobby's *other mind* had recognized that it had already marked her, and would be better served to let her go. It needed sustenance—fear, pain, and desire. These it prompted from the minds of its would-be saviors. It did not understand that it was committing suicide; it understood nothing at all of the consequences of its actions. The abhorrent thing living within Bobby cared only about fulfilling its needs, and because of its disregard for anything else, it, along with Bobby De Santo, died at 11:57 that morning.

Ronna was walking out of the operating room as she heard the flat-line behind her. The shrill whine of the machines as they indicated the cessation of brain and heart activity did not trouble her. Devoid of emotions, she glanced up at the clock and noted the time of death with cold efficiency.

The surgeon left the operating room and came to the main corridor, where she removed her face mask as she did not want her words to sound at all muffled or obscured over the long-distance phone lines. The bloody surgical smock was left in place. Ronna walked down the corridor and stopped at the first nurses' station, where she picked up the phone and dialed the number she had been given.

Chapter Six

Clint and Jeremy Tyler were in the midst of a little fun when the telephone rang. They decided to ignore it. Before them was prime, red-hot, Grade-A meat and they weren't about to allow it to go cold when they were in the middle of a feast. After the phone had rung seventeen times, Jeremy rose from the floor, picked up the receiver, screamed "Fuck you!" and slammed the phone down.

A few seconds later, after Jeremy had rejoined his brother and their prey, the phone rang again. Clint shook his head, looking up from the woman. Sweat covered his face and his long hair hung down in oily tassels. In a thick Southern drawl he said, "Will you take that fucking thing off the goddammed hook?"

"Can't, and you know why," Jeremy said.

"Goddammit," Clint replied, disengaging himself from the half-naked woman panting and crying out beneath him. She wore a light blue shirt, which had been torn open to reveal her small breasts. Her white shorts and panties were hooked around her ankles. The woman's running shoes were somewhere on the other side of the library. Surrounding them in antique mahogany bookcases were thousands of books that no one, except perhaps the servants, would ever read. The woman's face — teeth gritted, straining toward an orgasm — was beautiful. She had come to deliver a package to the Memphis House, their father's Southern Gothic mansion. To the Tyler brothers, she had possessed the irresistible attraction of a farmer's daughter torn from the pages of a *Playboy* supplement. Her honey-blond hair was partially braided and pinned back. They were taken by the woman's bright, innocent voice, deep, rich blue eyes, soft, perfect skin, and sensuous, full lips. Her glorious attributes had added up to something Clint and Jeremy wanted far more than the overnight package she had carried in her hands.

They had raped her.

To them, however, it wasn't rape. She was a human being, and because of her humanity, she had no more weight or substance than a flickering image on a movie screen. She was no more real to them than the arrangement of colored dots which coalesced on their television to form some porn star when they plugged one of their fuck films into the VCR. In the estimation of the Tyler boys, human women were good breeders. They were also *fun*. Killing them was fun. Screwing them was fun, particularly when they fought back and had to have the shit beaten out of them first. Sometimes they were dry and they had to be hurt inside before their blood and piss provided any decent lubrication. It was better to make them want it, or at least make their bodies want it. The victims would find themselves screaming for it while their minds were trapped, looking out from an orgasm-wracked prison over which they no longer had any control. The fear they radiated was far more pleasurable than the gyrations of their bodies, even though that felt decent enough.

The Brothers Tyler, identical twins with deep blue, almost violet eyes, long, angular, but pleasing features, hard, athletic runners' bodies, and the most chilling feral grins imaginable, called their pastime "sport fucking." Occasionally they murdered their victims, or programmed them to take their own lives a few weeks or a month after their ordeal. They didn't allow the women they had attacked conscious memory of their ordeal. Instead, they forced them to recall the incident in their dreams every night until their deaths. When they woke, the memory would vanish, but its effects would remain to drive the women into premature graves.

The spacious library where they were now was only one room in a fifty-five-room mansion which sported *two* guitar-shaped swimming pools. Two smaller houses sat close to the mansion. The entire complex was protected by concrete walls, electrified fences, motion sensors, bodyguards, video cameras, random aerial patrols, and the inhabitants themselves, creatures far more powerful than any human assailant. Priceless antiques and dozens of awards, gold records, and newspaper clippings were also in evidence throughout the Memphis House. The delivery girl had unexpectedly proven to be a virgin, and her blood was now soaking into the fabric of the gorgeous Persian rug beneath her.

Clint saw this, recalled that a video crew from *Lifestyles of the Rich and Famous* would be here to shoot the Memphis House tomorrow, and found himself driven into a frenzy. The incessant ringing of the phone and the screams of his victim only made it worse. "Do me!" she cried. "Do me, come on, baby, do me! Do me up the fucking ass, I want a cock in every hole I got, baby! I need you to come and pour it down my throat—"

It became too much for him. Clint and Jeremy had programmed her to say these words, delivering the entire scripts of a half-dozen porn films into the girl's mind. She was even hearing the overused, repetitive musical soundtracks from the videos and using the professional screaming of the porn queens as cues. The boys knew she wasn't experienced, and had had to give her something to say as they fucked her into the ground. It was just too much. The scent of the blood overwhelmed Clint. Jeremy cried out for his brother to stop, but his protest came too late.

Clint transformed, reaching an orgasm he splattered on the girl's stomach and breasts. His hands became talons and a mouthful of razor-sharp teeth sprang from his mouth. His brother considered reaching out with his power to stop his twin, but he knew things had gone too far. Clint's bloodneed exploded from him, washing over Jeremy. The brothers descended on the girl, tearing her apart in their frenzy.

When it was over, they looked at what they had done and started to giggle.

"Shit," Clint said, staring at the torn-open chest of the dead girl, wiping the blood from his mouth with the back of his hand. "I think I swallowed some of my own *jizz*."

"Wouldn't be the first time," Jeremy said. They laughed even harder until, at the exact same moment, they suddenly became aware of the phone's continued ringing. It hadn't stopped, but the sound had been drowned out by the thunderous beating of their hearts, which had become perfectly synchronized. In the midst of a kill, the mind and body of one brother seemed to melt into that of the other.

One night, several years ago, they had been given a terrible fright when they had accompanied their father, a member of the Parliament, on a hunt for a Wildling. The renegade vampire had wounded Clint, nearly killing him, and the shock had caused an identical, sympathetic wound to open in Jeremy's body. They had both been turned by this time, and they had quickly recovered.

Their father, Devin Tyler, had killed the insane, monstrous thing which had almost been their deaths. The experience had haunted them, and memories of it often returned after they had killed together. The possibility of their mutual deaths took some of the fun out of their games.

"I guess we better answer it," Clint said. The lines were designed so that if a phone went down or was taken off the hook, a red flag would go up and security would send a team to investigate. The guards were powerful Initiates, all aware of the Tyler brothers' usual practices. But Clint and Jeremy did not wish to be in the presence of more of their kind during the sensitive afterglow of a kill. Shielding their thoughts was too difficult.

Jeremy went to the phone. He picked it up, heard a woman's voice, and immediately recognized the slightly dulled tone of a human placed under a compulsion.

"I have a message from Bobby De Santo. Please confirm your identity by truthfully answering the following questions."

The computerized sound of the woman chilled Jeremy. His brother rose from the corpse at his feet, his power immediately snaking out to link the brothers' minds. The questions pertained to various kills they had made, verifying the dates, victims, and manner of death—certain bits of information only the Tylers could know. Normally, they would have been concerned that the person who had placed this compulsion within the human had been compromised and was using the mortal law officers to entrap them. That seemed unlikely with Bobby De Santo. Though he was just a kid, Bobby was even more dedicated to the fellowship of Immortals than the Tylers. Besides, no human law or morality could ever hold them.

"This is the message," the woman said. Without

pausing, she related Bobby De Santo's words.

Jeremy asked the woman to repeat the message twice. Clint nudged him with his power, prompting Jeremy to ask, "Bobby, how is he?"

"The patient expired at 11:57 this morning," the human said tonelessly.

Clint seized the phone from his brother and disconnected the line. "She was talking about those cunts the Du Prey bitch let go last year, the Wildling and her human."

Jeremy nodded. Alyana Du Prey's secret had been uncovered six months earlier, and the woman's mind had been flayed by several members of the Parliament, forcing her to reveal all that had occurred in San Diego with Danielle Walthers and her adopted human mother. Two members of the Parliament had died and Alyana had been in complicity with their murderers. Only a decree by the Ancients had saved Alyana, and her connection with the Parliament, though tenuous, had not been severed.

Clint raised the receiver and dialed the supervisor of first-floor housekeeping. He solemnly ordered a cleanup in the library. Initiates would assess the situation and determine the dead woman's other stops from her paperwork. They would masquerade as the woman and make a few of her deliveries, then park her van somewhere deserted and smear her blood around. Her body would be removed and cremated elsewhere.

Without pausing to pick up their clothes, the blood-drenched brothers walked from the room, took the elevator to the third floor, and powered up one of their twin personal computers. Jeremy logged on, inputing an array of private codes, then chose an item from the on-screen menu. The electronic disgorgement of tones followed by a burst of static served as a prelude to the establishment of the modem link to Adrien Cassir's mobile PC. Cassir was their father's personal manager, another power-ful Initiate. After Jeremy imparted the gravity of the situation, his father was summoned.

Devin Tyler phoned them on a secured linkup. Jeremy reported Bobby's declaration, then told his father that Bobby had died just before noon.

"Thet's a fuckin' shame," Devin Tyler said. "Bobby was a good kid. He was one of us, not like that fuckin' priss of a father he got stuck with."

Jeremy sensed from his father's tone that despite his fondness for Bobby De Santo, the man would enjoy making the call to Christian De Santo to in-form him that his son was dead. The elder De Santo might already know, but if not, Devin Tyler was going to have a blast telling him.

Then he recalled that De Santo was in partner-ship with Alyana Du Prey, the Immortal who had allowed Danielle Walthers and her human mother to go free after killing two of their kind. Both De Santo and Du Prey would have to be kept out of the loop for as long as possible. That meant the bitch who had made the call would have to be found and destroyed as quickly as possible.

Both brothers wished they could be there for it.

"Yew boys have done good," Devin Tyler said. "Real good. I'm gonna make some calls, try an' do this right, get something right special out of this fer yew two."

The line went dead and the twins stared at each other.

"What do you think?" Jeremy asked.

Clint smiled. I think there's some real good times ahead, my brother. Some *real* good times . . ."

Chapter Seven

Dani had been devastated by the news of Bobby De Santo's death. She had put herself and the safety of her entire family at risk to save the boy and her efforts had not been enough. The hole in his spleen had ruptured, though it had been partially healed by the boy's innate power, and he had died.

That had been the official story, in any case. But Dani had peered into the mind of Jack Taylor, who had been assisting during the operation, and she realized that Bobby had somehow regained consciousness during the procedure. He must have been terrified. Without thinking he had lashed out with his power and he had debilitated the humans who had been laboring to help him.

Dani blamed herself. She should have stayed with him. Instead, she had gone on another call, and had returned to find that Bobby De Santo had died at 11:57 that morning. The startling blast of euphoria that had overtaken her in the aftermath of the crash had been wrenched away.

Sitting alone in the cafeteria, Dani had rubbed at her reddened eyes. She had cried until there were no more tears, and had allowed Max to hold her in his heavy arms and rock her like a child.

Why had she left him alone? she wondered.

Why had she been so stupid? She knew from the way he had reacted when they had been trapped in the ruined aircraft that the demons in his blood could overtake him. If she had been with him, she could have helped him to fight them down.

"Seat taken?" a voice asked.

Dani looked up and saw the bright, pretty face of Sue Ritchie, her Chief Flight Nurse. Sue was thirty-one, but she was still carded at nightclubs. She was short, with a petite figure. Curly brunette hair framed her heart-shaped face, slightly pudgy and reddish cheeks, and genuinely pleasing features. She had compassionate green eyes. The woman was incredibly cute. Adorable. People teased her, saying that her unflagging optimism made the Smurfs look like nihilists in comparison. Despite her killer cheerfulness, she was a hard-edged, consummate professional when necessary.

"How you holdin' up, kid?" Sue asked.

Dani smiled weakly. The true Elizabeth Altsoba was older than Sue, but she referred to most of her people as "kid." As it was coming from Sue, no one considered it an insult.

"I heard what happened. Do you want to talk about it?"

Shaking her head, Dani said, "It's not the first time. I'm dealing with it."

Sue nodded.

"I appreciate it," Dani said, realizing how ineffectual her words actually sounded. "I'm going to be okay. I'm ready to fly, don't worry."

"Do I look worried?" Sue asked, her eyes practically twinkling.

"You never look worried," Dani groused. "Animatrons at Disney World show more concern."

Sue smiled, radiating love and comfort.

Dani frowned and looked away. Sue had been

87

with her when she had lost her first patient. It had been an old man in Sante Fe who had suffered a heart attack. There had been a spark of life within him, and Dani had done everything in her power as a human healer and as an Initiate to save him, but he had died anyway.

She knew what was coming. Sue was going to recommend counseling. Dani was projecting the false image of Elizabeth Altsoba, keeping Elizabeth's face calm and composed. She strained to maintain a relaxed aura. But when she had looked into her true face, in the mirror of the women's rest room, she had seen how white her flesh had become, how shaky her hands were. Initiates weren't the only beings on earth with empathetic powers. Despite Dani's best efforts to conceal her fragile emotional state, Sue had sensed that Dani was in trouble.

It was true. Pressures were building within Dani. Maintaining the illusion that she was, in fact, Elizabeth Altsoba was slowly becoming too much for her. Simple things like going to the bathroom or checking on a patient at the nurses' station seemed like a military operation to Dani, because she could not walk down a corridor or enter a rest room without first considering the placement of mirrors and using her power to assess the number of humans who might see her true reflection and learn her secret. The effort was draining. She would desire nothing more than to arrive home after her seven-in-the-morning-until-seven-at-night shift and sleep until it was time to get up and do it again, but she had other activities she performed at the hospital, studies that could only be conducted at night.

"Elizabeth?" Sue asked.

Dani forced herself out of her reverie. Her concentration must not waver, she reminded herself. If she became too distracted she might allow the illusion of Elizabeth Altsoba to fall away.

God, what she wouldn't do just to have time to relax, just to be herself for a while. But that was no longer possible. She could quit her job, of course, but she was too firmly entrenched in the Elizabeth Altsoba persona to abandon it. Besides, her mother and brother were depending on her. Sam couldn't work under her assumed identity, and she needed to be with Michael.

Dani looked at her supervisor and shook her head. "Kids are always the worst, aren't they?"

"Losing a patient is never easy." Sue placed her hand on Dani's wrist. "Did I ever tell you about my first?"

"No."

Sue's face became unusually solemn. "I was still an EMT. We responded to a call, a mother giving birth on a street corner. There were complications. I did everything I knew how to do, but it wasn't enough. We lost the baby first. The mother was hanging on, and we tried to get her back to the hospital in time, but a truck overturned and blocked an intersection. Traffic just swallowed us up. We couldn't get out in time. She died before we reached the hospital."

"I'm sorry," Dani said.

"It's all right. I mean, it's all right *now*. It wasn't then, not for a long time. All the high-risk maternity training in the world didn't prepare me for what it would feel like to wake up in the middle of the night and honest to God believe that my arms were soaked up to my elbows in that woman's blood. I had to get help."

"You think I should see the critical-incident-stress briefing team," Dani said.

89

"Do *you* think that's a good idea?" Sue asked.
"Maybe."

The hospital was such a major trauma unit that its employees saw most of the worst disasters of life. Dani's fellow workers, including flight nurses, emergency nurses, O.R. nurses, burn nurses, and the pediatric intensive-care nurses, often became shell-shocked by what they saw. The team helped those in crisis to talk through the situation, and assured them that they'd done the absolutely best medicine. Many times, a healer would have to be reminded that despite their best efforts, people were sometimes not going to be saved. The human disasters they saw on a regular basis often left them in a state where they needed to recover. Chaplains, counselors, and social workers were on the critical-incident-stress briefing team to help them talk through their traumas and then go on.

"You think I won't be able to handle it when my pager goes off?" Dani asked.

"If I thought that I would step in and relieve you right now. That's not what I'm doing. Part of my job is to watch for possible victims of post-traumatic-stress disorder. It's not easy to catch. Personally, I don't think you have anything to worry about, but it wouldn't hurt to see these people. Or if you just want to get together after work with me and talk about it, that would be okay too."

I wish I could, Dani thought. She wanted nothing more in the world than to sit down with someone other than her mother and explain what was going on inside her. When she spoke to Sam, her mother would become nervous and agitated. Sam had enough on her mind without having to worry about her daughter having a complete breakdown.

90

There was no one Dani could talk to, no one she could trust, and the isolation was driving her insane.

"Let's see how it goes," Dani said. "I'll let you know before I get off shift."

Sue gave her an expression that made Dani regret her words. The smiling brunette always knew when someone was bullshitting her. She seemed innocent and gullible. People who didn't know her constantly tried to get things past her. They learned that it was nearly impossible.

"One more pitch," Sue said, undaunted.

"Okay."

"Ten years ago there was a prison riot. A slew of people were brutally murdered. A critical-incident team had to be called for the pathologists performing the autopsies, because they had seen case after case of unbelievable acts that humans had performed on each other.

"I've talked to Max. I know what you saw in that airplane and I know what you went through to save that boy. The team could help put things in perspective."

Dani shuddered. She knew that she should just say yes and get it over with. But she didn't want to have to lie. She would have to endure the sessions as "Elizabeth Altsoba," not Danielle Walthers. She would have to remain in character, play the whole scene, and it would only make it worse.

There was one solution, of course. Two, in fact. She could agree to the sessions, then use her power to reach into her counselors' minds and have them pronounce, after an hour of sitting in blessed silence, that Dani—or Elizabeth—was perfectly all right. That would be a lie, of course. She had wanted to become a healer to help people. How could she help them if she was heading for a crash?

The other alternative was to alter Sue's perceptions, and make her change her mind about Dani's—no, *Elizabeth's*—state of mind. Tampering with the minds of others had become so easy for her. Most of the time she used her power without thinking, without considering the ramifications.

Bill Yoshino had used his power on her in this way. He had intensified her emotional need to serve his own purposes. She had given her virginity to him and became a monster to please him. He had offered her the acceptance she had always craved and for it, she had been willing to make almost any sacrifice. Richard Sterling had used his power to deceive her mother, forcing Sam to see him as the embodiment of everything she had ever longed for, everything she had ever needed or dreamed of having in her life.

It had been rape, in both cases, though Dani always found it easier to believe that her mother had been *raped*, and she had simply been *tricked*. What was the difference between what the vampires had done to them and what she was doing time and time again to so many humans?

Elizabeth's hands were trembling.

No! Dani screamed in the confines of her thoughts. Not Elizabeth's hands, my hands! They're mine, not hers. I'm not her! I'm not!

She looked over and saw that Sue's expression of concern had deepened. Dani trained her power inward and forced herself to relax.

"I have something to do today," she whispered. "But I'm off tomorrow. I'll come in then."

Sue squeezed her hand and said, "Have you eaten anything?"

"No, I haven't had much appetite."

"It's on me then," Sue said as she rose from the table.

"Okay," Dani said. "Thanks."

Watching Sue go to the food counter, Dani wondered what she would do about the appointment tomorrow. At least she had purchased herself a day to consider her options.

A moment ago, she had railed against the idea that she was, in some subtle fashion, becoming Elizabeth Altsoba and losing Danielle Walthers. That might not be so bad, she realized. Elizabeth was someone Dani had instantly admired.

Dani had taken years of memories and experiences from Elizabeth Altsoba. The woman had given them freely. She had understood that she would not live and she did not want the knowledge she had gathered to die with her.

Becoming a flight nurse had been difficult for Elizabeth. There was a long waiting list of people who wanted to fly and the hospital never accepted brand-new graduates. Only experienced emergency or I.C.U. nurses were looked upon favorably. Elizabeth went through the regular orientation, then signed up for the "casual pool." She was given the chance to cover for established flight nurses during vacations and sick leave. The nurse also acquitted herself well on the fixed-wing. She learned that the team was tight-knit. They relied on each other and their personalities needed to mesh. Elizabeth fit in perfectly. When an opening came up, she was given the job.

Even with her wild abilities, Dani could never have placed herself in this position. To qualify, she would have needed a Registered Nurse License, Advance Trauma Training, ACLS — Advanced Cardiac Life Support, and PALS — Pediatric Advanced Life Support. A flight nurse had to be up-to-date on intubations, and had to go to the O.R. and do some if they were rusty. They needed to be proficient in I.V. The hospital preferred certified emergency nurses. Special training in high-risk maternity was also warmly looked upon in a candidate. A bachelor of science and nursing degree was preferred but not required.

Becoming an R.N. would have taken a three- or four-year program. The four-year study would have given her a B.S.N., a bachelor of science and nursing. An associate program would have meant two years plus a year of clinical. The shorter route would have still made her an R.N., but it would have denied her many courses that would have helped to round out her education.

Dani had circumvented all the normal routes. She had the abilities and the knowledge that Elizabeth Altsoba had spent years attaining. She had performed admirably with her borrowed skills, saving hundreds of lives. That did not ease Dani's sense of being a pretender and a thief.

Elizabeth had been ambitious. Had she lived, she probably would have gone on to become a chief flight nurse. The potential was there for her to have been promoted to director of a program, director of emergency services, or a hospital administrator. Her death had been a terrible tragedy. A great loss.

A friend of Elizabeth's had been promoted to director of the recovery room due to her experience dealing with critical patients. The woman did not have direct staff supervisory experience, but she knew how to handle situations. That woman, Jane Fellows, had been a problem for Dani. She had culled the dead woman's medical training and experience, but not every aspect of her personal life. Dani decided that she could not continue the friendship thy way it had been. Using her power, she gradually created a distance between them.

Dani had been unwilling to become close with anyone. Fortunately, Elizabeth's concessions to sociability had usually consisted of going to the parties or events to which Jane dragged her. With Elizabeth and Jane estranged, Dani could remain on her own.

She hated the loneliness, even though she understood the necessity for not involving herself with anyone. When she was home with Sam and the baby, she had very little to do except immerse herself in her thoughts and her endless questions about the nature of her kind.

In her off hours, she had begun a series of private studies and she needed access to equipment, labs, and technicians. The vampires had told her that she was sterile, as were all women of their kind, Initiates or Immortals. Her first task had been to verify their claims. She would never forget the pain that had surged through her when Thomas Mowry, the doctor she had placed under her control to perform the tests, told her the results.

The vampires had not lied.

For a time, Dani became obsessed with discovering the cause for her condition, and finding some way to reverse it. She wasn't entirely sure that she would ever *want* to have a child, but the thought that she would forever be denied the possibility — that all women of her kind would be similarly denied — drove her to search for the truth.

She began with her blood, which was supposed to have been the source of her power as an Immortal. Dani placed two men at the hospital's labs under a compulsion to run every test they could think of on her blood. She had considered her unnatural healing abilities, how she had always been impervious to colds and flu, and had hoped that her blood carried some immunization factor that could be detected and isolated. Perhaps diseases like AIDS could be wiped out by the miracles hiding within her bloodstream.

Other than testing as Type O Negative, however, her blood was perfectly normal.

Further tests upon her physiology had proven that she was, in every way medical science could detect, a human woman. That did not explain how, a month earlier, she had been able to drive a scalpel into her forearm at two in the morning and wake three hours later without a visible scar. The technicians she had used as thralls had been present for this experiment. They had documented her rapid recovery, but they could not offer any explanations. She had healed the way anyone might heal, but the process had been rapidly accelerated. Dani had watched the time-lapse video the men had made, and had been stunned to watch her flesh heal so quickly.

Dani focused her attention on her own infertility, learning all she could of the various techniques used to overcome conditions similar to hers. She underwent tests that proved her to be completely resistant to all forms of treatment. Her eggs refused fertilization even outside the womb. This intrigued her for a time. She was certain that any artificially inseminated fetus would die within her body. Her power would find a way to destroy it. But as her blood had acted perfectly normal when it had been taken from her, her eggs should have followed suit. They did not. She wondered if they were suffused with her power. Perhaps the key to isolating the unique, mutant qualities she had inherited from her Immortal father, whoever that had been, lay in her eggs.

The tests had revealed nothing. Her technicians pointed out that her blood had been healthy within her body, as well as without. Her eggs had not functioned within her. There was no reason to believe they would suddenly become what she wished them to be simply because they had been parted from her. That discovery had shattered her hopes that one of her eggs could be removed from her body, fertilized, and placed within a human host for gestation.

Medical science had failed her. Her reasons for attempting to learn the physical origins of her power were not strictly altruistic. She considered the demon within her blood to be a parasitical organism, something that existed separately from her and acted to corrupt her body and her mind. If that parasite could be located, identified, and removed, she might find a way to cure her own condition.

Dani wanted to be free of the burning hunger that so often ripped through her, but she was not sure that she wanted to give up her paranormal abilities. She had become adept at the use of her power, and she would have felt blind if she were suddenly unable to glimpse the thoughts of others, powerless if she could not reach into the minds of humans and control their actions, or alter their perceptions. She was stronger than any human, and at times faster than she would have ever believed. Her ability to absorb massive amounts of information, retain all of it, and be able to instantly extrapolate in non-linear bursts of thought might also have been a product of her unique and inhuman nature. Without her gifts, she feared that she would be everything she had believed herself to be when she was a child:

Plain, ordinary, untalented, and unworthy.

Dani shuddered. She knew that her self-worth was not tied up in her powers; she drew strength from what she was able to do with them, the choices she had made in her life. She could have been like any of the others. The Initiates she had encountered seemed willing to give themselves over to their blood. They didn't want the responsibility of taking charge of their lives. Dani's mother had taught her the importance of being in control of what happened to her, and it had been that lesson and many others that had allowed Dani to make the lifelong choice she had made, to be a human.

She wondered if she had been fooling herself all this time. The constant series of violations she had performed on the minds of others had made her acutely aware that she could never be human again. She remembered the years in high school after she had been kidnapped by the Willis brothers, the serial killers who had murdered her best friend, Jami. The demon in her blood had been catalyzed into action on that day, and she had tortured one of the men who had taken her, then forced him to kill himself.

Her actions had been so terrifying to her that she had blocked the memories of those fateful twelve hours and had existed strictly as a human girl, with no parahuman advantages. Dani could recall what it had been like to be a human and nothing more, but those memories came with a tight, uncomfortable, claustrophobic edge. The thought of reverting to the limitations of a totally human existence made her recall what it had been like two months ago, when Max had dared her to try a sensory-deprivation tank.

Dani had lasted only an hour.

She knew that her motivations for being a healer also came from a deep-rooted loathing of her true nature, a self-hatred brought about by her love for her amazing and inhuman gifts. Dani had believed that she had come to terms with her murder of Madison, a human girl who had been her first friend in Beverly Hills. The vampires had deceived Madison and they had coaxed Dani to make the kill. Nevertheless, Madison's blood would forever be upon her.

By entering the life of a healer, she was taking the curse of her blood and using it to help those she might otherwise prey upon. She wasn't the first of her kind to walk this path. Jimmy Hawkins, the Los Angeles EMT who had helped Dani and her mother to learn what they would need to know of the Native American cultures to integrate themselves within the reservation, had told her of healers among his people who were also of the demon race.

Dani had been attempting to find others like herself, so that she could learn from them. Her "detective" work had led her to a woman named Candayce Lee, with whom she had an "appointment" after work.

Sue was coming back with two dishes heaped with angel-haired pasta in a cream sauce when Dani's beeper went off. The unit she wore was part of a multi-pager system. The flight crew, pilot, and security and maintenance people were alerted simultaneously. Lifeguard One was part of the citywide response team. The hospital's quality-assurance requirement was that lift-off time was five minutes or less from the initial call. They had not exceeded that limit once in the time Dani had worked for the hospital. It was understood that even if people were in the middle of taking a bite of a sandwich in the cafeteria, or working on a quality-assurance report, they would drop everything and run when their pagers went off.

"I've got to go!" Dani said, staring into the eyes of her supervisor. If Sue were going to intercede, this was the moment. Though Dani was badly shaken, she prayed that Sue would not hold her back. She might never be able to go on a call again if that were to happen.

"What are you waiting for, kid?" Sue said with a smile. "Trying to bring down our average?"

Dani bolted from the cafeteria, racing toward the stairs. There was no one in the stairwell and she took the stairs three at a time, five at a time, and realized that she was, in some impossible way, *flying*. Sam had said that the fallen Initiate Tory had been able to do this.

The moment Dani became aware of what she had been doing, she stumbled and cracked her knee against a step. She gripped the handrail, then pushed herself onward until she climbed the last flight of stairs and burst onto the rooftop helipad, which was monitored by security and equipped with a fire-suppression system.

Max was waiting for her. "We've got a drowned child in an irrigation ditch in Belen."

Dani nodded. Children were always playing in the ditches. Belen was thirty miles to the south. The town's name was Spanish. It meant "Bethlehem."

Another child, she thought, praying that they would save this one. It was a prayer she whispered to herself every time. Often, those prayers were answered.

This morning, they had not been.

Max looked at Dani and winked. "Freddy was in the head when the beeper went off. He got so excited he almost zipped himself up before he was

100

finished."

"Ouch."

"I'll say. It's a hell of a way to get circumcised that late in life."

Smiling, Dani shook her head. She wanted to kiss Max for not asking, "Are you up for it? Can you handle this?"

"There it is, let's go!" Max said as Freddy signaled all-clear to board the chopper. Dani followed Max, ducking beneath the wind created by the churning helicopter blades.

She thought of nothing but her job as they lifted off.

Chapter Eight

Ronna Kaye was walking around in a haze. She vaguely remembered the events in the emergency room, the chaos, and the death of the boy, and had no idea why she had left in the middle of the operation. At some point she must have gone to her locker, because she was no longer wearing a surgical smock. Her clothes were fresh and her purse was hooked over her shoulder. She wore jeans and a white tank top with no bra — she apparently had not been worried about gawkers staring at the tiny nobs that were her breasts — and sat on a bench in a crowded shopping mall somewhere on the other side of the city. Ronna did not remember driving there and she wondered if she had taken a cab. Maybe she had walked, or hitchhiked.

Christ, she had been rattled before, but never this badly. She had suffered some kind of breakdown. That was the only possible explanation. She would take a few minutes to adjust to her surroundings and calm down. Then she would find a pay phone and call the hospital.

The boy was dead. Criminal malpractice proceedings would certainly be brought by his parents. Her career had been ruined. She might even go to jail.

Ronna wished she could remember what had happened and why, but it wasn't possible for her. Instead she found herself thinking of the boy's peaceful face, the slight smile he seemed to display though he was unconscious, and her vow that she would do everything in her power to save him, the same vow she inwardly made before every operation she performed.

Realizing that she was about to cry, Ronna got to her feet and kept her head down. The sign for a rest room appeared at the same time as the boy's bloodied corpse. Ronna gasped and drew back as she saw the beautiful face of Bobby De Santo. He was wearing a hospital gown that was slit in the back. The gown's front was soaked through with blood.

He motioned for her to follow.

It's a dream, this isn't happening, Ronna told herself.

As if he had heard her thoughts, the boy frowned and shot a "gimme a break" look at her. Then he turned and merged with the crowd, which was surprisingly large for a weekday. She looked at her watch and saw that it was lunchtime. When she looked back to the crowd, the boy had vanished, but he had been replaced by Lisa Grimes, her closest friend, who had moved to Los Angeles two years earlier.

"Lisa!" Ronna screamed, breaking into a dead run to follow the woman. Lisa ducked into the entrance of a department store with Ronna only a few yards away. The woman walked around a clothing display and Ronna lost sight of her. Rounding the aisle where she had last seen her friend, Ronna expected to find Lisa standing there, waiting for her.

The woman was gone.

"Ronna, try to keep up," a man called.

She looked over and saw Lee Matteo, the twenty-one-year-old to whom she had lost her virginity twenty years earlier. He was turning his back to her, walking down the menswear aisle, and had given her only a fleeting glimpse of his face. She had recognized his voice instantly, though they hadn't spoken in ten years. His face was exactly as it had been in college, and his thinning hair was once again rich and full.

What am I doing, she wondered, realizing that she was allowing herself to be led by this impossible parade of figures from her past. She closed her eyes and put her hand on her forehead, trying to dispel the nightmare surrounding her. People jostled her and cursed at her as they passed. Her legs felt weak and she began to feel dizzy. Ronna's arm shot out and she prayed that she would find something upon which she could steady herself.

A pair of hands clamped over her arms and suddenly she was in no danger of falling. She opened her eyes and looked up into the face of a handsome security guard. He had thick wavy hair and perfect blue eyes. If he had not been wearing the uniform, he might have been mistaken for a model.

"I'm a doctor," Ronna said.

"Right now, I think you're someone who needs some help. Let's get you into the office. Get you off your feet before you pass out."

"Yeah, okay," Ronna said.

The man scooped her up into his arms and carried her through the store the way Richard Gere had carried Deborah Winger through the factory at the end of that movie she had seen a decade earlier. She thought it strange that no one seemed to notice them. They were an unusual sight.

The security guard took Ronna to the back of the store, carrying her effortlessly through a series of darkened corridors until they reached a large office with two desks, several comfortable chairs, and a couch. Harsh fluorescent light bathed the room. Paperwork was strewn on the desks, a time-card machine was nailed to the wall. A cassette player on the desk played a country-western tape. She recognized the heartfelt voice of Devin Tyler.

Ronna was gently placed on the couch and the security guard walked to a small gray cabinet, which he opened. He withdrew a first-aid box. "You said you're a doctor?"

"Yes," Ronna said, shaking her head. Her dizziness and fatigue were starting to fade. She looked up and saw that the large clock on the wall had been stopped ten minutes earlier and the phones on the desks had been smashed to pieces. A man's bare feet poked out from under the closest desk.

The security guard turned. Blood was spattered over the front of his uniform. He held the first-aid kit open and had removed a sharp kitchen blade.

"Time to operate, sweetie."

Ronna bolted from the couch and ran to the door, noting desperately that it opened inward. The security guard was faster than she was, incredibly fast, and he slammed the door shut, trapping her in the small room. She looked around for anything she could as a weapon, and the security guard grinned, as if he were reading her thoughts.

"I'd say this could be quick if you don't fight back," he said. "But that wouldn't be any fun."

Ronna was backed deep into the room. She found a pair of scissors on the edge of the second desk and scooped them up. Her knowledge as a surgeon might give her an advantage, though the thought of using her training to inflict harm on any living being made her ill.

"Ain't you a right bleedin' heart," the man said, his well-modulated voice suddenly degenerating into a Southern drawl. "Lookee here. Let me show you something."

Ronna watched in horror as the guard transformed, becoming Bobby De Santo, Lisa Grimes, and Lee Matteo. He giggled and allowed his features to run like wax, suddenly changing into a repulsive amalgam of all three, his flesh bubbling and changing.

"It's time to get this procedure under way," the guard said, resuming his natural appearance. "Sorry to break it to you like this, but the anesthesiologist got called away. It's just going to be you and me, snookums. Now let's see, do I want to start with a breast or a thigh? Well, I guess it don't matter much, I'll be cutting into all of it soon enough. Let's just —"

The deafening roar of a shotgun blast sounded. The security guard was rocked as the front of his shirt exploded in a hailstorm of blood and gore. He teetered for a moment, dropped the knife, then looked down at the ruined mass that had been his chest.

"Well *fuck me*," he said as he started to turn.

Ronna couldn't believe what she was seeing. The man should have been dead. She could see through a hole in his chest to the other side of the room, where a dark-haired pregnant woman stood with a shotgun. The woman primed the weapon and aimed it higher as the security guard took a step in her direction. The second shotgun blast vaporized his skull and he fell to the floor, dead at last.

The pregnant woman went to Ronna, transforming in mid-stride to a tall, flaxen-haired man who was dressed like a college professor with a tweed jacket, white shirt, and blue jeans.

"Are you all right?" he asked as he set the shotgun down and examined her, turning her quickly to check her front and rear, the way a parent might treat a child who had fallen.

Ronna couldn't respond.

"You're all right. I hated using the gun, especially with you so close. I was worried that some of the pellets might have sprayed you."

106

"I'm okay," she whispered. She knew that it was appropriate to say, *People must have heard the shots. They'll call the police. We should wait for them.* Those words seemed ludicrous after what she had just witnessed. On some instinctive level she understood that these beings, whatever they were, would have taken steps against being discovered. After all, her savior wasn't worried about the *sound* made by the gun, only its potential damage.

"You probably think you've gone out of your mind, don't you?" the man asked.

Ronna nodded.

"I'll be honest with you. It might be easier for you to keep thinking that." He held out his hand. "My name is Joseph. I work for a man named Christian De Santo. I'm a *friend.*"

Ronna took his hand, amazed that she had made it this long without passing out or screaming.

Christian De Santo sat in Ronna Kaye's empty apartment at a little after two o'clock in the afternoon. Jamie Vasquez, the man Christian had sent his son to Albuquerque to visit, had phoned Christian the moment he had learned that Desert Way Airlines Flight 2027 had crashed. By the time Christian had arrived in Albuquerque, he had learned from his friend that Bobby was dead.

Like Christian, Jamie had once been Parliament. The blood of the Ancients also ran in him. But it was not so fresh anymore. He had quit the Parliament half a century ago, and his tolerance to the light was now only slightly better than that of an Immortal who had never partaken of the Ancients' gift.

Jamie had sent his emissary—a human he had trusted—to the airport. Christian considered himself liberal in his thinking, but even he could not

107

get over his friend's ability to place his well-being in the hands of a human. His son might have easily controlled Jamie's human servant, a task that would have proven much more difficult if an Initiate who was older and more seasoned than his son had been sent. But Jamie had been betrayed by his own kind many times and he refused to put his trust in them.

The humans in Jamie's employ were aware of their master's inhuman nature. They respected and sometimes worshipped him for it, allowing Jamie to tamper with their minds and place shieldings in their brains in a way that Christian might never fully understand. These protective measures would supposedly make them impervious to the manipulations of the Immortals. Christian could not understand how this could be true. An Azreal Block was one thing. Perhaps Jamie's technique involved the same form of manipulation. Christian did not know and at this moment he did not care.

All he knew was that if an Initiate had been present during Bobby's last moments, the boy might still be alive. Christian had reconstructed the scene in the operating room from the testimony of several witnesses. He knew that the doctor had walked out in the middle of the operation, and had learned of the hysteria that had gripped the operating team, causing them to lose consciousness and allow his son to die. A cloud of fear had swept through the hospital during the last sixty seconds of Bobby's life. Christian knew at least part of what had happened. He had come to this comfortable midtown apartment to learn the rest.

Six of his people—each an Initiate—had been sent to find the physician who had walked out on his son's operation. He was confident that they would be successful in their task and would bring the woman to him.

Christian was angry at himself for not sending one of his Initiates with Bobby. The boy had survived the initial crash. Another of their kind might also have walked away. If an Initiate or another Immortal had been in the operating room, they could have countered Bobby's frenzy. They could have controlled his power for him. The boy might not have died.

Christian sat on the living room couch, his hands balled into fists. He wanted to cry. He remembered how it was to cry and he desperately *needed* to cry, but it had been centuries since he had last been able to do so. The tears would not come. They would never come, he knew. The loss of his beloved had been devastating for him. Her final words, her ultimate rejection of his feelings for her—such as they were, such as they *could be* for one of his kind—had nearly destroyed him. But learning that his own son had helped to bring about her death had made him strangely determined not to walk into the flames just yet. That impulse had almost overtaken him many times. Though Mia had been distraught, though her seemingly endless reserve of love and patience had finally been exhausted, he knew that she wanted, above all else, to save her son. Christian had been determined to stay alive until he found out if there was any shred of hope that this task could be achieved.

Jamie had promised to determine this for him. The Immortal was going to spend time with Bobby and pass judgment on the boy. Christian had not held out much hope, but he'd been driven to give his friend the chance to plumb Bobby's mind and find some degree of decency, something that Christian had been unable to discover within the child.

Decency.

The thought made him smile. Had he wanted to see decency as humans defined the term or as *his kind* defined the term? He couldn't say. Perhaps a little of both.

Bobby was dead now, and Christian had no reason to remain alive except to learn the answer to this one final mystery: Why had the surgeon not been affected like the other members of the operating team? Why had she been able to suddenly leave and make a phone call?

In Christian's mind there were two possibilities. The first was that Bobby had placed the woman under a compulsion. If that were the case, Christian wanted to know who the woman had called in his son's behalf and why it had been so important. The second was that another Initiate was present. If that had been the case, it might have been that person who had used their power on the operating team and caused his son's death.

Christian hung his head low, allowing his face to sink into his cupped hands. The second option seemed highly unlikely. Nevertheless, he liked the idea of having someone to blame, someone to find and punish for the misery he had endured.

Someone to *kill*.

Christian heard the key being unsteadily fit into the lock of the front door. The lock disengaged, the door opened. Ronna stood in the doorway. Joseph was behind her.

The vampire shuddered in anticipation as he rose and walked toward the woman anxious to learn the truth of his son's death.

Chapter Nine

Ronna Kaye entered her apartment. A beautiful man with dark, Spanish features stood before her. She was not surprised. Joseph had warned her that this man would be waiting. Her body was stiff, her movements robotic. It had not occurred to her that she was coping so well with the insanity she had faced today because Joseph had placed her under his control. The tall man walked away, releasing her, and Ronna Kaye, a lovely and frightened thirty-five-year-old woman with strawberry-blond hair emerged from the hollow shell that existed only a few moments before. Her body sagged and the dark man went to her, grabbing her before she fell to the floor.

"What in the name of Christ *are* you people?" she asked, shrugging off his arm as he guided her to the couch. She hated the weakness of her body.

"Something I fear you could never fully believe in," he said. "My name is Christian De Santo. My son, Bobby—"

"I know." Her tone had been icy. Under normal circumstances she would have shown nothing but compassion to a grieving parent. Instead, she felt terror and fury.

"Ronna, something terrible has been done to you," he said in melodious, hypnotic tones.

She sensed that he might touch her at any moment, but not in a sexual way. He might reach out and take her hands or caress her arm. The thought made her ill. A part of her sensed that they were not the same.

Ronna shuddered. Not the same *what?*

A feeling had overwhelmed her, one she had at first been unable to identify. Understanding came to her in the form of a terrible memory she had tried for years to repress. She was surprised to find herself tumbling down into that memory, her perceptions of the dark man and her own apartment suddenly vanishing:

Ronna was in college, working part-time for the Census Bureau as a field agent. It had been a quiet morning. She approached the next house on her list, a rundown two-story, and climbed the porch stairs. The front door was open and through the screen, she could see a long, dark corridor. The rug was stained and ratty. The wallpaper was peeling. She checked her clipboard and called, "Mr. Everly? Census. Hello?"

From around either side of the house, she heard the scittering of claws, the low, thunderous growls of animals rushing to attack. Ronna turned and was frozen by the sudden appearance of two black dogs who stopped at the foot the stairs. They were panting, saliva dripping from their maws. She knew that she could not escape them by leaping over the side rail of the porch. It was too far away. She wouldn't get more than a few feet before the dogs would bound up the steps and leap at her. She imagined the shock and pain she would feel if she ran from them and they took her from behind. Their claws would rip into her back as their weight dragged her down, knocking the wind from her.

Stay still, she told herself. Don't move. Be quiet and they won't attack. The first dog slowly climbed one of the steps with a lupine grace. They were coming. Ronna looked at the screen door from the periphery of her vision, wondering if it was locked. She had tried to keep her fear under control, but a part of her mind had said, why bother? That's the only thing holding them off. They can sense your fear, they're hungry for it, feasting on it.

The dogs came up two more steps.

No sudden moves. Calm. Still. Relaxed.

Panic seized her. She grabbed at the door, praying it would be unlocked, certain that she could tear it open even if it were *locked. Her fear and desperation would give her a burst of inhuman strength— the kind that allowed people to lift cars in order to save a loved one or themselves.*

The door was locked. She yanked at it hard, but it wouldn't give.

The dogs were on her before she could draw another breath. One bit her hand, the other her leg. Blood spurted as her hand came loose from the animal's mouth, but the dog was climbinq up on her, its claws biting into her belly and breasts, ripping, and tearing. Needles of agony shot through her as the dog went for her throat.

"Pandas!" a voice cried.

The dogs stiffened and fell away from her. She dropped back against the screen door, chest heaving, thanking Christ she was still alive. Suddenly, she heard the clicking of the screen-door lock and sensed a presence pushing against her from the other side.

"Come on, come on, step away from the door."

She angled her head and saw an old black man pushing at the door. Cautiously, she moved from the door, her legs pained and weakened. The door opened and the hounds brushed past her, chuffing happily as they padded inside and vanished into the house's darkened recesses. The old man shook his head and slammed the hard wooden door, locking it.

113

Ronna stood on the porch in shock, mumbling the word the man had used to control the dog's murderous impulses, "pandas, pandas, pandas," until she reached her car, which she locked herself inside with trembling hands.

She drove to a pay phone, nearly running down an innocent stop sign on the way. By the time the police arrived at the house, the old man had somehow gotten rid of the dogs. As the hounds could not be tested for rabies, Ronna had to endure several painful rounds of shots. Nothing was ever done to the old man or his dogs.

Ronna shuddered as she emerged from the memory. She could not look at Christian De Santo. Instead, she stared at the floor and recalled that many of her co-workers had expected her to quit her job, to shrivel up and become too frightened to execute her duties. But her friends knew how stubborn she was, and they were not surprised when Ronna continued to work for the Bureau. Despite her fully justified anger at the old man whose dogs might have killed her, Ronna's faith in the basic goodness of most people was not shaken.

Animals, however, were something else entirely.

Two weeks ago, she had gone to the house of a friend from work. She hadn't known that the woman she visited owned a full-grown German shepherd. Though Ronna was given the assurances of her new friend that the "puppy" was harmless, Ronna had excused herself and walked back to her car, somehow restraining the urge to run.

For five consecutive nights she had suffered nightmares of being torn apart by animals. She couldn't even pass a pet store in the mall without being disturbed by the strange *otherness* of the creatures.

Ronna had never experienced that sensation because of another human being before. Sitting with

114

Christian De Santo, she felt as if she were in the presence of something that was neither human nor animal, but somehow more ravenous and frightening than either.

"That is how you see me," Christian said, nodding thoughtfully.

Ronna stared at him and suddenly realized that he had, impossibly, been within her thoughts.

"Yes," he said, "perhaps that's all we are, rabid dogs who should be put down."

The surgeon stared at him in amazement. If he was looking for sympathy, he wasn't going to receive it from her. The logical part of her mind was struggling to reject what she intuitively understood was happening: She was sitting in her living room having a conversation with a creature that might have masqueraded as a human being, but was instead something entirely alien.

"Ronna, I understand that you are very brave, and very intelligent," Christian said. "I would like to be honest with you. I would like to tell you—"

"Fuck you," she said sharply, startling herself with the words. She rarely used such language. "I'm not going to be your confessor. Just do whatever you're going to do and get it over with. Sitting next to you is making me sick."

He was not angered by her words. A slight smile traced itself across his handsome face. It might have been viewed as a mocking, paternal smile, one of amusement, but instead it was clearly one of admiration with no trace of pity.

Ronna felt herself relaxing until it occurred to her that perhaps he had the power to *make* her feel whatever he wanted her to feel. She immediately put herself on guard.

"You know that I have been in your thoughts," he said.

She swallowed hard. "Yes."

115

"You understand that I am not human. You have probably gathered that my *son* was not human either."

Ronna nodded.

"What happened in that emergency room was not your fault. You must not blame yourself. Do you have any clear memories of those final moments?"

"It's all — blurred," she answered truthfully, realizing that he would know if she were lying.

Christian drew a deep breath. The amnesia would be part of any standard compulsion. He could get around that easily.

"One of my kind forced you to leave the operation. If you allow me, I can give your memories back to you, and prove that you were not at fault."

The dark man watched her closely. Ronna obviously blamed herself for the boy's death. She was numb at the moment, but the grief and recriminations were waiting for her just below the surface, and they would destroy her when they came.

"Allow me —" he began.

"All right. Yes. Just do it."

Christian reached out with his power and peeled back the layers of her consciousness with the skill of a surgeon at his prime. He caused her no pain or discomfort as he learned that his son had indeed been the one who had brought about his own death. Echoes of other memories came to him, reflections of Bobby's thoughts which the boy had carelessly lodged in Ronna's mind. He saw the efforts of Danielle Walthers to save Bobby and understood that she would have died to help him. In return, Bobby had wanted to destroy her.

Christian withdrew from Ronna's thoughts. There had been no decency left within his son. Had Bobby lived, Christian would have one day been forced to drag the boy into the flames with him. Now he would have to walk that path alone.

Visions of the Walthers girl and the fate that would befall her settled squarely upon Christian De Santo, and he made a decision. His son owed Danielle Walthers not one debt, but two. She had saved the boy's life and would now suffer for his betrayal.

The flames would wait while he fulfilled his son's obligations.

The touch of Ronna Kaye's hand on his arm surprised him. He suddenly realized that he had not withdrawn *completely* from her mind, and had allowed her to glimpse his thoughts. She was no longer afraid or angry.

"Show me everything," she said, contradicting her earlier vow that she would not be his confessor.

Christian allowed his life to unfurl for the woman. She saw his childhood, his dreams, and the fateful day when he became aware of his blood heritage and was forced to give up his days in the light. The centuries moved past while he remained unchanged. The blood, the terror, and the man's eventual reformation played out for her. The deal he had made to reclaim the light and his eventual decision to abandon the group known as the Parliament, despite the consequences, became real for her. She experienced all of it as if she were looking through his eyes, feeling his emotions, his inner conflict, his agony.

Suddenly it was over and she found herself sitting on the couch, staring into his eyes. "You're going to make me forget, aren't you?"

Christian gently caressed the side of the woman's face. "I will take care of everything. The memories of everyone who was involved in my son's death will be changed. Official records will be altered. I want you to go into your bedroom and go to sleep. When you wake up in the morning, life will be as you remembered it. You will know that you lost a patient,

117

but you will also know that you did all you could to save that patient. You will grieve as you might under normal circumstances, but you will move on, your future untarnished."

"I'll forget all of this?"

"Isn't that what you want?"

"I'm not sure. I think I'd rather remember."

"You could remember me in your dreams, if you like. Perhaps one day we'll meet again."

"No. You won't be alive long enough for that."

Christian looked away from her. From the corners of his eyes, he could already see the flames that would bring an end to his terrible existence.

"I want to remember," Ronna said forcefully. Her thoughts suddenly went to the animals that had attempted to rip her apart. She had wondered what would have happened if she had not shown them fear, if she had held her ground. They might have ripped her apart anyway or they might have hesitated and turned away. The question had haunted her. Today it would be answered.

"Very well," the vampire said, and for a brief moment, Christian De Santo felt the way he had 981 years ago, when he had healed souls, rather than devoured them.

Ronna was surprised as he kissed her cheek. His lips were warmer than she would have expected.

"Thank you," he whispered. Then he rose from the couch and left her alone in the apartment.

A few minutes later, Christian sat in the passenger seat of his rented Jaguar. His driver was waiting down the street. He opened his briefcase, took out his cellular phone, and dialed a number. He heard a series of clicking sounds as transponders across the United States bounced the signal through fifteen separate locations, then fed it through three different scrambling systems before it reached the private extension on his partner's desk in Los Angeles.

A woman answered. "Du Prey."

"Alyana," Christian said. "There's something you have to know. I want to negotiate a deal with you, then I want you to make some phone calls. I think you will find the deal to be mutually beneficial."

"I'm listening."

Christian De Santo repeated the message Ronna had given the Tyler boy, then outlined his plan. Alyana made several counter-suggestions, all of which he had anticipated as he had worked with her for almost seventy years and knew how she thought. He continued to be amazed that they had worked together for so long and had never became lovers or even *friends* in the traditional sense, though they looked out for each other's best interests. Each rationalized that they were only serving themselves by doing so. After all, together they were greater than they ever could be apart.

The unique symbiotic tie they shared had even allowed them to weather the trouble six months earlier, when Alyana's position with the Parliament became tenuous and her execution seemed likely. Christian was not certain that they would die for each other, but he often suspected that life separately would not be worth it for either of them.

He wondered if she would walk into the flames with him.

"Consider it done," Alyana said finally, as she struggled to keep the emotion from her voice. "Provided you can guarantee your end."

"Without a doubt," Christian said. The line went dead. He issued a mental summons and his assistant returned to the car.

They drove off in silence.

Chapter Ten

"So, what happened to the tape?" a hard voice asked. "You never gave it to me."

Peter Red Cloud looked up, startled. He had not heard Sam enter his video store. She was dressed in the rags of Paloma, the burned woman. The store was deserted except for them.

"Bread and Chocolate," Sam repeated. "You said that you came to my place to give me a copy of that movie. Where's the tape?"

Peter nodded and reached slowly behind the counter, paying special attention to the tension he registered in her body and the slight rise of her right shoulder. Her hand was in one of the deep pockets of her billowing dress and he had no doubt that she was clutching one of the Berettas. Drawing the tape out carefully, Peter held the cassette out to Sam.

She saw the handwritten label and said, "Put it in the VCR. Let me see a few minutes of it."

"No problem," he said, following her orders without hesitation. He knew she would shoot him if she felt she had been given provocation.

After the tape ran for five minutes, Sam drew her hands out of her pockets and rested them on the counter.

"Thank you," she whispered in amazement. "I saw this film with my daughter when we visited

New York one summer. I've wanted to see it again ever since."

Peter hit the stop button and handed the tape to Sam. This time she took it and placed it in her knapsack. "Surprise her with it tonight."

"I will."

An awkward silence suddenly developed between them. Peter was certain that Sam had been prepared for every contingency except learning that he had been telling the truth. She didn't want to believe what he had told her. Her life was complicated enough. Nevertheless, he loved her, and he wanted her to know that she no longer had to feel alone.

"How did you meet Elizabeth Altsoba?" he asked.

Sam was startled by the question. In the past few hours, she had come to regard Peter as someone who knew *everything* about her life. The discoveries he had made caused Sam to feel that she had no further secrets from him. That was ridiculous, of course. Peter knew nothing of the vampires. He believed, as everyone believed, that Elizabeth Altsoba was still alive. He was unaware that Dani had been present during Elizabeth Altsoba's dying moments, and that she had taken the girl's memories and assumed her life, using her power to make people see her as the Native American.

"That's a long story," Sam said.

"When you're ready to tell it, I'll be here to listen."

"What if I'm never ready to tell it?"

"I'll be here anyway."

Another silence, this one even more dreadful than the last. Sam tried to remember why she had come here, why she had once again entrusted her son to Dorothea's care. There was one possibility that she didn't particularly like, though it seemed the most likely explanation: When she had kicked in the door

121

of her house, her heart had been racing, and she had felt *alive*. The miracle of Michael's birth had changed her, softened her in ways she had never dreamed possible. She had not been worried by these changes. She knew that she would never let her guard down, never allow harm to come to her family through her own inaction or weakness. If a crisis came, she would once again become a soldier.

Peter's revelation had shattered her beliefs. She had allowed the life she had built for the last year to be brought down because of her own carelessness. In the beginning, she had always pinned dark curtains over the windows when she had bathed, but she had liked the feel of the warm sunlight on her body. It had been one of the few indulgences she had allowed herself, a luxury she craved.

Her heart sometimes pounded when she had been bathing and she heard the slightest noise from outside. The tension would fade as she would wrap her face in a towel and look out the window to see a stray dog running from the house. She realized now that she had enjoyed the little game she had been playing with herself; she had enjoyed it the way someone who thought she had nothing to lose enjoyed the sound of a sharp metallic click when she was playing Russian Roulette. Her appreciation of life would rise tenfold. Sam wondered if a part of her had wanted the dark times and the struggles to return.

For a brief time, from the instant she had read the note, she had believed the crisis to be upon her. In that moment, she had changed once again. She was able to abandon all she had worked to build within herself for the last year. She felt as if she had come back to herself and she had liked the feeling. More than liked it, she had *loved* it. Couldn't get enough of it. Wanted it like a junkie might want a fix.

That frightened her.

Sam was acutely aware of her son's perceptiveness. She worried about how her tone or her actions would influence him. The pounding, adrenaline rush of her brief encounter with Peter Red Cloud today had left her high, though she would have preferred to deny that fact. She felt that she had heard the joyous click of an empty cylinder and also felt ashamed to be in her son's presence. She had to leave. It wasn't until Sam was one hundred yards away from Red Cloud's store that she suddenly understood that she had not been wandering at all. She had *wanted* to see Peter again.

Sam liked this man. She was attracted to him. For most of her adult life, she had not been allowed to do anything that was strictly for herself. Caring for Dani and building her career had been her entire life. She would be almost sixty when Michael graduated high school. The thought of dying alone was not pleasant to her.

Sam closed her eyes. She couldn't allow herself to think like this. Her self-indulgence had cost her family once. She could not let that happen again.

In her mind, a bullet was being fitted into the chamber of a revolver.

"Peter, why do you think I'm here? Because you think Elizabeth's in trouble? You think I'm helping her?"

"No."

"Then you realize I'm in trouble. That I'm hiding."

"Yes."

The cylinder was being spun.

"Hiding is the only possible solution to my problem," Sam said. "I never believed I would say that to anyone, but it's true. I have a son and he's in

123

danger. I'd die to protect him. I'd *kill* to protect him. So would Elizabeth."

"I would do the same."

"No," she said, shaking her head. "Don't say that."

The cylinder was caught. The gun was against her temple.

"It's true," Peter said. "I love you. If it came to it, I would die for you and yours."

She looked into his face and saw the most earnest expression she had ever seen before. In that brief instant, she knew that he *was* telling the truth. She felt a strong temptation to tell him everything, and even entertained a brief image of Dani using her power to prove to him that her mother's story was true.

Her finger closed over the trigger. She pulled the trigger and heard the sharp metallic click of the revolver falling on an empty cylinder. But this time there was no sense of comfort or relief.

"I have to know that when I leave, you won't try to follow me," she said in a low, pained voice.

His gaze did not leave hers. "Is that what you want? To leave this place and forget what's happened?"

"Nothing's happened yet," she said, her heart racing once more.

"It doesn't matter what our bodies do. Love is not of the flesh. It's of the spirit."

"Pretty words, but they don't really mean anything."

"Yes, they do," he said. "In your heart, you know that I'm right. That's why you let me leave your house alive. That's why you came back here today."

Sam stiffened. "Peter, I have to know that when I leave, you won't try to follow. You have to forget about this. Forget about all of it. For my sake and for the sake of my children. Please."

"You have my word," he said, though the statement obviously caused him great pain. "Unless you change your mind."

"I won't. I can't." Sam looked away from him. "I'm sorry."

"I understand."

"There's no way you *can* understand," she said, surprised by the sudden desperation which had come into her voice.

"You need to talk, Sam. You need someone to talk to."

"I have . . ." she stopped. She was about to say "Dani." He had not asked about Dani. She wondered if he had somehow drawn the connection. *"Elizabeth* is with me. She only works three days a week. The rest of the time she's there to listen and to help out with Michael."

"It's not the same, though. It's not what you need."

"You can't possibly know what I need. I don't know what I need."

"You need to trust. You need to know that there is one person in this world who would never betray you."

Sam thought of Dani. "I have that."

"Do you?"

The question startled her. Dani had been closing herself off to Sam. She barely knew her daughter now.

"I hope that you will talk to me again before you leave," Peter said.

"I don't know," Sam said as she turned and left, suddenly aware that she might cry at any moment. "I just don't know."

Sam walked back to Dorothea's hogan, collected her son, and locked herself in her home. She cradled her son, keeping him close as she rocked him

125

and sang to him. On the walk, she had managed to shut down her emotions. Images of Michael's birth flooded into her, and she had decided that nothing could be allowed to occur that might one day put her son in danger. She had made sacrifices for him before, and she would do so again gladly. The thought of Richard Sterling or another of his twisted, monstrous kind raising her son was enough to convince her that she had chosen well.

The boy had his father's eyes, but he could be forgiven for that. Sam looked down at her son's beautiful features and caressed the side of his face. Michael was three months old, with sky-blue eyes and a tuft of dark hair. She grinned as he reached up and took hold of her finger. He held it in his tiny fist and moved it back and forth a few inches as he gurgled and giggled. Sam wasn't entirely sure if it was proper to attribute *giggling* to an infant Michael's age, but his face lit up and he always seemed ecstatic when Sam was with him.

"Hello, Bright Eyes. Hello, sweetie," Sam said, playing with his hand and making silly faces. "Yo, munchkin. Whose munchkin are you?"

Michael giggled and beat his hands together, dragging Sam's finger with him.

"You're *my* munchkin?"

The baby kicked his tiny feet in the air. Sam tickled them.

"I made you? I guess I did something right."

Sam thought of Peter once more. She tried to force him from her thoughts, but it was impossible. The man had innocently talked of the first time they would make love. That was a joke. Though Michael's father had not taken Sam forcefully, though she had been a willing sexual partner at the time, Sam had been a victim of rape.

Images from her days as a police officer came to her. When rape calls came in, at least one female

126

officer was generally dispatched. Sam had been sent to thirty-seven of these calls. She had comforted victims and convinced each of them to go through the ordeal of the physical examination in the emergency room. The women would have to stand naked, covered in blood and filth, while a dispassionate photographer made a record of their every bruise and cut. The eyes of those women haunted Sam. The victims hated her for the humiliation they were enduring, a trauma almost as damaging as the rape itself.

Sam had finally learned what it felt like to be on the other side of that terror and humiliation.

One day, on the way out of Peter's store, she had caught sight of the box for a film called *Love Bites*. It was a shlock horror film that Richard Sterling had produced. His name was still on the box. She had rented the tape and had felt incredible anger stir within her when she saw that the film had been lovingly dedicated to his memory.

It had been on the set of that film that Sam had first realized that she was falling in love with the man. He had come to her and their lovemaking had been magnificent. But it had all been a lie. Richard Sterling was a vampire. He had used her as a brood mare, placing his child within her as he manipulated her body and her emotions.

She had enjoyed killing him.

When he died, the compulsion under which she had been placed to protect the life of the fetus growing within her had been lifted. She could have had an abortion. That had been her choice, her *right*. She had marched in pro-choice rallies and worked security at abortion clinics to protect mothers who ran the risk of physical assault by pro-lifers. She believed in the freedom to choose. But Sam wanted this child and she had *chosen* to have it.

She felt a pang of guilt. Michael was not her *only* child. She could not love Dani any less because her adopted daughter had not come from her body. She might not have given birth to Dani, but she had given the baby life after her birth parents had abandoned her, leaving her to die in a garbage dumpster. After Sam had learned of Dani's blood heritage, she had suffered nightmares in which she had reconstructed the events of the night before Dani had been found.

She tried to forget about those terrible dreams, tried to block them out, but inevitably, images from them would return unexpectedly to slice across her consciousness with the cold, unforgiving deadliness of a razor in the hand of a lunatic:

A man and a woman approached the pea-green Dempsey dumpster in Tampa where Dani had later been discovered. The figures were lit only by the pale orange glow of the open bulb overhead. The man had dark, handsome features, and he wore a black, full-length coat over his expensive charcoal-gray suit. His golden eyes glowed in the darkness. The woman beside him had wild brunette hair and perfectly sculpted features. She was dressed in a long white gown and she carried in her hands a naked, screaming baby. Looking directly ahead, the woman was oblivious to the child's cries. As the couple walked forward, they passed through glistening crimson puddles lining the uneven surface of the parking lot. Blood splattered upward, soaking the lower half of the woman's dress. Soon it appeared that the blood had come from her body.

They reached the garbage dumpster and the dark man raised the lid. When he spoke, his wolflike teeth became visible. Snarling, he said, "Let her get taken out with the other trash."

Without hesitation, the woman tossed the golden-eyed infant inside the trash bin. The vampire al-

128

*lowed the lid to close, muffling the baby's screams.
He took the woman's face in his hands, which had
transformed to bone-white talons.*

*"You'll let me try again?" the woman asked, her
eyes filled with fear.*

*"Of course," he said with an inhuman laugh.
"You and all the others . . ."*

Sam forced away the memory of that dark
dream.

She had considered the events leading to Dani's
abandonment by her parents from every point of
view. Dani's human mother had not been killed and
left with her child. Dani had been placed in the
dumpster *alive.* This indicated to Sam that either a
scenario similar to the one which plagued her nightmares had actually occurred, or Dani's human
mother had not been placed under a compulsion at
all. The woman may have been abandoned by
Dani's Immortal father.

In her days with the Tampa police, Sam had seen
other abandoned children. Occasionally the parents
were found, and a few of those parents actually admitted their reasons for dumping their children in
the trash or in the street. One mother had been
completely dispassionate, stating, "He didn't want
me and the kid. Just me. Said if I wanted him, I'd
do something about the kid. I figured someone
would find the brat."

Most were not so forthcoming.

Thinking about this made Sam seethe with rage.
Dani might have died. Christ, the mother might
have *thought* Dani was dead at the time she abandoned her. No, that was giving the woman too
much credit. The mother might have been killed
elsewhere. Later, when the Immortal examined the
child which had been delivered to him, he had seen
that it was a girl and tossed her away.

The possibilities were endless and terrible. Sam

129

thought of how Dani might have been lost to her, and how empty her life would have been without her daughter. Dani was a human girl. She suffered, through no fault of her own, as a child whose parents were substance-abusers might suffer, inheriting their addiction. Dani's symptoms of this problem had not manifested until after her first period, and with the exception of one terrible day when Dani was sixteen, the girl had suppressed them until Sam had taken her daughter to Beverly Hills, where the vampires forced Dani to submerge her humanity in a river of blood.

The same thing could happen to Michael, if they were ever found.

Jesus, she didn't want to think about this.

She had to think about it. Peter Red Cloud knew her secret. Sam's instincts told her that Peter would keep their secret for the rest of his life, if that proved necessary. But she couldn't trust her instincts. With all that had happened to her, she knew that she could not trust anything but her love for her children.

You need to trust. You need to know that there is one person in this world who would never betray you. Even if he maintained his silence, there was always the chance that he could come in contact with one of the Immortals — or even an Initiate — and their power could be turned upon him. If they knew of the search for the killers of two members of Parliament, they would rape his mind, leave him shattered, or maybe even dead, after they extracted what Peter knew of the fugitives.

Dani would have to be sent to him. His memories would have to be changed. He would love her no longer.

He would be a threat no longer.

That was the cold, proper, logical assessment of the situation. There was something welling inside

Sam, however, something that didn't care about logic. It was a need that she had worried she would never again be able to fulfill.

She sat in her home, staring into the beautiful face of her son, and realized that she had no idea what she was going to do about Peter Red Cloud.

Chapter Eleven

Dani pulled up before the Glass Tiger Bar and Grill, and was amazed to find a parking space during happy hour. The tongue of sunlight darting between the rows of buildings lining the downtown area was harsh and burning, even through her sunglasses. The glare did not bother her. When she lived in California, she had made a religion out of working on her tan. Her darkened skin had faded in places, but her arms and face were taking a reddish cast from the amount of time she spent outside, on her job.

Dani locked up her shit-green Duster—or so her mother had proudly described the car when they picked it out—and looked at the vehicles lining the street. She had been worried that her wreck would draw too much attention, and was relieved to learn that she was in no danger of bringing the property values down. Judging from the collection of beat-up Hondas and oxidizing Fords, the clientele of the Glass Tiger was not the yuppie crowd at all. Dani missed Los Angeles, but she had been grateful to escape the barrage of BMWs that had constantly greeted her on the roads.

She was still feeling the incredible surge of relief that had moved through her earlier in the day when Lifeguard One had reached the drowned little girl. The child had been only five years old. Dani's heart had been racing when she had seen the child's unmoving chest.

They had revived her. She was going to be fine.

The last call of the day had been a traffic accident in Edgewood. A power line had been brought down and a man had been electrocuted. Once again, they had been able to save the victim, and this time the man would have died if Dani's powers had not been employed.

Dani left work feeling better about herself, energized and ready to face whatever trials still lay ahead of her. She had driven to the bar with the radio blaring, and she had sung along to anything that came on, whether she knew the lyrics or not.

After leaving her car on the street, Dani took a quick glance through the bar's window and saw that it was a blue-collar hangout, with twenty or twenty-five customers, mostly male. That meant she would be hit on constantly unless she used her power to deflect the attentions of the bar's patrons, or simply assumed a visage that was unattractive enough to keep them away.

Dani was no longer afraid to use her power. She felt exhilarated over her triumphs that afternoon and knew that she could reach out with her silver thread without concern. She was a healer blessed with a unique and powerful gift. If she occasionally chose to use it for her own purposes, that was her right and privilege.

Dani stepped inside and noticed the mirror behind the bar. That was not a problem. She walked directly to one of the booths lining the wall, keeping her back turned to the mirror. Her dark hair was braided and all she had to remember was to make whatever false identity she assumed possess the same exact hair and clothing. The face and the eyes were all that required shielding.

To all outward appearances, she was still Elizabeth Altsoba, and she decided that her somewhat plain Native American face would serve her well enough. If a problem arose, she would deal with it. Dani smiled pleasantly at a waitress.

"You know what you want, hon, or do you need a few minutes?" the waitress asked. She was a tall woman with auburn hair, out-of-control freckles, and a friendly but tough smile. Her name tag read, "Tabitha."

Dani noticed that there were menus on the table. She didn't bother to glance at the one closest to her. "Whatever's on tap. I'm meeting someone."

"Sure," Tabitha said, closing the small book she carried. "Be right up."

"Thanks."

The waitress left and Dani looked around as unobtrusively as she could. The woman Dani had come here to find was not seated at the bar or at any of the tables. The bar was L-shaped, and the small rear section held a pool table, a jukebox, and a couple of video games. The Glass Tiger was not large enough to accommodate a second room. Candayce Lee was either hiding in the ladies' room, or she hadn't yet arrived. Dani realized that she should have reached out with her silver thread and checked the waitress's memories. She decided that unless the Lee woman showed up first, she would do just that when Tabitha came back with her drink.

As she waited, Dani considered her reasons for hunting down the Lee woman. Dani felt like a predator. An animal stalking her prey. The sensation was somewhat exciting, Dani was ashamed to admit. She *enjoyed* using her powers in this way. She was pursuing her mother's old vocation, acting as a private detective. The phrase, of course, was oddly applicable in some ways and not at all apt in others.

The form of detection Dani applied *was* exceedingly private. She used her psychic powers to get answers and doctor the memories of those she had questioned to prevent them from ever being fully aware of her existence. But she could not really consider herself any kind of traditional detective, as she was only serving her own interests.

Dani had been hunting others of her kind who had chosen to use their powers to help humans, rather than prey upon them. She had read about faith healers who had performed miracles, and had discounted most of what had been documented. A few cases, however, were vastly intriguing to her. Last month she had read an article dated two years earlier, about a woman who had been on the street when a speeding pickup truck had blown a tire and came barreling up the sidewalk.

The woman, Candayce Lee, had been saved from death only by the fortuitous placement of a collection of objects rooted to the sidewalk—a *USA Today* stand, a cement garbage bin, and a pay telephone. The pickup had struck her, but its speed had been reduced by the buffers it had first demolished. Candayce Lee had been driven back through the glass window of a clothing shop. She had sustained internal injuries and broken limbs, but she had survived.

The worst damage should have been to her magnificent face, which should have been cut to ribbons by the glass. Those who saw the victim shortly after the crash had said that her face was little more than a torn, bloody mask. One had become sick at the sight of her. A man had broken from the crowd of onlookers, ordering people to call 911 as he tended to the woman. He had kept his back to the people and bent over Candayce Lee, staying with her until the EMTs arrived. Then the man had vanished into the crowd before he could be questioned. The EMTs had found no signs that the man had given Candayce Lee any form of treatment. Nevertheless, the woman's face had borne only a few noticeable lacerations. Her wounds had been so shallow they would heal and require minimal cosmetic surgery. Her blood pressure had been surprisingly level, and her injuries, though serious, would not prove fatal.

The onlookers, when questioned later, could not

agree on a description of the man who had gone to Candayce Lee's aid. Dani had been certain this man was another of her kind, an Initiate, perhaps even a fallen vampire, like herself.

For a time, Dani had become a full vampire. The first kill she had made occurred when she was under the influence of Yoshino. According to the conditions of their blood, Dani had needed to make a second kill, this time completely of her own accord, within three days. Yoshino told her that if she refused to kill again, and forever become an Immortal, she would die. Dani had tried to fight the need within her. With her mother's strength, she had succeeded. She had learned that the vampires had lied to her. Death had not come for her, she had simply fallen back to a state more powerful than that of an Initiate, but less godlike than a full vampire.

She wanted to know if her healing abilities had manifested because she had once been turned, or if any Initiate could perform the miracles she had learned to master. That question might have been answered last year, when she had befriended Marissa, a young woman who had been terrified of her powers. But Marissa's true father, a powerful Immortal named Richard Sterling, had turned his daughter before Dani could learn if Marissa shared Dani's healing powers. Sterling had set into motion a chain of events that climaxed with his own death and that of his daughter, and had turned Dani and her mother into fugitives.

Occasionally, Dani had entertained perverse notions of finding another Initiate and experimenting with them, but contacting other Initiates was a frightening prospect. The Parliament actively recruited half-vampires, promising that they would be turned by influential members of the vampire cabal. Though she had been able to utilize the *self-healing* powers of Bobby De Santo, Dani had no way of knowing if Bobby could use his powers to heal others.

Bobby had died and she would continue to grieve

136

for him. But she couldn't keep herself from wondering how she might have been able to go back and use the boy to fulfill some of her curiosities about their race had he lived.

Dani shuddered. What she had just been considering was monstrous. She recalled the mocking tone of Richard Sterling as he discounted Dani as any real threat because she was only an Initiate.

Little vampire, he had called her.

The society of Immortals was overrun with prejudice. Full vampires felt contempt for Initiates, and both viewed humans as little more than prey or breeders. Females of their kind, whether they had been turned or not, were considered useless as they could not reproduce.

Dani wondered if she had, in some way, surrendered to the inherent and repulsive sin of pride that marked their race. As a fallen vampire, did she feel herself to be superior to an Initiate who had not been turned? If that were true, how was she beginning to view humans?

Suddenly, Dani was shocked from her thoughts by the approach of the waitress, Tabitha. She wondered how often the woman was teased about her name. Dani couldn't help but think of the old *Bewitched* TV show, and she had to fight off the urge to wriggle her nose at the red-haired waitress.

Instead, she found herself doing something worse. She lashed out with her power, slamming into Tabitha with enough force to make the waitress shudder and nearly lose her footing. Dani used her wild talents to steady the woman, manipulating her body like an expert puppeteer. Tabitha set the mug of beer before Dani and looked at the golden-eyed young woman with a blank stare. Dani knew that in Tabitha's mind, the woman had suddenly been yanked out of her normal, waking reality, and was living in a Technicolor dreamworld.

Unable to resist the lure of Tabitha's fantasies, Dani

137

followed the woman into her waking nightmare:

The dingy, smoke-filled bar was lit only with neon. The patrons were outlaws, thieves, and killers—dark and sometimes handsome men with scars and deep, brooding eyes. A fat man in a T-shirt stood behind the bar, smoking a cigar as he cleaned glasses. From somewhere close came the call of a foghorn and the rattle of chains. The bar was on some ancient dock in a fog-enshrouded city. It was night, and Tabitha herself had changed. She no longer wore her light blue and burgundy uniform; she was clothed in a tight, body-hugging red dress that revealed the swell of her large breasts and displayed nearly all of her incredibly long and shapely legs. In reality, she did not have large breasts or long and shapely legs. But this was not reality. Even her freckles had faded. Tabitha caught her reflection in the mirror behind the bar and saw that she was stunning. Her hard edges had softened and her pale skin had darkened considerably. The woman's pushed-up nose was now a cute button nose, and her angular face was now heart-shaped.

Tabitha walked up to a man who might have been even more beautiful than she had he shaved his three-day stubble or dressed in decent clothing. His suit looked as if it had been slept in for several days, and his raincoat, hat, pants, and shoes were so wet that he might have fallen off the nearby pier for all she knew.

She wanted him desperately.

The man took off his dark sunglasses and revealed blazing golden eyes. "Have you seen this woman?"

Tabitha looked down and saw that he was holding the photograph of a gorgeous blond woman with wildly flowing hair. She might have felt some jealousy, but she knew that she was far more desirable than the woman in the picture. Moving forward, Tabitha pressed herself tightly against the man, pressing her crotch against his leg.

"What do you need her for when you can have me?" she asked, without inhibition or restraint.

"Maybe I want both of you."

Tabitha looked at the photograph a second time and smiled. The woman in the picture was beautiful enough to be an erotic film star. Tabitha had rented dozens of adult videos, and had never been entirely sure which sex she enjoyed watching more. Now that she looked the way she did, perhaps it was time to conduct an experiment. Her ex-husband had been a terrible lover, who had never allowed her to try anything. He told her what he wanted and became angry if she tried to do anythinq more. His attempts to satisfy her were dull and clumsy.

"You think you can handle that?" Tabitha asked, running her hand over the detective's crotch. The bulge she encountered and the fire she saw within his bright golden eyes gave her the answer she needed.

"Tell me about her," he said.

"Well. I've seen her. She comes in three or four times a week to meet her boyfriend. He works down the street, at the newspaper. I think he's the guy who draws the little spokes on the tires in those ads you see. Something like that."

"Has she been in tonight?"

"Not yet, but she's due. What do you want with her—other than the obvious?"

"I'm a vampire," he said. "She's my intended victim."

"Is that right?"

"It is. I went to Fossworth and Sons, where she works. They told me I might find her at the Glass Tiger."

"I bet you didn't expect to find me, did you?"

"No, I didn't."

Tabitha smiled lasciviously. "So, you're a vampire."

"That's the rumor."

"Do you want to suck me or do you want to fuck me?"

"Both."

The detective hiked up her skirt, heaved her on top of the pool table, and took out his throbbing member.

She threw her arms around his neck. Screaming, she drew him down into her. He laughed as she screamed, laughed as a dozen men surrounded them, urging them on, lining up for their turn. The golden-eyed man laughed and took pleasure in her every—

Scream, the woman was screaming, what was happening? Dani shuddered and was wrenched out of the fantasy world she had unleashed in the waitress's mind. She stood and found herself staring at a nightmare she had created. Tabitha had been placed on the pool table. A burly man with blue jeans around his ankles was driving himself into her, holding her ankles and keeping her legs locked in the crooks of his thick arms. Gathered around the table, some content to watch, others stroking themselves openly in anticipation, were almost two dozen men. The other women who had been present only a few moments earlier had vanished. Dani worried that they had been taken off to the bathrooms or the business offices by other men, but the only women she sensed were the waitress and herself.

Tabitha's screams, which had been of pleasure only a few seconds earlier, had suddenly turned to shouts of pain, fear, and rage. Dani was horrified. The woman was coming out of her dark, erotic fantasy into a harsh, cruel reality. Tabitha's dreams of being desired had been twisted. She might have found the idea of being taken by a handsome stranger in a public place extremely arousing, but she had been in control of that fantasy; nothing had occurred without her consent.

"No, please, stop," Tabitha cried, pushing at the curly haired man who pounded into her.

In the dreamworld, Dani had been the handsome stranger, the dark private detective. She was the one who had been *fucking* Tabitha. Somehow the lines between the fantasy Dani had released in Tabitha's mind and reality had been blurred, and everyone in the bar had become involved in acting out the scenario Dani had unleashed in Tabitha's mind.

The woman was being raped.

Dani was raping her, using the men in the bar as her surrogates.

With horrible finality, Dani realized that the crash had come. She had believed herself to be recovering from the blow of Bobby De Santo's death. She thought that she would be able to arrest the mental strain that was consuming her.

Instead, she had snapped, and Tabitha had paid the price. Dani had become everything she had despised.

The waitress had emerged from the fantasy. Her "lovers" either had not, or were so overcome with lust they did not care. They had awakened to find themselves in the middle of performing a gang rape and they were enjoying themselves too much to stop. Dani could not believe that in all of these men, there was no shred of humanity or conscience, that not one would be so vastly disturbed by what they were doing that he would try to stop it immediately. Instead, the rape continued.

Dani could not afford to wait to discover whether her power was still controlling the men, whether she had released some primal urge in their minds that even she could not control, or whether they were a group of would-be rapists who had been waiting all their lives to fulfill their desire to dominate women. The participants seemed further aroused by Tabitha's screams. Tabitha beat and clawed at the curly-haired man. Two other men grabbed her wrists and pinned her down. Someone slapped her. Sickened, Dani moved forward, lashing out with her power.

A part of her had engineered this event. The demon in her blood had wanted this and was reveling in the sheer pleasure brought about by the waves of fear and desire crashing through her as Tabitha was being attacked. She refused to be a slave to her blood, to her inhuman needs and desires.

A taunting voice inside her whispered, *But there is no demon, is there? We established that a long*

141

time ago, Dani. There's nothing here but you.

Dani shut the voice out. She couldn't listen. She had to save Tabitha.

The men were ignoring Dani.

She knew that she could hurt these men very easily, and she dearly wanted to do so. Killing them with a thought, bursting blood vessels within their brains, constricting their airways, stopping their hearts—the ways to kill a man with her power were almost endless, and the darkness within her screamed for her to take such measures. Instead, she blanketed the entire group gathered around the pool table with her power and uniformly severed their own links with their senses.

The man who had been pinning Tabitha down, slamming himself into her with regard for nothing but his own pleasure, fell away from her, suddenly unable to stand. Panic seized the men who had been cheering a moment earlier. Dani knew what they were experiencing. She had plunged each of them into the hell of total isolation, the same hell she had experienced in the sensory-deprivation tank two months earlier, at the hospital. They had no control over their bodies. Every man who had participated in the rape was now aware of nothing but his own thoughts. There were no sights or sounds for these men, no tactile sensations whatsoever. They could not hear their own screams, or feel their wildly beating hearts.

Dani felt smothered by the storm cloud of fear she had created by punishing the men in this manner. She wanted to run away from what she had done, but she could not leave Tabitha behind. Wading through the sobbing, shaking forms of the men, Dani gently lifted Tabitha from the pool table and carried her from the bar.

Chapter Twelve

The woman was crying and she allowed herself to be taken by Dani without a fight. Kicking open the swinging double doors, Dani realized that she had used enough force to cause them to fly back on her. She darted back, and when their momentum faded, she turned and pushed her way through the doors with considerably less effort and effect. She didn't realize how badly she was shaken until she got to her car's passenger side and found that she couldn't think of a way to reach into her purse and retrieve her car keys without setting Tabitha on the hood or the trunk. Such an act seemed too reminiscent of the first physical act in the rape the waitress had just suffered, when her "handsome detective" had placed her on the pool table.

"Christ," she whispered, almost in tears. First she couldn't open a goddamned door, then she couldn't figure out how to get her keys. She had an idea of what had happened to her. Sue had been worried that Dani might suffer the terrible effects of post-trau-matic-stress disorder. That may well have been the case. Sue had no knowledge of the other traumas Dani had suffered through before the loss of Bobby De Santo that morning. Before now, Dani had never fully considered the danger that was involved if someone with her powers were to suffer a nervous collapse.

143

Her human personality had retreated and the demon had emerged.

"I didn't do anything, I didn't do anything," the red-haired waitress chanted. The sun had become a deep red orb. The sky was streaked with pale silver, purple, and orange. Dani didn't think she had been in the bar long enough for twilight to descend. A terrible thought occurred to her: Perhaps the man who had been inside Tabitha when Dani came to her senses was not the first. The gang rape might have been in progress for as long as an hour before Dani regained control of herself. Several men might have taken Tabitha.

"I know you didn't do anything, I know," Dani said, intense waves of guilt washing over her. This was her fault. All of it. She thought that she had the demon under control, and instead, she had let her guard down long enough to become a slave to it. "I need to set you down. Can you stand?"

Tabitha nodded and Dani gently set the woman on her feet. The waitress's legs wobbled and Dani held her around the waist for support as she found her keys and unlocked the door. She scraped the paint around the lock several times before she was able to insert the key. This was insane, ridiculous, horrifying. Dani could not believe this was happening. She checked her watch and saw that she had been in the bar for an hour and ten minutes.

"Oh, God, this isn't possible, I couldn't have done this," Dani whispered, and suddenly an image came to her. She saw herself sitting in the bar, a terrible smile on her face as she watched one man after another take the waitress. The image became even more repugnant as she saw herself reach between her own legs and touch the fiery wetness of her sex.

Four customers came to the bar from the street and were turned away by Dani's power, their perceptions and desires altered instantly.

Dani forced the image away and nearly put her fist

144

through the passenger-side window. Then she became aware of Tabitha, and knew that she had to stay in control. Now and forever she would have to be on constant guard against what was inside her.

"It'll be all right," Dani said, the words sound hollow even to her. "Come on."

Helping Tabitha into the passenger side of her Duster, Dani took another look at the dying sun and felt no comfort from its fading light. She closed the passenger door and walked around the back of the car, afraid to look into the face of the woman she had violated. Pausing outside her own door, Dani wondered what in the hell she was doing with this woman. She had no idea where to take her. They could go to the police, but how could Dani explain what had happened? The waitress probably needed medical attention. Dani had training and vast knowledge, but she was afraid to touch her. Using her *power* after what had just occurred was out of the question.

Dani cranked the ignition, pulled away from the corner, and heard a car horn blast as a white four-door swung around her. She wasn't thinking; she had nearly pulled into oncoming traffic.

Christ, it was all going to hell. Everything was going bad and she couldn't get control of herself.

A hand closed over hers and Dani looked sharply to the right, where Tabitha sat. The woman's expression revealed an unexpected wellspring of strength.

"Take me away from here. Please," Tabitha said.

Dani nodded, checked for traffic, then pulled onto the road. She realized that for the first time in what seemed like years, Dani was out of her mother's presence, out in the real world, and was not using her power at all. The discovery startled her. She should have masked her presence in case she was seen carrying Tabitha out of the Glass Tiger. The Duster and its tags were also a problem. To make everything worse, she was not projecting the false visage of Elizabeth

145

Altsoba. The true face of Danielle Walthers had been exposed.

She had one option and only a few seconds to exercise it. The car was pulling away from the bar. If she was going to use her power, she had to do it now.

Dani decided to take her chances.

As she drove through the streets of Albuquerque, she stole a few glances at Tabitha. The waitress was looking up at the sunset. The back of her hand was resting on her trembling lips and she was clutching her stomach with her other hand. The enormity of what had been done to her was becoming apparent. The woman's face had become pale.

Dani went for a few blocks before she decided to stop fooling herself. She was not taking this woman to any emergency care center. Not yet.

A memory came to her. Last year, she had been driving to a date with a gorgeous young detective named Ray Brooks when she had become involved in a major traffic accident. The crash itself, plus its bizarre aftermath, had left Dani a mess. Her mother had come for her and had insisted that Dani get behind the wheel once more, drive them home, then drive them to the beach the next morning. Her rattled nerves were no excuse for avoiding the wheel, in her mother's estimation, and the woman had been right.

Fuck you, she thought, *the last thing I need is a goddamned "Get back on the bicycle" lecture.*

Her anger aside, Dani knew that there was no other choice. She would have to remove the memories of what had happened from the waitress's mind. There was no way she could live with herself knowing that this woman would be plagued with nightmares of the rape for the rest of her life. Both Dani and her mother had been raped. They had suffered terribly and would continue to suffer so long as they lived.

But she would have to use her power. She would have to enter Tabitha's mind once again. It would be a second violation.

146

Bullshit. She had seen emergency room teams strip off the clothing of unconscious victims, not for their own perverse pleasure, but to ensure that they could reach the damage the victim had sustained and help them. Dani would be in control of her power. She would use it to heal Tabitha. It wouldn't make up for the terrible act she had committed, but she would be compounding Tabitha's injuries by allowing the woman to suffer.

Dani could heal Tabitha's physical and psychic wounds, even if it meant staying with the woman and using her medical knowledge and whatever stolen supplies were necessary to help her. Soon, she would have to use her power to put the waitress to sleep, so that she could go back and deal with the men she had left behind. Their memories would also have to be stripped and replaced.

The longer she waited, the worse it would be. Dani knew that. Nevertheless, she kept driving, and chose to keep the waitress's mind from the attack she had suffered by doing things the human way, speaking directly to her, not invading her thoughts.

"I was wondering," Dani said.

"Uh," Tabitha said.

Dani stopped. She was about to ask why the bar had been named the Glass Tiger. That would have been incredibly stupid. All she would have done was remind the woman of the trauma she had just endured. So what was she going to talk about? she wondered. Ask the woman what movies she had seen recently? If she went to college? What her family was like? Did they approve of the man she'd married, then later divorced? Dani already knew too much about the woman; she knew things that no human being could ever know, unless they had investigated her past or asked her direct questions.

Earlier, Dani had been feeling entirely superior to humans, though she wasn't entirely willing to admit that to herself. But when she thought of the quiet power and dignity she had seen in the eyes of this woman, even after the horror the waitress had just endured, Dani felt ashamed. Humans had none of the advantages of her kind. They could not look into the minds of others to tell if someone was telling the truth. Humans could not manipulate the perceptions of others; they had to rely on what God had given them. They had to trust. Most damning of all, Immortals could not live without humans, while mortals had no need of her predatory race.

She finally understood which race was superior.

"Jesus, I just can't do this," Dani whispered as she squeezed the steering wheel, acutely aware of Tabitha sitting beside her, waiting for Dani to ask her question. They were stopped at a light, and Dani looked around to see that they were somewhere in a rundown part of the city. She hadn't realized where she had been heading. Darkness had enveloped them and Dani had switched on her headlights, but she didn't remember either of these events.

The light changed and Dani tried to spot a street sign. She was thinking about the men back at the bar. They might be recovering from her attack by now, or others might have wandered in and found them. She had not gone into their minds deeply enough to take their names and addresses. They might as well have been animals that she had whipped into a frenzy. They were lost to her, she now realized, and several of them might have seen her true face before she had taken their perceptions from them.

The darkness within her attempted to rise in consolation, putting forth the possibility that they could have been driven insane by what she had done to them. If that were the case, she would have nothing to worry about.

Suddenly, the woman beside her began to gag. Dani looked over in alarm and realized that Tabitha had clamped her hand over her mouth and was about to become sick. A boarded-up 7-Eleven loomed be-

148

fore her on the right and she turned into the parking lot. Tabitha clutched at her door as Dani threw the car in park. The woman found the handle, opened the door, and stumbled out of the car, falling to her knees as violently wracking dry heaves ripped through her.

Without killing the engine or shutting off the lights, Dani raced from the car and came around to see Tabitha crouched before the headlights, her face buried in her hands as she sobbed hysterically. The hot, searing, white light bathed her hair and made her appear ethereal.

"Tabitha?" Dani asked, looking around to see if there were any humans on the street. There were none. The street was mainly residential and no cars were in sight. Dani went to the side of the waitress, whose red hair appeared almost ghost-white in the searing brightness of the headlights.

The woman's grief and horror at her situation reached out to Dani, but she fought away her hunger. The speed with which it retreated surprised Dani. She felt different, more in control, as if she had been away from herself and had just returned.

"Tabitha, I know there's nothing I can say. I know there's nothing I can do to make up for this. Hell, you probably don't even understand that it's my fault."

"Not your fault," Tabitha whispered, her voice sounding strange as it filtered through her hands, which were still closed over her face.

"I'm going to have to do something."

"Yes."

Dani bit her lip as she coiled her power. She was going to use her wild talents to learn where the woman lived. Then she would take Tabitha home and get her cleaned up. Later, she would remove the woman's memories of the rape. Dani thought of her mother, who would be getting worried about now. Dani had said she'd wouldn't be too late. Her mother would have to understand.

"I'm sorry," Dani said, reaching out to put her hand on Tabitha's shoulder.

"I'm not," the woman hissed, taking her hands away and turning sharply in Dani's direction, so that the headlights revealed her features.

Dani's legs turned to water as she stared at the impossible sight before her. She gasped and fell backward, removing her hand from the other woman's shoulder as if she were worried about being burned. The waitress's hair had changed. It was no longer a rich auburn, it was platinum-blond. Though it was still short, it was now spiky. The woman's freckles had vanished, and her flesh was now porcelain smooth and clear. Her plain features had stretched and reformed into those of a European fashion model who did not need or care to wear makeup. She had a sharp, perfect nose, oval face, perfect cheekbones, stunning eyes, and rich, sensuous lips. Dani recognized her instantly.

"Angel?" Dani whispered, nearly choking on the word.

The vampire rose. "You know it."

Dani stared at Angel's wildly grinning face. This was impossible. She had seen Angel die. Then it slowly came to her: Actually, she had *not* seen Angel die. She had seen a building she believed Angel to be within blown to hell.

Refusing to accept that this was happening, Dani employed a final burst of maniacal energy and raced for the driver's side of the Duster. Her hand was on the door when she felt Angel slam into her from behind. The wind was knocked out of her as she was thrown against the car door. Dani tried to lash out with her power, but she felt a terrible burst of pain in her mind that left her momentarily dazed. Angel withdrew and Dani slid down against the car door and fell to the pavement.

Shaking, Dani regained her breath and attempted to rise.

"You want to get up?" Angel asked as she grabbed Dani by the hair and arm and lifted her into the air. "How high do you want to go?"

As if she were handling a child's toy, Angel flung Dani straight upward. The golden-eyed woman screamed as she found herself climbing into the air. Dani rose ten feet, fifteen feet, and wanted to scream that this was impossible. The vampire sailed up beside her, catching Dani from behind, grabbing her roughly. Angel hugged Dani tight, encircling her former friend's waist and pinning the young woman's arms. She yanked both of them upward — fifty feet, a hundred feet, twice that — describing elegant patterns in the air. Then she arced around and sent them downward aiming them at the roof of the Duster.

"Wheeeeee!!!" Angel screamed in a mocking, childlike fashion. She veered off at the last possible second, nearly driving them into the side of the boarded-up convenience store. The vampire swung around, pirouetting in midair, and swung Dani around, unmindful of the young woman's screams. Angel brought them upward, then drove them downward, and finally settled on a dizzying, pendulous motion. "What's the matter, hon? You wanted to fly again, come on! Enjoy yourself! Let go!"

"Fuck you," Dani managed to whisper.

Angel flung Dani toward the front window of the Duster, which shattered on impact. Dani fell away from the car, rolling over the hood until she once again fell before the car's headlights. She was vaguely aware of Angel's descent, and the clicking sound of the woman's heels. The vampire wore Tabitha's waitress's uniform. No, Dani thought. There was no Tabitha. It was Angel all along. The whole thing had been a lie.

Angel grabbed Dani by the back of the neck once more, yanking her head back, exposing her throat. Dani had a glimpse of Angel's hand, which had transformed into a razor-sharp talon, and tried to coil her

151

power. The attempt failed. She looked into Angel's grinning face and waited for the vampire to rip her throat out.

"That's enough."

Dani was startled to see Angel's expression change. The insane glee the vampire had exhibited only moments before vanished as quickly as her talons, which retreated into delicate human hands. A soothing warmth entered Dani's mind as she felt something dark and loathsome flee. Understanding came to her as she sensed the approach of the *others*.

Looking up, Dani saw four figures descend to the ground, surrounding Angel. The car's headlights bathed each of them as if they had levitated before a spotlight. She recognized Alyana, whose resemblance to Isabella, the first vampire Dani had slain, continued to startle her. The other three Immortals were all males, extremely handsome and powerfully built. She guessed that they were members of the Parliament, like Alyana. Dani only glanced at them. Her gaze returned to the dark eyes of Alyana. The last time she had seen the Immortal had been over a year ago, at a resort in San Diego. Isabella had been Alyana's adopted daughter. Sam and Dani had only been allowed to live because a part of Isabella—her memories, her touch—remained within Dani. Some of Alyana's final words to Dani returned to her:

Others of our kind may not be so forgiving. I will do what I can, but there are no guarantees that I can keep the truth of what has happened from the other members of the Parliament. They may come for you one day, and if they do, I will be powerless to stop them.

Dani turned her gaze back to Angel. It had not been the demon that had resurfaced within Dani, it had been Angel, manipulating her power and her perceptions.

Angel's cool, businesslike facade crumbled as she laughed and said, "Don't you *wish*."

"This has waited long enough," one of the male vampires said.

Dani nodded. She knew that it was over for her. The members of the Parliament had only stopped Angel from killing her because that honor had been reserved for one of them. She thought about Sam and Michael and how she had let them down. They needed her, depended on her, and she was about to die in this lonely place. She did not want to think about what they would do to her mother and brother, but horrifying images flooded into her mind. Scrambling to her feet, Dani steadied herself against the car and waited for the attack.

The vampires did not move. They were going to draw it out, wait for Dani's fear.

Dani turned her gaze to Angel and whispered, "So you found someone new to order you around. You always were a weak-willed little cunt."

Angel took a step forward in anger, then relaxed, realizing that Dani was attempting to goad her. She smiled and unfurled her hands at either side of her body, once again transforming them into talons. "What you've just experienced, Danielle, my sweetie, was a test of the emergency broadcasting network. And you know what, hon? You just failed, big time. . . ."

Chapter Thirteen

"All right. Tell me about the goddamned finger."

Peter Red Cloud smiled and opened the door to his home, allowing Sam to brush past him and go inside. She was dressed in Paloma's most attractive and colorful robes and scarfs. The makeup was removed the moment he closed the door behind them. Sam slipped off the baggy layers of clothing. Under them, she wore dark shorts and a white top.

Peter's house was a threadbare adobe, much like her own. Sam had expected to see movie posters lining the walls, but none were in sight. The man did not take his work home with him. His furniture was sparse, a ratty couch and recliner, a pair of old fold-up tables perfect for TV dinners, a mattress in the corner, a shower basin, and a stove. Sam had visited prison cells that had more character. There were no photographs on display. She wondered if he had any stashed away, and if so, what the subjects would have been. She knew almost nothing about Peter, and most of the Native Americans she had dealt with over the last year were reluctant to volunteer anything about themselves. There was no reason to believe that Peter would be any different.

It was early evening. Dani was late and Sam had left Michael with Dorothea. She could not explain why she had felt the need to see Peter once again, but it had been a compulsion she had found impossible to resist. He had answered the door wearing blue jeans which displayed his small hips and a white T-shirt that showed off his strong upper torso and muscular arms. His feet had been bare.

Candles had been lit. The room was awash in a delicious warm orange glow.

"Would you like some dinner? I could heat something up," Peter offered.

"I'm not hungry," Sam said. That was a lie. She had been unable to eat all day. Standing here with him, she felt herself begin to relax. Her stomach growled, as if on cue.

"Are you sure?"

"Maybe later."

"If you like. Want to sit down?"

She looked at the couch, touched the cushion to make sure a spring wasn't about to leap out at her, then sat down. It was comfortable and soft, exactly what she had needed. Peter sat in the recliner, though he remained perched on the edge, his face pleasant and inquisitive.

"I'm glad you came," he said.

"I'd be happier if I knew why I bothered."

"Would you like me to tell you?"

"Sure. Why don't you?"

"You came because you know, deep down, that everything I've said to you is true. And you also feel a little off balance. I know so much about you, but you don't know anything about me."

Shit, she thought. No one had ever been able to read her the way this man could. "So tell me."

"Not much to tell."

Sam laughed. She knew he was going to say that.

"I was born on the pueblo. My parents died when I was very young. I became a man here and got a girl pregnant when she was only sixteen. My Amy had a little girl. We got married and she got pregnant again before I shipped out for Viet Nam. I was over there when I found out that she had lost the baby. A shaman convinced her that she was cursed. It upset her so much she hung herself.

"Later, I talked to the Anglo doctor. He said she was rhesus negative. I was positive. Our first child, Caroline, had been healthy, but during the birth, her bloodstream produced something called *agglutinogen,* a substance that destroyed our son's red cells. The bottom line was that her own blood destroyed her child and Amy couldn't face that."

"What happened to your daughter?"

"She died of a fever when she was five. I left the pueblo and moved to California. One of the survivors from my unit helped me to get a job." The salt-and-pepper-haired Native American smiled. A rarity. "I worked there for seven years. The white world offered me little comfort. There was only one place I had ever known peace. I came home and met a woman named Marietta. We fell in love and were married a year later.

"Marietta suddenly decided that she wanted to go to the city. She was tired of this life and admitted that she had been attracted to me because I had lived away from the pueblo. She had hoped that I would tire of it once more and take her away. I told her that I could not go with her. I was not the same man away from this place, these people.

"My wife changed before me. She said that I was a coward. She could not understand how I could tolerate life on the pueblo after all I had been through. This place should have been what the Navajos called a ghost-house to me."

Sam nodded. She understood the custom of many Navajos to seal up the house where someone had died, leaving only one small opening through which the spirit could escape. Places where people had died were considered forbidden as the ghosts were generally still trapped there and the living risked contamination by their spirits.

"She died from cancer. The last days of her life

were spent in the terminal ward at the University Hospital in Albuquerque. She would joke that she finally got away from the pueblo at least. It was a terrible death. She suffered. I've had years to think of what I would do differently. I realized that by denying my wife her dream, by not caring about her needs and placing them above my own, I helped to weaken her spirit and allowed the demons to plant the disease that killed her."

Sam stared at him in shock. "You allowed this?"

"I did."

"That's bullshit!" Sam shouted, suddenly angered. "How goddamned self-centered are you anyway? Your wife can't even get cancer and *die* without it being a direct result of something you did. I had to watch my mother go insane as her brain was eaten by her disease. It would have been easy to blame myself—hell, she even screamed at me a dozen times that it was my fault. But I know now that it wasn't. There wasn't anything I could have done to keep my mother from dying and I didn't do anything to make her sick in the first place. What you're talking about is the most self-serving crap I've ever heard.

"Where do I fit into all this? You think that if you make some noble sacrifice on my behalf, that's going to even things up for what happened to Marietta?"

Peter stared into her dark eyes. He was silent.

"I mean, I know—look, I'm sorry. I know I'm not coming off as sympathetic to your losses. Two wives and two children. That's terrible. I'm sorry. But I think in ways you blame yourself for each of them. Am I right?"

Peter said nothing. His expression was unreadable.

"You were away from the pueblo. If you hadn't been, you could have kept Amy from killing herself, right?"

The man did not even blink.

"Caroline had a fever and she died. Maybe she would have gotten better medical care if you had taken her from the pueblo. The fever wouldn't have killed her. Or you were off doing something and she had been left with the elders. They let the fever go too long, or had a shaman do a singing to bring it down, but that didn't work. Then you rushed her to the hospital but it was too late."

Peter's gaze was unflinching.

Sam found herself talking louder. Peter's lack of response to her words had enraged her. "Then you lose Marietta to cancer—the woman is *raped* by this disease—and you think that if you had given in to her demands, everything would have fucking been *all right?*"

Peter leaned forward, staring at Sam's beautiful face. She was on the verge of tears.

"No," he said. "I do not believe that. And it is exactly the same for you. Or it should be."

Sam went pale. "What are you talking about?"

"You are torturing yourself for something that was not your fault. Michael's father raped you."

Fear gripped her. "I never told you that."

"You didn't have to. I didn't tell you what I did in California. I was a police officer."

"Christ," Sam whispered.

"Just like you."

"No, not like me," she said, rising from the couch, turning in a vain effort to hide the tears that had started to descend from her dark eyes. "I never used to go in for entrapment."

"None of what I told you was a lie."

"Fuck you," she said, wondering why she was not gathering her disguise and running from his house. She had turned from him, but she had made no effort to flee. "You lied to me. Everyone lies."

"I love you."

"Worst lie of all."

"You know that it's not."

"Fuck yourself."

"I want to spend my life with you."

"Liar."

"You wouldn't have come to me tonight if some part of you didn't trust me."

Sam shook her head. She now understood why she had come to Peter. In ways she could not reveal to him, she had saved him from undergoing the same form of violation she had suffered. It had been in her power to have Dani enter his mind, alter his perceptions, and edit his memories. But she had not allowed that to happen. Because she had rescued him from undergoing the same form of psychic rape she had endured, she felt an intimacy with him that he could not understand or appreciate, and would only misinterpret if she tried to explain.

"Don't trust you," she whispered. "Can't trust *anybody.*"

"Because everyone betrays you. Everyone hurts you."

"Yes." She was crying openly.

"Everything I told you is the truth. For years I allowed myself to believe that it had all been my fault. But you were right. None of what happened was my fault. And what happened to you wasn't your fault either."

"You don't know what happened."

"Tell me. Then I'll tell you what happened to my finger. I've never told anyone the real story."

"How will I know if you're bullshitting me or not?"

"You'll just have to trust me."

"Jesus," she said, covering her face. She sat down on the couch. "You really want to know." It was a statement, not a question.

"Yes."

"Everything."

"I want to know."

Sam told him as much as she dared. She described the case Richard Sterling had hired her to investigate and her immediate attraction to the man. It would have been impossible to describe the exact nature of the violation without revealing the existence of the Immortals — which might have seemed ridiculous to someone who had never been exposed first-hand to the monsters. Instead, she described Richard Sterling's uncanny ability to become whatever she would need whenever she needed it. She told Peter how Richard had charmed away the fears she had spent twenty years nursing, and how everything he had said and done had been a lie.

"He used me," she said, wanting desperately to tell Peter how Richard had been able to take control of her body, alter her perceptions, dominate her will, and twist her emotions. "He took me for everything he could get out of me."

Worst of all had been the Azrael Block. She had been present when another human who had been placed under Sterling's control had acted out the final sequence in his "programming." The man had suffered an attack that was so violent it ended with the man biting off his own tongue and suffering a heart attack. Sterling had placed an Azrael Block in the man, a death command. One had been implanted within Sam too. The vampire wanted to ensure that Sam could not abort his child and would bring the baby to him in a year's time.

She recalled the first anniversary of the Azrael Block's impregnation. Dani had held her hand all night, and when the day had passed and nothing had happened, Sam finally believed that the compulsion under which Sterling had placed her had died with the man.

She wanted to tell Peter all of this. Only then could she be free. But it was too great a burden. How could she trust him with the knowledge? He might think that she had gone insane. She could picture him quietly starting procedures to have the authorities take Michael from her. No matter what he imagined he felt for her, he would place the child's welfare first. In his place, she might do the same.

Instead, she described the physical torture she had endured for the last year. Her sleep had been sporadic, at best. Getting to sleep would take forever and if she woke in the night it was almost impossible to fall back to sleep. On the rare occasion when she was asked about her exhaustion, she would write it off to having an infant in the house. In truth, Michael rarely troubled her at night.

Then there had been the nightmares. In her dreams, she would constantly relive the morning when Richard Sterling made love to her. The dreams were not simply a replay of the traumatic event, as the sex itself had not been anything but a joyous release when it actually occurred. In the nightmares, Sterling took her by force, beating her into submission, making her perform horrendous acts and somehow causing her body to respond with pleasure to them while her mind screamed in agony. She endured stomach pains, tension headaches, and incredible bouts of anxiety for no apparent reason.

To compound these symptoms was the constant reminder that she had lost all control of her life. She could not be Samantha Walthers because of what Sterling had done to her. For the sake of her son, she had to remain in hiding, unable to seek counseling or become involved in programs that might have helped. She knew that statistically, nearly three quarters of the rape victims who volunteered at rape crisis centers recovered from the most violent symptoms. That was not an option she could explore in her new life. If she hadn't had Michael, her emotional life would have consisted of fear, depression, humiliation, embarrassment, and anger.

"It wasn't your fault," Peter said soothingly. "None of it was your fault, Sam."

"Easy for you to say."

"Do *you* think it was your fault?"

"I let him into my life. I wanted him. He didn't throw me down and tear my clothes off. I fucked his

161

goddamned brains out like some stupid kid. Christ, when Dani lost her virginity to that bastard Yoshino, I thought, she hadn't learned anything from my mistakes. Then I turn around and let the same thing happen to me."

"That's the first time you mentioned Dani. Where is your daughter now?"

Sam swallowed hard. "It wasn't safe for us to stay together. She's okay."

"Yoshino's the man who was killed in the explosion at the warehouse. The drug dealer."

"Yes," Sam said, remembering the story that had been given to the press.

"You don't hate him," Peter said.

"What? Who?"

"Richard Sterling."

"What the fuck have I been saying? Of course, I fucking hate him. I hate him more than I've ever hated anyone in my life."

"That's not true."

"Jesus, what the fuck do you know about it?" she screamed, suddenly unable to restrain herself. "You think I don't hate that son of a bitch? I killed him, all right? I set him on fire and shot him in the head seven goddamned times. What does that fucking sound like? A Valentine's Day card? A goddamned Hallmark greeting?"

"It sounds like you were pissed. That's good. Remind me never to get you that pissed at me."

"This isn't funny."

"No, it isn't."

"My only regret is that I can't do it again. I wish he were here right now so I could blow his fucking head clean off."

Sam stared at Peter. She had just confessed to murder. He hadn't seemed at all surprised. Nevertheless, now that she was looking at him as another ex-cop, she recognized the process that was going on in his mind. He knew that she was on the run. Now he

162

would believe he knew the reason: Richard Sterling's murder. In time, he would investigate the man's passing and would learn that, according to the public record, Sterling had not died in the manner Sam had described. The contradiction would bother him. He would continue his investigation. That might draw attention from the vampires and lead them back to the pueblo.

Of course, she had no guarantee that he would try to learn the truth. Peter had left the white world and his position with the police behind. Their conversation earlier came back to Sam:

What happened to Michael's father?

He died.

Was it what he deserved for the way he mistreated you?

As a matter of fact, it was.

Then it's good that he died.

"There isn't a day that goes by that I don't want to see him die," Sam said slowly. Her sudden outpouring of emotions had frightened her.

"That's because you only killed his body," Peter said, tapping his forehead. "Up here, he's still got power over you. In your mind, you're keeping him alive."

"Bullshit."

"It's true. You know it is. If it wasn't, you would have walked out of here long before this."

"Fuck you!" Sam cried.

"Do you see him in me?"

"Yes."

"In all men?"

"Yes. Especially his kind. I want to kill them all."

"You don't. You don't even hate him, not the way you should. There's someone else you hate more."

Sam's chest was heaving. What in the hell was he talking about? The only other person involved in the situation had been Dani, and she could never hate Dani.

163

Nevertheless, Dani had entered Thomas Begay's mind and had placed him under a compulsion to believe that he enjoyed her bread. The girl could argue that it had been a small thing, that it had hurt no one, but that was not true. Even if Dani had performed this task for no motive other than wanting to ensure her mother's happiness, what she had done was wrong. There was no fine line dividing the lesser or greater evils of invading the sanctity of someone else's mind unless it was absolutely necessary.

What was Dani becoming that she could so casually perform this task and say nothing to her mother? How many other people was she using her power on, and for what reasons?

Sam shuddered as she considered her daughter's actions.

"It's you, Sam. You hate yourself," Peter said.

She got up. "This shit I don't need."

"It's true." Peter rose and touched Sam's arm. "You should have been able to see through this man. You should have seen him coming. But you didn't. He tricked you."

"Shut up."

"He was everything you had been keeping your guard up against for twenty years and he walked right in. You let him walk right in and take over."

"Shut up! That's not true."

"Sure, it is. He wanted you and you let him have you."

"You weren't there. You don't know what it was like for me. I didn't have anything. Not anything. I hadn't let myself feel anything for a man in twenty years."

"Why not?"

"Because I had to protect Dani."

"Your daughter needed you and so you denied yourself."

"Yes."

"Your son needs you now and so you will do it

164

again."

"Hey, I'll tell you, Peter. This is *not* the way to my heart, all right?"

"I think it is. You denied yourself because you were afraid. You didn't want to risk getting hurt again. Dani was your excuse. Michael is your excuse."

"Drop dead."

"You seemed to think your heart was taken from you. But you know that isn't true. What do you feel for Michael?"

"I love him."

"And Dani?"

"I love her. What are you getting at?"

"What about yourself? How do you feel about Samantha Walthers?"

She could not answer the question.

"You *hate* Samantha Walthers," he said. "Samantha Walthers was weak. She allowed Richard Sterling to trick her. She should have known better but she did everything wrong, she opened herself up to the wrong man, and now *you* have to pay for it. Admit it, Sam. You loathe yourself. You despise yourself."

Sam was shaking. Everything Peter said was correct. She had been unwilling or unable to admit any of it to herself.

Until now.

"I have to leave," she said hurriedly.

"Don't you want to hear about my finger?"

She shook her head. At this moment, she didn't give a flying fuck how he'd lost his middle finger.

"Ask around. There are stories all over the pueblo. I can tell you a few. Then I'll tell you the truth."

"Some other time," Sam said as she gathered Paloma's dress. She suddenly had need of the disguise. All Sam wanted was to hide herself away in her new identity and never again have to look at herself. Peter had held a mirror up to her and she had hated what she had seen.

"Running away isn't going to fix anything," Peter

said. "Believe me, I know."

"You don't know *anything*." she said, though they both realized that Peter had cut to her core and had revealed much of what she had been denying to herself for the last year. Sam had thought that by not talking about what had happened, it would somehow get easier. But that hadn't been the case. The longer she held the truth inside her, the more volatile it became.

She had attempted to adopt not only the physical disguise of Paloma, but also the serene inner self of this invented woman. Again, it had not worked.

She had confessed Richard Sterling's murder to Peter. There had been no amazing catharsis. She didn't feel any better. Nevertheless, now that she had started, the urge to tell him everything, to share with him all that had happened over the last few years, had become overwhelming.

Stop me, she thought as she pulled her scarfs over her face. Don't let me leave here without telling you.

Peter watched her, his hard, proud features revealing only the love he had professed for her. He wasn't going to force her to do anything.

Thank God, she thought. Her earlier instinct had been correct. It might be possible for Peter to live with the knowledge that Sam was a killer. Murder was a part of the natural world. No one, however, could be expected to believe her incredible stories about the vampires without first encountering the Immortals and learning the truth for themselves.

She stopped and turned. "You can't go to the police."

"I won't. I would never betray you."

"You have to forget what I told you about Sterling."

"I can't do that. Every moment we spend together is precious to me. What you reveal about yourself matters more to me than my own life. I can forget nothing."

166

"Promise you won't do anything about it. Don't make inquiries. If you do, you could bring the people I'm running from down on me."

"It's not the police, is it?" he asked. "You're not running from them."

"No," she said as she walked to the door. "I'm not running from them."

"The police cannot protect you?"

"They can't."

"I cannot protect you?"

"No one can."

He nodded. "Then you have my word. I will be silent."

Her relief was palatable. "Thank you."

"What about my story? How I lost my finger?"

"Save it for another time."

He nodded. "Another time, then."

She turned and left his home.

Chapter Fourteen

Dorothea Odakota cradled the baby in her arms. She was a fifty-three-year-old round-faced woman with a stocky build and a kind demeanor. Her thick black hair was streaked gray, and her eyes revealed a strength that could only come from living through hardships and confronting adversity. Her hard, deep blue eyes softened as she gazed at the burned woman's child. The baby was the most well-behaved infant Dorothea had ever seen. The only time Michael ever cried was when he was ill, and those incidents were extremely rare. The plethora of minor sicknesses that most children his age endured seemed to have made a detour and gone around him, striking instead at other children at the pueblo with redoubled ferocity. She had often remarked to her husband that it was as if Michael had received some special blessing from the gods.

That was ridiculous, of course. His blood clearly marked him as not of the people. His mother may have been Spanish—though Dorothea suspected this was a lie, despite the woman's fluent grasp of the Spanish language—but his father was an Anglo, no matter what Paloma said to the contrary. She could see it in Michael's features and his beautiful, sky-blue eyes.

Dorothea had been surprised by Paloma's late night visit. The burned woman had apologized profusely for her intrusion and had seemed more agitated than Dorothea had ever seen her. In all the time Dorothea had known the woman, Paloma had never asked her to watch the child at night. She didn't ask what was wrong. Paloma was an extremely proud woman and would not beg for assistance unless she had no other choice. Dorothea knew that Paloma would feel terrible at having to ask the favor, and did not want to make the woman feel worse by attaching a price to her services: *Tell me what's going on if I'm to help you.* Nevertheless, she was curious.

Dorothea said that she was only too grateful to take Michael for the few hours Paloma would require. The burned woman kissed the baby, played with him for a few moments, then regarded him with her warm, loving eyes before she departed. Dorothea could sense Paloma's distress, and was surprised that Michael had not done the same. She expected him to be unruly at the change in his routine, or to cry over his separation from his mother. Instead, he was serene.

At times, Dorothea had the sense that Michael enjoyed being near the distress of others. Dorothea and her husband had been embroiled in an argument once when the child had been with them, and she had been terrified that their harsh words would disturb the baby. When they had gone to check on Michael, he was smiling and laughing, moving his tiny hands as if he were trying to applaud. At the sight of Michael's too-cute-to-be-believed antics, their anger had fallen away and they had embraced. Michael had seemed even happier at this.

Later that same night, long after Paloma had come to retrieve her baby, Dorothea had entertained a strange and wonderful thought. She'd wondered if Michael had somehow been responsible for quelling the anger she and George, her husband, had felt. That was impossible, of course, nothing but an idle fantasy. The thought was comforting nonetheless. That night, she had slipped into a beautiful dream of

169

a time and place when the *old ones* walked the earth and bestowed miracles to the true people. One of these old ones cured the sick and brought peace to several warring nations. He was a dark-haired man with Michael's sky-blue eyes and beautiful smile.

Cradling Michael now, feeding him from the bottle his mother had left, Dorothea thought of the first time she had met Paloma. Elizabeth Altsoba had committed what many had considered an ill-thought-out act by bringing Paloma to the pueblo. A wide mix of people lived in Isleta. If Elizabeth had studied the various reservations and chosen one for Paloma's residence based on the varied races living there, Isleta might have seemed like a very good location for her. Naturally, it had been Elizabeth's only choice as she had come from Isleta. But unfortunately, life on the pueblo had not been particularly pleasant for Paloma. The woman had gone out of her way to avoid the attentions of the many who wanted to visit and see the child, and she had insulted a few too many of the wrong families. If she had wanted to be left alone, she would certainly have her wish.

Completely alone.

Dorothea had remembered how it had been for her when she had left the res for a time and returned with her husband, George Odakota. He was a Sioux. She had felt the sting of losing many women who had once been her friends. Over the years, she had reached a friendly accord with them, and even considered many of them trustworthy. It was clear, however, that she had committed a serious breach and would never again be considered in the same terms she had been before she left the pueblo. The frustrating part was that nothing was ever said directly to her. All the indications that she had been ostracized were subtle ones, and if she had confronted the other women directly, they would have acted shocked and hurt, and they would have treated her even worse because she had made such an insulting accusation.

170

There was no way to regain what had been lost, she simply had to live with it.

When Paloma had needed help, Dorothea had been the only one to reach out to her, even though she knew that she would be tempting even more scorn than she had already acquired. She had no regrets and found that she was quite intrigued by the woman. Paloma would go on about her days as a child in Puerto Rico, telling stories and expounding on Puerto Rican customs. But these reminiscences seemed hollow, as if she were telling them only to help establish that she was indeed Paloma Corazon, something she did not have to do, unless, perhaps, she was *not* that woman.

No matter who she was, or why she was here, the burned woman was honorable and strong, and she deserved not only Dorothea's friendship, but also her loyalty. Dorothea had sensed that if she herself were in trouble, Paloma would not hesitate to come to her rescue.

A scratching at the window shocked Dorothea from her reverie. She walked with Michael to her window and looked out to see a nightmarish face looking back at her. The woman shuddered and froze, wanting desperately to look away, but the eyes of the monstrosity waiting outside the window held her. She could not take her gaze from it, even though she knew instinctively that it wanted to bore into her mind, steal her thoughts, and reach deep to violate her. To stare at the creature's gaze was to give it power over her. She had to look away. For her sake and for that of the child she held in her hands, she had to look away.

It was impossible.

The creature had her and she was powerless against it.

Dorothea studied the face outside her window. There was nothing else she could do. Its small, marblelike eyes were dark. Simmering red fires burned within their depths. The fur covering its face and elongated snout was a bright silver. The creature's lips were pulled back in a feral grin, revealing rows of razor-sharp incisors.

The face staring at her was that of Coyote, the Trickster. The body beneath the neck was primarily human, though tufts of silver fur lined its chest and arms. She could not see its legs and she wondered if they were human or those of a beast. The monster's hands were talonlike, the fingers stretching forward like ivory daggers. Silver fur covered the backs of the creature's hands.

She knew both the religions of the Spanish Catholics who once held this land and of *the people*. It was believed among many Native Americans that Coyote and Silver Fox created the world. Dorothea had wrestled with the myths and images of both religions and had come to the conclusion that the old stories employed symbols, and were not to be taken literally. The Catholics believed in a single Creator. Her people felt God was divided, with equal parts of good and evil, order and chaos, wisdom and foolishness. The Coyote represented all the baser halves of the equation. Countless myths were told of the creature whose selfishness often resulted in the pain or loss of others, though he generally employed clever and entertaining means to bring about a victim's downfall.

Coyote was standing outside her window, watching her with dark, hungry eyes. Furtive movement behind Coyote made Dorothea jump, but she did not take her gaze from the creature. There were others that were like Coyote, a blend of man and animal, and they were outside, accompanying the Trickster. She heard them scratching at the door. One of them had climbed the ladder and was on the roof, dancing. The concept of such a beast performing a dance made her heart thunder, but Dorothea did not allow her mind to break under the strain of the impossible sights and sounds surrounding her. She heard the howls of the creatures, wondered why no one was coming to help her, and guessed that there were a half-dozen of the beast men surrounding her house. Her husband had gone off with his friends for the evening. She was alone and terrified.

The scratching sounds bit into her and she flinched as she heard the pounding of heavy hands on the walls.

"You are not real," she whispered. "You're some kid with a mask and gloves. Not real."

Coyote tilted his head slightly and seemed hurt. He reached up with his talons, gripped each side of his face, and pulled his head apart. The front half of his skull split down the middle and broke into two clean and neat pieces while the back half of his skull remained intact. Dorothea screamed as the creature's bloody skull transformed and somehow presented his brain box, the bone shoving the organ right up to the window for inspection. Then he undid the damage, melding his head back together so swiftly that Dorothea did not have time to look away before the two halves of his face joined together and his piercing eyes bore into her and held her once more. Coyote shrugged and raised his hands up in a gesture that seemed to say, "Well? Are you satisfied *now?*"

Dorothea's reply was a strangled "What do you want?"

She shuddered as Coyote pointed at the child in her arms. She screamed as she heard the door splinter, crack, then burst inward.

Dani was powerless to prevent the vampires from frightening her friend. They were contemptuous of all religions, though they claimed their origins to be dependent upon that of the Christians. She was too tired, drained, and horrified to worry about it, but if she had the strength, she would have added complete hypocrisy to the sins of her race.

Her face was bruised and bloodied from the impact with her front windshield. A sharp, constant tongue of pain had burrowed into her skull and remained there. One of the male Immortals held her with his power. She could do nothing, say nothing, and, if it came to it, *think* nothing that her captor did not allow. He was Parliament, and he was on his guard against her. They knew that she and her mother had killed five of their kind and they were being suitably cautious. Of course, Sam and Dani had killed Sterling with Alyana's blessing and assistance. From the looks the woman had been giving her, Dani knew that she could expect no further help, no quarter, from the Immortal.

The man holding her was Devin Tyler. Dani had been stunned when she had finally taken in the faces of the male vampires. Tyler was a country-western singer whose latest release had achieved stature rivaling that of Garth Brooks. He was a *Kennn-tuck* as he liked to refer to himself, proud of his heritage and his home state. The man had a face capable of reflecting the pain and aspirations of Americans everywhere. His jaw was suitably square, his eyes green and arresting, his cheekbones chiseled, his mouth surprisingly soft and pleasing. Framing his handsome face was long brown hair tied in a ponytail and partially hidden under an Orioles baseball cap. He wore a brown leather jacket, white shirt, blue jeans, and snakeskin boots.

"Christ, I want to get this shit over with," he had growled a half-dozen times on the drive out of Albuquerque in a cheap, stolen van. Dani found it all the more disturbing to listen to talk of her imminent death when it was spoken by a voice she had long associated with caring and compassion. Though Dani was not a major fan of country music, she had enjoyed what she heard of Tyler's releases.

The next man was Ted Lewis, the owner of a nationwide chain of fast-food restaurants. Taking a cue from Dave Thomas of Wendy's fame, he had starred in his own series of whimsical commercials to promote his restaurants. He was taller than Tyler, a bit stockier, and he looked remarkably like an American version of John Cleese. His self-deprecating humor had made his ads a great success, his restaurants an even greater one. He had gentle gray eyes and a soft, slightly jowly face, though his nose was solid and pleasing. His cheekbones made one instantly wonder if he had resembled a Greek god when he was a young man. He wore a striped shirt and red tie under the dark blue jacket of his expensive suit.

The last man was Allen Henkle, a real-estate broker who could be seen late at night on a host of informercials, sitting poolside in Maui as he instructed people on the ways of becoming financially independent. Henkle had curly black hair, a sexy mustache, and heavy Italian features. At first glance, he had reminded Dani of Ray Brooks, a police officer whose death she had inadvertently brought about. Henkle was a bodybuilder, with thick arms and a barrel chest. He wore blue jeans, a black turtleneck shirt, and black Reeboks. The sleeves of his shirt had been pulled back to reveal a tattoo of a phoenix on his powerful left forearm. He wore a ring with a similar crest.

Dani felt very odd to be in the presence of these men, particularly under her current circumstances. These were high-profile people. The type she had never expected to actually meet, but felt some fondness for, based on their public personas. She had not anticipated their appearance as her executioners.

Something else about them bothered her. Most vampires were turned when they were very young, but these men appeared to be in their later thirties, or early forties. They had either been turned much later, or the Immortals were not immortal at all, just extremely long-lived. It was bizarre and contradictory to think of an Immortal aging and one day — even if it

175

took a millennium or two—dying of old age, but that would follow if her suspicions about these men were true.

Dani was all too familiar with Alyana and her breathtaking beauty. She looked similar enough to Isabella to have been the woman's sister by birth. Alyana did not appear old enough to have been Isabella's mother. At most, she looked thirty. Her onyx eyes were highlighted by a changing array of blood-red flecks, and her pale European features seemed to shine in the darkness. The stunning dark hair of the woman reached to her shoulders and part of the way down her back in cascade of elegant waves. She wore the same clothing she had worn the last time Dani had seen her, a long black leather trenchcoat and black leather boots. What she had on underneath, Dani had never seen. The rings, earrings, and necklace she wore hosted the most expensive of diamonds. They caught the moonlight and glittered as she moved.

Dani suddenly realized that she was having a difficult time keeping her thoughts on any given subject for more than a few moments. She had to look up, study what was before her, and remind herself what was happening.

She was standing at the doorway to Dorothea Odakota's home. The door had been kicked in by Allen Henkle and he had already gone inside. Alyana had been the one who had stood at the window and played with Dorothea by forcing the woman to perceive her as the Coyote-creature. The pettiness of what she had done seemed out of character for Alyana, who, like Isabella, generally embodied restraint and quiet elegance. It was as if she had been putting on a display for the benefit of her companions. Perhaps that was so. Alyana had gone in too. Angel and Ted Lewis stood behind Dani, flanking Tyler. Angel had changed in the van, removing the waitress's outfit she had worn as "Tabitha" and slipping her sensuous

176

form into a black leather miniskirt with a matching jacket and boots. She wore a diamond-studded corset and choker.

"Go on, goddamnit," the singer commanded as he jabbed at Dani's mind with his power. She heard him spit on the ground as she followed his orders, having no power to resist.

She walked into the dark, poorly furnished home and saw Alyana cradling Michael in her arms. A surge of outrage passed through her and she tried to leap forward, to take her brother out of the Immortal's hands, but the most she was able to achieve was to take two steps before Tyler's power clamped down on her and drove her to the floor. She looked up at the emerald eyes of the singer and saw that he was startled. He hadn't expected her to be able to slip free of his control, even for an instant.

Angel came to him, reaching around from behind to caress his chest as she bit his left ear, then said, "What's the matter, *pard?* This one a little too feisty for you?"

Screaming in rage, Tyler grabbed Angel's right hand with both of his and tore her from him, running up to the wall and stopping less than a foot away as he swung Angel around the way he might a baseball bat. He slammed her body against the wall and laughed as he heard the sharp crack of breaking bones. He released her hand, but not before giving her arm another twist that provoked a second, terrible crack.

Angel's head lolled as she looked up and said, "Again! Again!"

Tyler raised his heavy boot up over Angel's head.

Dani watched, horrified not only by Tyler's brutal, homicidal rage, but by the control he was continuing to exert on her, despite his insane anger. Then she thought of the remaining male vampires, Henkle and Lewis — Christ, they sounded like a comedy act — and decided they were picking up whatever slack Tyler was leaving. She stared at Angel's grinning, bloodied face, and knew the woman's head would be crushed if Tyler brought his steel-reinforced boot down.

"Stop!" Alyana screamed.

Tyler hesitated, his boot poised inches above Angel's face, his entire body trembling with rage, and he stomped down hard less than an inch in front of Angel's eyes. The platinum-blond vampire did not blink. Her wicked, catlike grin returned.

"Fuckin' A!" Tyler screamed as he backed away. "Whut is this!? Whut is this shit!? Dammit!"

"Devin, you know the rules," Alyana said softly, but with a ring of authority.

Dani watched the green-eyed country-western singer as he stared at her, his chest heaving, his lips pulled back to reveal a collection of jagged teeth. His hands had also transformed. Finally, he looked down and away.

Ted Lewis, who had been silent until now, went forward and put his hand on Tyler's shoulder. The man shrugged it off with a feral snarl.

"This is what we *agreed* to," Lewis said.

Dani almost smiled. The man even chose his inflections as John Cleese might. The smile faded as she remembered that her brother was literally in the hands of the Immortals.

"Fine, fuckin' fine," Tyler said as he spun around and pointed a finger in Angel's face. The platinum-haired vampire had not moved. Her stillness had been a result of her injuries, nothing more. The woman's back had an odd shape, and her arm was twisted at an unnatural angle.

"Devin," Alyana warned.

Tyler ignored her as he screamed at Angel, "Yew are our *bitch,* do you understand thet? You don't speak unless you're spoken to and you shore as hell never talk to me like thet less'n yew wanna be sent back to that fag-ass bastid De Santo in a whole score a' fuckin' boxes, yew understand me, bitch?"

Angel frowned. "I'm not exactly clear on what a 'bastid' is and the difference between a regular one and a 'fag-ass' one, but I think I get the general drift."

Tyler slapped her. "Yew know whut I think a' bitches like yew an' that fuckin' Du Prey tramp over there? I think yer only good fer one fuckin' thing. Yew know what that is?"

"Explaining what the really big words in Doonesbury mean first thing in the morning?" Angel asked.

Tyler took her face in his hand, pressing his fingers and thumb into the hollows beneath her cheeks. "If yer real lucky I may let you gimme a fuckin' blow job later. I bet yer the type who takes it down nice and deep and likes to feel it explode in the back a' yer throat, ain't that right, yew fuckin' little cunt?"

Angel stared at him defiantly and said, "Why don't you just fuck me up the ass, pard, just like you do your little-boy roadies every night?"

"Thet's it. Yer fuckin' dead." He drove his talon toward her eyes, but Angel was faster than he expected. She slid out of his way, then brought her own boot up between his legs, kicking him with enough force to make him howl in agony. His pain did not last long, however, and he was about to take another shot at Angel when the comedy team of Henkle and Lewis grabbed him and dragged him from the platinum-haired vampire. Dani watched, hoping the vampires would slip and release their hold on her, but it never happened.

"Get your shit together," Henkle said in the same voice he used in his self-help seminars.

"Fuck," Tyler said as he looked to Alyana. "This whole fuckin' thing is yoah goddamned fault in the first place. If yew had just killed this fuckin' slut and the human like you were supposed to in the first place, I wouldn't have had to cancel Baton Rouge tonight. Do you know how much I fuckin' *like* doin' Baton Rouge? I got my goddamned fuckin' start there. Those people have always been kind to me there, and what do I have to fuckin' do? Goddamn cancel on them at the last minute. And with my schedule, I'm not going to be able to get back there for another six months. I gotta do fuckin' Viva Las Vegas for the next three weeks. Least I'll have my boys meetin' me there tonight. Still, do yew know how much thet fuckin' pisses me off!?"

Alyana said nothing.

"I don't know, I just don't fuckin' get it," Tyler said. "Any of us do the kind of shit you did and get caught, they'd have fuckin' taken a year to pull us apart. They'd have fucked every hole we had with blowtorches, then poked us some new ones. But yew, Miss Du Prey, yew pull this shit and the Ancients goddamn forgive you."

"On condition."

"Yeah," he said ruefully. "On fuckin' condition." He shook his head. "Look, get on with it, all right? I want to get the fuck out of here and away from the pussy stench a' yew goddamned bitches as soon as I can."

"You better listen up, Dani," Angel said. "This is all about you. You're the whole reason why all these important people have been dragged away from their lives to act as dogcatcher. I mean, we're bitches, right? That would figure, wouldn't it? Dogcatcher, bitches — get it?"

Alyana fixed the young vampire with her dark gaze. "You've said enough."

Nodding, Angel fell silent, leaving Dani to look down at Dorothea. The older woman had curled herself up into a fetal position and was crying uncontrollably. Dani wanted to comfort Dorothea, but she couldn't move. The vampires retained complete control.

"Look at me," Alyana said.

Dani did as the woman asked, surprised that she was being given an option, rather than a command. The minor freedom she had just been awarded went no further. Dani tried to move any other part of her body and found that she was still frozen in place.

"A year ago I made a mistake," Alyana said with the finality of a judge delivering a death sentence. "Tonight, it's my duty to rectify that error."

Dani shuddered as she heard several of the other vampires begin to laugh.

Chapter Fifteen

"That's enough," Alyana said, silencing the others.

Dani had heard Alyana talk in this tone before. Alyana was a powerful businesswoman, as powerful as any of the men in the room, though she did not share their exhibitionism. All emotion had retreated from Alyana's voice. She was delivering a ruling as she might in a boardroom, stating the cold facts without pleasure or discomfort. Dani suddenly felt like a product line that was about to be discontinued.

"In the brief time since Bill Yoshino released your memories and allowed you to become one with your true nature, you have shown remarkable progress in your development as an Immortal," Alyana said to Dani.

"Puh-lease," Tyler said. "Thet is such bullshit."

Henkle and Lewis stood near him, but they no longer held him in place. Angel remained on the floor, allowing her healing power to course through her.

"Let her talk," Lewis said.

"It'll go faster that way," Henkle added.

"Fuckin' fine, whut the hell do I care?" Tyler spat.

Alyana spoke once again to Dani. "My daughter had the right idea. You needed to be weaned away from your human tendencies and inhibitions. Samantha Walthers raised you to be weak, to deny your blood heritage. If the current situation were allowed to progress unchanged, she would do the same thing with the child I hold in my hands. That cannot be allowed."

Dani closed her eyes. She had been doing everything she could to avoid any thought of her mother. When she had seen the vampires drive past her home and go to Dorothea's, she had feared that Sam was also here. That had not been the case. Sam had left Michael with Dorothea, something she never did at night. She wondered if the vampires had already killed Sam, or taken her hostage. They might have learned Sam's habits and decided to allow Dorothea to care for the child while they went into the city to finish with Dani. But why would they bother to play the games they played with Dorothea? It didn't make sense. Sam had gone off, that was all. Perhaps she would be able to elude the vampires. The thought gave Dani some comfort, until she realized that Sam would never allow the Immortals to keep her child without a fight, even if it was a battle she could not win.

Alyana whispered, "Listen to me, Dani."

Dani focused her attention on Alyana, though it was difficult. The power the vampires employed to keep her their slave and make her docile interfered with her ability to reason properly.

"You can be redeemed. If you can learn to forget about what Samantha Walthers tried to teach you, you can embrace your blood heritage and come over to us. I honestly believe that, Dani. I've been inside you enough to know. What happened tonight with you and Angel told me I wasn't wrong."

Dani felt the power holding her subside just enough to allow her to respond. "I don't know *what* happened tonight."

"Of course you do. You walked into a bar and engineered a mass rape so that you could feed from the fear and desire of your victims. I know what's in your head, Dani. You're thinking, *This is bullshit, but so long as you're alive, you have a chance to save*

183

Walthers and keep her child from us. You have to stop thinking that way. It's not our power that's making it hard for you to focus your thoughts. You're drunk on all you've consumed tonight."

"It was *Angel,*" Dani said insistently. "She made all of it happen."

"No. It was you. All Angel did was help you let your guard down so that you could give in to your true nature and do what you *wanted* to do. I'll let you in on a little secret, Dani. Angel didn't have to do much at all. You were a very willing victim."

"That's not true!"

"Yes, I'm afraid it is," Ted Lewis piped in, just as cheerily as he might on one of his TV commercials.

Dani did not look at the man. She was suddenly reminded of the old Monty Python sketch with John Cleese and the Department of Arguments and Contradictions. Jesus, how could she be thinking of something like that now? Maybe she *was* drunk in some strange way. Drunk on fear. That couldn't be right. She was being manipulated by the Immortals. *Everything* was being manipulated by them. She wondered how could she trust anything her senses — human or otherwise — told her. Suddenly, she felt all vestiges of Alyana's power fall away from her. She fell to her knees, disoriented.

Get up, fight, do something, she screamed in her head, but she didn't have the strength.

"I have been authorized to deliver a proposal to you," Alyana said. "The terms are as follows: You are responsible for the deaths of two members of the Parliament. As there are a finite number of seats — so to speak — in our Parliament, you have created two openings which must be filled. Membership in the Parliament is a highly sought-after honor among our kind. There are six possible candidates, but only two openings. To select which candidates will be allowed to join our ranks, we have devised a method for the candidates to prove their worth.

"They will be set against you, Dani. You and the human you insist on thinking of as your mother, though her blood is not in you."

Dani felt relief surge through her. Sam was alive.

"The candidates have been told that they must kill *both* of you. One of the tasks of the Parliament is the slaying of Wildlings, and you, Dani, are that. You murdered two members of Parliament."

"You were going to take Michael," Dani said, overcoming the sluggishness of her thoughts to recall that terrible morning in San Diego, one year ago. "I did it because you were going to take my brother. I don't have any regrets."

"You will," Alyana said.

"Fuckin' right yew will," Tyler spat.

Ted Lewis shook his head. "God knows, you will."

"Amen," Allen Henkle added.

The comedy team of Henkle and Lewis grinned at each other. Alyana cradled Michael in her arms. Dani was surprised and more than a little frightened to realize that despite all that had happened, the baby had not cried even once.

"The hunters will seek their prey in teams. The first team will be released at nightfall tomorrow, giving you and the Walthers woman something of a head start. The second team will be allowed to come for you the following night. Should you survive against all four . . ."

"Wait," Dani said, determined to sound as dispassionate as Alyana. "You said there were *six* candidates."

Behind Dani, Angel lifted herself off the floor and cut a quick glance at Devin Tyler. When she spoke, she continued to mock his thick, Kentucky drawl. "I'm damn glad to know my partner hasn't forgotten her readin' and 'rythmitic, I shoarly am."

"No fucking way," Dani whispered.

"Yes, way!" Angel cried with a perverse giggle. "You and me, we're the fifth and six candidates."

185

"Parliament," Dani said, the full meaning of Angel's words seeping into her. "You people would want *me* in the Parliament?"

"Don't fuckin' push it," Tyler said. The emerald-eyed singer spat on the floor. *"Want* is far too strong a way to put it. Alyana an' the Ancients are crammin' this down our fuckin' throats."

"It would be your choice, of course," Ted Lewis said amiably.

Dani shook her head. "I'd never agree to that."

"If it's any comfort to you, that's what just about everyone on this side of the equation thought too," Allen Henkle said, sounding more like a real-estate broker than an Immortal. "I advised the Ancients to think this through more carefully, move slowly, and render a judgment only when they were certain. But they've said yes to these terms."

"So they're supposed to kill you too," Dani said to Angel, recalling the nightmare she had just been put through at the Glass Tiger. "Good."

"It's not that simple," Alyana said as she continued. "The hunters do not *have* to kill Angel. She has committed no crimes. They will kill her in self-defense, if that is necessary. They will also slaughter her to better get at you and your mother. If she survives and the two of you do not, she will go back to her position as assistant to my business partner, Christian De Santo."

The name finally broke through to Dani's muddled consciousness. The boy, the Initiate she had saved in the plane crash, was named Bobby *De Santo*. She remembered the brief contact she had endured with the darkness inside him. He had learned her secrets, and his loyalty had evidently been to the Immortals, not the woman who saved his life.

Dani looked to Alyana and asked, "What happens to my mother if she and I both survive? What happens to Michael?"

"The Walthers woman will be forgiven her trespasses and allowed to live without fear of repercussions. She will have her freedom. The child will be raised in a more suitable environment."

"With you."

"Doubtful. I'm not the domestic type. The child will be delivered to his new home tonight. You will never see him again."

"Unless you become Parliament, that is," Ted Lewis said in a warm, supportive tone.

"Give you some incentive, I guess," Allen Henkle added.

Dani looked at Angel. The vampire's arm and back had healed. "You're already Parliament. You were out in sunlight and you didn't burn."

"Blood of the Ancients, babe. Well, once removed. There still ain't nothing like it."

"I don't understand."

"Christian De Santo has it. He passed some on to me. Of course, I don't have what they have—you know, the *good stuff*, the undiluted, pure-as-honey, one-hundred-percent blood of the Ancients. I just have a smidgen of what they've got. Even so, I've got to tell you, hon, it's a blast. An absolute, fucking blast. I've haven't had this much fun in a *long* time."

"What you did to me at the bar—"

"Hey, all they said was get you out of there," Angel said with a laugh. "They didn't say how. I thought I'd be creative."

Rage moved through Dani, and she wondered if she could make it to Angel before one of the older Immortals once again placed her under their control. She wanted to kill the grinning, platinum-haired vampire. Then she realized that she had seen this expression on Angel's face many times before. The woman was trying to get to her, that was all.

"The *truth* is," Ted Lewis said in his bright, friendly voice, standing with his hands behind his back in a stance that eerily recalled John Cleese, "what you went through *was* a test."

187

"Yes," Allen Henkle said, "a codicil to the contract. We had to know if there was any hope at all of bringing you around to our way of thinking. Angel said you failed that test, because your human side reasserted itself and you became guilty and repulsed at what you had done."

"Not so," Ted Lewis said, brushing his receding black hair back into his scalp. "The important thing is that we were shown that deep down, you're just like us. Alyana was right about you."

Dani shuddered inadvertently. A hand clamped down on her shoulder. Angel stood beside her.

"God, Dani, you're such a pisser. I'm not the enemy. Hell, girl, we're partners. The sooner you get used to it, the better."

"Get to the good part," Devin Tyler said, drawing out good so that it sounded like *goooo-ooood*. "I wanna see the bitch's face."

Dani knew that what he really meant was that he wanted to taste her fear. She steadied herself for yet another blow. "Come on, Alyana. Tell me."

"Each of us is here because we have personally sponsored one or more candidates for Parliament."

"Sponsored? You mean—turned?"

"In a way."

"Devin Tyler has put forth his twin sons, Ted Lewis and Allen Henkle have favorites of their own. My partner, Christian De Santo, while no longer a member of Parliament, has shared of himself with Angel. And you, Danielle, are my choice."

Dani struggled to keep the fear away. At first, she had thought that the Immortals had taken their candidates as Initiates and made them into full vampires. But Angel was already a vampire, and knowing the prejudice of the Immortals against those who have not been turned, that theory seemed far less likely. Another possibility came to her, and this time she was unable to stave off the terror.

They meant to turn *her*.

Dani thought about what her life had been during those few days when she had been an Immortal. If not for her mother's willingness to sacrifice herself to protect her child from the darkness within, Dani might have surrendered to the demon in her blood.

It had almost turned out differently.

She had *almost* been driven by her bloodneed to murder Samantha Walthers.

Dani did something she had not done since she was a child. She fell on her knees and began to pray. The Immortals surrounding her broke into hysterical laughter. Dani ignored them and their taunts.

"God is merciful, God is good," Dani whispered desperately. She had studied the curse of her blood through every scientific means available, and she had been led to the inescapable conclusion that the source of her power was not strictly related to the body; it had to be a product of some other form of energy. That energy was either some type of physical phenomena humans could not yet grasp, but which Immortals could instinctively access and manipulate, or it was of the spirit, the essence of her immortal soul. If the latter were true, the vampires' stories of their origins relating to the blood of Christ and wishes of Lucifer to have his own spawns upon the earth could also be literal.

God, therefore, was real. If that were true, He would not turn his back on one who so desperately needed His help.

"Bullshit," Devin Tyler said as he planted his boot in the center of Dani's forehead and sent her sprawling. She fell hard, landing only a few feet away from the weeping form of Dorothea Odakota.

"I'm on record as having doubts about this entire operation," Henkle said ruefully. "Serious doubts."

Tyler spat on the floor beside Dani. "God helps those who help themselves, yew stupid little slut. He stood by and let His only begotten son get nailed to a fuckin' cross. Yew think He's gonna charge right in

189

here and bail out yoah sorry ass? Think again, cunt."

She knew that her thoughts had been open to the Immortals, and she wasn't entirely sure that she had truly hoped for divine intervention, but for the sake of her mother and brother, she'd had to try.

"Do her," Devin Tyler said to Alyana. "I'm fuckin' tired of this."

The elegant, dark-eyed vampire crouched before Dani and said, "This is your choice. I fought for you to have this option, but if you can't *live* with this, then perhaps it would be better if you were to *die* with it instead. I promise you, your death, and that of Samantha Walthers, will be merciful."

Mercy.

It was what Isabella had taught Dani. Their kind had the power to be merciful. She remembered reaching into the dying minds of Isabella and Marissa, blanketing their fears with the comforting warmth of her power, allowing their minds the fantasies of their most private and special moments when their flesh was being ravaged and destroyed, their lives ended.

Dani was afraid. She wanted to think of herself as being strong enough to face this moment with the dignity and resolve Marissa had shown, but she couldn't bring herself to do it. She recalled telling Marissa that it had to be done, while there was still enough of the human inside her to know the difference between the mercy of death and the horror of her existence as an Immortal. Now that she was being faced with the same decision, she found that she was not as brave as she wanted to think.

"Decide, Dani."

A brief flicker of hope flashed into her mind and she struggled to hide it from the Immortals. They captured it and examined it as they might a firefly under glass.

"So you think yew can live with making the change, then at the end of three days not making another

190

kill," Devin Tyler said, still out of breath from his laughter.

Dani looked around and saw that Angel and Alyana were not laughing. She knew why Alyana was attempting to preserve Dani's life: A part of Isabella's memories, her life, continued to exist within Dani. But Angel's reaction surprised her. The platinum-blond vampire seemed unusually solemn.

"That's another condition of the deal," Alyana said. "You must remain of our kind. You must make a second kill within three days to avoid reverting. If you don't, you and your mother will remain the hunted, and the full power of the Parliament will be brought down against you. When the two of you are found again, your deaths will be horrifying and seemingly endless."

Shattered, Dani looked over to Dorothea, her friend. "Not her."

"Yes," Alyana said. "This is punishment, Dani. Punishment with a means for redemption, but *punishment* nonetheless."

"A stranger. Someone else."

"We're not here to make it easy on you," Allen Henkle said. "You don't dictate the rules. We do."

"Fuckin' shit or get off the pot," Devin Tyler growled.

Dani stared at the older woman cowering on the floor and remembered when she had been turned the first time. Bill Yoshino had eased his power into her and it had been Madison who had died. Her friend. Dani's only comfort was the knowledge that if she had not taken Madison's life, one of the others would have done it, and they would not have employed mercy.

"That's not applicable in this case," Ted Lewis said, his bright smile never fading. "If you choose the less difficult route and accept your death here and now, the Odakota woman will live. We'll even take away her nightmares."

191

"Such a deal," Angel said softly.

Dani knew the rest of it, the part the vampires were not mentioning. Dorothea would live, but Samantha Walthers would die. To save her mother and herself, to live long enough to rescue Michael from the Immortals, she would have to take an innocent life.

Dani tried to think of what her mother would have done, if the choice had been killing Dorothea or allowing her son to be raised by monsters, with no hope for redemption. She was grateful that at least her mother hadn't been forced to make such a decision and live with the guilt that would follow.

"Dorothea stays where she's at," Dani said. She reached out with her power and could sense that the older woman believed herself to be in a room populated by nightmarish creatures, half-human, half-beast. The vampires would never allow her to bestow mercy upon Dorothea, but at least the woman would not be aware that she was dying at the hands of a friend.

"Whose feelings are you worrying about?" Alyana asked. "Hers or your own?"

Dani lowered her eyes. She knew the answer. If Dorothea died her way, Dani would find it easier to live with the memories of the woman's death.

Tyler checked his watch. "Can we puh-lease get this movin'?"

"Decide," Alyana said. "This is your last chance before the decision is taken from you."

Dani was ashamed at the slight flutter of relief that brushed against her heart like the wings of some delicate and fragile creature. If they made the decision, if they forced the change from Initiate to Immortal upon her, she would not be responsible for what happened.

She sensed, however, that the decision would not go that way. The choice the vampires would make for her would be the death of her mother and herself.

"All right," Dani said, hating herself for her weakness. She wanted to believe that it was self-sacrifice that spurred her decision, not fear and the need for self-preservation. But she knew she would never be certain.

"Sheeeitt-fire!" Devin Tyler hollered. "About fuckin' time!"

Dani bit her lip as the vampires crowded around her, Angel remaining at the back of the room.

To her credit, she did not scream when they touched her.

Chapter Sixteen

Samantha Walthers was walking home from Peter Red Cloud's house, not especially worried about going through the darkened streets of Isleta on her own. She was armed, and she could handle herself if she were attacked. A part of her *wanted* a confrontation. She needed a simple, black and white equation in her life rather than the endless vista of grays that stretched out before her.

She had faced terrible adversity in her life, and a part of her had thrilled to it. If someone wanted to hurt her, she would stop them, and perhaps hurt *them* instead. She looked around. The streets were deserted. All the potential serial killers, thieves, rapists, and God-only-knows what else had already gone to bed, apparently. Or they considered the pueblo either sacred ground or beneath their notice.

For Sam, it would have been much easier to deal with a no-nonsense attacker than to struggle with the concept of once again allowing herself to trust someone other than her daughter. Peter was a strange man, but he seemed honest and deeply honorable. Appearances meant nothing, however. If Peter wanted her trust, he was going to have to earn it.

To make everything even worse, Sam was concerned for her daughter. Dani had retreated so far within herself that Sam found it almost impossible to tell what was going on inside the young woman's mind. There had been a time when her daughter could not lie to her, could not hold anything back. But that had been before the trouble had begun, before the job offer from Halpern and Weiss and the move from Tampa to Beverly Hills. The darkness had come upon them in the form of Bill Yoshino, Isabella, and their brood. For a time, it had lifted, then the vampires had returned. This time it had covered them in a shroud that would never be lifted. From that time of ultimate horrors, however, had come a blessing so indescribably sweet that it nearly brought tears to Samantha Walther's eyes when she thought of it.

Michael.

She could endure anything for his sake. The miracle of his life helped to put hers into simpler terms and she desperately wanted that purity in her existence. She had possessed it once, or thought she had, in the days before the move, and would have given almost anything to have it in her life once again.

Or so she believed.

Sam was three blocks from her home when the vision crashed down upon her, sending her to her knees. For a moment she thought she had gone insane. Reality had dissolved around her and reformed so that she was looking at something that resembled a cheap photographic effect, a double exposure. She continued to see the houses of the pueblo, the street, even a pair of dogs at an intersection fifty feet in front of her. But these images were ghostlike, and another set of strange, shadowy, insubstantial images also imprinted themselves upon her perceptions. Sam felt that she was existing in two places at one time. She knew that she was kneeling on the street. The rocks and soft earth could be felt underneath her fingers. A slight chill cut through her.

Despite the evidence of her senses and the absolute logical certainty that she had not been magically teleported to another place, she could see that she was *also* kneeling within the main living quarters of Dorothea Odakota's house. The older woman was lying on the floor, curled up in a ball. Five figures stood, staring down at her. Sam's heart shriveled as she identified the watchers. She knew all of them, though she had only seen two of them on television.

Dani was there, and behind her was the dark and beautiful vampire Alyana, of the Parliament. Sam shuddered as she saw her son in Alyana's arms. Another woman was present, and Sam was comforted by this woman's presence. It was Angel, the spiky-haired vampire who had been with the pack that had first attempted to seduce her daughter. Angel had been dead for two years. Sam had killed her, rigging the warehouse the vampires used as a lair to explode, catching the creatures within. That meant this scenario was not real, it was not actually happening. Why Sam was seeing it at all, she couldn't explain, unless her mind had finally snapped. Also present were two men who were television personalities, Ted Lewis and Allen Henkle. She wondered why Mister Rogers hadn't been thrown in too. His appearance would have made the absurd conglomeration complete.

Still, as much as she wanted to dismiss the vision, her daughter and her friend were at the heart of this unusual cabal. Sam tried to rise and found that she didn't have the strength. She wanted to go home, to collect her son from Dorothea—if Dani had not yet gotten home and done that herself—and make sure that everyone was perfectly safe. Snarling in frustration, Sam attempted to pull herself up once more. She rose to her watery limbs and fell face-down on the dirt road. Sleep stole over her. As hard as she tried to fight what was happening to her, she was powerless to resist as the streets of Isleta lost their solidity and a dreamworld formed around her.

From the height at which she observed the events transpiring before her, Sam realized that she was not kneeling or lying down. In fact, she was standing up-

right, and was slightly shorter than she was in reality. A hand moved up before her face, a man's hand, and she realized that she was looking out of someone else's eyes. She could not feel what this person felt. Though she could see nothing in front of her except the room and its bizarre inhabitants, Sam felt the cold ground pressed against her face. She had no control over what was happening. She was a passenger in someone else's head.

Sam watched, horrified, as Dani agreed to something, some kind of deal, which brought intense pain to the young woman. Dani took off her jacket and her white blouse, but left her bra in place. Sam was startled when her perspective suddenly changed and she heard a booming voice cry out in approval. Her host was moving closer, presumably to get a better view.

"Yay-haw! Now that's what I call a pair 'a tits!"

She recognized the voice. Devin Tyler. He was the last member of the group and she was witnessing events through his eyes. Jesus, this was weird. Why in the hell was her daughter getting undressed?

The vision grew worse. Infinitely worse.

Michael was handed to Angel, who stood off to the side and frowned as she looked at the baby's face, a flicker of a smile striking her hard but sensual features. Then Angel looked away from Michael and watched as Alyana began to touch Dani the way a lover might. Sam felt repulsed as she saw the woman embrace her daughter from behind, running her hands over Dani's bare arms and shoulders. Alyana kissed Dani's neck gently, then began to caress her breasts.

"Girl-fuckin'!" Tyler screamed. "God bless the fuckin' U.S. of A., baby! Hay-ooowww!"

Allen Henkle turned in Sam's direction. "Keep it down." She realized he was talking to Tyler, not her.

"What's the matter? You two queer or somethin'? got some full-tilt pussy action goin' on here. Maybe

197

we'll get some!"

"Just imagine your prick is VVlcro and you tore it off and left it at home, okay?" Henkle said.

"Shit, you boys ain't no fun at all. But I guess yoah right. If we keep talkin', we ain't gonna be able to hear all the squishy sounds. Normally I don't eat fish, but this ought to be pretty damned entertaining!"

Sam suddenly felt as if she were going to become violently ill. This was her daughter these bastards were talking about. Her Dani!

She watched as Dani began to respond to Alyana's caresses. The young woman's golden eyes opened and her nostrils flared as she ground her ass against Alyana's thighs and moaned with pleasure. Dani cried out as her right nipple was squeezed by Alyana. The woman's left hand went to Dani's crotch and closed over her sex.

No, Sam thought, no, I don't want to see this!

She could not look away. The option was not open to her. The red flecks in Alyana's eyes grew larger and more intense, and soon, both women's eyes burned like torches.

I don't want to see!

Suddenly, Alyana transformed. It happened so quickly that if Sam had been afforded the possibility of blinking her eyes, she might have missed it. Alyana's hands became talons, her teeth wolflike incisors. The woman closed her mouth over Dani's neck and the girl cried out, shuddering as if an orgasm had torn through her. Blood leaked down from the wound that had been made in Dani's neck and fell into the crevasse between Dani's swelling breasts.

You want it, Alyana said, though she did not speak. The words had been projected so forcefully into Dani's mind that everyone in the room had heard them in their heads. At Dani's feet, Dorothea stirred, looked up, and screamed.

Inside her own mind, Sam also screamed as she watched Dani become what Alyana had become.

A monster.

Dani's hands elongated and became ivory claws. Her teeth metamorphosed into a mass of jagged, needlelike daggers that glinted in the soft light of the room. Dani reached down and took Dorothea's hand. The older woman was begging and pleading for this nightmare to end. Sam echoed her desperate cries.

Laughing, Dani shook her head, made a kissing motion, then jammed her talon into Dorothea's chest, shattering the older woman's breastbone. With one hand anchored inside Dorothea's twitching body, Dani brought up her other talon and sliced it cleanly through Dorothea's neck, severing the woman's head. Dorothea's lips were still moving as her head fell to the floor with the same terrible plop as a deflated basketball.

Dani leaned forward, opening her mouth wide to receive the jutting stream of blood from the corpse's exposed neck. She tore Dorothea's heart out and bit into it, rubbing the blood over her breasts.

Allen Henkle and Ted Lewis began to applaud, but their hands and teeth transformed too. They raced forward, thrilled at the sight and smell of fresh blood. Tyler went forward quickly, reaching out with curling ivory talons. Sam's perspective changed as he ran.

Dani screamed again, but not with terror.

With delight.

Sam was wrenched from the vision. She found herself lying on the street, face-down, and heard a roar. Looking up, she saw a dark van heading straight for her. She rose up onto her feet as she was bathed in headlights and dove out of the way of the speeding vehicle, skinning her knee and falling to the ground once again. The van's rear door shot open and Sam saw the grinning, hyenalike face of Devin Tyler. He waved good-bye as a two-year-old might, his wrist limp, his hand flopping up and down in a blur.

"Bye-bye! Bye-bye! Bye-bye! Bye-bye!" he called in

a mocking, childish voice. Then the door slammed shut and the van sped into the night.

Sam wanted to run after the van, to return to Peter's house and get his car, anything. If the vision was real, if she hadn't gone insane, Tyler's companions would be in that van with him. They might have Dani and Michael as prisoners.

It couldn't be real, it couldn't have happened, it couldn't —

She started to run, but a searing pain in her mind brought her down. The sensation was not unfamiliar to her. She had known this agony and far worse when Richard Sterling had used his inhuman power to place her under various compulsions. There was no physical way for her to follow the vampires.

It was real, Sam thought. Good God, help me, help us *all*, it was real.

She became ill on the side of the road, emptying her stomach. Her skin became feverish and a taste like iodine stung her lips. Blood.

Blood everywhere.

She had bitten her tongue. It didn't matter. Nothing mattered.

Something moved behind her.

"Mom?"

Shaking, Sam turned to face what had been her daughter.

Chapter Seventeen

Sam knew at once that this was not her daughter. It looked and sounded like Dani, but it wasn't her.

"Which one are you?" Sam asked.

Dani's face blurred and was replaced by that of Angel.

The vampire grinned. "Hey, Sam. How's it goin'?"

"You're dead," Sam said, realizing how stupid the words sounded the instant they left her mouth. She couldn't very well be standing on the side of the street with Angel if the vampire had been blown apart in the warehouse two years ago.

"Not," Angel said, planting her hands on her hips. "Oh, and you can lay off the 'Oh God, this isn't real, this can't be happening,' because it is real, it is happening, and God, apparently, doesn't give a fuck.

"Furthermore, your daughter still loves you, even though she's a basket case. And what the hell, I'm kind of fond of you too."

Sam considered the weapon she carried, and wondered if she could kill this creature before it reached out with its power and shut her down.

Frowning, Angel said, "Hey, come on, I've had enough of the Wild West shit with Tyler. We're not going to have a showdown in the street. You know"— Angel suddenly shifted to a low voice, imitating an announcer on a televised golf match—"well, Sam Walthers is carrying a load of shit, including a 9-mm

Beretta. Her opponent has only the powers of a god. Gee, I wonder who's gonna win this one, Chet? I dunno, Bill."

Sam was silent, waiting.

"Just don't be stupid any more than you have been, okay? I don't really want to be here any more than you want me here, but the only way I can get what I want is by helping the two of you to survive, and all this bullshit is just wasting a lot of time that we don't have anymore."

"Where's my son?"

"Gone. All gone."

Sam's entire body tensed.

"He's alive, he's fine, and he's the last thing you should be worrying about right now. Ah, well," Angel said with a deep sigh. "I figured you would want to have this little talk sooner or later. I guess it's better if we get it over with before I take you to see Dani."

"Fuck you."

"I didn't think you'd be up for it this soon, but okay. You want me to start or do you want to start?"

Sam was rigid.

"Come on, a little joke, lighten up. Now, to begin with, unless you're a complete moron — and at times I have my suspicions — you know that none of your neighbors have come out to help you because I'm not letting them see or hear us. So we can say whatever we want without having to worry about it. We could even rut like pigs out here in the street, if we were so moved. Sorry, I don't mean to keep bringing everything around to sex, but I've always had this thing about older women. You make me hot, what can I say?"

"As little as possible."

"Ohhhh, now I'm hurt. You want me to shut up? Fine. I'll take you to Dani right now. How does that sound?"

Sam couldn't bring herself to answer. The image of Dani killing another human being had been the most terrible sight Sam could ever have imagined. It could have been a lie; the vampires might well have put the vision in her mind simply to torment her. Or it could have been only Angel. She could have engineered all of this for revenge. The Parliament might not have come, Michael could be safe—

"You're going to drive yourself crazy if you keep thinking like that," Angel said. "Snap out of it!"

Sam felt a stabbing pain in her mind, which was as brief and sharp as a slap to the face. Even in the sting of the blow's aftermath, Sam could not help but rifle through possibilities, both good and bad, to explain what was happening. After all, the evidence of her frail, human senses was always suspect when she was in the presence of one or more of the vampires.

There were two explanations that were the hardest of all to take. The first was that Dani had snapped and she was causing all of this.

"Sure, it's Dani pretending to be me pretending to be her," Angel said. "That sounds real likely, Sam."

The second was that this was real.

"Bingo, stupid. Look, for the sake of speeding things up, why don't you just go along with the assumption that all of this is really happening. If it's not, you haven't lost anything. If it is, you might save your own life."

Sam stared at the vampire. "All right."

"I want you to know, there's really no hard feelings about what happened in L.A. That's rare for me. Usually, when people try to kill me, I get *pissed off*. But the situation with Yoshino and Isabella was becoming intolerable anyway, so you actually did me a favor."

"You weren't in the building."

"Right. I had been sent for some take-out. We knew Izzy was going to be coming back with Dani and she was going to *need* to *feed*. So I went out."

"Why didn't I see you?"

"I could be *nasty* and tell you that I made it so you

203

couldn't see me, but that's not true. You were parked outside the warehouse and you kept falling asleep, remember? You weren't out for long, a minute or two at a time, but you were losing it. I came up to the car and even flashed my tits at you, but you were out cold. I was gonna run inside and tell Bill, or just drag your sorry ass in with me, but I decided to take a little peeky into your head first. And you know what I found out? That you were going to blow up the building and kill my entire family. Fortunately for you, I'm not big on family, so I decided it was time to cut my losses and let that asshole Yoshino and that stuck-up bitch Isabella — I really didn't call her Izzy back then, but I do it now because I know it pisses Alyana off — deal with you himself. He went boom! Big boom. Went boom, all fall down. Fuck it, who cares, right? Ancient history. I've always believed in living for the moment. Lately, though, I've been thinking about the future. The last thing I've been doing is worrying about the past. You and your Missy Morose daughter could learn something from me, you know?"

"So what now?"

"Dani went into Albuquerque to get a hotel room. I told her I'd round you up and bring you along. Things are going to get hot around here real soon. Dorothea's husband is due home from Bingo Heaven — or whatever the fuck it's called — any time now. Come on, I'll fill you in on everything that's happened along the way. Or, if you want, I could just put it in your head."

"No."

"Might save some time."

"Go to Hell."

"Eventually, hon. Eventually."

Angel turned her back on Sam and motioned for her to follow. Sam considered going for her gun and attempting to take off the top of the vampire's head, but she could always do that later. She hoped.

"So," Angel said as she approached the nearest car

and tore open the locked door, "it's like this . . ."

Dani sat in the darkened hotel room, wondering how she was going to face her mother. If she had felt drunk with power before, she was absolutely swimming in it now. She could not get the image of Dorothea's pleading eyes out of her mind. A part of her thought it was hilarious, and that frightened Dani even more.

The door opened and Sam appeared, Angel directly behind her.

"I'm home, sweets!" Angel shouted. "Miss me?"

From the doorway, Sam caught sight of the young woman sitting on the couch and shuddered. Angel had not lied. The vision Devin Tyler had placed in Sam's mind had been true. Dani's flesh had gone pale. Her eyes were dark and deep-set. She looked like a junkie in the early stages of withdrawal.

"Mommy?" Dani said in a voice that was slurred, guttural, and monstrous.

Sam felt as if she had been slammed in the chest by a shotgun blast. The searing realization that Dani was no longer human made Sam want nothing more than to wake up from this nightmare which had become her world.

There had always been a possibility that Dani would succumb to her inhuman side once again, but it was one Sam had discounted as being minute, especially after the ordeals they had shared for the sake of the baby. She had believed that Dani would never allow herself to be *turned* ever again.

How close had her daughter been to seeking out another of her kind and allowing an Immortal to transform her? Sam wondered. How many times in the past had she wanted to reclaim what she had lost? Sam now realized that the darkness living inside Dani had always been struggling to break free. She did not want to know how many times Dani had been

205

tempted to give in to that temptation. Warring voices erupted in her head:

This thing is not my daughter.

But it is.

My daughter died when she became this monstrosity.

That isn't true.

Sam knew that wasn't true. Nonetheless, Dani was no longer human. The evidence was sitting before her.

The tears of the shuddering, golden-eyed young woman were blood-red. Sam understood *logically* that Dani had sacrificed her humanity only because she had believed herself to be left without options; Dani had allowed herself to be perverted in this way to save her mother and brother. In a cold, analytical way, Sam understood that, and if she could have turned off her emotions and listened to her logical side, everything might have been all right. She might have been able to take her daughter into her arms, a task she now found impossible. As much as she wanted to—as much as a *part* of her wanted to—she couldn't bring herself to touch Dani.

"Mommy?" Dani begged piteously. "Don't hate me, Mommy. Oh, please, *God,* don't, oh, please—Mommy!"

Sam opened her mouth, but she could not speak. She felt something hard and dead inside of her.

"Mommy!"

"Oh, God, Dani," Sam said as she turned and ran from the room.

Angel watched. The vampire considered looking at Dani and saying something along the lines of "Looks like she didn't take it well, *sweets,*" and was surprised by her own willingness to allow the jibe to die, stillborn behind her lips.

"Oh, fuck," Angel said, realizing she would have to be the liaison between these two. She wondered if a seat in the Parliament was really worth all this.

Samantha Walthers had shut herself up in the bathroom. Angel considered using her power to retrieve her, but humans were fragile, and she sensed that this one had been pushed just about to the brink. Angel knocked on the door.

"Walthers? Come on out. The three of us have to talk."

Puking sounds issued from the room.

"Shit," Angel muttered. She hesitated for a moment, realizing that she was hearing dry heaves. "You've got ten seconds to answer the door. If you don't, I'm taking it off its hinges. I won't give a fuck if it's locked or not. You're pissing me off and I want to *break* something!"

Noise came from the small room. The doorknob slowly turned. Angel half-expected Sam to emerge pointing a weapon in her face. She was prepared for it. Taking control of Walthers the moment she posed a threat would be no problem. The door opened and Sam stood there, chest heaving, flesh pale.

"I don't need you to help me talk to my daughter," Sam said in a low, determined voice.

"Good," Angel said brightly. *This* was the woman who had taken out Yoshino. She had been getting worried.

"Get out and let me talk to her alone."

Angel shrugged.

"Go!"

The platinum-haired vampire grinned. "You know, the two of you are really sand in my pussy."

With a laugh, Angel walked to the door. Sam followed the woman, ignoring the kiss Angel blew her and the slight wiggle of the vampire's ass. She slammed the door shut behind Angel and bolted it before she crossed the room and went to Dani.

Kneeling before her daughter, Sam placed her hands on Dani's knees, and squeezed them lovingly. Then she took hold of her daughter's hands, kissing each of them in turn.

"Sorry," Sam said.

"I'm sorry," Dani blubbered. "Dorothea's dead, she's dead, I killed her, oh, God—"

"Hush. Shhhhh. Shhhhh," Sam whispered. "Don't. I know. I saw it happen."

Dani's eyes grew impossibly wider. Her own vague recollections of the murder were enshrouded in a blood haze. She recalled the aftermath, however, the terrifying moment when the demon, happy and sated, retreated to sleep, and full awareness came upon her. The sight of Dorothea's mangled corpse, her staring eyes, her face locked forever in an expression of betrayal and fear, would never leave Dani.

Something deep within her was not so sure about that. It laughed and told her of the thousands of faces that would supplant Dorothea's. She was a true killer. Now that she had been given a taste of blood, she would never stop. Her list of victims would be as endless as her life span.

Dani refused to listen to that mocking voice. She cried to her mother that she was sorry, chanting the phrase though she knew how hollow and trivial those words actually were, as if "I'm sorry" could make up for the loss of a human life.

To Sam, however, those words held infinite importance. They meant that Dani was still in control. Her body had been transformed, but Dani was fighting the change, and she was winning.

Sam hated to admit it, but Angel had been right. Hysterics would achieve nothing. Guilt, anger, regret—these emotions served a purpose. They might allow Dani to continue the inner struggle and remind herself why, from this point out, she had to fight down the demon in her blood.

At the moment, Sam could see the incredible grief Dani held in her eyes. She knew that the young woman didn't need those feelings thrust upon her from without. Within, she was engulfed by them. She needed her mother's love and forgiveness.

Sam suddenly recalled when she had believed in her

daughter so much that she had locked herself in the basement of the Malibu house for the last day of Dani's "incubation period." She had been willing to die if necessary, but a part of her had believed that no matter what horrors had overtaken Dani, no matter how twisted the girl's perceptions of reality had become, deep down, Dani was a human girl. Her daughter. Dani could never be anything otherwise.

At that time, however, Sam had not actually witnessed Dani in the act of murder. She had not seen the orgasmic frenzy in which the girl had writhed as she took the life of someone who trusted her. The glee and the incredible shrieks Dani had delivered when she had savaged her prey had disgusted and terrified Sam.

Though she was ashamed of her own emotions, Sam could not deny that she was afraid of her daughter. That was something she had never felt before. She had known that for a short time, Dani had been the same as Bill Yoshino, Isabella, Marissa, Richard Sterling, and so many thousands, perhaps millions more, but she had known it as cold data that she could store as a computer might. She had seen Dani in full transformation, seen the feral hatred in the girl's face, heard her threats to kill her own mother. Sam had been able to distance herself from those horrors because this was her daughter. She had fed Dani at night as a baby and walked her to school years later. The feel of Dani shuddering in her arms after her ordeals in her teenaged years was still fresh.

Those memories had helped Sam to survive when she had last seen her daughter transformed into a monster. They were still there, but they had lost some measure of the emotions that had been tied to them. Her beautiful, bright memories had been eclipsed by the grotesque image of Dani killing their mutual friend, Dorothea.

"Honey," Sam said, "we're going to have to work together on this thing. You're going to have to tell me

209

everything you're feeling, and when you start slipping, you're going to have to tell me that too."

"Yes, Mommy," Dani said between sobs. She had regressed to a childlike state, retreating from the horrors she had committed.

Sam decided that even though it would be easier to control Dani while the girl was in this state, her daughter would be worthless to them in a crisis. That would have to change.

"Dani, listen to me. I know what you've done and I know why you did it. But Michael won't have a chance unless we get him away from those bastards. I need you to be strong for his sake. Can you do that?"

Dani nodded slowly. "I'll try."

Sam thought of Peter's words. "You're angry at the wrong person, honey. They knew that if they forced you to make this decision, you would blame yourself instead of them. They're counting on your being incapacitated with guilt. You've got to rise above that. If we get out of this, and get away somewhere with Michael, then I promise, we'll both get help. Somehow we will, I swear it. You're not the only one carrying around a lot of anger. The thing is, if we keep blaming ourselves for what's been done to us, instead of trying to get the hell out of this hole we've been thrown into, then we're giving them exactly what they want—complete power over us."

Dani looked up, her cloudy eyes starting to clear. Slivers of gold burned within them.

"We've got to take back our lives," Sam said. "And right now, the only way to do that is to stop doing everything by their rules."

"Yes," Dani said, her tone suddenly razor-sharp. "What about Angel? Can we trust her?"

"We don't have much of a choice, honey."

"She did things to me. I want to pay her back too."

"After this is over."

"All right," Dani said, the childlike edge to her

words replaced with a devastating fury and a disquieting air of delight.

Sam nodded and went to the door. It opened before she could touch the knob. Angel walked in, grinning.

"Sorry to eavesdrop," the vampire said, "but when you've got the Blood of the Ancients running in your veins, you could be standing a couple of blocks away and it wouldn't matter. The whole goddamned world is open to you. It's better than CNN."

Sam nodded. Dani had been turned by Alyana. That meant her daughter also possessed the Ancients' gift. Both Dani and Angel had power beyond that of a normal vampire. Dani's only disadvantage was her lack of experience. Angel could help her to master her new powers. They would be needed in the battle ahead.

"So, are we ready to get started? Tit-beating all done?" the vampire asked.

"Yes," Sam said.

"Good. I've got some new Ren and Stimpy tapes in my bedroom and I want to get to them before we take off."

"I think this will be more entertaining," Sam said, laying out her thoughts to the vampire.

Angel fell over laughing. "Shit, that's great!"

"Mom?" Dani asked, unwilling to use her power unless it was necessary.

Sam's body tensed as she said, "I was thinking about the terms Alyana laid down. We've got one day before the first team of hunters, Devin Tyler's sons, come after us. They expect that we're going to use that time to run and hide. To pick out some place in the desert where we can make a stand."

"Yes," Dani said hesitantly.

"Why the hell should we? We know they're in Las Vegas. Why not take them out *before* they can come after us?"

"Yeah," Angel said as she picked herself up from the floor. "A fucking preemptive strike!"

Dani shuddered. "But Tyler's sons are only going to be in Vegas because Devin's there. Are you saying that we take *him* out too?"

Sam turned to Angel. "I have no problem with that. What about you?"

Angel thought of her treatment at the man's hands. In an icy voice she whispered, "Why the hell *not?*"

For the first time in a long time, Samantha Walthers smiled.

Part Two
Where the Shadows Run from Themselves

"I'll tell you how to beat the gambling in Las Vegas. As soon as you get off the airplane, walk right into the propeller."

—Milton Berle

Chapter Eighteen

Dani crouched in the shadows with the others, remembering what it had been like when she had been a child. She loved to play, but not little-girl games. Jami and Lisa Evans, the twins who were her best friends, cared about dolls and playing dress-up, or learning the new dances from television shows. Dani preferred watching old movies starring Laurence Olivier or Grace Kelly. She could stare for hours at the image of the woman who would later become Princess Grace, wishing that she had the woman's beautiful blond hair and impossibly soft skin.

When Dani wasn't with Jami or Lisa, most of the children avoided her. But there had been one little boy, Emile, who would stay in Tampa with his grandparents during the summer. Dani loved spending time with Emile. They would find discarded old boxes and build forts, or they would pretend to be superheroes and race around the neighborhood. Emile didn't mind her golden eyes. It didn't matter to him that the other children seemed to hate Dani, and by virtue of his association with her loathed him too. When the summers came, Dani could leave the taunting of her schoolmates behind and lose herself to the fantasy worlds she and Emile would create.

Often, they would sit around reading comics or *Mad* Magazines. Emile liked to collect the old black and white horror magazines of the sixties and seventies. He especially liked *Eerie,* with its gamut of sympathetic monster heroes who would inevitably turn the tables on their tormentors. Dani also enjoyed them, though she felt the exploits of the barely clad Vampirella were a bit farfetched. She loved going with him to the used bookstores when his grandmother felt up to taking them, particularly Haslam's in St. Pete. Sometimes Dani found true-crime magazines. She would read them, imagining that her mother was a part of the stories, bursting in on whatever nastiness she was reading about and saving the victims.

The best times came when they sat in the darkness of Emile's attic, trading scary stories or talking about their parents. They sat in their cardboard fort, which had been covered in heavy blankets to prevent the harsh afternoon sunlight from intruding. The only illumination would come from the beautiful custom-crafted candles Emile's father made for a living. Emile never said it, but Dani could sense that the boy was scared of his father and mother and he lived for the summers when he was allowed to get away from them. Dani told him the *secret,* that she was adopted.

Most of the neighborhood knew that — it was common knowledge to anyone who had lived there years earlier, when Samantha Walthers had found the infant in the garbage dumpster and saved her life. Emile had had no idea. She told him, fearing the worst, hoping for the best, and he sat quietly, then began to cry. He said that he wished *he* had been adopted by another family. Dani held him, and found herself crying with him, though for different reasons. She could not explain to him how terrible it was to know that the people who had given birth to you didn't want you, that they had thrown you away with the rest of the trash.

She loved Sam. The woman *was* her mother. But there was always a part of Dani that was aware that this was not the way things were supposed to have been. She had another family somewhere, and they did not want her. It would have been worse, of course, to have grown up with parents like Emile's, who took advantage of every opportunity to be rid of their child. There had even been the summer when Dani and Emile had gone skinny-dipping, and she had seen the pair of deep scars that had been gouged permanently into the boy's back, and the network of smaller scars in his flesh.

No matter how bad it was for him, however, at least he knew where he belonged. He had secure footing beneath him. Dani cried that afternoon because she feared that she would never find anyone who understood what it was like to feel so apart from the rest of the world, despite the love she had been given every day. Dani and Emile never spoke of it again, and when she was eleven, Emile's grandparents moved.

Dani never forgot the smell of the slightly dilapidated cardboard fort, the strangely comforting odor of rot. She always smiled when she thought of the day when Emile's grandmother caught them up in the fort with the candles. The woman had been certain they would set their sanctuary afire and insisted they use flashlights only.

Dani knew the fort could never be destroyed. That safe place would live forever in her heart. After she had killed Dorothea, she had crawled back into the fort, and had been shocked to find that it offered no comfort. The candles had burned brighter this time than they ever had before, and they set the flimsy cardboard walls on fire. Dani had fled from the fort, terrified of the flames, frightened more than she had ever been in her life by the bright, searing light.

Sam, Dani, and Angel had come to a small private airstrip in search of a fast and hopefully undetectable means of leaving Albuquerque and making it to Vegas. Dani had suggested Lifeguard One. She could get access to the chopper, and she knew how to fly the craft. Her mother had gently, but firmly, made it clear to Dani that this was not a wise choice. They wanted to leave the city quietly. Stealing a valuable medical-relief helicopter would instantly make them targets.

The golden-eyed young woman knew that she was being spoken to as if she were a child, but she didn't mind somehow. There was a safety in the innocence of childhood, a sanctuary she craved almost as badly as she desired the blood and terror of another victim. If she were a child again, she would not possess the godlike power and the inhuman hunger that threatened to drive out her sanity and release the dark, animal *thing* that lived inside her, the demon she had been attempting to deny for years.

The demon that was her blood.

Dani had been silent as Sam and Angel had debated on ways to get out of the city. The Parliament's decree had been worded loosely enough to leave it open for a frightening array of interpretations. According to the rules of engagement, the Tyler twins would not be allowed to come after Dani until nightfall of the following day. But there had been no clause to prevent *agents* of the twins from tracking them and leading the hunters directly to their prey.

They had lost precious time determining that they were not being followed directly. Nevertheless, they were convinced that watchers would be placed at the city's main airport. Even if they had been physically disguised and psychically shielded, the Initiates or Immortals used by the Tylers would be aware that others of their kind were booking a flight, and records would be kept of their destination. They would be followed.

Angel had suggested a less direct method of travel. She had worked briefly for drug runners in Los Angeles. The routes, pickup and drop-off locations, and even the names and likenesses of the operatives in their nationwide network were captured in her inhuman memory. Their planes would fly low to avoid radar, and their crews were human.

Easy prey.

The airstrip, which amounted to a runway, a bunker for the plane, and a separate small building used as a business office, was thirty-five minutes outside of the city. The privately owned plane was utilized for commercial tours of the desert during the day.

According to their regular routine when Angel worked with the them, the drug dealers would have no scheduled runs for the next few days. Sam, Dani, and Angel would be all right unless the strip had been closed, the pilot had been busted, or the plane was engaged in a private charter, which was unlikely at this time of night. All they would have to do was walk in, place the pilot under a compulsion, and take off.

Dani had no hope that it would go so smoothly. Despite Angel's claims that a pilot was kept there on duty twenty-four hours a day in the event of an emergency, Dani was certain that the office would be abandoned. Angel had driven for the last mile with the headlights turned off. It was pitch black and Sam was worried that they would drive off the road. But Angel claimed that she was sending out her power and registering the perceptions of small animals along the roadside, gauging any possible disturbances up ahead through their eyes. Dani thought that was a load of crap, but she hadn't felt up to challenging the vampire.

They had parked a thousand yards from the office and covered the remainder of the distance on foot. Sam had instructed Angel to send out a blanketing haze that would distort the perceptions of anyone who might see them. Dani had waited for Angel to say something like, "What do you think I've *been* doing?" or something equally snide and condescending. She knew that the platinum-haired vampire had already been covering their approach.

Angel had nodded. That had been her only response. She had been unusually quiet since they had reached the airstrip and that worried Dani.

Now they were crouching in the shadows outside the business office and Dani was having a difficult time concentrating. She wanted the comfort of her safe place, the darkened cardboard fort she had built with Emile, but it had been reduced to ashes. There was no smoldering wreckage she could cling to, no dying embers left of the warm light it had once provided. It was dust, nothing more.

"Dani, are you listening?" Sam said insistently.

She looked up. "What?"

"We're going in. Wait here."

Dani looked at Angel. The expressionless vampire flexed her long, ivory fingers. She seemed wired tight, anxious to get moving. Nevertheless, she was standing at Sam's side, taking orders from the woman as if that were natural for her. The restraint she displayed was so out of character for the vampire that it caused Dani to shudder. She did not want to leave her mother alone with the creature.

"No," Dani said. "I'll go with you."

"If you're up to it."

"Yeah," Dani replied absently. "Sure."

Moments later they stood before the locked door of the front office. It was dark, but through the glass window in the door, light could be seen from the back room, which had been converted into sleeping quarters. Angel reached out with her power and reported what she had sensed. The pilot was there, watching a syndicated episode of *Family Ties*.

"Do you want me to bring him out to unlock the door?" Angel asked. "If not, I can kick it in. Either way, he's got to be put under. How do you want it?"

Dani looked to her mother. The woman did not seem to like the idea of taking control of the pilot's mind. On the drive, Sam had argued with Angel that they could pay the man and charter his plane the way anyone else might. Angel had reminded Sam that the man might not go along with their wishes, and he would later be able to identify them. They did not have much time and it would be faster and easier to take the pilot immediately and get on their way. Sam was aware that the vampire did not have to be looking at, touching, or even in the same room with her subject to place them under a compulsion. With one command, Angel would make the man her slave.

Dani stared at Angel, amazed at the moderated behavior of the vampire. Angel seemed like a dog that had been whipped, its spirit broken. Dani wondered what she had missed. The vampire noticed the way Dani was scrutinizing her, snarled, and looked away.

"It's not going to *hurt* him," Dani said, and realized that her tone was petulant, that of a child. She was also disturbed to note that she was defending Angel's position. Her mother looked at her sharply, and she realized that Sam was agonizing over committing an act that Dani had performed so often that it had become meaningless to her.

"Dammit," Sam whispered, surrendering to the inevitability of it all. "Take him out, but no bullshit."

For the first time in the last hour, Angel's eyes came to malicious life. With a laugh she said, "Little ole me?"

Angel's power lashed out with such ferocity that Dani received a taste of the intense, burning agony the vampire projected into the pilot's mind. She felt as if she were plunging into a churning, spitting sea of lava. Fires licked at her mind. The flames that had consumed the safe place within her thoughts returned and seared away her reason. Her identity fell away. She dropped to the ground, grasping her head as she screamed for the pain to stop. Suddenly it did stop, and the complete emptiness she faced was somehow more terrifying.

"Oh, I'm sorry," Angel said, looking down at Dani. She had pronounced the word *sahr-wwweee,* like Bugs Bunny in a Warner Brothers cartoon. "I should have warned you."

"What did you do to her?" Sam screamed as she grabbed Angel and attempted to drive the vampire against the wall. The Immortal could not be moved.

"You'll hurt yourself, stop it," Angel said as she pushed Sam away with the lightest brush of her power. Sam fell back. She went to Dani, who was lying facedown in the dirt, and turned the girl over.

Dani's head was beginning to clear. She wondered why her mother had not checked on her first, instead of launching herself at the vampire. Which did Sam care about more, Dani wondered, having someone upon whom she could vent her anger or seeing to the safety of her child? The woman's concern seemed almost like an afterthought, and that hurt Dani nearly as much as the psychic backlash she had endured from Angel's attack on the pilot.

"Honey, are you all right?" Sam asked.

Dani shrugged off her mother's hands and rose to her knees.

"I'm fine," Dani said, unwilling to look at her mother. "It wasn't me."

Confusion washed over Sam. "What are you talking about?"

"The pilot," Dani managed to say.

Sam's gaze shot to Angel, who was giggling madly. "What did you do?"

Angel shrugged. "If you're going to do them right, you've got to clean them down to the bone. I guess it's just a habit with me. A little wasteful. After all, we're going to have to strip him out again later, now that I've done this. It's still safer."

Sam had no idea what the woman was talking about, but understanding burned in Dani's eyes.

"She wiped out his entire personality," Dani said, "all his memories. Everything."

Sam attempted to absorb this. The enormity of it staggered reason. They hadn't even walked in the door, they hadn't even *seen* this man, and already his life had been destroyed because of their contact. "You killed him."

"Not exactly," Angel said. "The body's still good."

Sam attempted not to shake as she turned to face Angel. "Get out of here. We're not going to deal with you. This was a mistake."

"You don't have a choice. Neither do I."

"This man's dead because . . ." she faltered. "No reason. He's dead for no reason."

"He's not dead," Angel said.

"He might as well be," Dani said.

Angel winked. "Don't get all stressed out. I just thought we'd share. Y'know, a little female-bonding thing. Show both of you how things are done in the real world."

"It doesn't mean anything to you?" Sam asked. "Doing this to a human being?"

Angel frowned, scratched her neck. For a moment she seemed lost in deep concentration. She shrugged. "No, I don't think so. Dani, does it mean anything to you when you fuck with someone's head?"

"I don't do what you just did," Dani said.

"Oh, I see. What I did is different."

"That's right."

Angel drove her hand through the glass window in the door. Shards of glass struck the floor inside as Angel reached in and unlocked the office door, then withdrew her hand.

"Come on," Angel said. "There's something I want to show *both* of you."

223

Chapter Nineteen

The vampire's hand was bloody. She had cut herself. Raising her wounded hand in Dani's direction, Angel said, "Wanna lick this off for me?"

Dani stiffened. Within, she felt the lumbering, sated demon that was her bloodhunger shift in its slumber.

"Why are you doing this?" Sam asked. "I thought we had an understanding."

"Jesus," Angel spat as she opened the door and led the others inside the office, "an understanding. I hate when you try to fucking sound civilized, you know? I've been inside both of you, deep down. I know what both of you are. Neither of you have *anything* on me."

"So that's what this is?" Sam asked. "You're feeling insulted? We think you're shit, we're acting superior, and you want to put us in our place?"

Angel hesitated before the doorway to the bedroom where the pilot's body lay. "I'm feeling that both of you are so goddamned ignorant and self-deluded that you're gonna get yourselves killed and fuck everything up for me. That happens, I'm not going to get what I want. You both need a little education. This is the first lesson."

The platinum-haired vampire went inside and stood at the foot of the bed where the pilot lay. He was a tall, lanky man with thinning blond hair grown long to cover his receding hairline. His face was soft and gentle. The pilot wore a green flowered shirt and white shorts. He was barefoot. Angel went to him and ran her finger along the underside of his right foot. His body jerked slightly, an involuntary reflex.

The man was alive.

"See what's in his head," the vampire said as she clamped her strong hands on Dani's shoulders and shoved her forward. "Go on, do it."

Dani looked to her mother. Sam bit her lip and nodded. The golden-eyed young woman reached out tentatively with her power. Her bright, silver thread touched his mind and she retreated instantly. "It's a vacuum. There's nothing there. It's hungry. It wants to suck up anything that comes near it."

"How can it be hungry if there's nothing there?" Sam asked.

"I don't know, okay?" Dani said, angered. "How the hell am I supposed to know anything? I don't know what she did!"

Angel shook her head. "Sure, you do. You do this all the time. You just do it so fast it doesn't occur to you to break it down and really look at it in stages."

Dani went to Sam. "I want to get out of here."

The vampire sat on the bed before the comatose man. "Fine, go. Get out of here. Do exactly what they want you to do. Lie down, spread your legs, and let them fuck you again. I mean, you don't mind if you bleed a little bit, right? You could even take it up the ass from them again, I'm sure they won't object."

Sam detached herself from her daughter's grip and stood before Angel. Impatiently, she asked, "What is this?"

"I told you. A lesson. Your daughter can do what I just did. She can do it to someone who's attacking her. She can do it to the Tylers, if she's willing."

"I'm not doing *that*," Dani said, terrified.

"Keep talking," Sam said to Angel in a low, contemplative voice.

"Mom, don't," Dani pleaded. "Don't make me."

Angel plopped on the bed beside the pilot. "You seem to think I've burned away everything that made this man an individual. Everything that made him human and intelligent. That's not true. It all still exists up here." She tapped her forehead. "I can put it back any time I want."

An odd sense of detachment closed over Dani. She no longer felt threatened by Angel's words. Instead, she was intrigued. Dani drew on her medical knowledge, considering the lightning storm of electrical activity in the brain, the imprinting of memory, the vast biological "circuitry" that allowed the existence of memory, reason, and emotion—in short, identity. She had sensed that when she was changing the perceptions of a human, she was altering their brain chemistry to some degree, but she had never been able to ascertain the exact nature of those changes. It became enough to know that she could do it when it was necessary.

Angel was suggesting that the elements making up a human mind could be removed en masse from the physical body, edited, then replaced. That was absurd. Belief in such a theory would mean accepting the existence of a separate consciousness apart from the body.

A soul.

Angel smiled. She had been listening to Dani's thoughts. "You got it, sweetums. The best thing is, they're really *tasty.* Num, num. Good vittles, Mom!"

The cool, scientific immersion in reason that Dani had experienced suddenly fled. She felt once more like a frightened child with nowhere to run and she screamed, "Stop it! Shut up!"

"Come on, Dani. Stop acting like you still have your cherry. Uncle Bill took that from you a long

226

time ago. I mean, it's not like you've never tasted one of these before. A soul, I mean. You had a fine old time with Dorothea a few hours ago. Madison a while back. Jacob Willis when you were still a kid. And *who* was that other one?"

"Mom, make her stop."

"Dani—" Sam began.

"That's right," Angel said, snapping her fingers. "I remember now. Altsoba. Elizabeth Altsoba."

"That's not true. It's not *true!*"

"Come on, Dani. You know what you did. You just don't want to remember it the way it actually happened. You've got a history of burying memories. Or did you forget that too?"

Trembling, Dani thought of that terrible morning when she came upon the car wreck bearing the bloody forms of Elizabeth Altsoba and her dead boyfriend. She knew how it had happened. Elizabeth had told Dani to take her memories.

Angel's power sliced into Dani's consciousness. She heard the vampire's voice in her mind: *Is that how it really happened, Dani? Or is that how you want to remember it?*

Another memory approached. Elizabeth Altsoba, covered in blood, begging for mercy, release. Dani shoved it away. This memory wasn't real. Angel was using her power to place it within her mind. Dani would never have taken Elizabeth's identity from her if the woman hadn't told her to do it. She would be a monster if the truth were anything but that.

Dani raced away from that other memory and suddenly she felt a wall cracking within her mind. For a horrifying instant, she glimpsed something she was not consciously aware existed within her mind. Another memory. An entire library of memories. Untold volumes. She wanted to run from these memories, but they closed over her before she could get away.

She was a madman named Jacob Willis, a serial

227

killer, receiving a surprise birthday party for his thirtieth year. Black balloons, a tombstone on the cake. Streamers. His house was filled with friends and his only surviving relative, his brother. Beneath his jacket, the blood of a little girl who would be the next victim of the brothers was drying against his chest. Over the laughter and applause of the partygoers, he could hear her cries as she clawed and scratched him before the chloroform put her under. His hand throbbed with the sympathetic memory of her wildly beating heart thumping against him as he touched her chest.

Dani attempted to slam the door shut on this memory. It faded quickly, but its echo remained.

Willis was alive. The killer who had trapped her when she was a child continued to exist. His body had been destroyed, but his essence had taken refuge within Dani.

The demon had a name and a face. It was Willis. She had taken him. He had corrupted her.

She was innocent. It had been him all along.

He was the demon.

No, Angel whispered in her mind, *the demon existed before you consumed Willis. It's a part of you. It is you. Accept it.*

Then why are you showing me this? Dani screamed in her mind. *I don't want to know that this is inside me. I don't want to remember his memories, feel his feelings. Make it go away!*

I can't. Only can do that. Angel laughed. Her tone suddenly shifted to that of a game-show announcer. *But wait, there's more!*

Within Dani's mind, there was an eruption of flame and several fissures opened in her memories:

She was Dorothea Odakota, five years old, playing on the res with the other children.

She was Madison Avery, living in the streets until a beautiful dark man named Bill Yoshino found her and took her to a better life.

Dani felt as if she might go insane at any moment. *Please, make it stop, I don't want to know, please!*

Too late, Angel whispered. *Too late.*

More fissures opened.

She was Isabella Giancarlo, after she had murdered Vasari, her husband, half-insane, convinced that she was a monster, until Alyana Du Prey found her and changed her life forever.

Dani could bear no more. *Please, God, no!*

For a moment, Dani was able to retreat into her own memories, but they offered no comfort. She saw the face of Elizabeth Altsoba once again. The woman was pleading with Dani to stop.

No, Dani thought. She had been pleading for Dani to *make* it stop. To take her pain away. To see that her knowledge and experience did not go to waste.

Don't do this to me! Elizabeth Altsoba screamed.

Dani turned from the false memory and tried to cling to what she knew was real. She had not taken anything that was not freely given. Elizabeth had asked Dani to help her. Dani had not preyed upon her. That was a lie Angel was attempting to drive into her mind.

Is it? another voice asked from deep within her, the harsh and brutal voice of the demon.

Fleeing from her own wildly distorting memories, Dani suddenly found herself enveloped by one of the stolen memories she possessed of Elizabeth Altsoba.

I didn't steal anything, Dani thought, I only took her knowledge, I didn't take any of this.

Nevertheless, a sweeping vista of memories engulfed her. She fought against the maelstrom of images that comprised the life of a woman she only met once, as the woman lay dying, and clawed her way out, one memory at a time. She saw Elizabeth as a teenager, an infant, approaching thirty. Finally she was near the surface of the woman's memories. She only had to endure one more and she would escape.

She was Elizabeth Altsoba, losing her virginity. She screamed with the pain of entry as her boyfriend raised himself above her and cruelly rammed himself into her, unmindful of her cries and protests.

The walls between her memories and those which she had stolen from her victim blurred. Suddenly the face of the man above her blurred and changed. She was no longer recalling Elizabeth's first sexual encounter. This time it was her own.

Bill Yoshino strained above her, driving himself into her as his eyes burned a luminous sky-blue. His lips curled back and a mouth filled with razor-sharp teeth was visible. The hands which had touched her so tenderly transformed into bone-white talons that punctured and tore the sheets. Blood soaked the bed and his lower torso.

The pain was horrible. She felt as if she were being ripped apart within, and also sensed that her conscious mind was unaware of all that was truly happening. Dani had believed that she was receiving pleasure, not pain, and after a time, sensations changed to bear that out.

Yoshino had remained a monster the entire time he made love to her.

"No!!!" Dani screamed, breaking from the array of memories Angel had loosed in her mind. She had known that Yoshino had been inside her mind when they had made love, and later concluded that the romantic, gentle, and painless encounter she recalled was, in part, a fiction. The young woman had no idea that the true memory had been burned within her mind, waiting for her to one day seek it out.

Sam moved forward, pulling Dani into her arms. Her daughter was weeping. Staring at Angel over Dani's shoulder, Sam said, "Why are you doing this?"

"Because she has to learn, and I don't have the time or the inclination to make it easy on her. Right now, she's worthless. She's like you. I could bend her, I could break her. I could do both of you at the same time."

"You goddamned bitch," Dani hissed. She could not banish the dual sets of memory in her mind concerning Elizabeth Altsoba. For the last year, she had been plagued by guilt over her acquisition of the dying woman's memories. Angel had sensed that. The vampire had known that Dani would consider it an ultimate horror if she were to learn that her own memories could not be trusted, and she had, in fact, raped the dying woman's mind.

"Fine," Angel said, disgusted. "You want to keep deluding yourself? Go ahead. But this is what's been tearing you apart. You did something shitty. So what? At the time you felt you were doing it for a good reason. Admit it to yourself, feel like crap if you want, and move on. Life's too short for this."

"I did not do that to Elizabeth Altsoba!" Dani wailed. "You're making me think that. It's not true."

Sam shook her head in confusion. "Dani, what are you talking about?"

"She's fucking with me, that's all," Dani said darkly. "That's all she's good for."

Dani wondered if Angel were attempting, as she had at the bar, to make Dani accept her blood heritage. When she thought of the false set of memories concerning Elizabeth Altsoba, she felt a certain tranquility that had not been hers for the last year. Angel claimed that it was the strain of denial that was harming her. A part of her almost wanted to give in to these dark imaginings, embrace them as if they were true. Finally, she would be at peace with herself.

She would also be a monster, a creature no better than Angel. At least she would no longer be divided. Perhaps that had been Angel's intent. Dani fought the seductive lure of this line of reason, suffusing herself with anger at the vampire and all of her kind.

231

Your kind, the demon whispered. *Your kind too.*

"You're mad?" Angel asked. "Good. Do something about it. Take me on."

Dani stared at the woman, her golden eyes blazing, then turned away and buried her face in her mother's chest. Sam stroked her hair gently.

Angel absently ran her hand though the hair of the man whose mind she had consumed. "Hey, Sam, you're not saying what's bothering you either. You want me to put it in her mind?"

Before Sam could object, the words slammed into both her mind and that of her daughter.

The bread. The bread was a shitty thing to do. That's all I had and you made it nothing but a lie.

Dani cried out and wriggled away from her mother's embrace. "Oh Jesus, I'm sorry, I'm sorry."

"There we go, a little cleansing of the soul," Angel said cheerily. "Let it all come out. Isn't that nice?"

"Why are you doing this?" Dani screamed.

"You refuse to get it, don't you?" Angel asked. "You can't reconcile what you've become — hell, what you've *been* all along — with the image you've always had of yourself. You're the good girl. You don't do those things us bad girls do. But you've been doing them and you want to do them all the time. So you need a reason why you shouldn't just give in to the voices in your head and tear the hell out of this man. Or out of Sam. Or any human. They're all the same, right?"

"Stop it," Dani cried.

"Nope. You need a reason and I'm giving you one. This is what it's really like when you take a victim. When you make a kill. What did you think the purpose of it was, Dani? What you get out of it? The blood? Wildlings make that mistake. You know better than that. It's not even the fear and desire. It's even more than the rush you get by completely taking

232

control of someone else's life, by being God to them with the power to kill them or let them go. It's more than that, sweets.

"You eat their fucking *souls,* Dani." She grinned. "You laugh, you cry, and they become a part of you. So don't do it any more or else you'll be like me, and you'll have hundreds of them living in your head."

An idea flashed into Dani's mind. In disbelief, she said, "You're trying to help me hold on to my humanity?"

"Sure."

"Why? If I revert, the deal is broken. I'll be hunted again."

"Well, let's say I want to delay it for a while. You see, Dani, you're a natural. If you give in now, you're not going to give a fuck about what we have to do together to survive. You're going to do what I did. You're going to go on a spree."

"No," Dani whispered, "I wouldn't."

"Sure you would. You love it. You keep forgetting, I know what's inside you. I know how much the two of us are alike."

"That's enough," Sam said.

The vampire laughed. "Not really. She's going to have to use her power, and that's going to make her hungry. She needs to remember all of this when she gets hungry, or else she's going to blow the whole fucking deal."

Dani shook her head. Angel could not be telling the truth. Dani knew that she possessed the memories of her victims because she had been in their minds as they had passed on. Her brain made copies of their remembrances and stored them, the way a computer might. She had not torn their essences from them at the point of death and taken them within herself. That was impossible and too horrifying to even consider.

"Is it?" Angel asked. The vampire tapped the skull

of the man lying beside her. "You know there's nothing in there, don't you? Say the magic word and . . ."

Suddenly the pilot sat up in bed, gasping for air. He looked at the women surrounding him. "Jesus. Who the hell are you people?"

Dani stared at the man in shock. He was restored. Fully restored. She didn't have to access his mind to know that. The urge to pass out was overwhelming, but she fought it. She hugged herself.

The mind cannot exist separately from the body, she told herself. It was physically impossible.

Suddenly, she remembered the car accident in Los Angeles. She had been driving the Karmann Ghia. It was destroyed. There had been a little girl and her mother. The child's name was Hazie. The woman would have died, but Dani had healed her. Dani had linked their systems and used her own body's inhuman chemistry to help inspire changes in the woman's physiology. For one brief, startling moment, Dani had found herself looking out of the woman's eyes at her own body. She had physically made that same out-of-body leap once in the past. Why was it so hard to accept now?

Without warning, the pilot leaped from the bed, pulled open the drawer of his nightstand, and drew an automatic. Before he could aim the weapon, Angel was on him, slapping it away and crashing his head against the wood. He slumped to the floor, holding his head and moaning.

"Well, enough of this slow-mo crap, kids," Angel said. "Let's watch the tape in real time, shall we?"

Before Dani could object, Angel lashed out with her power again. This time Dani sensed a slight flickering of pain, nothing more.

The pilot rose from the floor, put the gun away, and went to his clothes cabinet. Sam had to dart out of his way. The man was oblivious to the presence of the women.

234

"He can't hear or see us," Angel said. "It's impossible for him to perceive us in any way. He's decided, all on his own—or so believes—that he wants to round up some fine Vegas trim. So he's going to fly there tonight, under radar. He's done it before. Outside the city, he's going to change his mind and put down, because he's going to feel ill. Then he's going to turn around and come back here. He'll refuel in the morning, kick himself for not going on and getting laid, then forget the whole thing.

"Is that a little more palatable, ladies?"

Dani stared at the vampire. Angel had reconfigured the pilot's mind with amazing speed. Dani felt completely alert and in command of herself. She knew that she was no longer going to be able to hide in the sanctuary of her own delusions. Suddenly she drew down shields within her mind and denied Angel access to her thoughts. The vampire recoiled. Angel had apparently not expected such an immediate show of power, or that Dani would become aware so quickly of the vast power she had at her disposal.

"It's true, isn't it?" Dani asked. "For once, you're not lying."

"Uh-huh," Angel said casually.

Sam touched her daughter's arm. "Honey, are you all right?"

"Yeah, Mom. Better than I have been in a long time." That was not a complete lie. She would never feel good about herself again. Trusting herself after what Angel had showed her would be impossible. But she was infused with a calmness she'd thought she would never regain, a sense of purpose she had lost. Angel had raised questions in Dani's mind, and she refused to lie down and die until she had the answers to those questions.

Was the darkness a part of her, or was it something that preyed upon her and corrupted her? *Had* she been corrupted at all? What was the truth?

235

Dani smiled and glanced in Angel's direction. If Angel was telling the truth, then, in her twisted way, she was actually attempting to do Dani a favor. On the other hand, if the vampire was lying, Dani would kill her for what she was doing. Dani made a decision. She would follow the conditions laid out by the Parliament and save her mother's life, even though that meant condemning herself to life as an Immortal.

Then she would renegotiate the deal.

"Let's go," Dani said, gesturing in the direction of the pilot. The man had gathered his flight gear and was walking out the door, still oblivious to their presence. "We've got a flight to catch."

Chapter Twenty

On the flight to Vegas, Dani told her mother all that had occurred between Angel and herself in the pilot's bedroom. She had made a promise to Sam that she would hold back nothing and she had no intention of breaking that promise. Once Dani was finished, Sam placed her arms around the young woman, and did not let her go until the pilot began to prepare for their landing. They said nothing else. Words were unnecessary. The simple gesture of love was enough for both of them.

Angel remained surprisingly quiet. Her silence reminded Dani of the event that had directly preceded Angel's attack on the pilot. The vampire had been subservient to Sam, and when Dani had noticed this, Angel had become a monster, taking out her anger on the pilot and Dani. The image of Angel at Sam's side instead of Dani's had startled the golden-eyed young woman, and she could not purge it from her thoughts.

Dani had avoided the view through the nearby windows. She didn't want to see the ground rushing past. It would have reminded her that if she chose, she could leap from the plane in mid-flight and take to the air on her own power. For years she had dreamed of once again doing exactly that, but now she was afraid of the very thing she had coveted. Angel had been right in one regard. Dani would have to use her powers, and when she did, the hunger would return.

The pilot brought the plane down well outside of Las Vegas, on a deserted airstrip that was also owned by the drug cartel that employed him. The landing was rough, but that was not unexpected. There was no one to greet them, and for that, all three women were grateful. Once the heavy strongboxes of weapons that Sam had collected were unloaded, the pilot took off again.

"You're really carrying a lot of shit," Angel said as she sat down on one of the two silver chests. The vampire patted the side of the box. "I bet some of this is the same crap you used to take out Isabella."

"Yeah," Sam said distractedly as she looked around. The area was a wasteland. There was no civilization in sight. "The shotgun's still in there."

"Cool."

Dani shuddered as the desert breeze cut through her. She felt annoyed at having to worry about something as mundane as being cold, and suddenly her body chemistry altered and she felt as if she were burning up.

"Jesus," she whispered, alarmed at her impossible control over her own physiology. Then she thought of the startling tasks she had seen the members of the Parliament perform, and realized that it was possible that many of these same functions were not beyond her own abilities.

"What's wrong?" Sam asked.

Dani told her.

"We're going to find a way out of this," Sam promised.

"I know," Dani said. She checked her watch. "Right now we have to get into Vegas. It's almost one o'clock. Thanks to that *cunt,* we're stuck in the middle of the desert with no transportation."

"You know what has to be done," Angel said. "There's a road not far from here. We'll have to hitch a ride."

238

Dani looked at her. "Not far? Maybe it's not far if we had all night to walk it. We don't."

"Well," Angel said, clasping her pale hands on the edge of the strongbox between her legs and rocking back and forth as she grinned. "I guess that means one of us will have to fly there, then bring the car back. I've flown once tonight. You know what that does to one of our kind."

"It's draining."

"So I'll have to feed."

"You would anyway," Dani said.

"I dunno. Or you could do it. You wouldn't even feel it after the meal you've had."

Dani flinched.

"It's up to you," Angel said. "I don't have a problem with going, but I've already told you how it's going to turn out. It's up to you. I can live with a little blood on the seats if you can. Doesn't matter to me."

Sam touched Dani's arm. "Is she telling the truth?"

"I don't know. There's no way to tell for sure."

Angel crossed her arms over her breasts. "This distrust thing is getting a little old."

"You want our trust?" Sam asked. "Do something to earn it. You promised not to hurt the pilot."

"I didn't. I told you, I just did what any of us do when we play with someone's head. I just slowed it down some so you could see what was really happening."

"Bullshit."

The vampire sighed. "You know, if you thought about it, you'd see that I don't have any reason to lie. It's not in my best interests. But you can believe whatever you want. Reality is however you want it to be. I don't give a fuck. I'm too tired and hungry to care."

"I thought part of being Parliament was never getting tired," Sam said. "Never getting hungry."

The vampire curled up her lip in frustration. "Well, I *am* hungry, all right? Does that offend your fucking

239

little human sensibilities? Too goddamned bad. Dani got to feed. The others got some. Everyone got some. But I didn't. I was taking care of your brat. I was shielding your precious Michael. That's fine. I didn't mind. That's what I was supposed to do. But this is different. I've gotten a taste for it and it's hard to give it up after that's happened.

"Besides, neither Dani nor I is Parliament yet. We've got the Blood of the Ancients, sure, but it's *once removed*. The hunger's still there. The need's still there. But there's a hell of a lot more that goes with it. Dani knows that, it's all inside her, but she won't let any of it out. She's still the same as she was when she was first turned because that's all she can handle. And like I keep trying to tell you, that's not good enough for what we're going up against."

"So why send her out now if she's not ready?" Sam asked.

"There's no other way to make her ready. Do you know how many people are in Vegas? The way those humans think? She'll have fear, desperation, and lust pressing in on her from all sides. I can't protect her. I can't be the one doing everything for everybody. If she can't handle this, she shouldn't be going on from here."

"Stop it!" Dani shouted. Both women froze. "Stop talking about me as if I wasn't even here."

Sam and Angel waited. Dani could sense that her mother had taken the words of the vampire very seriously. She wasn't the only one.

"I'll go," Dani said. "I'll do it."

"Honey, what if—" her mother began.

"It's my decision," Dani said with a ringing finality.

Sam bit her lip. She suddenly realized what her daughter was agreeing to, and she wanted to go on the run again and this time make damn sure the vampires never found them. Then she thought of Michael.

Jesus, she didn't want to have to choose between her children, but if what Angel had suggested about Dani was true, then her little girl would soon be lost to her forever, no matter the outcome of the next twenty-four hours. Memories of Dani killing Dorothea flashed into her mind. Michael might still have a chance. She had to survive to try and save her son. That meant both she and Dani would have to be strong enough to face the Parliament's challenge.

Sam watched as Dani turned and walked into the darkness. She was swallowed up quickly. A few moments later, Sam heard the sound of a sharp wind that was somehow different from the breezes that blew in the night.

The wind faded and was gone.

It had been as glorious as Dani had remembered. There had been no hesitation, no awkwardness or fumbling around. She had flown in her dreams for two years. Dropping the barriers between dream and reality proved to be effortless. She had wanted to fly, and so she had flown. Her body had changed, becoming somehow lighter, and she had lifted into the darkened skies. The sensation was perfectly natural to her. She had laughed as the wind had blown her long hair into her face and she had tried to blow it away, only to have it softly slap back against her, obscuring her vision. Dani brushed it away, wishing she had possessed enough sense to have her mother braid it for her before she attempted this.

She had no idea why she had been afraid of this. If she was going to suffer through the living hell of this existence, she might as well enjoy the few rewards it had to offer.

Suddenly, she sensed what she had been waiting for: A car was coming down the endless, relentlessly straight road below her. She reached out with her power and allowed her silver thread to wrap itself around the minds of the car's driver and passenger. A man and a woman on their way to Vegas to get married.

It was too sweet.

Dani dropped to the road, transforming, gaining solidity until she had the full weight and mass of a human once again. She touched the ground gently and silently strolled to one side of the road. Memories assailed her. Two years ago, when she had first been turned, she had stopped a car that turned out to be a police vehicle. The cop, Hal Jordan, had later been killed by her companions.

The thought was a sobering one. Dani had to keep herself under control this time. She had to ignore the temptation of reaching deeply into the minds of the humans and making their worst nightmares a reality.

The hunger was already returning.

In moments, the car's headlights were visible. Dani thought of the humans within as vessels for the most wondrous delicacies she could ever imagine. Fear, desire, pain, and death.

The car whipped past her. She had decided to let it go by, just as she should have allowed Jordan's car to pass, when she suddenly recalled the terrified face of Dorothea Odakota. Her silver thread was still wrapped around the passengers of the gray Taurus that had passed. She pulled the thread tight and the car screeched to a halt.

Trembling, Dani walked to the car. The man and woman inside the Taurus sat with their hands in their laps, staring forward with blank expressions. Dani watched them for long moments, then reached down and tore open the passenger side door, descending on the bride-to-be.

Sam had been sitting with Angel. The vampire had proposed a game of cards. Though they didn't actually have cards to play with, Angel claimed that she could make Sam believe she did, and she promised that she would play fair.

She always did, after all.

Sam passed on the game.

"Just trying to get you in the mood for Vegas," Angel said, leaning back and snapping the bones in her fingers. She performed this act with such vigor that it sounded as if she was actually breaking her own bones, then causing them to instantaneously heal so they could be damaged once more.

To Sam, the frightening part was that she knew Angel could do exactly that if she wanted, and so could Dani.

"Who the hell are you, really?" Sam asked finally, to break the silence. Dani had not yet returned. Terrifying possibilities were racing through Sam's mind with every passing second. She had to do something to avoid thinking, even if it meant actually *talking* to the vampire.

"I'm just a dream," Angel said, an oddly contemplative look clouding her face. "I'm not real. I haven't been real since 1953. I'm just the Velveteen Vampire, only I don't give a shit about being real again. I like it just fine this way."

Sam looked at Angel closely. The vampire looked young enough to be carded in nightclubs. She knew from Dani that the vampires claimed to be incredibly long-lived, and they never aged once they were turned.

"What happened in 1953?" Sam asked.

"The lights went out. Everything got real dark."

Sam nodded. "That was your last year as a human being?"

The vampire grimaced. "It would have been, I suppose. If I had ever been a *human being* to start with."

Sam was about to ask another question when Angel raised her hand.

243

"Let's not play this game, all right? You know everything you have to know about me. It's not all that interesting anyway."

"That's fine," Sam said, inwardly dreading a return to her worries over her daughter.

Unexpectedly, Angel said, "I'll tell you one thing, if you really want to know."

There had been a nervous tinge in the vampire's voice.

"Sure," Sam said.

"I was a rock and roll chick for a while. Then the fucking Big Bopper stole one of my tunes, man. Pissed me off. Problem was, when they told me he was taking that plane, I didn't know who else was on it. I thought it was just Lardo. I mean, I was flying real high after I did it, y'know. The Bopper wasn't, but I was. Then I found out that Buddy Holly and Ritchie Valens were with him. Talk about waking up one night and having your whole life turn into the shits. I mean, I liked those other two guys. They were just getting started. Shit."

"Wait a minute," Sam said, "you're trying to tell me that you're responsible for the deaths—"

Her words were interrupted by a brilliant white light that exploded only a few feet from where they were sitting. Angel fell back, off the weapons cache, and landed square on her ass. Sam drew one of her Berettas.

The lights cut out. Sam suddenly became aware of the sound of a motor idling. A gray Taurus was parked in front of them. The driver'sside door opened and Dani stepped out.

"Just wanted to see if I could do that," Dani said. The golden-eyed woman wore a pair of sunglasses she hadn't owned before. There was no one else in the car.

Angel broke into hysterical laughter. "You fucking got me! Fuckin' A!"

Sam stared hard at her daughter. The young bru-

244

nette seemed to be holding herself straighter. The self-doubt that had been plaguing her seemed to be gone. Something else had taken its place. A strange bemusement, a dark, animal confidence.

"What did you do?" Sam asked.

"I covered my approach. I wanted to see if I could get close without either of you spotting me."

"That's not what I mean."

"You know the saying," Dani said. "Ask me no questions."

I'll tell you no lies.

"What did you *do?*" Sam repeated, her stomach suddenly awash with acid.

Dani removed the sunglasses. Her golden eyes burned in the darkness. "I took *care* of it. That's all that matters, right? The job was done. Fuck it."

"Works for me," Angel said happily. "Let's load this stuff and get the fuck out of here."

"Dani, you can't just come back here and—"

"Either you trust me or you don't!" Dani screamed. "If you don't trust me, then there's no sense in any of this, is there?"

Sam shuddered. She wanted to tell Dani that she was not simply using her as a weapon in her fight to rescue her son. If the words had come, she would have explained that she would die for either of her children, but that Michael had to come first, at least for now.

She could say nothing.

"Come on, gang," Dani said as she unlocked the trunk, then walked past her mother and lifted the heavier of the silver cases as if it were weightless. She went back to the trunk and dropped it inside, causing the vehicle to rock on its axles.

"Viva Las Vegas," Angel said, taking the other box and jamming it in the back seat. The vampire got in beside it. Dani slipped into the driver's seat and slammed the door shut.

Sam watched her daughter and suddenly felt a light brushing of wings graze her consciousness. It was not unlike the dark wind that had followed Dani's earlier departure.

Coming? Dani whispered in Sam's mind.

Jesus, Sam thought. Dani rarely did this.

We're going to a place where everything's a risk. You were willing to gamble on me once. Are you willing to do it again?

"Yes," Sam whispered. "Always. I love—"

That's enough.

Sam hesitated for a moment, then got in the car with the vampires.

Chapter Twenty-one

They saw the glittering lights from the desert.

As they passed the borders into the city, Sam felt as if she had crossed into a nightmare of pulsing lights, twisted art deco architecture, and monstrous, self-perpetuating glitz. Casinos and hotels rose up into the dark, desert sky like monolithic elder gods wearing blazing, sequined jackets. It was as if the set designers from *Blade Runner* had channelled the spirits of the mad Roman emperors and together they had designed a city that sported more excess than any other place on the planet. The streets were packed with traffic. Pedestrians massed outside the various hot spots and congealed on the sidewalks.

Earlier that night, Sam had felt strange about leaving Isleta behind and driving into Albuquerque. She had been on the reservation since the birth of her son, Michael. Dormant cells in her body seemed to have been awakened. Suddenly, she had been alive once more.

Driving into Las Vegas, she felt as if she had been killed somewhere along the line and her soul had been dispatched to a hell created by a latter-day Hieronymus Bosch, using neon and flashing lights rather than brush strokes to create a nightmarish vision of purgatory.

Sam looked over at her daughter and wondered how the veritable explosion of fear and desire existing within the city was effecting her. Even to Sam's human senses, the pounding, driving need of the Vegas gamblers was evident, a dark, amorphous cloud that permeated the air and settled into her every pore. She was uncomfortable. Dani had to have been in torment.

The golden-eyed young woman seemed perfectly fine. Completely unaffected.

Angel sat in the backseat, absently humming Ritchie Valen's "Donna."

On the drive into the city, Dani had been extremely vocal. She had devised a plan to kill the Tylers that was brutally direct. Angel had argued that Sam's role in the assassinations was unnecessary. She was only a human. They should find a safe place for her somewhere in the city and leave her there until the job was over.

"She comes with us or it doesn't happen," Dani had said in a tone that was not to be argued with.

Angel had eventually withdrawn her objection. For a time, Sam had been been comforted by her daughter's insistence that her mother come with them on the "hit." Dani was afraid of what she might do if she was left without her mother's support. She needed and wanted Sam with her.

Then Angel had raised another point: "Devin Tyler's a paranoid fuck. He's made enemies. The casino he's playing at has cameras coming out of the fucking wahzoo. He's bound to have some of his people looking over the shoulders of hotel security."

Sam had reminded the vampire that she had packed stage makeup kits, wigs, and clothing in with the artillery. "Tyler's not expecting us to show up in Las Vegas. So long as we disguise ourselves, no one will pick us out of the crowd."

The platinum-haired vampire had one last problem and it had turned out to be the killer: She had worked as a guard to Christian De Santo. It was standard practice for guards to perform blanket scans of the immediate area to make sure no one who had a grudge against their employer got anywhere near them. Dani and Angel could fool those readings. They could put up shells—surface identities that would bounce any casual psychic look-sees. But Sam couldn't do that, and if one of them had to do it for her, then they would have to reveal their core identities.

"Yeah," Dani said with a nasty grin, "we wouldn't want anyone to think we were anything other than a couple of white-chick vampires out looking to score a good time."

"Right, yeah," Angel said. "That's exactly right. I've been to Vegas before. It's crawling with our kind. The place is like a fucking buffet. Whatever kind of prey interests you, you're going to find it there. No one's going to give a shit about us. They *will* notice a human who not only knows about our kind, but is planning on offing as many as she can get in her sights."

"I know how to get around that," Dani said, and went on to detail an augmentation to her initial plan that left Sam covered in a light, cold sweat.

Sam sat back to consider her daughter's words. The proposition was horrible. Richard Sterling had invaded Sam's mind and had forced her to be his slave. He had raped her. Dani's plan amounted to little more than a replay of that event, with Dani—or worse, Angel—assuming Sterling's role.

Sam would have to submit to having her identity pressed down into the depths of her mind while a new persona was temporarily imprinted. For a time, she would honestly believe herself to be someone else, with a completely different life. She would be responsible for smuggling the weapons inside the hotel, but she would be unaware that she was performing this task. A flamethrower could be in her hand and she would believe it to be some innocuous item—a hair dryer, a can of roach spray, God only knows what. At a prearranged time, her false identity would fall away and once again she would become Samantha Walthers.

Logically, Sam understood that this was the only way to get close to the vampires without being detected. Dani could shield her, but the act would defeat Dani's own disguise. Nevertheless, she was sickened by the idea of once again having her mind defiled by the touch of an Immortal, even if the vampire in question was her own daughter.

"It won't be the same," Dani had promised, showing her first real hint of compassion since she had returned from securing the Taurus. "This isn't something that's being done without your consent. If you don't want to do this, then we can do what Angel said and leave you to take care of the fallback until we get there."

The fallback, Sam thought. They would have to arrange for a hiding place within the city before they attempted to take on the Tylers. In the best-case scenario, the kills would go perfectly and they would escape undetected. Even if that occurred, it would not be long before Devin Tyler himself was coming after them. They would need to be able to dig in and hold their position while hunters searched for them.

Her priority was to stay alive for Michael, but she could not leave her daughter to face the monsters alone. The vampires were incredibly powerful, but they were also arrogant, particularly in their views of humans, and she had used that arrogance against them in the past. Sam's presence could be the deciding factor in her daughter's survival. She had to be with Dani, even if it meant exposing herself to the threat of the vampires.

Conversely, if anything went wrong, the Immortals could do to her what Richard Sterling did to her, and they could do it with numbing speed and ferocity. She could be transformed into a weapon against her own child.

No, she thought, recalling her ability to override Sterling's control in his hotel room a year earlier, when his daughter was about to hurl Dani off a twenty-story balcony.

Sam made her decision and prayed that she had made the correct choice.

"Good," Dani said.

Sam stared at her daughter. The golden-eyed young woman had spoken the word with such pleasure that a part of Sam wondered if her daughter had another reason for wishing to submit the woman to this treatment.

You're being paranoid, Sam told herself. Suddenly she was terrified of losing her daughter, and not altogether certain that this had not already occurred. She was ashamed to admit that she had casually checked the car for any signs of a struggle. It was impossible for her to forget about the car's previous owners.

Dani was right, of course, when she said that Sam either trusted her or she didn't. For the last year, her daughter had given her life to protect Sam and Michael, even at the risk of her own sanity. When she had been faced with the possibility of a painless death, or a torturous, guilt-ridden existence as the one thing she despised the most, Dani had chosen the only course of action that would save her mother and give her adopted brother a chance to escape being raised by the Immortals.

Sam wanted to believe that she trusted her daughter, but she would have felt better if Dani had simply told her what had occurred on the roadside.

They had been in Vegas for only a few minutes before Dani announced that they were running on fumes and needed to fill up before they went any farther. The gas station they stopped at was lit up like a ten-dollar whore. Signs advertised that slot machines could be found in the convenience store behind the pumps.

Angel got out of the Taurus and opened the door for Sam.

"Thanks," Sam said cautiously.

"Y'know," Angel said, "I read that some of the bathrooms out here have condom dispensers shaped like slot machines. Course, you're a winner every time with those. I dunno, I thought it was kind of funny."

Dani made a display of ignoring the exchange.

She's jealous, Sam thought with a startling burst of insight that she instantly attempted to dismiss. *Could* Dani be jealous of Sam and Angel? That was insane. If Sam had the opportunity, she would make up for her mistake two years earlier and turn the vampire into ashes on the desert winds.

But was that really true anymore? Angel might have been a stone bitch, but at least she was honest, and she was at peace with herself. The inner conflicts that had been raging within Dani all her life did not seem to touch Angel. In some ways, she was very much like Sam. The vampire knew what she wanted and she went after it. That was all.

"You fill it up," Dani said acrimoniously, and tossed the keys to Sam. "I'll go pay."

"Lemme get that," Angel said, taking the keys from Sam's hands, unlocking the gas tank, and inserting the premium unleaded nozzle into the tank.

Sam wanted to ask Angel why she was being so decent toward her, but she didn't want to push it. Angel had explained that she did nothing that was not in her own best interests. For some reason, she had decided that acting like less of a shit than usual was the way to go. Fine.

A series of beeps sounded. The digital totals on the pumps cleared and Angel squeezed the nozzle. She hummed another Fifties tune while she pumped gas.

252

"Ever been to Mel's Diner?" Angel asked. "In L.A.?"

"Sure, I know it," Sam said. She had taken Dani there on their first week in Los Angeles for authentic fountain-style Cherry Cokes.

"I love that place."

"Yeah, it was cool," Sam thought, recalling that she thought she had walked onto the set of the Happy Days Diner when she first went inside.

"Um-hmmm. Takes me back. I worked in a place like that once. You know, the checkerboard floors, waitresses on roller skates, all that shit. I used to skate around and shit. It was fun."

"Really? I worked at a McDonald's when I was in high school. It was the shits."

"Different era. I'm older than you are."

"Yeah," Sam said, and suddenly shuddered. She crossed her arms over her breasts and hugged herself.

"What is it?" Angel asked.

"Nothing."

"This is weird, isn't it? Just talking?"

"Yeah," Sam said. "Pretty fucking strange."

Angel nodded, and went back to humming her song. She finished filling up the gas tank, set the pump back on its cradle, then locked up the tank and waited for Dani to emerge.

Without looking at Angel, Sam said, "She didn't do it, did she? She didn't hurt whoever owned the Taurus?"

"I don't know."

"It's important."

"Really, I don't know. I can't tell. She's got shields up that are as strong as anything I've ever seen. I'm not sure anything less than the Ancients could get into her head now if she wasn't letting them."

"Jesus."

Sam watched as Dani paid the man at the register and emerged from the convenience center. Suddenly,

253

a black pickup with five howling teenagers whipped through the parking lot and cut in front of Dani. The truck came within a foot of slamming into her with its front grill.

"Hey, watch where you're fuckin' goin' man!" one of the greasy-haired teens shouted.

Dani had been looking down at her wallet, stuffing her change back inside, an arrogant move in any major city. Sam had taught her better than that. She knew to always put her money away inside the store, not out on the street where someone could snatch the wallet from you.

"Stupid cunt!" another cried.

Sam watched with mounting fear as the golden-eyed teenager looked up slowly and smiled at the boys.

"Oh, shit," Angel whispered. "The last fucking thing we need right now is to draw attention to ourselves."

Ahead, Dani jammed her wallet in her jeans and turned to face the collection of youths, who looked like extras from a Nirvana video, as they got out of the pickup. They wore torn jeans, filthy T-shirts, and mud-drenched sneakers. Their faces were marred with stubble and acne scars, and their hair fell into their faces. Beneath their anger lay a magnificent, nearly irresistible feast of fear and desire.

She wanted them.

"What's the matter?" Dani asked. "You shitfaces aren't getting any? You're all pent up?"

"Fuck you," said the first one, a blonde wearing a "Cthulhu for President" T-shirt, as he shoved at Dani savagely. His obvious intent had been to knock her to the ground. She didn't budge.

Twenty yards away, at the pumps, Sam started toward her daughter. She had wanted to break into a run, but Angel came up beside her and whispered, "I can handle this."

Sam believed her. They walked in the direction of the golden-eyed young brunette casually, not revealing that they were with her. Suddenly, Angel became aware of the unnatural waves of emotion flowing from the teenagers. She stumbled and Sam caught her.

"This isn't right," Angel said, "this isn't the way it's supposed to be."

Ahead, Dani ignored her mother and the other vampire. She laughed at the stringy-haired teen. "Fuck *me?* You couldn't pay me enough. Now, to fuck you over, that's something different. I can help you there."

Reaching out with blinding speed, Dani took a fistful of the teenager's hair and wrapped it around her hand several times. Before she could yank it from his head, another of the teens moved forward and hissed, "Blood of the Ancients."

"Fuck," the lead teenager said, the intense, searing cloud of fear that had risen from the group of youths and suffused Dani suddenly vanishing.

Dani released his hair and stepped back.

"We didn't know," the teenagers said. "The Advocacy rules, man, okay? Peace."

"Yeah, we don't want any trouble," said the second teen.

"Right," Dani said. "Sure."

The youths went inside the convenience store and Dani turned to face Angel and Sam.

"What the hell was *that?*" Dani asked as she allowed herself to be led back to the Taurus by her mother. On the way, she glanced inside the pickup and saw a radio dispatch unit and a small console that looked like a computer terminal.

"I don't know," Angel said, genuinely shaken.

"Well, you're supposed to be the big, fucking authority, you know everything—"

"Just get in the car," Sam said. "I want to get out of

here before those kids get a really good look at us and what we're driving."

Dani fell silent and snatched the keys from Angel. In moments they were back on the streets. Walls of brilliant light surrounded them as they passed signs that read "Sassy Sally's," "Today, all jackpots doubled!" and "Glitter Gulch." Above the last sign was the famous neon cowgirl.

Dani looked over her shoulder at the vampire, though the car was still in motion. "Come on, Angel. You said you've been here before. You knew all about Vegas, that's what you said. Explain this—"

"Dani!" Sam screamed.

Ahead, a red Datsun had suddenly changed lanes and cut them off. Without bothering to look back at the road, Dani cut the wheel to the left, squeezed into a narrow space between two oncoming cars, and avoided the Datsun.

Sam had seen Alyana perform this trick once before. The vampire's assistants had been sending out their power, watching the traffic through the perceptions of other drivers and passing instructions directly into her mind. Sam wondered if her daughter was even aware that she was doing the exact same thing, and wondered if it had been her own perceptions that Dani was using as a guide. She decided to keep her gaze on the road at all times.

"Two of them were Initiates," Angel said. "The others were Immortals."

"Yeah, I finally figured that out," Dani said. "They were all pros at covering up that fact."

"They were *vampires?*" Sam asked, alarmed.

"Yeah," Angel said, severely shaken. She had obviously not expected anything like this.

"What did they want?" Sam asked.

Angel shifted uncomfortably in the back seat. "I don't know. They didn't seem to be after us. They were trying to draw out any of our kind. I don't have a fucking clue why."

"That's why I'm asking," Dani said. "Why don't you know what's going on here?"

"I dunno," Angel said. "It's been a while. I guess there's been some changes."

"How long?"

"I don't know exactly—"

"How long?"

The vampire frowned. "What year was it they impeached Nixon?"

"Jesus," Dani said, turning around and settling her gaze on the traffic ahead. "Your information's twenty fucking years out of date! Who knows what the fuck is going on out here now!"

"All right," Sam said. "Take it easy. Angel, what's this *Advocacy?"*

"That one's easy," Angel replied. "They sensed the Blood of the Ancients. So did I. Dani's shields started to fall apart when she got pissed."

"Fuck you," Dani whispered.

"You've got to watch that. It's the hardest time—"

"I said fuck yourself!"

"Not unless you're going to watch and diddle yourself too," Angel said in a low voice, but there was no real enthusiasm in the taunt. "Does anyone here still want to know about the Advocacy?"

"We should have dusted them," Dani said stiffly. "We should have torched all of them."

"Dani," Sam said, horrified by her daughter's words.

"They have radio equipment in their car," Dani said. "Microwave transmission computers, just like a cop would. That means they're in touch with someone. It's their fucking job to draw out those like us and report on us to someone. We should have kept them from doing it."

"I still haven't said much about the Advocacy," Angel muttered from the backseat. "I suppose I could just start fucking myself now and save some time, if this bullshit is going to go on for much longer."

"Go ahead," Dani said to the vampire.

"What about the Advocacy?" Sam asked.

"Being an Advocate means that you've been turned by someone with the Blood of the Ancients. You're in the second circle, a candidate for a place in the Parliament. There's been a lot of dissension in the ranks. The only way to get into the Parliament, which everyone wants, is to become an Advocate first. The only way to do that is to suck the ass of a member of Parliament, or get born into the position, which is the more common way of doing it. An Immortal off the street has almost no chance, and there's an underground of pissed-off vampires that wants to change things.

"By saying they support the Advocacy, that bunch of shitfaces was lying down and exposing their stomachs to us. They wanted us to know that they believe in the current rule. The underground will get burned, like it deserves. I'm an Advocate, she's an Advocate—"

"Wouldn't you like to be a fucking Advocate too?" Dani snarled as she guided the Taurus through traffic. "Can we get past this shit long enough to think about going back and nailing those fucks before they turn us in?"

"Dani, this isn't you talking," Sam said.

The golden-eyed vampire yanked the car off the street, into a rare parking spot. She threw the car in drive and turned to her mother. "It isn't me? Then who is it?"

Sam said nothing.

"Oh, shit," Angel said. "I hate this tit-beating crap."

"Shut up!" Dani wailed, then looked back to Sam. "What do you know about it? I don't even know

258

what's really inside me? How in the fuck can *you* possibly presume to know?"

"Because I'm your mother. I raised you—"

"All right, *Mom*. Explain this to me. We're here to commit premeditated murder, but that's okay, cause we're just going to fuck up a couple of lousy vampires. I mean, they're all shit, they deserve to die just because they exist, right?"

"You know, we could stop and get a drink," Angel suggested. "Get a nice couple of Cherry Cokes. Chill out."

Dani screamed, "So if you take that one step farther, I'm a goddamned vampire, so I should be killed too!"

"No," Sam said, somehow biting back the tears that were threatening to burst from her. "You're my baby, you're my little girl. I love you."

"What makes me any different from *her?*" Dani cried hysterically as she thumbed back at Angel.

"You're human. You didn't want to become this."

"How do you know she did?"

Angel set her head against the window and closed her eyes. "I'm out of this. Don't make me a part of it."

"Come on, Mom. Think. What makes a vampire so goddamned bad? They have to kill to survive. Right?"

"Yes," Sam said, biting her lip hard enough to draw blood.

"How is that different from what you're doing? From what you've always been doing and what you've always taught me? I knew fucking judo when I was ten. By the time I was twelve you were teaching me to crush a man's instep if he came after me. For my sweet sixteen you taught me how to fire a goddamned gun! I mean, shit, this isn't exactly a normal situation, you're not what I could call an average parent. Stop passing judgment on me when there really isn't any difference between my kind and your kind. We both just do what we have to do to survive."

Silence erupted in the parked car. Finally, in a low, trembling voice, Sam said, "I've never harmed anyone who wasn't threatening me or the life of someone I cared about. I've never gotten off on killing."

Dani stared at her mother in shock. "I didn't *want* to hurt Dorothea."

"I saw the whole thing. You had an—you—"

"It gave her the big one," Angel suggested.

Silence again.

"Think whatever you want to," Dani said, turning away from her mother. "It doesn't matter. All that matters is going in and killing a couple of bastards who are getting ready to kill us, right?"

Sam swallowed hard. "No, that's not all that's important."

"But it's the bottom line."

"Yes."

"So if those shitheads back there radio in our descriptions to God only knows who, we're dead. Their continued existence is a threat. The threat should be eliminated."

Angel leaned forward. "There's a lot of Advocates."

"Female ones?" Dani asked.

"We make the best lays. I doubt they're going to say anything. They're probably worried about *us* reporting *them* for hassling us."

"That sounds right," Sam said, wiping at her eyes, attempting to control the tremor in her voice. She was losing her daughter. She was losing everything. "But it still doesn't explain why they're here or who's paying them."

"You're a detective, Mom. Figure it out."

"I'll try."

Angel pointed directly ahead. They were stopped near a Best Western with a lit vacancy sign. "Maybe we should just set up shop and go do this thing."

"Yeah," Sam said, her thoughts suddenly leaping back to Dani's preposition. She loved her daughter more than she loved her own life. Nevertheless, she was terrified by the prospect of allowing Dani into her mind after the blowout they had just endured. Dani's expression had been one of feral hatred, and Sam could no longer tell if that anger was directed outward, or inward, or if it even mattered.

"Let's rock and roll," Angel said.

Dani put the car in reverse and pulled back onto the street.

"Rock and roll forever," Dani whispered as they traveled a half-block, then turned into the parking lot for the hotel. "And forever, and forever."

They parked and went into the hotel.

Chapter Twenty-two

Pamela Tyree handed her car keys to the brightly dressed valet, along with five twenties. She was a beautiful, statuesque blonde with short-cropped, perfectly styled hair. Her dress was basic black, her jewelry sparse but elegant, her eyes dark and penetrating. The woman had graciously accepted the hand of the college-age valet as he had helped her from her car, and she now stood with him before the entrance to the opulent and towering Buccaneer Hotel and Casino. The handsome, dark-haired valet was dressed in the wardrobe of a sanitized cinematic pirate, complete with an eye patch, knee-high black boots and leggings, and a garish shirt open to the waist to reveal his well-defined chest.

"I have personal belongings in the trunk," Pamela said. "I want them handled gently and brought to my room immediately. You'll need help carrying them. That's why I'm giving you the other twenties. Consider them a down payment and don't skimp on the help. If I'm satisfied, I'll remember you very well when I'm ready to check out."

"Thank you, ma'am," the valet said in his smooth, melodic voice. He may have been dressed as a pirate, but to Pamela, he sounded like a disgustingly polite Disney World employee. "I'm certain all will be to your satisfaction."

"So am I," Pamela said as she turned her back on

the valet and walked to the front entrance of the hotel.

Inside, she went to the check-in desk. The hotel carried the pirate motif throughout its environs. The walls were curved wood, with panels that could be slid back to reveal views of a raging ocean or a pirate battle at sea. An authentic cannon was set in the center of the lobby, which was filled with people even so late at night. Hotel employees wandered around in full pirate regalia.

Pamela waited her turn at the registration desk, and soon made it to the head of the line. The clerk at the desk was a dark-haired, chesty young woman wearing a soft blue sleeveless top tied off beneath her breasts and a host of sparkling rings and silver jewelry.

"Pamela Tyree. I called in a reservation."

The woman tapped into her computer console and frowned, revealing a network of lines that had been covered under pancake makeup. From a distance, she seemed twenty-five at most. Up close, she could have been twenty years older.

"I'm sorry, I don't see it."

"Are you Lisa? I was told to ask for Lisa. I was told today was her birthday and I was supposed to tell her *happy birthday.*"

At once, the registration woman stiffened. Her eyes glazed over. She punched a new series of codes and nodded.

"I have a vacant suite on the executive level."

"Wonderful."

"It's funny, I *thought* we were full up."

"Things have a tendency to fall into place for me, I guess."

"And how will you be paying tonight? Visa, MasterCard, Discover—"

"Cash. I hate plastic."

"I don't blame you."

Pamela paid for the suite, exchanged a few more pleasantries with the woman at the desk, and explained that she had already made arrangements for her baggage. Along with her room key, she was handed a map of the casino and its grounds.

"If there's anything you forgot to pack, we have a twenty-four-hour shopping mall in Quadrant C. You should be able to find it, no problem, but if you need help, just ask any of our employees. They'll be happy to assist."

Pamela nodded. The hotel and casino consumed a city block. Finding her way could be confusing.

"You'll find a coupon in your information pack that entitles you to half off on all Vamp products, including their hot new jeans line and fragrances."

"*Vamp* products?"

"Yeah, you know. First there was voguing, then there was vamping. I'm sure you've seen the commercials. The actress in the red dress at the old-style Hollywood premiere walking down the runway, strutting her stuff, putting on a show for the paparazzi. She gets ignored because some hot young thing in the crowd is wearing Vamp Jeans and all the photographers flock to her. You know the one. Everyone's seen it."

"Okay, sure."

"Are you here as part of a convention? We have several going on."

"No. I'm meeting a friend from out of town. We haven't seen each other in a while." That was a lie. She had been completely alone for the last five years, since her husband had divorced her. The trip to Vegas had been a last-minute decision. Vacation time had come up, use it or lose it, and she had been lonely. She'd told everyone at work that she was going to Vancouver to visit her relatives, but in truth she *had* no relatives. In fact, she had no real friends. Her sole motivation for coming to Vegas had been to lose herself. She had even traveled under a false name and paid cash the whole way to avoid leaving a trail. For the next ten days, she wanted to allow whatever might happen to happen. She had been tired of sleeping alone, and wanted to go somewhere that she could find a man, have sex with him, and never have to worry about seeing him ever again. It was cold and brutal, but there it was, and she had no intention of apologizing. Her black dress had shown her cleavage, and she had enjoyed seeing the flickering gaze of the valet as he noticed her full, firm breasts.

"Do you want me to check on your friend's reservation?"

"No, thanks. I'd rather just be surprised."

"Then have a nice night!"

Pamela turned and walked to the elevators.

Dani and Angel watched the exchange. It had gone off exactly as planned. No one would suspect Pamela Tyree of smuggling 105 pounds of weaponry into the hotel. Her clothes cabinet was stuffed with explosives, guns, portable flamethrowers, and even a teargas launcher. Pamela was also ignorant of her actions. She had no idea that only an hour earlier she had been Samantha Walthers, and in twenty-two minutes she would become that woman once again.

Angel had been hesitant to use her power in the hotel after the bizarre encounter with the stringy-haired teens at the gas station, but Dani had convinced her there was no choice. They had confirmed Devin Tyler's whereabouts by picking up a newspaper, and finding a full-page ad for his limited engagement at the Buccaneer. To learn his room number at the hotel, they would either have to look into the mind of a hotel employee or attempt to hack into the hotel's computer system. The latter was out of the question as none of them had enough experience with computers.

Sam had not wanted to risk calling her friend Alex in Los Angeles because she assumed the vampires had all of her past acquaintances under surveillance. Besides, it would have still proved necessary to place one of the registration people under a compulsion to give them a room on the same floor as the Tylers. Angel had taken care of this part. So far, they had gone unnoticed.

Both vampires wore physical disguises. They only used their psychic abilities to alter the manner in which their facial features were perceived. The cameras, which were everywhere, would see their true images, and neither of them wanted someone to notice a vast discrepancy between their recorded images and the illusions they were projecting.

Angel had once again assumed the persona of the seductive saleswoman from the Los Angeles clothing shop. She had not told her companions what occurred the last time she had pretended to be this woman. It might have been bad luck, she had reasoned. A long blond wig covered her spiky hair, and soft blue contacts disguised her eyes. She wore a white jacket and skirt, an aqua slip and bra beneath. Her shoes matched. The entire outfit had come off the rack at the Victoria's Secret in the Forum Shops at Caesar's Palace.

The vampires had been amused by the vaulted sky that covered the vast shopping mall. Every three hours, the artificial sky changed from dusk to dawn. They'd spotted several Immortals staring up longingly at the ceiling. The Forum had seventy-four stores, including Louis Vuitton and Gucci. Animatrons of the Roman gods greeted shoppers, or sometimes became involved in spirited discussions with each other.

Dani had stuffed her lustrous, wild hair into another blond wig, thinning her dark eyebrows so that she didn't look like a peroxide blonde. Her contacts were a deep blue. Over her thin, white turtleneck and black, stirrup pants, she wore a double-breasted creme-colored jacket with padded shoulders and covered buttons. Both she and Angel carried running shoes in their bags.

They watched Sam get on the elevator and waited until they saw the valet get on with her, supervising two assistants who actually carried the heavy clothes cabinet. It would be delivered to Sam's room moments after she arrived.

Dani glanced at her watch. "We've got time. Let's check out the tables."

Angel nodded. Until now, they had been standing around, looking as if they were waiting for someone. With a sigh that was completely in character, Angel turned and followed her companion.

They passed through a long wooden hallway lit by electric torches. Floorboards creaked beneath their feet. Concealed speakers hissed the rushing sounds of the ocean. A gaggle of young women passed them, each drunk out of their minds. Fair game for any predator, human or otherwise.

Ignoring the signs for the convention center and meeting rooms, they came to the vast gambling hall, which had been styled to resemble a Daliesque version of Madagascar, one of the most notorious pirate havens in history. Sealed glass cases with relics from pirate ships dotted the floor, along with roulette wheels sitting on tables that looked like sections of shattered hulls rising from the floor. Hucksters passed out flyers concerning the next night's floor show. Traditionally dressed blackjack dealers were intermingled with scantily clad women who proudly told everyone they were pirate "wenches."

"Come on, ye salty dogs!" shouted a gaudily dressed pirate who was attempting to entice business to his craps table. "How about you, sirrah? Missy? Are you game? You look like you might be . . ."

Dani and Angel realized they were somewhat overdressed. Many of the people crowding around them looked as if they had been sleeping in their clothes and had not even thought to bathe for weeks. Almost everyone carried plastic buckets that *chinked* with quarters, dimes, and nickels as they walked past. Dani was reminded of the George Romero film *Day of the Dead,* and its shopping-mall zombies.

Endless rows of slot machines stretched before them, three quarters or more occupied by people who stared, entranced, at the prize screens and seemed completely detached from reality. Mechanically, they dug their hands into their buckets, fed money into the machines, and pulled the levers. Occasionally they would collect a jackpot and immediately scoop those coins into their buckets and begin the cycle again. Or they would get up, their change evaporated, and stumble off to get more.

Handsome men and women dressed in the blinding costumes of another age's plunderers walked past, carrying trays of drinks they would distribute for free, helping the clientele to get thoroughly plastered so they wouldn't care how much money they lost.

The casino was a factory with desperation as its major product. Chronic gamblers darted here and there, anxious for their next chance to recoup their losses. Dani decided that if Walt Disney had opened a theme park in Hell, this would have been it, complete with loud, obnoxiously dressed, rude-beyond-*belief* tourists. On the street, she had seen a straggly-haired man walking around with a placard that read, "God is dead, Wayne Newton is bankrupt!" She had laughed then. Now she saw new levels of meaning in the street prophet's words.

Months earlier, she had seen Bono from the rock group U2 on an MTV interview one night at the hospital, when she had been waiting for a call. He had said, "Chance has replaced faith. Casinos are the new cathedrals."

If this was the new religion, then it was already a debauched one, its servants willingly offering up their bodies and souls for defilement. The casino was dimly lit and cavernous. The designers did not want people to be able to see one another very well. Only the brilliant, glowing lights of the slots and their flashy, gold-trimmed and sequined frames offered any illumination. Some of the machines could be run by plastic debit cards, but these were generally ignored. People wanted to feel the coins pass into or from their fingers.

They were as hopelessly addicted as the Immortals.

Nevertheless, a part of Dani reveled in all she found here. Both she and Angel ignored most of the showy aspects of the casino's floor and concentrated on the delicious waves of ambient fear and desire that suffused the room. Despite the laughing, festive atmosphere, the civilians who had come here to gamble radiated an irresistible aura of desperation. Dani found herself staring contemptuously at the human prey, imagining which of them she would take, if she only had the time.

"Don't forget why we're here," Angel whispered.

"Of course not," Dani practically *breathed*. "We're here to have a good time. Isn't that right?"

The shell personas they had erected to fool casual scans by others of their kind revealed them to be a pair of Immortals from Atlanta who had come to Vegas for a vacation. Angel had visited Atlanta three weeks earlier to perform a job for Christian De Santo. She refused to discuss the nature of that assignment, but she had come away owning the full memories of three humans, two of them female. The vampire had edited those core personas and used them in the creation of their new identities.

Angel had tried to be alert to the presence of their kind in the casino, but if her senses were correct, Im-

269

mortals and Initiates were everywhere. It had been difficult to pick out their exact locations among the swelling tides of fear and desire that had blanketed the entire complex, but the vampires were there. She had not mentioned this to Dani. The last thing she needed was the golden-eyed twenty-year-old panicking and allowing her shields to fall. Angel was prepared to take over for her at any time, but the effort would drain her, and her own hunger was becoming a difficult animal to master.

"The grand prize!" another huckster wailed. "A hundred thousand dollars in gold, brought to you in an authentic pirates' treasure chest!"

"I think I see *my* grand prize," Dani said with a biting, malicious giggle. "Right over there."

Angel did not have to turn. She could sense what Dani had been talking about. The prey that had interested her companion was a handsome young Japanese man dressed in a stylish black suit. A white silk scarf had been puffed out and placed meticulously into the jacket's front.

He could have been Bill Yoshino come to life.

Angel checked the time. "I think our cover's set. We better get out of here if we're going to make it in time. The executive level is sealed off, we're going to have to get an employee to put their ID key in the elevator to get us up there."

"Kiss, kiss, sweetie," Dani murmured, oblivious to Angel's warning. She lashed out with her power, sending it forward like a whip and instantly retrieving it.

The Japanese man shuddered and looked around sharply.

"Oh, good," Dani said. "He's *human*. And he's innocent. This is going to be fun."

"Shit," Angel hissed. Dani was drunk with power. She was losing herself to her true nature. The vampire had already done what she could to wake Dani up to the horrors of a continued existence as an Immortal.

270

For a time, she believed that she had gotten through to the young woman.

This is your brain, honey. See? Nice and normal. Now this is your brain after you've made a kill:

Hell, damnation, fear, horrors beyond imagining, the eating of souls, death may never come, no release, and they're inside you, the dead live again and come for you when you sleep!

Any questions?

Her warnings were apparently not enough. She couldn't risk giving Dani a refresher course. Not here, in this crowded casino. If it became necessary, she would go on without Dani, and attempt to salvage what she could of the operation.

Suddenly, Dani's ravenous hunger seemed to fall away. She turned from the Japanese man and released him. "I don't want this."

"Good."

Dani looked at the time. "We've got to go."

"Yeah, we do." No fucking shit, Angel thought.

They were halfway to the door leading back to the main part of the hotel when a dark, powerfully attractive man stepped in front of them. He was dressed as a blackjack dealer, with a white shirt, black vest and bow tie, and bands around his upper arms. His skin was swarthy. He was a Native American, a Zuni most probably. The dealer's hair was dark and wild, longer than Dani's and magnificently sleek. His face was pantherish, with strong cheekbones. He had a thick perfect nose with flaring nostrils, wide, sensuous lips, and a square jaw. The dealer was powerfully built, with a barrel chest and small waist. The black silk pants he wore seemed to have been painted on his muscular legs.

His eyes were the reddish-orange of a desert twilight. In his long, sculptor's fingers, he held a deck of cards.

He was a vampire and he had *made* them.

271

"Come with me quietly," the dealer said, "or every one of our kind in this place will turn their attention on you and sand your brains down to nothing before you can make a move against me."

Chapter Twenty-three

Dani was terrified.

The dealer, who had identified himself as James Yuwai, had taken them to the Fiddler's Green, one of the many lounges inside the casino. The Green had been designed to replicate the deck of a pirate vessel. The rail that should have dropped them into the ocean instead led to the bar. Surrounding them was a beautiful, sparkling sea, a breathtaking three-dimensional hologram complete with glass sculptures of mermaids, monsters, and mythical gods. A stunning fountain rose up to one side of the bar, and beneath its churning waters lay a collection of shining gold pieces.

Dani tried not to look at her watch. To her credit, she had not allowed the walls protecting her shell persona to collapse. James saw them as Rachel Porath and Elise Sieverson. He had only employed the lightest of surface scans on them; had he made any true effort to scour their thoughts, he would have discovered his mistake.

Briefly, Dani's thoughts flickered to her mother. Right now, the woman would be unpacking her clothes closet. She would believe that she was putting away her various dresses and shoes when, in truth, she would be outfitting herself for battle.

The Tyler twins were in their suite with a couple of young women they had picked up in the casino. An entourage followed them. That meant guards would be outside their door. At the prearranged time, Samantha Walthers, believing herself to be Pamela Tyree, would leave her room wearing a long jacket to protect her from the chill outside. She would stop near the Tylers' guards, lift each of the shotguns she had slung over her shoulders, and fire at the faces of the guards. Then she would become her true self once more.

Dani and Angel were supposed to be there when this occurred. More than two guards might be present, and they would also have to deal with the Tylers themselves. The young women had planned to psychically tear apart the remaining guards at the same moment Sam made her attack, then instantly assume the identities of two of them. Dani and Angel, posing as the dead men, would project the illusion that they had killed the potential assassins, but not before some of their people had died. The instant the Tylers dropped their guard, Dani and Angel would take them out. If that did not happen, Sam, whose presence they would continue to disguise, would shoot at least one of the twins, startling them into giving their psychic assailants an opening.

Sam's mind had been programmed for only one contingency: If the phone rang and it was either Dani or Angel, her programming would be defeated and she would pack up her weapons and wait for further orders. Without that call, Sam would shoot the guards whether Dani and Angel were there or not. Then her true personality would be revealed, and she would either be killed or captured. The way it looked now, Dani and Angel would be trapped at the bar with James when Sam was taking on the Tylers and their guards, and nothing could be done about it.

Ironically, it had been thoughts of Sam that had driven the bloodlust from Dani in the casino. Though she had spent two years intensely denying the facts,

Dani had felt that she had been cheated out of the opportunity to kill the man who had raped and deceived her. In a way, she had resented her mother for denying her that chance. When she had seen the Japanese man in the gambling hall, and known that she could kill him in any manner she chose, she'd realized that it would not have changed anything. Even killing Yoshino himself would not have healed her. Sam had been given the satisfaction of setting Richard Sterling on fire and pumping seven bullets into his head. That had not ended Sam's nightmares.

Her mother had been right. It was time to stop being a victim. Time to take back her life. She no longer wanted to be a slave to anyone or anything, including her own bloodlust. Her mother had saved her body and her soul countless times. Dani had to repay the woman with something more than the agony she had recently inflicted upon her. Somehow, she had to make it up to Sam.

But now she was trapped.

Dani looked at the startlingly handsome Native American. He was young, her age. Or so he appeared. He held himself with confidence, and he seemed to be tranquility incarnate. She could not picture him feeling love or hate. James Yuwai seemed to be in perfect harmony with himself and his surroundings.

He was also a professional.

What that meant, exactly, Dani could not explain. But she could sense that whatever he was about to say was part of a spiel he had delivered many times in the past.

The bartender brought James a glass of mineral water and asked Dani and Angel if he could get them anything. They declined the offer and he vanished. The lounge was packed, but the intense emotions that had permeated the casino were muted here.

"I thought we should get away from all that business," James said. "If you're not used to it, trying to think in all of that is very difficult."

"In all of what?" Dani asked.

Beside her, Angel kicked her ankle. Hard.

Dani understood. They had to get away from this man as soon as possible. It was best to let him have his say without asking questions or encouraging him to talk longer than he had already planned.

"You've never been here before," he said. "You're not in the Net. You don't work for the company. That means you don't understand about this place. I don't just mean the casino. I'm talking about Las Vegas as a whole. Immortals own a large interest in this city. There are rules that must be followed." His fiery gaze seemed to burn into Dani. "What you were about to do would have amounted to a serious breach of etiquette, and management gets very upset by visitors who don't mind their manners. Especially here. This is the first casino the Ancients have actually built. They're very sensitive about this place.

"Out-of-towners, rogues, and loners are always showing up here thinking they can come in and make their fortune on the tables. It's the same thing in Atlantic City and Rio. They don't know that the Ancients have a lot of money in these places, and get a lot of revenue from them.

"To help protect their investment, the Ancients use Initiates and Immortals as dealers to help control the wins and losses and keep the frenzy alive on the floor. They're also used as security officers and spotters. It's important to corner newcomers in the casinos or when they first arrive in the city. The airport, bus stations, and car-rental offices are filled with our kind who are on the payroll. Teams of baiters roam the streets, sending out enough raw emotion to make any unsuspecting Immortal want to swallow them whole. Those in the Net can recognize and avoid them without any problem."

Dani nodded attentively. She tried to imagine how her friend Nina from college would have told her to react in the circumstances. Nina had taken acting courses.

Look it from your character's point of view, Nina would have reminded her. *You're Rachel Porath. You came here for a good time and you've been busted. Everything seems okay; in fact, this guy is kind of gorgeous. If he wanted to take you somewhere and hurt you, or lock you up, he could have done it already. Don't seem antsy. You're supposed to have all the time in the world. Try to relax. If you don't, you'll never get away from this man.*

Dani forced her body to unwind and reached over to take a handful of peanuts from the bar. "Jesus. I didn't realize this place was so complicated."

"I'm a spotter," James explained. "My job is to get the new blood on the side and explain how the system works. That's what I'm going to do for you now. Stay away from the tables. Don't go near the human employees. You're allowed to feed all you want on the fear and desire anywhere in the city, even the casinos and hotels. But you must not bring physical or emotional harm to humans without express permission."

"What if you can't help yourself?" Dani asked hesitantly.

"That's not an option for you. If you think you're in trouble, I can get a ride for you to the airport, get you on the next flight out. Are you in trouble?"

"No."

"For your sake, I hope you're not lying," James said, pausing to take a sip of his mineral water. "You can apply to join the company, if that interests you. There's a variety of positions open. All of them offer a salary, lodgings, and a regular allocation of approved victims. You'd be amazed at how many of the loners want to join up. It makes them feel as if they have an extended family. But if we took everybody,

277

eventually there'd be more of us here than there are of them. The humans, I mean."

Dani smiled nervously, as her character might. She glanced at her watch and wondered what her mother was doing right now. Loading the shotguns, probably. Putting on the support harness over her dress. She would be completely ignorant of what was really happening.

They had told her to stay in her room until the appointed time. The only thing that would keep her there now was a phone call from Dani or Angel to abort. But they could not get to a phone, and that was one glaringly obvious contingency that Dani had not thought of when she had constructed her mother's assumed persona and programmed her actions. Dani had been angry and her anger had made her sloppy.

They were down to minutes before her mother would leave her room.

"In terms of what's available, there are the positions I already mentioned," James said. "In addition, prostitution is legal here. Take a look at the couple at the end of the bar. The woman in the green dress, the balding man she's talking to? She's one of ours. That's another career choice some make. But if you're an Initiate or an Immortal and you want to whore in this city, you have to work within the prescribed system. Keep your rates within acceptable levels, never leave your customers so rattled they won't come back for more, and give the standard kickback to the hotel. Twenty-five percent, I believe. If you want to get on the health and insurance plan it's another ten percent, right up to fifty percent if you want to get on the official payroll and have your room supplied by the company.

"The competition is extremely rough. I know. I tried it for a time. I always get more out of the emotional ride, but that's just me."

278

"Yeah, I'm the same way," Dani said absently, feeling as if she might pass out at any moment. *She had to reach a phone!*

"You probably have an idea that organized crime also has a major interest in Vegas," James went on. "That's true. We work with them. Any hits that have to be performed are left to the Immortals. The Ancients also want the streets kept safe. Immortals are used to ferret out the human crazies and dispose of them quietly.

"If you have any kind of degree in communications or management, there are always straight jobs available. Also, the Parliament sends its people here from time to time. You can be a tour guide, a gofer, whatever they need.

"Just between us, most of them are real pricks. They expect a lot more than the job description, and once you get mixed up with them, it's difficult to get yourself out of it. That's not to say Immortals aren't always jumping at those temporary openings. Every one of them hopes to get a shot at being chosen as an Advocate."

Dani noticed her watch. In one and a half minutes, her mother would leave her hotel suite and walk to the Tylers' door.

"I don't know, I have the feeling I'm leaving something out," James said. He frowned, then reached into his breast pocket and drew out a card. "If you have any questions or problems, call me. Don't hesitate."

Dani regarded Angel, still attempting to cover her anxiety.

Sensing their desire to be on their way, James nodded. "Yes, that's it. You can go."

"Thank you," Dani said as she got off her bar stool.

"Hold it," James said sharply, his hand lancing outward to grasp her arm. "I just remembered. I al-

279

most forgot to tell you the most important part."

Dani waited. Even Angel was distressed.

"What I've told you is not to be taken as a list of requests. These are *laws*. If you break any of the laws I've told you, there will be penalties. Severe ones. Physical and emotional pain the likes of which you probably never even dreamed existed. Keep that in mind before you attempt to take a victim. We have a preapproved list and those candidates are matched up to employees in need."

"We'll be careful," Angel said.

"Yeah, thanks," Dani added.

James nodded and turned away. Dani and Angel were almost to the door of the lounge, anxiously scanning for a house phone, when James suddenly appeared before them once again. He had moved almost as fast as a member of Parliament.

"I forgot to ask you," James said. "Are you ladies set for a place to dig in for the night? Dawn will be here before too long."

"Yeah, we're set," Dani said, wanting desperately to reach out with her power and hurt this man if he stopped them one more time.

"Well," James said, smiling slightly, "you have a good night, then."

They reached a house phone in the lobby. Frantically, Dani punched in her mother's room number.

The phone rang a dozen times. No one picked up.

They were too late.

Chapter Twenty-four

Pamela threw her bag over her shoulder and loosely belted the sash of her long, black coat, questioning why she had felt it necessary to wear the somewhat heavy jacket in the first place. It was not raining outside and it was not particularly cold. Nevertheless, she had felt obligated for some bizarre reason to put on the coat. It hid the lines of her body, and that defeated the purpose of her visit here.

Ignoring her logical objections, Pamela finished with her belt and checked herself in the mirror. Perfect.

Another feeling coursed through her. The phone. It should have rung—she wanted it to ring, desperately needed it to ring. Of course, that didn't happen. The notion had been ridiculous. She knew no one in the city and no one knew that she had come here. The front desk had no reason to call her. Why would her phone have rung, and why should that have been so incredibly desirable?

Pamela left her suite and heard the door lock behind her. She didn't mind leaving the collection of rooms behind. They had been decorated in the most tasteless fashion, with gaudy, glitzy lights and color, and windows shaped like portals in a ship. If she had been the callous, questioning type, she would have assumed management was attempting to send people screaming from these horrible rooms, driving them down into the gambling pit below.

Fortunately, she wasn't a negative person.

When Pamela had first come to her room, she had passed several long-haired men wearing black funeral suits with red power ties. They had seemed surprised to see other guests on this level, and had murmured something about talking to the "fucking little slit" at the front desk.

Pamela had a mental block about such language, though, perhaps because she had once been married to a man who had used swear words in just about every sentence. As far as she had been concerned, that was unnecessary and wasteful, a terrible butchering of the human language. Vulgarity for vulgarity's sake, nothing more.

The men were standing outside that same door when she emerged from her suite. This time they smiled at her. A chill passed through her. These were hard men who smiled only out of malice, never from joy. Three stood near the door, all with slicked-back hair, weightlifters' builds, designer suits and sunglasses.

Her hands sunk into her long pockets. She was not aware that the pockets had been neatly scissored out of the fabric and that her fingers were closing over the hard stocks of shotguns. In another few seconds, she would be upon the men. She would pull her hands back, her fingers locking into the triggers of the weapons, and raise them up. Her long black coat would rise like a showgirl's hooped skirt in a Wild West revival. Then she knew they would fire, and in the aftermath of the twin blasts, Pamela Tyree would cease to exist.

A sharp, frightened scream escaped her as someone grabbed her from behind and hauled her back. She could not see her assailant. Her view was of the hallway, and it receded with impossible speed, as if she were suddenly a passenger on a subway car sailing in reverse. She heard a door burst open behind her, smelled the fetid breath of her attacker, certainly a man, and continued to scream.

One of the guards waved "Bye-bye."

Her view changed as she was dragged into the stairwell next to the bank of elevators. The door leading back to the corridor slammed shut with remarkable finality. She was thrown against the wall. Instinctively, she allowed her body to go limp, so that when she struck, she would lessen her injury.

How in God's name did I know to do that? she wondered after she had hit the wall and slid to the floor.

"Come on," a dark voice said. "Gimme, gimme, gimme, *gimme!*"

She almost laughed. A strained, crazy giggle. The line had been from a Bill Murray movie. The one where he was a guy who drove his psychiatrist crazy.

No, that was wrong. That was too insane to be true. She was thinking about movies because they had been her whole life for the last year. They had been her conduit to civilization, to reason, to the life she had left behind.

What? she asked herself. She hadn't left anything behind. Her life had been dull, that was true, but she had not been in hiding.

Or had she?

"I'm not fuckin' kidding!" the unseen man snarled. *"Gimme!"*

Suddenly, his hands were on her. She wailed in pure terror, all conscious thought driven from her mind, a dark, primal fear erupting from her, "Holy Mother of Jesus, Holy Mother of Jesus!"

"Ummmm," the man said, his tone nasty, but satisfied. *"Much better."*

Pamela realized what was happening. The man was

going to force her to do things, he was going to touch her in terrible ways.

He was going to *fuck* her.

The word rankled in her consciousness, and it had no basis in truth. Her husband had liked her to say that word. He had liked her to breathe it out while he clumsily rammed himself inside her. He had wanted her to scream that word like an animal and tell him how much she wanted him to do it to her, faster or slower, harder and deeper.

He had taunted her about the scars on her back.

Perfezione e solo perfezione se esso cicatrizzarsi.

Richard had whispered those words into her ear as he put her on her knees and took her from behind, screwing her the way dogs would do it. He had made her his dog, made her want it, made her believe that he was something he was not.

Perfection is not perfection unless it is scarred. He had scarred her, all right. She had been scarred for life. She saw her husband's face. Blond and handsome. Sunburned. William Hurt in *Body Heat,* without the mustache.

Richard Sterling had not been fucking her. He had not been making love to her. There was another word for it.

Rape.

He had been *raping* her, he had gone into her mind and made her feel things she thought she would never feel again, made her want him more than she had ever wanted another man in her entire life.

You can do anything to me. Anything you want. Those words had gone through her mind and he had heard them, because he had violated much more than just her body.

Pamela felt as if she were disintegrating. Her husband had not been named Richard Sterling. She had not been raped.

What was happening to her?

Suddenly, her assailant grabbed her shoulder and yanked her around to face him. Before she registered anything else about him, she saw his blazing eyes, bone-white, talonlike hands, and razor-sharp, animal teeth.

"What the fuck?" the vampire whispered as his hand closed over something hard and cylindrical that was buried beneath Pamela's coat. He yanked it forward just as Pamela Tyree vanished and a completely alien presence took over her body.

Samantha Walthers felt the shotgun being yanked forward. She had expected to feel as if she had been emerging from a deep sleep, groggy and slow-moving, but that had not been the case at all. Instant clarity of reason filtered through her. She had no idea why she was in the stairwell with this monster. He didn't look like one of the guards she vaguely recalled from Pamela Tyree's perceptions. She also did not care.

Her hand was still in her cut-away pocket. The trigger of the weapon brushed her fingers as its stock was yanked forward. She jammed her fingers into the trigger guard and curled them. The vampire did the rest for her as he pulled the weapon to him.

An explosion tore through the stairwell. The lower part of Sam's coat was blown apart. Her elbow jerked back into the wall, impacting with a sharp pain that caused an ice-cold finger to be driven through her consciousness. The vampire was blown back, a huge chunk of his midsection vaporized. The shotgun had not caught the monster squarely in the stomach, unfortunately. The creature's spine had been damaged, but it had not been severed. Part of his hip had been shattered, with white bone and stringy red gristle jutting from his wound. Four of his ribs stuck out above a curling, steaming mass of entrails that moved like snakes, attempting to keep themselves from untangling on the floor.

"Fuck me," the vampire whispered, looking down at himself. He was a young man dressed in a bright pirate's outfit, with stubble on his perfect cheeks, and absolute shock on his Adonis-like features.

Better you than me, Sam thought as she raised the other shotgun, leveled it at the creature's neck, and fired before the monster could overcome his surprise and use his power to take control of her.

The vampire's head was blown from his body as his neck exploded in a hailstorm of gore. The lips of his severed head moved as the head was blown upward, sailing on the rim of an invisible geyser, twisting in midair to arc leftward, fall over the guardrail, and disappear into the darkness below. A nasty splat sounded from somewhere close.

"Jesus, fuck," Sam whispered, finally noticing that Angel and her daughter were not with her. The Tylers' guards would have heard the blast. They would be on her in seconds. She dragged herself to her feet and was startled as a yawn came over her.

This was fucking ridiculous, she thought. It was true that during the last day, she had been put through some of the worst hell of her life. She knew that she needed sleep desperately. The cold, needle-like pinpricks of exhaustion covered her flesh and made every cell in her body want to slow. For some reason, the adrenaline rush she was counting on had failed her. She was about to die and she couldn't keep herself from yawning.

Sam considered her options. If she turned and ran, the vampires would catch her. They could reach out with their power from a distance and take control of her body and her mind. Better to make a stand here and take out one or two more of the bastards before they had her. It was doubtful that they would kill her outright, once they realized who she was. Not if Dani

286

was still alive, anyway. They would probably hold her, rape her mind and body a few dozen times, then use her as bait for her daughter.

The thought of being used as a weapon against her own daughter was too horrible to consider. She had clung to the idea that so long as she was alive and her children needed her, she could endure anything for them. Those were not casually tossed off sentiments. She knew the exact form of the terror and punishment to which she would be subjecting herself.

But the vampires could burn away her mind — do to her what Angel did to the pilot she'd attacked outside of Albuquerque. If Angel had been telling the truth, the vampires could eat Sam's soul and use her body as a tool to victimize her precious Dani. They might even keep her body alive for the next twenty years and use her as some kind of tool to control Michael. Sam wondered if it would be better to cheat them out of the pleasure. Kill herself before they could have power over her again.

She heard voices in the hallway. They were coming in person. That made no sense. They could have taken her from a distance. The moment they heard the shotgun blast they should have used their power to ascertain the nature of the threat. Finding Sam to be nothing but a human, they should have savaged her mind with their wild talents and put her down. For some reason they were moving with incredible caution. Their motive eluded her.

She heard a noise from below. Someone, human or otherwise, was coming up the stairs. Footsteps also sounded from above. Others were descending. The Tylers' guards were in the corridor, somewhere on the other side of the door. The vampires were going to trap her.

Again, why not use their power? This made no sense. They had an advantage they were not using.

Jesus, baby, I'm sorry, Sam thought, considering her daughter. But I don't see any other way.

Anchoring herself against the guardrail, Sam readied one of the shotguns and plunged her hand into her heavy handbag, drawing out a lump of grayish-green clay with a digital timing device. She punched in ten seconds, darted forward to slam the explosive against the door, engaged the unit, and waited for it to be over.

Chapter Twenty-five

Ten seconds.

She was going to die.

Force the terror away. Think about something else.

Closing her eyes, Sam recalled her daughter's face when she had returned from securing the car in the desert. She had to believe that Dani had not harmed whoever had owned the car. Nevertheless, earlier that night, Sam had been unable to bring herself to look inside the glove compartment when she had the chance. She did not want to see the name of the man or woman listed on the automobile's registration, and she had been terrified at the prospect of finding pictures of him or her.

Nine seconds.

It had all gone to hell and Sam had no idea how that had occurred. She had been under the compulsion of her daughter to believe herself to be Pamela Tyree. The weapons strapped to her were a testament that part of the plan had gone correctly.

What had gone wrong?

Eight seconds.

She was never going to hold Michael again. He was going to become something as terrible as Bobby De Santo. The child was too young to remember her, and his new parents would never tell him his real name or anything about his true mother.

I love you, Michael, she thought. I'm so sorry.

Seven seconds.

The sounds were getting closer. Footsteps from above. Voices in the hall. Movement from below. Soon.

Why in the hell couldn't she stop yawning?

Six seconds.

She wondered if Heaven and Hell existed and if they did, where she would end up. Walking into Hell would not be so bad if she knew that Richard Sterling was there, and she could spend eternity paying him back for what he had done to her.

Let it go, she thought, knowing that was impossible.

Five seconds.

Peter Red Cloud stood naked in her home, exposing not only his body, but his heart and soul. Sam's instincts had told her the truth. He loved her. And given time, she might even be able to love him.

One thing was certain. If it were in his power, he would give her all the time in the world.

But it had not been in his power.

Four seconds.

Dani's first word had been "boobie." Once the girl had said it the first time, she could not say it often enough. Sam had been sure to thank her partner at the time, a cop named Rick Ciovelli, for hanging over the crib calling her daughter that name so often that it had stuck in the child's brain.

He had retired and opened a bait shop in Sarasota. Smart man.

Three seconds.

The first of the vampires appeared at the head of the stairs. A dark-haired man in a pair of blue jeans and a loud shirt. The monster saw the explosive device on the door, realized what was happening, and leaped off the stairs, flying for the unit. As the vampire passed overhead, a wind erupted in the stairwell behind her. Someone screamed Sam's name.

Angel.

Two seconds.

Sam felt hands upon her, dragging her back, over the guardrail. She did not resist. Her body once again went limp and her heart leapt into her mouth as she was yanked backwards, into the air. Her view receded wildly and she felt as if she were on a roller-coaster car streaking in reverse. She passed Dani, who gripped the handrail. Her daughter was staring at the vampire who was about to tear the detonator from the explosive.

"Like fucking hell," Dani snarled, and lashed out with her power.

One second.

Angel and Sam dropped down the half-story flight of stairs, whipping around on the straightaway for ten feet, down again, never once touching the ground.

Her daughter was not following them. She had passed out of view.

"Dani!" Sam screamed.

But it was too late.

Detonation.

A blinding white flash seared Sam's consciousness, divorcing her from physical reality. For an instant she was certain that she was dead; then a series of images exploded in her mind. Each of the images had been viewed through her daughter's eyes. Sam experienced a vast kaleidoscope of memories that strobed past so wildly she could only discern a few of them with any true clarity. Two images repeated more than any others.

In the first, Dani was a child, sitting in a candlelit cardboard fort with a boy Sam had to strain to recall. The image was so vivid that Sam could almost smell the fort's rotting walls and the sweet fragrance of fabric-softener from the blanket used to block out the attic sunlight.

That image was superseded in repetition only by

one that was infinitely more disturbing to Sam. The memory was from only a second earlier. Through Dani's eyes, Sam saw the vampire who had launched himself at the explosive device. The monster suddenly recoiled as Dani's power struck him with such force that his consciousness was seared away. The door leading from the stairwell burst open, snapping off its hinges to spin like a revolving door. A trio of men in dark funeral suits stood in the now-exposed corridor, and behind them, she saw two shirtless young men wearing black leather pants. They were identical twins, with blond hair that stretched at least part of the way down their back. The Tylers. They had someone with them.

The door spun around once more. The explosives were now back on Dani's side. Beyond the guards, the twins moved and she caught another glimpse of their companion.

Peter Red Cloud stood next to the Tylers, his eyes glazed, his face practically expressionless.

They have him, Sam thought. They took him to use him against me!

The door spun once more, the explosives now facing the corridor. They went off in the faces of the guards and the door was blown back, directly at her.

In her mind, Sam screamed and the vision abruptly ceased. She was back in her own reality now. Angel was attempting to fly away from danger while carrying Sam. Behind her, the stairwell exploded with a thunderous crack and the walls shook. An invisible fist slammed against Angel, causing her to lose the sleek, sensuous lines of her flight. The vampire grunted as her back was slammed against the wall and she lost her grip on Sam. Both women fell to the stairs, toppling half a flight to another landing before the roof collapsed. Debris dropped toward them. Angel scrambled to her knees and shoved Sam out of the way, sending the woman into a roll down another half-flight of stairs. Sam lost one of the shotguns.

The other dug into her ribs. Miraculously, it did not go off.

Sam hit the wall behind another identical landing and came to a stop. She wanted to scream her daughter's name, but the wind had been knocked out of her. A vague awareness that Angel had been struck by several chunks of debris and could very well be dead settled over her, but she was more worried about her daughter. With a tearing, shuddering gasp, her breath returned. She tried to stand but her ears were still ringing, her equilibrium shot. A concrete pebble struck her foot and she looked up to see a figure approaching from the darkened, debris-ridden stairs above. The pale orange fluorescent light on this level had been destroyed, but there was still some illumination from the landing below. It sent the shadows running.

Sam reached for her remaining shotgun and raised it with trembling fingers.

"Don't be naughty," a familiar, taunting voice said. When the owner of the voice stepped into the soft orange glow, Sam was amazed by the powerful waves of relief that moved through her. Angel carried Dani's limp body in her arms. The golden-eyed teenager was bruised and bloodied, but she was also alive. "Let's not fuck around. We have to get out of here."

"Yes," Sam said.

Dani's gaze fell on her mother. The young woman's lips drew back as she sensed the blood that covered Samantha Walthers. She came to sudden, vicious life, clawing and scratching to escape from the iron grip of the vampire.

"Whoa, doggie," Angel said. *Shit!*

Sam drew back in fear, and that caused her daughter to become even more frenzied. A sudden, startling insight gripped Sam. This was *not* Dani. The creature Angel struggled to restrain was what Dani had referred to as "the demon." Whether that was a splintered personality stemming from Dani's own mind, or

293

a separate, parasitical creature, it was not her daughter. It was the embodiment of everything Dani had wanted to deny in herself. This had been the ravenous creature that had been loosed to kill Dorothea.

Dani was innocent.

Angel had wanted to integrate Dani's personality with this *thing*. That was the expedient solution to making Dani into a soldier who would fight to achieve the goals Angel shared. It was also the worst idea they could have come up with, because this *thing* had no reason to fight. The demon's concerns were not the same as Dani's. It was an animal that only cared about consuming and existing. Occasionally it had borrowed vestiges of human personality from Dani and had attempted to control her by stabbing at her weaknesses. But it was separate from her, though it existed in her body.

"Give me back my daughter," Sam said in a low, controlled voice. Sam was not only Dani's mother. She was, perhaps, the only person to whom the demon would listen.

The creature stiffened.

"*You're* my daughter too," Sam said. "I know that now. But if you're going to live, it's Dani who has to be in control. Give her to me."

Dani shuddered and the demon receded. Angel grinned and released Dani, who sprang toward her mother and embraced her. They held each other, tears streaking both of their faces.

"I didn't do it," Dani said. "I didn't hurt those people on the highway. I made them decide to go hitchhiking back home. That's all I did. But I could feel that goddamned thing inside me the whole time. The demon wanted me to cut them to ribbons, but I faced it down. I won."

"Why didn't you just tell me?" Sam asked.

"Because, when I came back and saw your face, I knew you were afraid of me. I realized you didn't expect me to win. You didn't think I had it in me. I got so mad at you. You're not supposed to give up on me."

"I didn't. I love you, sweetheart."

Dani stared at her mother longingly. She wanted to say those words in return, but they wouldn't come.

"It's so hard to keep the demon from getting out," Dani whispered.

"I'll help you," Sam said, wondering if there was some way to destroy the demon and leave her daughter sane.

"That's great," Angel said. "It's a fucking shame Michael Landon's not around to film this wonderful, fucking Kodak moment. Now can we please get the living fuck out of here?"

Sam nodded in relief that was so powerful it practically made her giddy. That feeling was shredded into nothingness as she thought of the image Dani had glimpsed before the explosive went off. The vampires had Peter Red Cloud. When Sam had first encountered the man, her immediate thought had been that he was a thrall of the Immortals. That had not been true at the time. She would wager her soul on that fact. But they had him now, and it was her fault. When Devin Tyler had been in her mind, he had scoured it for information and learned of Peter's existence. They had kidnapped him before leaving Isleta.

Another person to save. One more reason to live.

"I'm going to need some help," Sam said. "I don't think I can walk straight. I feel kind of sick—"

Suddenly, she heard the sound of footsteps from the stairwell below.

More were coming.

Angel also heard the noises. The vampire looked like hell and she knew it. She was tired and trembling, her face pale and drawn.

"Great," Angel snarled. "I *have* to be wearing formal shoes for this."

Dani looked down. "Me too."

The vampire laughed. In seconds, the sounds of

running feet echoed through the landing. Suddenly they stopped.

"They're flying," Sam whispered, raising her shotgun. She prayed that she would be able to aim, fire, and actually hit something. There were no guarantees, considering her condition.

Angel nodded and looked to Dani. "You know why they're not using their powers, right?"

"Yes," Dani said, feeling an odd camaraderie with the vampire.

"Well, I don't have a clue," Sam said.

"No time, we'll tell you later," Dani said.

"Aren't we optimistic?" Angel remarked. "By the way, the ones that got fried, their minds were kind of tasty, didn't you think? I guess this is old stuff for you, but for most of us, it's not often we get to snack on our own. Not like you have."

Dani shuddered.

"Kidding, kidding," Angel said. "Sensitive, all of a sudden, I tell you."

A dark wind sliced through the silence.

Angel's smile fell away. "You know the truth. Use it."

Suddenly, a team of Immortals burst from the lower stairs. Dani was startled to recognize one of them as James Yuwai, the dealer. If it hadn't been for him, the Tyler twins might be dead right now instead of their guards. Beside James was a bald, shirtless man wearing a bandana, black tights, boots, and a plastic cutlass. Dani and Angel were about to attack when a noise came from above.

CHU-CHUKK!!!

One of Tylers' guards was on the stairs. The lower half of his right arm had been taken off by the explosion, and part of his skull had been seared to the bone. He had found Sam's shotgun, primed it, and was using the stump of his severed arm to level the weapon.

Sam felt a fluttering of wings brush across her consciousness and immediately thought it was her daughter. She recalled a similar sensation when Dani had placed her under the compulsion earlier that evening. The sensation vanished. The gunman on the stairs swung his weapon in Dani's direction. Sam aimed at him and fired as his weapon went off. The vampire's face exploded and he was spun around by the impact. Sam turned and saw that his shot had not struck Dani or Angel. It had taken the vampire beside James square in the chest. The Immortal struck the floor, arms blown back, eyes wide and imploring as he turned to his partner.

James turned his back on the women, transformed his hand into a talon, and tore his partner's head off. He did not lap at the geyser of blood that erupted from the corpse. Nor did Angel, despite her ravenous bloodneed.

Sam stared at the vampires in confusion. Only a few seconds passed before anyone spoke, but those moments seemed to stretch on forever. Angel, Dani, and James stared at one another and came to some strange understanding.

They were talking in their heads, Sam realized. She was only human, she could not hear the dialogue that was passing back and forth.

"Shit," Angel said, shaking her head. "This is good. Really good."

"What in the hell is going on?" Sam asked.

"He can get us out of here," Dani said. "And take us to a safe place."

"Why should we trust him?" Sam asked, terrified by the thought of placing her life in the hands of a stranger. "How do you know he's not just doing this to save his own ass, or to get us somewhere that we can be put down nice and quiet by the Tylers?"

"*I* think we can trust him," Dani said, her voice low and remarkably steady, despite the sheen of sweat that had suddenly broken out on her brow.

"More will be coming," Angel snarled. "I swear to

God, Sam, if you don't get moving I'll turn your lights out for a while and drag you."

"Don't go near her," Dani said.

"It's all right," Sam said. She knew it was odd to think this way, but she was certain the vampire would do nothing to harm her. If Sam refused to go, Angel would stay at her side. She wondered what she had done to cow the vampire to such an extent.

"You might as well trust me," James said. His shirt was soaked with blood.

Dani shuddered. Her need was returning.

"Even if you kill me, you'll never get past all the Immortals in this place. You've got nothing to lose by coming with me."

Sam looked at her daughter. The madness could set upon her again at any moment. The blood soaking Sam's clothes and that which had been splattered on James when he had killed his partner were going to drive the young woman into another frenzy if she wasn't given something else to occupy her.

Sam thought of her son, her daughter, and the man who had made her stop running away from her problems. Because he had cared about her, Peter Red Cloud was suffering the utter hell she had been willing to sacrifice herself to avoid.

The others were right. Even though they might end up dead if they went with the young Zuni dealer, they would *certainly* be killed if they did not.

Angel offered her hand to Sam. Dani stood with her back turned to the others, hugging herself.

Nodding, Sam took the vampire's hand.

Chapter Twenty-six

Before they left the stairwell, James dipped his hand in the steaming blood of his former partner and scrawled the words "END THE ADVOCACY — THE BLOOD SHOULD BE FOR ALL!"

"Why are you doing that?" Sam asked.

"They'll think it was the underground. Hits like this have been common over the last year. They won't suspect you now."

Sam knew enough to hold back her further curiosities. Cautiously, she followed James, Dani, and Angel, and felt Angel's power snaking into her mind.

Have to shield you. It's the only way, Angel whispered.

Sam gave her unspoken assent, and soon they were standing outside the door to the sixteenth-floor corridor.

Pointing at Sam, James commanded, "Take off the dress. It's dripping with blood." He stripped off his own bloodied shirt and handed it to her. "Act drunk. I'll be escorting you and your friends out. I'm allowed to give up a victim once in a while if a potential employee is about to lose their shit. That's our cover. It'll look like the three of you have been having a little party and I'm making you take it outside. Clean off your face. The monitors are black and white, the blood might not look like much on them, but I don't

299

want any hungry staff members getting more of a whiff than is necessary."

Sam nodded and removed her dress without hesitation. "Are you sure they're going to buy this underground stuff? Aren't they going to be suspicious that it was a group of women?"

"No, women are the underground's backbone. Over the centuries, they have been denied the most. You better leave the gun here too. There's no way to hide that on the monitor."

Sam was loath to leave herself so defenseless, but her daughter nodded urgently and so she complied.

"Let's go," James said.

They went into the hallway, took the main elevator down, snaked through the chaos on the main floor, and escaped through a series of corridors designated for employees only. James was questioned only once, and his cover story was believed.

Outside, they piled into his Jeep and sped away from the casino. In the rear seat lay an old pair of jeans and a dark sweatshirt James had been wearing when he had worked on his jeep a few days earlier. Sam put the jeans on, surprised that she had to pull them tight to button them. The Zuni's waist had been even more narrow than her own, and *she* was in practically perfect condition. The sweatshirt was fine.

They drove for twenty minutes, left the strip, and came to an office complex with several buildings that, according to the signs out front, housed only a small number of businesses. James took them into the parking garage, herded them into an elevator, and removed a hologram-imprinted credit card from his wallet. He inserted it in a slot in the control panel and the doors immediately hissed shut.

The elevator lurched and Sam's earlier concerns about a trap returned. Though they had entered the elevator on the ground floor, they were dropping.

"What the hell is this?" Sam asked.

300

James was stone-faced. "You'll see in a second."

They descended three levels, then came to a stop. The doors opened to reveal a long, antiseptic corridor. Gray carpeting, walls, and ceiling, with burgundy trim. They stepped into the hallway and Sam became aware of the long stretch of steel-reinforced doors with control panels beside them—exact duplicates of the basement door at the Malibu beach house. That room had been designed to hold Wildlings. Sam had visited prisons before. This place resembled one to an uncomfortable degree.

"You're still worried," James said, sensing the human's growing fear. "Don't be."

Sam looked back at Angel. The vampire had promised to shield Sam's thoughts from the Immortals. But Angel looked as if she were going to collapse.

"Don't give me those fucking doe eyes," Angel said with a Billy Idol sneer. "I'm fine."

Dani, who had been walking beside Angel, also seemed weakened. The failed attempt on the Tylers and the strength she had been forced to manifest to keep the demon under control had brought the golden-eyed young woman to the verge of physical exhaustion. Sam felt no better.

"A mobster—I'm not sure which one—built this place a while back," James explained. "He had been nervous over the bomb testing in the desert. Something could have gone wrong, he reasoned, fallout could have wiped out everyone on the strip. He wanted a place to run and hide if anything happened. The government had these places, why shouldn't he?"

The dealer led them to the end of the corridor, where it split off in two directions, then guided them to the right. Soon they came to another door, and he once again used his security card. A small green light appeared on the control panel and he pushed the door open, leading the others into a darkened room filled with banks of computer consoles and television monitors. Sam had read all the Tom Clancy thrillers. She felt as if she had just stepped into the computer control center at the C.I.A.

The room was twenty square feet with all the technology crammed against the walls, the center left open to give it a spacious, non-threatening feel. A half-dozen black leather swivel chairs were placed before various workstations, but only one was occupied. A red-haired woman turned in their direction. Her face lit up when she saw James.

"Hey, you big, swingin' dick," she said.

"Lily."

Her expression softened. "It's not happening, is it?"

"I'm afraid it is."

"I thought we'd have more time."

"I know."

Lily turned and smiled at the others. "Welcome to the end of the world, whoever you are. Friends, I assume."

"Yes," Dani said, breaking her self-imposed silence.

The red-haired Immortal rose to greet the others. Her power coiled within her. Dani and Angel tensed.

"Don't get too close," James said to his friend in warning. "They've been burned pretty badly. It's best if you don't try to go where you're not wanted."

Lily nodded, withdrawing her snakelike tendrils of power. "Opening ourselves up, opening our minds — it's customary. No offense intended. Come on over. I'll show you the layout, if there's time."

"There is," James said. "But not much."

A terrible sadness clouded Lily's pretty features. She had soft eyes that seemed to reflect the glacier-like green of the LEDs and monitor screens, and translucent skin. Her shoulder-length hair framed her fragile, innocent features and pale lips. She wore jeans and a black turtleneck. A clipboard sat beneath

302

her workstation, along with a spattering of reports and diskettes.

"Okay," Lily said, somehow regaining her earlier brightness. "I'm going under the assumption that you're completely uninitiated. Fair enough?"

Sam nodded. Dani looked to one of the computer screens. The information flashing by went too quickly for her to follow. Sam found a swivel chair and sat down. Dani and Angel did the same. James continued to stand.

"This is the Nursery—also referred to as the Net," Lily said. "It's almost all self-automated and a big part of it is self-contained. Modem lines from locations worldwide transmit data to and receive reports from screening stations throughout the U.S. and Canada. We access those stations through safelines with blockers that can defeat any attempts to trace where the information is going or to intentionally or otherwise contaminate the core with any type of virus."

"That fucking clears that up," Angel said darkly, her mood growing worse by the moment. "Can we have this in English, please?"

"That *was* in English."

James ran his hands through his wild hair and pulled up a seat. "Maybe we should start at the beginning. Everyone has questions. Sam most of all. Let's get everyone's questions settled and maybe that will be enough."

"Wait a minute," Dani said. "Just because we agreed to come *with* you and work *with* you doesn't automatically put you in charge."

"Absolutely not," James said.

"The last thing any of us fucking need is to get rescued from our own stupidity by, y'know, the *man,* like in some goddamned movie." Dani's eyes practically glowed with anger.

"I'm not trying to do that," James said, his voice somehow soothing without being condescending. "If

303

I had known what the three of you were up to when you showed up at the Buccaneer, I would have at least *offered* to help you. Instead, I got in the way, and I ruined everything for you. But it's not too late to fix it for all of us."

"All right, enough of this," Sam said. "James is right. I have questions. I think it's time I got some answers. I'm tired of not knowing what's going on. I've heard of the Net before. Richard mentioned it. I'll admit I'm curious, but what's bothering me the most is trying to figure out how the hit went to hell. It was a simple, clean, effective plan. What went wrong?"

"I think I've mostly got it figured out," Dani said. "The bottom line is that I fucked up. When it came to decide whether Angel or I would use our power on you, it was me you picked. I've had Angel inside my head before. I can understand why you didn't want her in yours."

Angel sat back and smiled at James. "They really love me, they just don't want to admit it."

"But we all might have been better off," Dani admitted. "I was pretty crazed when I went inside your mind. I didn't follow through on everything we discussed. I was thinking that you didn't trust me, and I was pissed off. So I ignored a lot of what you told me to do. Angel wouldn't have done that."

Angel looked down at her hands and shrugged. Her face was set in an oddly contemplative manner. "You never know. Shit, I never know what I going to do next. Takes the fun out life if you plan too far in advance."

That was bullshit, Sam was beginning to realize, but she let it pass.

"I didn't install all the fail-safes you wanted," Dani said. "If I had, everything would have been fine. I was acting like some goddamned kid and that nearly got us killed."

"We're here now," Sam said as she took her daughter's hands. "We're alive. We'll both know better next time. And there *will be* a next time. That's all that matters."

Dani nodded.

"The two of you give me cramps," Angel whispered.

Again, the remark was ignored. Dani said, "I turned you into the exact perfect prey. The Tylers' guards complained about having Pamela Tyree on the floor with them. You had been scoped out on the way in, just as we had expected, but not for the reasons we had figured. The Immortals had the choice of going through a potential hassle in moving your room, or simply adding you to the list of available prey and moving you up to the top slot. Then they sent an Immortal who was slated to feed tonight to get rid of you."

"Jesus," Sam whispered.

Dani told her mother all that had happened in the casino, including her temptation to murder the man who reminded her of Bill Yoshino, and her reasons for placing her growing hunger under control. She detailed the encounter with James, and passed on the information he had shared with her about the city.

"Yeah, it's fucking Vampire Central here," Angel said, looking even worse than she had a few moments ago. Her eyes were becoming sunken and dark, despite the contacts, and her fingers seemed to be growing longer, sharper, becoming talons with an eerie leisureliness. "I didn't have a goddamned clue."

Sam squeezed Dani's hand. "Why didn't the Immortals use their power against any of us at the casino? You and Angel both said you knew."

"The better question," James interjected, "is why your daughter and her friend decided they could trust me." He turned to Dani. "I'd like to tell her, if I may."

305

"Yeah," Dani said. "I didn't mean to be a bitch before. I think we're all still pretty shaky."

"So am I," James confessed.

Dani stared at him. The swarthy-skinned Zuni seemed as calm and at peace as ever. She wished that she could find that peace within herself. In many ways, James Yuwai was remarkably attractive.

"Me, I'm fine," Angel muttered. "I'm just about ready to do my fucking Jane Fonda workout."

James regarded Sam with his burning red eyes. They were the color of a swirling, angry volcano. Earlier, they had merely seemed burnt umber, with slivers of pure crimson. "There is a movement going on within our society. When I use the term 'society,' I am not talking of the human world, but that of the Immortals."

"All right," Sam said.

"More than a millennia ago, when the Ancients saw their children conducting wars among themselves, they decided that there must be laws. Without laws there would be anarchy. The primary law they established was that Immortals must not kill their own. The Parliament was created to enforce this law. It was their task to risk their lives to track down and punish any transgressors."

"Punish," Angel said contemptuously. "You mean *kill*."

"Yes. Members of the Parliament would subject themselves to terrible danger—particularly in the case of Wildlings. And by that I mean the most pure definition of the word. Over the centuries, the word 'Wildlings' has come to be associated with any of our kind who kill their own. When it was first coined, it meant those who went insane because they could not reconcile their human and Immortal aspects."

Sam resisted an urge to glance at her daughter. Dani stiffened anyway, somehow sensing her mother's thoughts.

"Yeah," Dani said. "Maybe that is what's happening to me. I dunno."

"In return for putting their lives at risk to enforce the laws of the Ancients, the members of Parliament were greatly rewarded. Immortals who wished for an easy route to money and power coveted positions in the Parliament. This is still the case. But only a certain number of Immortals are required for Parliament.

"It was not always an elite group. In the beginning, contests were staged to determine the worthiness of the candidates and these contests were open to all. I can think of one such contest that held as its goal the acquisition of the cup of Lord Antonius, the first of our race, used to capture the blood of Christ. It had been stolen by the enemies of the Ancients."

"The Grail?" Sam asked. "The fucking *Grail?*"

"Through the ages, legends become distorted. What I have been told may have been the fiction, to some degree. All that matters is that after a time, the contests were no longer open to all. Members of Parliament wished to give their seats to their sons, or to their chosen successors."

"The Advocacy," Dani said.

"Yes. Those of us in the underground want to bring about a new order. We believe in the system as it was first created by the Ancients. The concept was correct, but the execution is no longer working. The Parliament has become corrupt. With the exception of a few *splashy* hunts that are performed strictly for show, the 'shit work'—the actual hunting and destruction of Wildlings—has been relegated to lower-echelon Immortals and high-powered Initiates. Amazing promises are made to these gullible idiots, but any real follow-through is very rare."

"If the Ancients are so powerful, why haven't they put the Parliament down themselves?" Sam asked.

"That might have been possible once. No longer.

When it comes down to it, the Ancients are three old men who were once the young, vital sons of Antonius. They have more to fear from the Parliament than the Parliament does from them. With age has come incredible power for the Ancients, but even that power would not be enough to save them from the combined forces of the Parliament, their own bastard creation.

"The Parliament makes no move against the Ancients because these three old men have one saving grace: the gift of their blood. It is a gift that must be freely given. That keeps them safe and secures their seat of power in our society.

"Those of us in the underground want a return to the old ways. For the last year, attacks have been made against the members of Parliament and their Advocates. The Immortals who attacked you at the casino thought you were a member of the underground. They were afraid to reach out with their power, afraid to stick their heads into the maw of some psychic trap. Many of their kind have been killed that way."

Dani swallowed hard. "Both Angel and I learned about the underground from the minds of the guards who were killed. It all just kind of flowed out of them when they died. We caught enough to understand what's been going on."

Lily spoke. "We want to abolish the Parliament and replace it with a new organization that will be fair to all, not just the chosen few. One in which women won't be treated as if they're worthless. Right now, Alyana Du Prey is the only woman who's ever been admitted to Parliament."

Angel rose to her feet unsteadily and turned her back on the others, pretending to become engrossed in the information racing by on one of the monitors. Strings of computer-coded messages were mirrored in her darkening eyes. "Of course, if you're successful,

308

then the leaders of your underground get the first shot at the blood of the Ancients. Nothing really changes."

"Not true. We'll leave it to the Ancients to devise a new method of selecting those who will become the chosen enforcers. It will be open to all."

Angel spun around, enraged. She was in full transformation, her teeth and talons bone-white and razor-sharp, her eyes aglow. "That doesn't *work* too well for me. By your definition, I'm an Advocate. So is Dani. That blows your feminist revolution shit out of the water."

"Not at all," James said calmly. "No one in the Parliament except Alyana considers that either of you have any chance to survive. And if you do, Devin Tyler will find a way to have you killed that won't come back around to him."

Angel snarled. "You don't know much about me, do you? With or without your help, there's no way in hell Dani and I are going to lose. But if things go your way, I get cheated out of what I've been working to achieve. I have *no intention* of starting at the bottom again."

"You might as well leave right now then," James said. "Turn us in. Protect the Parliament. Save Devin Tyler."

Angel shuddered. Her lips drew back in a horrible smile. "Well. I really did want to see that fucker squeal like a stuck pig when he sees what's left of his little boys."

"Then stay with us," Lily said. "Help us. We'll do everything in our power to see the favor returned."

Angel looked to Sam. "Are you buying this?"

"I'm not sure."

With a powerful effort, Angel drew back from her transformation and slammed down into her chair. "Let me know what you decide. You know what I want."

Sam regarded James. "Tell me why you got involved with us."

James nearly smiled. "You can provide us with the one thing we've never been able to get on our own — an audience with the Ancients."

"Oh," Angel said. "That's nice. I wasn't aware I had their fucking phone number."

"You might as well," Lily added. "You have Alyana Du Prey and Christian De Santo on your side. They're two of the most powerful members of the current regime. You can get to them, and they can get to the Ancients."

"But De Santo left the Parliament," Angel said warily.

"You never *really* leave the Parliament," James said. "Once you have the blood of the Ancients, you're part of the fraternity forever. The three top money-makers for the Ancients are Alyana Du Prey, Christian De Santo, and Devin Tyler."

"Son of a bitch!" Sam shouted. "That's how it get's decided?' Who *makes* the most?"

"That's how the Advocates are given preference, yes."

"I didn't think a music career could net that much," Dani whispered.

"That's just a part of it. Devin was the one who got the Ancients into Vegas in the first place. The music was just a perk for him."

"Sure," Lily added. "Why do you think no one talks about the corporate sponsors for *his* tours?"

"What about De Santo and Du Prey?" Angel asked.

"Their company turns one hell of a profit," Lily said. "Investment, finance, liquidations. Between that and Vamp Products —"

"No fuckin' way," Angel said. "The jeans? The perfumes?"

"Sure. What do you think the De Santo and Du

310

Prey company is all about? The fun part is that VAMP is an anagram for the Vegas Association for Money and Power. They don't have that on the books, of course."

Sam frowned. "I'm having a real hard time believing that we just *lucked into* meeting with you people."

"Luck had very little to do with it," James said, "though I will say the odds were in favor of this happening. We have people *everywhere* in the Parliament and the Ancients' various holdings. It's the only way to affect a real change, doing it from the inside."

"I'm still not clear on exactly what it is you're doing, or what this place is all about," Sam admitted as she gestured to indicate the expansive room.

"The Net is two things," the dealer said. "It's the cornerstone of the Parliament's power. It's also the home of all the people who want to bring the Parliament and the Ancients to their knees."

"What a coinkee-dink," Angel said.

"She's right," Sam said. "How the hell could you have infiltrated to this level?"

"A lot of careful planning and misdirection. We've made dozens of seemingly disorganized, random attacks on the members of Parliament and the Advocacy to make our enemies think we were a bunch of amateurs, no real threat. In the meantime, we were busy getting up next to them."

Lily laughed. It was a high, sweet sound, devoid of the bitterness that tinged her words. "There's a downside to it. The Parliament hasn't taken any real stance against us because they see great value in us. They can kill one another, wage wars just like the *old ones* did before there ever was a Parliament, and blame the killings on us. For that reason, the Ancients aren't exactly receptive to contact from us."

"Lily, why don't you explain about the Net?" James asked gently.

She nodded. "In English?"

"Yes, please."

With a sigh, Lily said, "This complex has a variety of uses. Primarily, it's the home of the On-line Immortals, which is just our own little name for ourselves. If one of the Ancients, a member of Parliament, an Advocate, or a Second Tier Member—"

"Excuse me?" Sam asked. "Second Tier?"

"Immortals who have built their own fortunes and aren't a part of the Parliament."

Richard Sterling was Second Tier, Sam realized. "But if they have money and power, why worry about the Parliament?"

"Blood of the Ancients," Dani said. "They want to walk in the daylight."

"That's right," Lily said in her warm, sisterly voice. "If any of those people need information, if they need official documents 'produced' or filed in any database, we can do it. We're plugged in worldwide. We have access to all levels of government, and not just the U.S. The Ancients have been happy as all get-out ever since we've found out how to backdoor into Japan.

"We keep all records on 'daytime humans' and all likely candidates for those positions, both human and Initiate. Several hundred detective agencies in the States do nothing but collect this data for us. Generally, they have no idea what's really going on, though there are some agencies run strictly by Immortals and Initiates. Two members of Parliament are corporate attorneys, we've got an Initiate who's a state judge—it goes on and on. We keep track of all the detail work out of this office.

"The really important thing is that we also control the money flow. I mean—it's all crunching data these days. Everything comes through here. That's why it was so important to place members of the underground in this facility."

James put his hand on the redhead's shoulder. "Lily's the best we have. She has it worked out that we can suck every dime out of the assembled members of Parliament with a single command key. Clean out their assets, redistribute them into our own dummy corporations, and take them down before they know what hit them. Then our people go after them, destroying what's left of their lives."

Just like Alyana did to Richard Sterling, Sam thought. "I don't know. If this place is so important, why were we able to walk right in? There's no security. Nothing. What's to stop someone from coming in off the street?"

"I was watching," Lily said, pointing at one of the monitors. "I could have burned all of you in the elevator or at damn near any point between there and this office if I thought that necessary. Of course, I'm not the only one watching, or the only one here. The moment James inserted his card, a dummy security program was run, a computer simulation of an Immortal who's actually been dead for a while, but no one knows it. James uses his power to project that image in case he runs into anyone in the hall. That's pretty unlikely, unless we're changing shifts, but we're always careful."

Sam scowled. "This is too much. Even if all this is true—"

"It is," Lily said. "We've been working at this for years. I could spend the next two days explaining all the technical details to you. But you said you wanted it in English."

"You haven't heard the best part," James said. "The Ancients are here in Vegas. All three of them. Devin is their golden boy. They've come to show their support. They've been given the top three floors of the Buccaneer."

Lily nodded excitedly. "If we can contact them and get their *approval* before we move against the Parliament, then it'll be all over for Devin Tyler and the rest of those bastards."

"You won't have to run anymore. You'll be protected," James said.

Sam ran her hand over her brow. "You're telling me there's a war that's about to explode and we're the lit fuse that's going to set it all off?"

"Exactly."

Sam thought of the way she and her daughter had been hurt. For an instant she saw Peter's face flash before her.

"Yes," Sam said. "I'm willing. Dani?"

The golden-eyed young woman nodded and looked to Angel.

"Cool doggie," the vampire said, then collapsed from her chair.

Chapter Twenty-seven

David Farmer decided that he had been kissing Leo's ass long enough. Two years ago, he had arrived in Las Vegas a child in the ways of the Immortals. Before he had even gotten out of the airport, he had been swept up by a team of spotters and indoctrinated into a nightmare world that had never ceased to fascinate him. At first he'd thought it was all a joke. He had been nineteen and aware that others existed with the strange powers he had possessed. But the one time he had tried to make contact with others of his race, they had turned from him, but not before delivering a searing, psychic lash that had left a permanent scar in his memory.

In his innocence, David had called those like himself *Kingers,* after the gifted and sometimes tragic characters in Stephen King novels, which he had consumed voraciously. It was a term he had never quite been able to abandon, even when he had learned the truth about his race. The damned heroine of *Carrie,* the father from *Firestarter,* the boy from *The Shining*—they had gifts that were similar to his, though none of them equaled his power. Nevertheless, he had been an abandoned child, and all of his life he had longed to feel like part of some family. David had been fourteen when he had been sent from the orphanage to his last foster home. The Sheffields had told him that he was old enough and strong enough

315

to take part-time jobs and bring in some extra money for them. His new "father" had also had other uses for him. Secret and painful uses.

The boy's powers had manifested in a darkened bed slick with his own blood. He had been beaten when he had attempted to save himself from Tony Sheffield's attentions. The man had been about to violate him when David released something he would never have believed to be inside himself. A monstrous new ability. With it, David had decimated the man's mind and saved himself.

The official verdict was that Tony Sheffield had suffered a stroke. David had been returned to the orphanage, but nothing was ever the same for him again. It took him less than a month to gain control of his new talents. He knew that with his power, he could get practically anything he desired. It would have been a simple matter to terrorize the staff and the other kids, and he would have enjoyed it too. He could have hurt them all, driven them to commit any act that would have amused him.

For that very reason, David had been extremely pleased with himself for choosing to continue his life much as it had been. He used his power only to ease the frightened, crying new kids into sleep, or to protect the weaker children from the tyranny of their elders. He had hoped that if Mr. King ever met him and became aware of how he was using his incredible abilities, the man would have said, "All right, David!" and been proud of him.

David had also used his powers to ensure that he was not sent to any other foster homes. When he had been younger, he had dreamed of escaping the orphanage. That had changed when he had discovered his blood inheritance. The orphanage was no longer a prison for David. He could leave any time. On his frequent trips into Los Angeles, he had seen kids his age and younger living on the street. In comparison, the orphanage was not a cruel place. It was run by caring, overworked people who sometimes made mistakes. Sending David to the Sheffields had been one such mistake, but he had forgiven them. Something terrible had occurred in the Sheffield home. A dark, twisting *thing* had taken root in David's mind, but from that horror, a strange and wonderful fruit had sprung. David's former resentment of the orphanage had turned into pure love, because he now considered it not only his home but, in a way, his *creation,* a work of art that he could constantly mold into something better and brighter.

At the age of sixteen, David had begun his fundraising efforts for the orphanage. This was not an official activity, of course. He had grown tired of the other kids not having all they needed. When he walked around the malls, he would occasionally peek inside the minds of shoppers, see that they were about to spend twenty or fifty dollars on *junk* they didn't really need, and plant in their heads the compulsion to instead write out a check to the orphanage. Within a year he had graduated to corporate chairman, and had expanded his efforts to include other charities he found worthwhile.

His life had been enriching and complete. Then Gail Stevens had entered his life. She was sixteen, and would only be staying at the orphanage for a short time. Her parents had been killed in a gruesome car accident and her only living relatives, her aunt and uncle, were on a cruise. They would come for her as soon as they could make it back to the States. In the meantime, Social Services had placed her at the orphanage.

The moment David saw her he knew that he could not live without her. He had never been in love before. From the night Tony Sheffield had molested him, he had not been able to stand the touch of another human being. His power had been his salvation. It had allowed him to be close to others without giving them even a shred of intimacy in return. To all outward appearances, he was shy and withdrawn, a tall, blond-haired youth who could have been considered handsome if he showered, brushed his unwashed, stringy hair out of his face, and went to a dentist now and then.

Gail had been magnificent. An angel. She was short — four-eleven-and-a-half, according to her paperwork — but she had a perfect hourglass figure, a heart-shaped face, and a smile that spoke not only of strength, but also salvation. His salvation. He felt that he could stare at her sparkling blue eyes, rich chestnut-brown hair, and devastating lips and cheekbones forever.

She had been terrified of him. He had loved her, and in return, she was afraid of him. There had been no reason for her to regard him with wide, fear-filled eyes, or to hurry off in the other direction when he approached, but it happened every time. The day came for Gail to leave, and David decided to talk with her before she left. He had cleaned himself up and put on stylish clothes he had stolen from the mall. David had made himself so presentable that most of the others at the orphanage didn't even recognize him. It made no difference to Gail. She was still afraid of him.

David promised himself that he would not use his power on her. Forcing her to love him would have been wrong. But he wanted to know — he felt he *deserved* to know — why she was acting this way.

He looked into her mind, immediately withdrew, then ran from the orphanage and never looked back. What he had seen in Gail's mind had not been anything he could easily catalogue or explain. He had thought that perhaps he had reminded her of someone who had hurt her, or that maybe she really cared for him, but was afraid to admit her feelings, even to herself. Her parents, whom she had loved, had died. The girl might have been afraid to love again, or to love so soon after her terrible loss.

The truth was worse than anything he could have imagined. It was as if she could somehow sense that he wasn't the *same* as her. He wasn't even human. For that, she hated him. Had it been in her power, she would have killed him and felt nothing but relief. He had uncovered within her a cruel animal form of intuition that he had been oblivious to in the minds of other humans. In that shattering moment, he suddenly realized she was right. He wasn't a *Kinger*. David was nothing like those poor, helpless humans who were cursed with extraordinary powers. His gifts stemmed from his blood, which was anything but human. Gail had been *absolutely right*. Love was out of the question. They were natural enemies.

At some point after he had left the orphanage, David's mind had shut down. The horrible rejection he had faced had been too much for him to bear. He had awakened months later to find himself living in the stylish apartment of a stunningly beautiful young woman named Carry Hyde. He was sitting on her couch, naked, and she and another woman in her early twenties were both licking his pulsing, erect cock, pausing only to flicker their tongues at one another. In his last conscious memory, he had been a virgin. The events of that afternoon proved that was no longer the case. He surrendered to the sensations and took both women as if he had been making love for years.

Later, he learned that he had enslaved the women. They were his to utilize sexually, whenever he desired them, and they made money as models to help support his somewhat extravagant life-style. That should have bothered him, he knew. But these were only humans. They weren't his kind. Buried deep in their psyches, both women had urges to be used. Those

319

impulses stemmed from feelings of inadequacy and a lack of any true tenderness in their lives. David exploited their needs, and eventually became resentful of the arrangement he had created. So long as he depended on humans for his material needs, he was as much a slave to them as they were to him.

He decided that he should have his *own* fortune.

At times, when he was alone, he wondered how Mr. King would view his current actions. Not that it mattered, really. Mr. King was only a human, though he wrote with such an unerring ability to perfectly detail the inner workings of other's minds that David wondered if the author might be one of his kind. The thought had amused him, and it had been on his mind when he had boarded the plane for Las Vegas.

Two years had passed quickly. He now worked for an Immortal named Leo Grisham, a man whose ass he had been kissing for far too long. David was a *baiter*. He roamed the streets of Vegas in a black pickup, hunting down Immortals and Initiates who did not know the rules of the city. Five of his kind dressed like drugged-out headbangers and crowded into the pickup four nights a week. Leo was one of the three Immortals in the pack. David and a man named Jocko were still Initiates, despite Leo's promises to turn them.

David knew that Initiates were valuable to the Immortals. They could walk in the sunlight and perform tasks others could not, including finding the daytime haunts of stray Immortals who had been warned to leave the city and had remained. David had burned nineteen of these in the last two years. Every time he watched an Immortal die, he had fantasized that it was Leo.

Tonight, Leo had put David in his place for the last time. They had stopped a strange young woman at a gas station, a golden-eyed Immortal whose attitude marked her as exactly what they had been commissioned to hunt out — a stray, unaware of the city and its laws. Leo had challenged her, and had nearly lost his life for his efforts. David had recognized the blood of the Ancients within the woman. She was an Advocate. They had let her go.

David had not been satisfied. He had wanted to file a report. Leo had told him to shut the hell up and put that thought out of his mind. They would be lucky if the Advocate did not make a phone call about *them*. God only knows where her sponsor was situated in the Parliament. If the man who had mingled his blood with hers was powerful enough, he could order all five members of their pack mind-flayed for the affront they had performed.

"Forget about it and hope she does the same," he had warned.

David said he would do that.

He had been lying.

The pack had nailed another stray — it seemed to be the night for them — and the rogue Immortal had run from them. David had joined the pursuit with the others, then fell and twisted his ankle. Leo had called him a worthless pussy, and the rest of the pack had gone on the hunt without him.

When they were gone, David had returned to the pickup and used Leo's computer access code to get into the Net's database. He fed in the general description of the Advocate he had seen and waited for a matching reference to appear.

No match.

David smiled. His instincts had told him that something about this woman was wrong. Somehow she possessed the blood of the Ancients, but she wasn't a member of the Advocacy. He knew that she couldn't be Parliament — the only female in that group was Alyana Du Prey. Everyone knew that.

The creation of Advocates was strictly regulated. Each Parliament member was allowed two Advocates, no more. The Net database revealed that all openings in the Advocacy were filled.

Someone in Parliament had been very bad indeed. They had shared the Ancients' gift with an Immortal who was outside the Net. According to the laws of the Ancients, clandestine little deals like that were strictly prohibited. Those who broke the Ancients' laws — even members of Parliament — faced terrible penalties. By reporting on what he had learned, David could make a powerful enemy.

He could also make some important friends.

Going through proper channels was out of the question. Leo would either continue to ignore what had been learned and punish David for not following orders and backing off, or he would walk into his supervisor's office and take full credit for David's efforts.

David considered sending the information on the Net. That would be the quickest way. If the golden-eyed Immortal had come to Las Vegas to start any kind of trouble, it would be best to put out an immediate alert to secure her.

He accessed another menu and checked the bulletins for disturbances. What he learned troubled him deeply: Members of the underground had made an attack on the Buccaneer. At least two of the assailants were thought to be women.

Sweat erupted on his brow.

If the golden-eyed Immortal was involved in this, the information he had to impart would rise substantially in value. His fingers touched the keyboard and a dagger of guilt ripped through him.

In his mind, he had been able to justify his treatment of humans: He had embraced them and they — in the person of Gail Stevens — had painfully rejected him. Those of his own race had opened their arms to him, telling him that he was part of a larger family, a fraternity of orphans, but they had lied. The Immor-

322

tals had abused him almost as badly as Tony Shef-field.

David's loyalties were in a state of flux. The underground wanted to change things. They wanted to bring about a return to the old ways and make the blood of the Ancients a possibility for anyone, not just a select few. That sounded good to David.

But no one could really say if the underground *existed*. Many of the Immortals had found it convenient to blame their own crimes on the movement. Perhaps it was nothing more than a fiction created by the Parliament itself to excuse their own blatant disregard for the Ancients' laws.

Nevertheless, when David read the reports about the underground's attacks on the established regime, he felt that anarchy was coming and their civilization would soon be torn apart. The Immortals might not exist under a fair system, but it was one that had worked for a millennium.

David drew a sharp breath. He was about to type in a personally signed alert message when he heard sounds from outside the pickup. The others were coming back. He exited the system and settled into the passenger seat.

Suddenly, his door was ripped open and hands fell upon him, dragging him from the pickup. Psychic shields had been raised in his mind all evening. They did not waver now. The others had no idea that he was panicking, certain that Leo had seen his treasonous act and was about to punish him for it.

The other members of the pack threw him to the ground and pounced on him. They ripped his clothes from his body. He fully expected them to tear out his throat at any moment. Instead, they smeared him with the blood of the Immortal they had killed, made "kissy-face" motions at him, then piled into the pickup and sped away.

He sat there, naked and shivering, for almost a

minute. Then a pair of blinding headlights appeared behind him. He spun and saw that the pack had returned.

Leo hung his head out of the driver's side window. "You missed a good one, you fucking pussy. Get in!"

They didn't know, he thought. He lifted himself up and climbed in the back of the pickup. When his shift was over, he would find one of the Immortals who worked for the visiting Ancients and tell *them* what he had learned. They would wonder why he had waited, and he would explain that Leo had told him to forget about seeing the golden-eyed Immortal. If David's suspicions proved to be correct, Leo would get flayed for his actions. The thought made David want to grin, but he held himself back.

They drove for close to an hour. The Immortals relived every detail of their kill and busted David's balls for not being with them. He didn't mind. Even being cold and stinking of blood wasn't so bad, considering what the dawn would bring.

David would do everything in the light, when Leo was sleeping in the underground housing provided by the company. The Immortal would have one hell of a surprise waiting for him when he came to work the next night.

Thoughts of the books he used to read returned to David. When he had been unaware of the brutal, unforgiving nature of the humans and their inability to accept anything that was not *exactly* like *them,* he had wanted to be like the protagonists of Mr. King's novels. He had even identified with the poor teacher who inherited precognition in *The Dead Zone.* That man died, but he did so for a selfless and noble purpose.

David realized that he had been looking at those stories from the wrong perspective all along. His race had nothing in common with the bold, self-sacrificing heroes of those novels. Instead, they were much more like the unrepentant bastards Mr. King had also described so well.

But there was a difference between fiction and fact. In real life, the bad guys *won*.

Chapter Twenty-eight

Lily was about to join the others in restraining Dani when an alert flashed across one of the main monitors.

Everything happens at once, the Immortal thought. Seconds ago, the situation had been completely under control. Samantha Walthers, her daughter, and their protector had agreed to aid the underground. Then Angel had fallen to the floor and had been overtaken by an unexpected and violent fit of hunger. Dani had been vulnerable. Angel's desire for sustenance had reached out from the Immortal and touched off Dani's bloodneed.

The golden-eyed young woman had been driven into a frenzy. She had transformed as Sam had gone to her, and her talons had raked across her adopted mother's arm before James had grabbed her. Sam drew back in shock and James forced Dani to the floor.

"Lily!" James called. "Put her down, now!"

The red-haired Immortal suddenly paled. "I —"

"There's no choice, do it!" James shouted. He had wrapped his strong arms around Dani from behind, pinning her arms to her side, then pushed her down on the rug, lying on top of her back to hold her. The demon had escaped once more. It was struggling to bring up its legs and plant its knees for leverage.

James suspected that it would try to use its power of flight to drive him toward the ceiling or into a wall. It desperately wanted to free itself and attack the human.

Sam turned to Lily. "Wait!"

But the Immortals ignored Sam. Lily balled her hands into fists, twisted her expression into one of absolute concentration, then issued a short, tight scream.

Dani fell limp, her body instantly returning to its human state. James slid from her.

Lily buried her face in her hands and screamed, "Why did you make me do that? *Why?*"

"There was no choice. I'm sorry," James said as he sat beside Dani and absently brushed the long blond hair of her wig from her face. Sam knelt beside him.

"Is she all right?" Sam asked. "What did you do to her?"

"She's fine, for now. I just hope she stays under until we can get something into her."

They both turned at the sounds of sobbing. Lily was crying tears of blood. On the floor a few feet away from the red-haired Immortal, Angel lay unconscious and shuddering. Her convulsions were lessening.

"Something in her?" Sam asked as she took one of her daughter's limp hands. Dani's pulse was racing. "What the hell are you talking about?"

"She's hungry," James said. "Both of them are hungry. They need—"

"They don't need anything!" Lily cried suddenly. "Shut up!"

"Lily . . ."

Sam nodded sharply in Lily's direction. "What's her problem?"

In a soft whisper, Lily pleaded, "James, get them out of here."

"I will. But I'll need your help."

"Get one of the others. Go."

"Then you'll be here alone with them."

"Oh, Jesus," Lily said, wiping the tears from her eyes, gasping as she saw that her hands were stained crimson. She glanced back at the monitor, rubbing her hands on her jeans. "I've got incoming to deal with."

James returned his gaze to Sam's dark, inquisitive eyes. "Lily doesn't . . ." he stopped. "It's difficult to explain."

"What isn't about your fucking race?" Sam looked down at her daughter. "What did she do to Dani?"

"You probably don't want to know."

"The *fuck* I don't want to know. What did she do?"

"She severed the link between Dani's conscious mind and her body. It's not an easy trick. I've only seen a few who could do it."

"Severed," Sam murmured, trying to force away her terror at the connotations racing through her mind.

"That's a bad way to put it," Lily said without turning around. Her calm, professional tone had returned, though a trace of her earlier disquiet was noticeable. " *'Blocked'* is better. It's only temporary. She'll claw her way back up, but hopefully not for a little while."

"Then she's all right?" Sam asked, returning her gaze to James.

"She's fine."

Sam nodded at Lily. "What's her story? Is she an Initiate or an Immortal?"

"I don't want to discuss Lily's condition—"

"I'm an Immortal," Lily said, keeping her back to the others. "But I don't kill."

"How do you live if you don't—"

"I hate to complicate everything, but we've got a situation," Lily said, cutting Sam off sharply.

"What is it?" James asked.

"I've got a spotter who's entered the Net. He fed in Dani's general description."

"Shit," Sam whispered, recalling the pack of baiters who accosted Dani at the gas station.

"Fortunately, I've rerouted all inquiries so that they come to me. You wouldn't believe the flags that have been attached to any potential sightings of you or your daughter. For the past six months, it's been like people spotting Elvis for the *National Enquirer.* The Net had both of you in nearly every state in the Union. A slew of foreign countries too. You've cost the company one hell of a lot of money."

"Good," Sam said. "What about this inquiry?"

"He wanted to know if she's an Advocate."

"That makes sense," James said. "The baiters sensed the blood of the Ancients in her."

Sam looked to James quizzically.

"Your daughter shared the events of the last few hours with me when we were in each others' minds, at the stairwell in the casino. She also gave me the details on your overall problem. I shared some of it with Lily when we first walked in."

Nodding, Sam asked, "Lily, what are you doing with this guy?"

"The program's already done it. It told him there were no matches found. So far, he's done nothing else. He's entered no alerts."

"Why would he?"

"Because she has the gift of the Ancients but she's not listed as a member of the Advocacy. The used I.D. shows a *Leo Grisham.* That means our Mr. Grisham may be considering that some member of Parliament has broken the laws of the Ancients, and he may be deciding to use that information for his own benefit."

"I thought you said you had all inquiries routed to you. Why didn't *you* answer the request instead of letting the machine do it?"

"Because I got a little distracted. The system has an automatic override on manual responses. If you wait too long it intercedes. If it didn't, its response time would go way down."

"What do we do now?" James asked.

"I'm going to stay right here," Lily said as she tapped at her keyboard. "If Grisham enters an alert, I want to be ready to intercept. I've just routed any processing from his I.D. code directly to my terminal. If he puts out a warning, I'll make him think it went through, then crush it."

"Good, Lily," James said.

"Do me a favor," Lily said with a slight shudder. "Get everyone out of here. Rooms Three-eighty-one, Three-ninety, and Three-ninety-two are wide open. The last one has a monitor system. I'll set it up so you can keep an eye on the other rooms. The corridor's clear. I'm going to seal all doors and close off elevator access on this floor until you're done.

"Now go. I've got work to do."

Sam and James carried Dani to the first room, which had plush teal carpeting, gray walls, and a twin-sized bed with black sheets and covers. A television with 280-channel capacity sat in an alcove in one wall, a beautiful aquarium filled with exotic fish and lit with an eerie greenish-white light in an alcove in another wall. A reading desk with a few novels of classic literature, a silver-framed mirror, an adjoining bathroom and shower, and a clothes closet finished out the room. Soft white panels in the walls provided varying amounts of light. Open cabinets revealed a home entertainment system with a CD player, VCR, Nintendo, and a laptop PC. A hidden panel that James slid back revealed a small refrigerator packed with drinks. There was also a well-stocked food-storage area.

"Some of our kind never get over human hungers," James explained.

"Wait a minute," Sam said. "You mean, this place is like a *dorm* for Immortals? You have people coming in and out of here every day?"

"We have dozens of facilities like this one. But don't worry. This level is highly restricted. Management requires all rooms to be kept stocked and ready in the event of any disaster. A hold over from the bomb-threat days, I suppose."

"But the other two levels above are crowded?"

"Yes," James said. "They're teeming with our kind during the day, but I gambled that the place would be deserted until an hour or so before dawn."

"Jesus." Sam considered the effect that being so close to so many Immortals could have on her daughter. But there was nowhere else to go. If this "Leo Grisham" decided to warn others about Dani, an intensive search would begin throughout the city. Eventually, the vampires would find the room they'd rented at the Best Western. That might occur anyway, depending on how badly they wanted the people who had launched an attack on the casino.

They settled Dani into the bed. The Native American's seeming detachment had somehow comforted Sam. She had seen the way Dani had been looking at the breathtakingly handsome Zuni, and she did not want her child to be hurt once again.

"You take care of Angel. I want to stay here with Dani," Sam said.

"Your daughter could come around at any time," James said. "It won't be any different from before."

"You don't know that."

"I'm not willing to take the chance. Even if I was here with you, I might not be fast enough or strong enough to hold her this time."

"All right," Sam said reluctantly.

331

"You'll be able to watch her on the monitor. Let's get Angel."

After returning to Lily's office, Sam and James collected Angel and secured the vampire in a room that was identical to Dani's. Lily had keyed an access card for the particular rooms Sam would be visiting and handed the card to the human. Sam and James went to the last room Lily had mentioned and found its design to be only marginally different from the other two. Instead of a bed, it had a plush sofa and loveseat. A touch-tone phone and several remote units sat on an ornate glass table. Sam dropped down into the soft couch. James picked up the remote, turned on the console television that lay across from them, and punched in Dani's room number.

"You'll be safe here," James said. He went on to describe the remote's various functions, including a multi-imaging system that would allow Sam to do split screens, watching both Dani and Angel's rooms simultaneously. She could also relegate either or both of those images to a small box in one corner of the screen while she punched up any of the satellite channels.

The swarthy-skinned man walked to the door.

"You're leaving?" Sam asked.

"I need to spend some time with Lily. And there are arrangements that have to be made for Angel and your daughter."

Sam tensed. "What kind of arrangements?"

"I told you. They're hungry. They need sustenance."

The Zuni's detachment was suddenly no longer a comfort to Sam. "You're going to bring humans here for them to kill."

"Of course."

"You can't do that."

"There's no malice. It's just a necessity."

"Dani's newly turned. She hasn't made her second

332

kill yet. If she can hold out, she'll be human again."

"Odd," James said. "She didn't mention that part to me."

Sam thought once more about the occupants of the car Dani had secured in the desert. Dani claimed that she had not harmed those people. But what if Angel had been correct and Dani was once again deluding herself?

"You can't do this," Sam said. "I don't want any more innocent people to die."

"I don't mean to offend or upset you," James said, "but I haven't been bound by the restrictions of human morality for quite some time. The natural order must seem shocking when you realize that your kind is no longer at the top of the food chain."

Putting it bluntly, Sam thought, yeah, it scares the shit out of me.

"You were human once," Sam said.

"I was."

"Is it natural to be a predator? Is it natural to have to kill to survive?"

"Of course," he said without hesitation. "Your kind does it."

"To animals."

James was silent. His look said *exactly so*. He turned, and was about to put his access card into the inner control pad beside the door when Sam bounded from the couch and stopped him.

"Two years ago, Dani had been turned. She was in bad shape, struggling not to make a second kill. Isabella did something with her. Shared blood. Something. It got Dani through. Can't you do something like that?"

"That *might* work for Dani. Not the other one. Angel either feeds or she dies. It's incredible that she stayed conscious this long in her condition. Besides, what you're describing is dangerous. It's something lovers do. It bonds us."

"You do it for Lily," Sam said. "That's how she avoids making kills."

"I'm not the only one who tends to her needs. Lily is loved by many."

"Loved? Bullshit. Your kind can't *feel* love. You can't feel anything decent. Protecting Lily is in your own best interest. That's why you do it."

"Whatever you say."

"I love my daughter. I want her back. You can help me. I've already agreed to help you."

"And in return, we're saving your lives."

"It's not enough. Besides, if Dani makes another kill and she snaps, she won't be *able* to help you. She won't be able to do what you need done."

James thought about this. "The blood isn't what's really important. It's the essences that are joined. Your daughter might feel—violated. I have no wish to make her hate me the way she hates Bill Yoshino."

"That's your problem," Sam said.

"Or it could go another way. If I do what you ask, she may not *want* to become human once again. And she has the blood of the Ancients in her. I do not. She might not be able to stop once we've begun. I could be killed. If that happens, she will never be your human daughter again."

"Have Lily with you. She can help."

"I can't ask her to do that."

"You don't have any choice. You need all three of us to cooperate. If I hold back, so will Angel."

The Immortal's face became hard, his eyes a bright crimson. "I could *make* you help us. Dani and Angel would never know."

For the first time since she had been locked in the room with the swarthy-skinned vampire, Sam felt afraid.

"They have the blood of the Ancients," Sam said. "They'll know."

James took a step forward. "Maybe."

334

"Do you really want to chance it?"

The Immortal stared at her, his eyes seeming to burst into flames that quickly receded. "No. You win. Remind me never to play poker with you."

"It's not likely."

James nodded. "A kill must be brought for Angel."

"No more innocents," Sam said.

"No," James agreed. "No more innocents."

Chapter Twenty-nine

"You should get some sleep," Lily said over the phone. "When you wake up, it will be over."

"No," Sam said stubbornly. She was yawning almost continuously, despite her steady intake of junk food and Cherry Cokes for the last hour. She had been surprised to find that she had been starving. A kitchenette with a microwave lay down the hall. Lily had reprogrammed Sam's card for access for the additional room, then phoned her when the halls were clear.

Sam was beginning to question if there were really any other Immortals in the complex.

"There are," Lily had cautioned. "But you don't want to see them and you *don't* want them to see you."

Lily had also programmed Sam's monitor system to allow for a view of Lily's control center. Sam watched as Lily and James discussed the problem of Leo Grisham. She phoned Lily's extension by punching in the four letters of the woman's name and was placed on a speaker phone. Together, they agreed that a team should be sent to neutralize Grisham before he could talk.

"Funny," James said, looking up at the camera lens. "You have no compunction about killing our kind, though both our races are born of human women. I suppose the inherent contradiction is lost on you?"

"I suppose so," Sam had answered.

Calls were made. Details given. The killing was bought and paid for with a promise:

"Sure, I can tape that for you," Lily told one of the assassins. "No problem."

The call was terminated. "An Initiate worried about missing *The Young and the Restless.* Seriously."

Sam did not bother to respond to this, though it gave her an idea. "Call me when you're ready."

She hung up, went to the entertainment center, and found a three-pack of TDK blank videocassettes sitting next to the VCR. Stripping the plastic from one tape, Sam inserted it into the machine and experimented. To her relief, she was able to record whatever appeared on the monitor, including the split-screen images.

She watched Dani's image on the television. Her daughter stirred occasionally, twisting around in her sleep. Nightmares seemed to plague her. Sam believed that the young woman would soon wake.

Ten minutes later, her phone rang.

"They're here," Lily said coolly.

Sam felt sickened. Lily was referring to the Immortals bringing Angel's kill. She suddenly wished that she had not eaten.

The red-haired Immortal had already voiced her outrage at having to be a part of the ceremony James had agreed to perform with Dani, and she seemed intensely disturbed by the very idea of Angel *feeding* within the complex. Lily had been concerned that those of their kind who were present and not members of the underground would *sense* the killing and come to investigate.

James had promised that the Immortals who were bringing the kill would remain in the room to soak up whatever psychic energies were released by Angel and

337

her victim. They would ensure that no others of their kind would become involved.

"You should be pleased by this much," Lily said. "The man they're bringing in is a rapist."

"That was enough to put him on the list?" Sam asked in surprise, considering the casual manner in which the Immortals viewed such violations.

"The woman he attacked was the daughter of a made man, a Mafioso. 'The Ancients punish those who bring harm to their allies.' A Vito Corleone line if ever there was one, huh? James said you watch a lot of movies. Me too."

Sam had no interest in Lily's feeble attempts to become friendly. "How do I know you're not just telling me that?"

"I don't care if you believe me or not," Lily said, then slammed the phone down. Sam continued to watch the control room on her monitor. After a brief, heated exchange with James, Lily followed the long-haired Immortal from the room.

Sam touched the "PLAY" and "RECORD" buttons on the VCR and forced herself to watch what happened next.

Angel looked up as her door swung inward. The fear stench rose from the human who was driven into her room. She found it delicious and felt energized by the mounting terror of the dark, sleazy-looking man who had immediately fallen to his knees and begun to beg for his life. Swinging her legs over the side of the bed, Angel looked to the Immortals who had escorted the prey inside.

"You gonna join the party?" Angel asked. "I usually get pretty hot after I get going."

The Immortals laughed. One of the men was a dark-haired Scot with an imposing brow and a pleasing, sardonic expression. He wore jeans and a T-shirt that read, "Hey, yeah, let's *save* those fucking whales!"

The other was a handsome black man dressed in tight, black leather pants and boots, with silver chains dangling from his belt. His hands were encased in fingerless biker gloves. He wore a "Vampyr!" T-shirt. The word "Quest" was painted on his sunglasses.

"A party? Would that we could, darlin'," the Scot said in a mock mournful tone. "Maybe later."

"Yeah, first we've got to read Harry here his last rites," the black Immortal said.

The victim had not stopped crying and begging. Angel pursed her lips and made a kissing motion at him. Then she turned to the vampire clad in black leather. "Quest?"

"His real name is Lester," the Scot said.

"I like it," Angel said, then turned back to Harry. She crouched before the man and ran her fingers along the underside of his jaw. "Oh, I'm sorry, were you feeling neglected?"

Suddenly, Angel's hand transformed into a talon. She drove her index and middle fingers upward, piercing the underside of Harry's jaw, and dragged him onto the bed. Blood leaked from his mouth and his system was immediately thrown into shock.

"Let me do something about that," Angel said as she descended on the man.

Dani was lost in a dream. She had no idea that she had stolen the dream from Dorothea Odakota's mind when she had taken the woman's life. In the dream, Dani saw a vision of her brother, Michael. He was an adult, an Immortal with sky-blue eyes, who united the warring factions of their race and healed the spiritual wounds that had been inflicted on their kind when he was an infant.

339

Suddenly, Dani was lifted from the comfortable environs of the dream. She struggled to stay firmly ensconced in the safe, warm arms of her borrowed fantasy, but she was dragged away.

Someone—or some *thing*—was in her mind.

She lashed out with her power, but this move had been anticipated by her attacker. It raced past her defenses, burrowing so deeply within her mind that she could not harm it without bringing boiling waves of pain upon herself.

Dani waited, then heard its voice.

You know me. You know that you have nothing to fear from me.

Yes, Dani thought. That was right. She *did* know this man.

I can help you, James Yuwai whispered in her mind.

The statement made no sense to Dani. She was fine. *I don't need your help.*

Look outside, James urged. *Come out and see what has control of you.*

Reluctantly, Dani attempted to leave the darkened void of the featureless mindscape and take command of her body.

For an instant, she found herself in a small gray and green room with James and Lily. She was kicking and screaming, lashing out wildly with her taloned hands, biting at their flesh like an animal. Her attempts to arrest her body's movements failed miserably.

Once, her mother had attempted to describe the anger that had welled within her when Richard Sterling had taken command of her body, but words had failed her. Dani now understood her mother's agony and rage. She was a prisoner in her own flesh, unable to make a single movement, or restrict a single motion made by her body. The demon had gained ascendancy. It controlled her body and it was not about

340

to release Dani's flesh until it had fed and sated the incredible need permeating every fiber of its being.

When Dani had been in college, she had absorbed chapters of texts relating to various form of drug dependency. She knew that psychoactive drugs inspired an ever-spiraling pattern of need and desire within the user. The more you took, the more you wanted. She recalled a study in which a rat that had to press a button for cocaine would relentlessly pursue this one activity, ignoring its body's need for food, sleep, water, and sex. If the cocaine supply had not been taken away, the rat would have done nothing but consume until it died.

The demon was the same way. Its bloodneed had blinded it to all else. That was why the demon had wanted to integrate with Dani's personality. In its lucid moments, when it was not being fed, it had sensed that the one activity it loved above all else—the destruction of others, the taking of life—could also bring about its own demise. It needed Dani to sometimes hold it in check, or let it out to feed. Had it been in control, it would take victim after victim, its appetite growing with each kill.

Dani thought of Isabella in her final moments, when her personality had been burned away and *her* demon had been all that remained. Dani had set that creature on fire. Left in its current state, her own demon would have to be put down, trapped in the sunlight, burned to death. If that were to happen now, Dani would also suffer. She *had* to break free.

The taking of Dorothea's life and the knowledge that its power was practically boundless had driven the demon into the open. Now that it was there, Dani wanted to kill it.

Suddenly, she was batted down by the demon, driven back into the recesses of her own mind.

You can't kill it, James said. *Not without killing yourself. What you're fighting against exists within all of us. You can only control it by accepting it, by allowing its essence to merge with your own—*

No! Dani screamed. *Let me die! I don't want to live like this. Just let me die!*

I can't let you do that, James said. *I need you.*

Then the miracle happened.

Sam watched from her room. In one section of her screen, Angel viciously tore the life from the man Lily had sworn was a rapist. In another, she saw Dani's struggle against James and Lily suddenly cease. The young, golden-eyed woman settled back and gently touched the side of James's face. Then she pulled back her lips, eased him to her, and covered his throat with her mouth. Blanching, Lily turned away and left the room.

Dani could not believe what had occurred.

The demon had retreated. It had somehow overcome its own cravings and had allowed Dani to regain control of her body. A wild thought crossed Dani's mind, and when she considered it fully, she knew that her assumption *must* be correct. She had been terrified of the corrupting influence of the demon. It had never occurred to her that maybe it worked both ways.

The demon *had* changed her. She too had changed *it*.

Before the catalyzing incident that had first allowed the demon to emerge, Dani had been a frightened child, unwilling to try anything knew, afraid to trust and to take chances. Then a man named Willis had kidnapped her. His brother would have murdered her, as he had murdered her would-be rescuer, but Dani's power had manifested and she had destroyed the man.

342

The demon had empowered her.

But she was only a child. A sixteen-year-old girl with the blood of a serial killer on her hands. Dani's mind could not make the leap from innocent, repressed child, to liberated, in-control killer. She had been unable to take responsibility for her actions and so, in her mind, she had denied what she had done, and had submerged the demon. A bit at a time, however, the monster had climbed back to the surface, and had finally exploded outward to freedom when Bill Yoshino had made love to Dani, then turned her into an Immortal.

The demon had known that it was not free. It had tried to warn Dani that she would end up as nothing more than a slave to Yoshino and Isabella. When Dani had later been trapped in the basement of the Malibu with Sam, facing that long, terrible night in which she would either have to kill her adopted mother or relinquish her hold on her new existence, the demon had retreated far enough for Dani to make her own decision.

The monstrous entity had not craved a return to isolation, but it had known that Dani was still not ready. If she had gone insane, it would be left without a host. Dani had fought the demon and won many times, and over the years, it had become interested in more than its own survival. While the demon had brought a wildness and a stunning freedom to Dani, she had delivered an element of purity to the demon that had changed its basic nature.

The bloodneed was within her. That could not be denied. It affected both Dani *and* the demon. But she had passed enough of her strength to the creature within to allow it to fight its cravings as she might, to press the hunger down far enough for Dani to once more be in control.

Dani now understood so much about herself. But the question Angel had raised was not resolved. What had she done to Elizabeth Altsoba in the desert?

Two warring sets of remembrances existed in her mind. In one, Elizabeth Altsoba had willed her memories and experiences to Dani. In another, Dani had eaten the woman's soul. She tried to look at those memories, to establish which was the truth, which the lie, but they were hazy and indistinct, shadows that ran from themselves. The harder she pursued them, the farther they would go. She would have to wait for the true memories to come to her, and the false recollections to be burned away forever.

Dani's consciousness fully emerged and took hold of her physical form. She was not surprised to learn that she had not reverted. Her body continued to hold the characteristics of her inhuman condition. Instinctively, she knew what James offered, and felt a strange tenderness toward him as she bit into the flesh of his neck and felt their consciousnesses slowly meld. She was not afraid to open herself completely to this man, and in return, he gave without hesitation or restraint.

Angel lapped at the blood that had splattered on her arm. In her killing frenzy, she had stripped off her clothing and covered herself in blood. Crimson steaks covered the walls. The plush carpeting had been ruined.

Even Quest and the Scot had been shaken by Angel's horrifying display.

"I sure as hell hope you people have a cleaning staff," Angel said with a maniacal giggle. "Cause *I'm* not mopping this shit up."

The Immortals regarded one another. The Scot even managed to smile.

But it was a very *weak* smile.

* * *

Lily watched everything on her monitors. She felt more comfortable there. The sight of Angel making her kill had stirred something within the red-haired Immortal. Once, long ago, she had been as much of a monster as Angel.

Then the dark man had come into her life. Lily understood Samantha Walthers's pain. She had lived through an ordeal not unlike Sam's. The dark man had broken her. Made her less than she had been, less than a human even. She couldn't say his name, couldn't even bear to remember his face.

The dark man was dead. James had killed him for what he had done to Lily.

She turned her gaze to the next monitor. James and Dani might as well have been making love. He was within her as deeply as was possible for one of their kind, and she was within him the same way.

Lily knew that the sight should have been enough to bring her to the brink of jealousy and madness. It was true that she was "tended" by others, but James was the only man she wanted in her life. She was going to lose him. His body language, the manner in which he was giving himself to Dani—far more completely than he had ever given himself to her—told Lily that he would not come to her bed again after this.

She should have been enraged. Instead, she felt nothing but sadness and loss.

"Good-bye," she whispered, touching James's image on the screen. "I—"

Lily is loved by many.

Your kind can't feel love.

She knew what she wanted to say. Three simple words. But it was impossible for her. The words would not come.

Nor would her tears.

345

Chapter Thirty

Enough, James Yuwai whispered in Dani's mind. *Stop. You must stop now, before it's too late.*

Dani allowed James to pull away from her. The gossamer strands that had woven their minds together gently released and their consciousnesses separated.

"That wasn't what I expected," Dani whispered, her eyes closed. She had been lying back and he had leaned over her. Her beautiful, golden eyes fluttered open.

"No," James said, turning his back to her and rising from the bed before she could see him properly.

Suddenly, she felt the hot wetness on her face and neck. Blood. His blood. She felt powerful and alive, her every nerve bursting with energy.

James was hunched over, holding onto the wall for support. "I've got to go. Lily's going to need me."

"Yes. All right."

Fishing out his access card with trembling fingers, James could not manage to get it into the slot on the control panel. Dani thought about going to help him, then decided against it. Finally, James managed to insert the card. The door did not unlock.

"Someone must be in the hall," he said.

They waited together in silence. A minute later, the door popped open. James left the room. The weighted door swung back and sealed behind him.

A single, driving thought moved relentlessly

through Dani's thoughts as she went into the bathroom, turned on the light, and saw her own bloodstained features in the mirror:

He didn't want me to see him like this.

She washed her face. Before they had shared blood,
he would not have cared how she saw him. Her humanity had brought it all back to him. She would
never forget the secrets she had glimpsed in his mind.

*When he had been a teenager, more than a century
earlier, living with his tribe, he had been promised a
wife. She had loved another warrior. James had felt
desire for his betrothed that was stronger than any
passion he had ever known. His power had manifested and he had used it to kill his rival. When the
woman he wanted realized that he had the power to
break her will, to force her to love him, she had exposed him. He had been branded a demon and exiled
from his people.*

*Years later, after learning to survive with his
strange abilities, James felt he could no longer stand
the loneliness. Using his power, he transformed himself into a member of the Oglala tribe. When Sitting
Bull sent word for all tribes to join him at the Little
Big Horn, James had accompanied his new people.
Later, he had followed the Oglala chief, Low Dog,
and fought against Long Hair, the man white eyes
called "Custer." Long Hair's soldiers had been slaugh-
tered, and it had been a great victory for his people,
but for James, that battle had had a price:*

His life.

*He had been mortally wounded on the field of bat-
tle. Had he been human, he would have died. Instead, his innate power had kept him alive, though
his body was still and appeared lifeless. No one had
come to collect him. No one had helped him. Of
course, this had been because none of his people had
recognized his true face. His psychic disguise had
fallen away. For James, bitterness replaced reason.*

347

He surrendered to feelings of hatred and betrayal. They kept him alive and gave him the strength come nightfall to somehow lift himself from the field of battle and stumble off, traveling nearly a mile before he collapsed. Perhaps he was a demon. He would die in the desolate lands, with the spirits of his kind. Those he had considered his own, the humans, would not be given the honor of being present for his dying breath.

His demon father arrived that night. Startlingly, the man had been dressed as a blue coat. That was impossible. He had seen all of Long Hair's men die— felt their deaths. Then he remembered. The blue coats had been broken into three groups of soldiers led by Custer, Reno, and Bentine. An hour after Custer, the last of his regiment, had fallen, Low Dog had taken his people on a final assault against Marcus Reno and his men. Captain Frederick Bentine and his men had returned to strengthen Reno's troops.

Not one of Custer's men had turned and fled. The same, apparently, could not be said of those answering to Reno. At least one had escaped, and he dismounted and knelt before the fallen, disinherited Zuni.

"It hurts, don't it?" the demon father had said. "I can make it better. I can make it so nothing ever hurts you again. What do you think about that?"

James Yuwai, who had then been known as Shadow Walks, because of his unerring ability to close in on an enemy and take him before he was aware of his presence, had given himself to his demon father.

It wasn't until he had allowed his consciousness to merge with that of Danielle Walthers that James had learned that his demon father had lied. He had been hurt. Tearing himself from Dani's mind had been torturous for him, though it had to be done. He would have died otherwise.

All things considered, that might have been preferable. When he had been within her, he had once
again been able to feel love, compassion, and selfless-
ness. These emotions were not simply distant memories that he could long for and never again possess.
For the first time in more than a century, he had
known more than the hollow echo of love, and it had
nearly destroyed him.

Dani went back to her bed, put her face in her
hands, and began to weep.

Sam hit the STOP button on the VCR. She had
been afraid that after James had finished with Dani,
the golden-eyed young woman would be as she had
been two years earlier, when Isabella had shared
blood with her. Dani had been willing to do anything
for Isabella, including sacrifice her humanity. Sam
had intended to show the tape to Dani. She had
wanted Dani to see Angel killing the man in the other
room, and had hoped that any romantic notions Dani
had about her existence as an Immortal would be destroyed by witnessing this display.

Her instincts now told her that would be unnecessary. Sam had no idea what had passed between her
daughter and James Yuwai, but she was certain that
Dani's ultimate salvation was now in the young woman's own hands, and nothing Sam could do or say to
her daughter would make any difference.

Sam's thoughts drifted to her son, Michael. She
wondered where he was right now, and what the Immortals were doing with him. A terrible ache grew
from the pit of her stomach and suddenly overwhelmed her. A searing, intense, fireball of dark
emotions exploded within her, making her wish to
drop to her knees and plead for deliverance from the
horror that had become her life.

No, she thought. She had to be strong. Her loved
ones were counting on her. There was someone else in

her life, a man who had promised that he would die for her, if that was necessary, to prove his love. God only knows what he had already suffered because he had cared for her. She couldn't allow him to endure any more.

Sam rewound the tape, picked up the phone, and dialed Lily's extension. She knew better than to contemplate doing something "cute" with the tape, like trying to smuggle it out of the complex and get it broadcast on CNN. Lily was certainly monitoring her actions and could just as easily listen to her thoughts.

"It's time," Sam said. "We need to talk about exactly how this is going down. One thing. I have a new condition, and it's non-negotiable."

"You want to put all of us at risk for what? Some human?" James bellowed.

Dani had been stunned to see the absolute rage that had overtaken the Native American. Angel, Quest, and Liam, the Scot, had come for her. Dani had removed her wig, showered, and changed into a pair of Vamp jeans and a creme-colored top that had been laid out for her by one of Lily's helpers when she had been in the shower. Angel had been similarly attired. They had joined Sam, Lily, and James in Lily's control room.

"Don't you understand?" James snarled. "It's perfect. You don't have to leave this complex. You're safe here. Nothing is going to happen. All we need is for you to make a phone call and convince either Christian De Santo or Alyana Du Prey to escort Lily to an audience with the Ancients tonight. That's all you have to do. There's no risk. When it all explodes, you'll be here. Protected."

"You don't think the Parliament's going to realize that the damage was done here, at the Net?" Sam asked.

"We'll have you moved somewhere else by then."

"What about my son?"

"We'll find him," Lily said. "I've been tracking the movements of all the Immortals who went to Isleta."

"Alyana took Michael."

"Even better. All we have to do is ask her where he is. She's not going to keep your son from you. That might have made sense before, but it's all about to change. After tonight, our entire society is going to be different."

"What about the Parliament members your people can't destroy?" Angel asked. "They're going to want revenge. I know *I* would."

After having watched the platinum-haired vampire take her prey, Sam could not bring herself to look at the vampire. Thinking back on it, Sam was stunned to think that she had actually started to feel sympathy for this thing. A strange closeness had been developing between them, and it had grown out of more than the intimacy of risking their lives together. Watching Angel kill the rapist had driven away any feelings of warmth Sam might have had for the Immortal.

Angel did not seem to notice Sam's withdrawal from her. She was too high on the blood she had taken, the life she had consumed.

"The surviving members of the Parliament will demand some place in the new order," Lily said calmly. "They'll realize that even the blood of the Ancients eventually wanes."

"After forty or fifty years," Sam muttered.

"Immortals view time differently than humans," James said, his anger slowly abating. "They'll know that if they want to keep the gift they've been given, the ability to walk in the light, they'll have to fall in line. You will be safe.

"If, on the other hand, we go after the Tylers again, as you're suggesting, and we end up harming the

351

twins, Devin Tyler will make hunting down and killing each one of us his personal crusade, no matter what the Ancients command. It's too risky."

"I know you're just worried about your friend," Lily said. "I understand that. But the Ancients will be grateful to us. They'll grant any request we make."

"You don't *know* that," Sam said urgently. "Have you thought about what happens if De Santo and Alyana say no? Or if the Ancients don't sanction your plan? What then?"

James and Lily were silent.

"You've been building up to this for a long time," Sam said. "Are you really going to step down if three old men get worried and tell you no? This is happening whether they agree or not, isn't it?"

"Yes," Lily said in a strange, icy tone. "It is."

"Then Peter's going to get caught in the middle."

"The twins will be gone by tonight," James said. "They'll have flown out to chase after you and Dani. There's no reason to confront them."

"There's *every* reason. They're going to take Peter with them. What do you think they'll do to him when they find out that their father is either dead or ruined and Dani and I were involved?"

"It could be worse," Angel said cheerily. "Leo Grisham could talk."

"He won't," James said. "Our people are waiting for him."

"Why do you care so much about Peter?" Dani asked suddenly. "You hardly even know him."

"I know enough," Sam said, surprised by the jealous edge in Dani's voice.

"The hell you do!" Dani said. "What if you get killed? Who's going to take care of Michael? You can talk about tough choices all you want, but when it comes down to it, he's the reason we've gone through all this, isn't he?"

"Yes. That's why I want you to stay here."

"Good fuckin' deal," Angel said. "No offense, but the hysterics are getting on my fucking nerves."

"I'm not a kid," Dani said. "If anyone should stay behind, it should be you. What happened at the casino should tell you that much."

"You're right," Sam said. "But I'm going anyway." She pointed to James. "As far as I'm concerned, their play doesn't happen unless they back mine."

Angel moved uncomfortably in her chair. She had drawn her legs up beneath her and rocked slightly, a warm, happy smile upon her stunning face. "One last problem. Let's say we make the calls. The underground doesn't need us anymore after that."

Sam nodded. She had considered that. "We'll tell whichever one we get, De Santo or Alyana, that they are not to make the pitch to the Ancients until they've spoken to us and we're safe."

"Uh-uh. If De Santo or Du Prey agrees, it's going to be because of the larger issues, not to save our asses. That's not going to fly."

"Then we get Peter out first. Now. And when we get back, we make the calls."

"No!" Lily cried. "There's not enough time, and security is going to be too tight."

"It'll be worse after nightfall," Sam said.

"If you go back into that place, you'll never get out again," James said. "We were able to take advantage of the confusion last time. This time, everyone's waiting for an attack. Security will be sharp. You won't survive.

"The best thing to do would be to take them on the way to the airport. They'll be most vulnerable when they're in transit, and they won't leave until tonight. If they did, they'd be cheating."

"He's right," Angel said. "It would make them look like a couple of pussies."

"Fine," Sam said. "But we still have this little trust problem. How do we know the underground won't

353

screw us over the second we give them what they want?"

"I have an idea," Angel said as she rolled her chair side-by-side with Lily's and put her arm around the red-haired Immortal. "Since you and Dani are so intent on staying together on this one, how about I go with Lily? The Ancients are going to need to look inside her mind to see that the underground's proposal is really possible. If anything goes wrong, at any time between now and her meeting, I'll slit her fucking throat."

"They could still go through with their attack on the Parliament," Sam said.

"They could do it right now, if they wanted," Dani said in a low, tired voice. "But they won't. Not until they at least get a *chance* to talk the Ancients into agreeing. Angel's right. This is the best way."

Sam looked at James.

"Yes," he said in a dark, angry voice. He glanced at Dani with a strange expression. The flesh of his throat had healed where she had torn it open, but a light patch of pinkish skin marked the area. Concern flared in his eyes. He spoke to Sam, but his gaze remained riveted on her daughter. "All right. But I come with you. I'll even give you Quest and Liam to make up for Angel, if you want."

Dani bit her lip and thought of what they had shared. She knew that although James had been frightened by what had happened, he desperately wanted to experience it again. He would do everything in his power to preserve her life.

"Yeah," Sam said. "That works."

In the back of the room, Liam nudged Quest.

"Hear that, my black friend?" Liam whispered in his heavy accent.

"Call me your 'black friend' one more time and I'll tear off your head and come down what's left of your throat."

354

"Promises, promises," Liam said wistfully. "In any case, we're being *given away.*"

"Shit," Quest said with a laugh, "and here I thought I'd have to wait for my fucking wedding."

Angel made the call to Christian De Santo. He listened to the underground's fevered plea and told them to call him back in an hour, he would have to think it over. They phoned him again at the appointed time, and both he and Alyana were on the other end.

The deal was struck. Arrangements were made. The line went dead.

Angel turned to Lily, giggled, and said, "Come on, honey. Let's get some sleep."

Chapter Thirty-one

Earlier that day, Dani had walked in the sunlight. The memory was the only one that kept her sane that night as she sat in a dark van that had been provided by the underground. She waited with James and her mother for the Tylers to leave the hotel and casino. Quest and Liam were in another car, keeping a much closer watch.

Leo Grisham was dead. His threat had ended. The Immortal had been executed at nine o'clock that morning. Lily explained later that it had been too late for any of their operatives to get into the room of "Pamela Tyree," but she'd had people pick up the Taurus and reclaim the rest of their weapons and gear. Then the vehicle had been stripped and burned. James's Jeep had received identical treatment. The Immortals would soon recognize his complicity in the attack and come looking for him. Though he had adored that Jeep, he understood the necessity for its destruction, and had stiffly nodded and said, "We all make sacrifices."

The room at the Best Western had been populated by two Initiates who were company employees and members of the underground. When they had been rousted by others of their kind searching for the terrorists who attacked the hotel the previous night, both women had had durable alibis for the time of the attack. They'd said they were in other relationships and had taken the room for the privacy it afforded them.

When Lily had been complimented on her expert handling of the situation, she had shrugged and said, "It's my job to take care of the details."

Dani had later found herself alone with James.

"None of that was necessary," James said, referring to the lack of faith that had been shown by Samantha Walthers and Angel and the renegotiated deal that had been struck. "After what happened with us, I wouldn't do anything to harm you. You must know that. Even before, there was no intent —"

"I understand, but my mother didn't, and there's no way she ever could. I appreciate what you're doing for her."

"She's wrong, you know. She's going to risk getting all of us killed."

"I know," Dani said. "The thing is, she would do the same if it were for me or for Michael."

"And you would do it for me?"

Dani lowered her gaze. "You don't have to ask that."

"But your mother wouldn't put herself at risk to save any of our kind except you. What happens if you come over?"

"I don't know," Dani said. "I really don't want to think about it."

James paused, then said, "You're going through with this. The sun's out and you're going outside."

Dani nodded. She was terrified by the prospect, but she insisted that it was necessary. She had to be certain that the blood of the Ancients would truly protect her. It was close to eight in the morning when James went with Dani to the elevator, handed his access card to her, and promised to wait. The Immortals who made their home in the underground were safely in their rooms.

She rode up in the elevator and tensed as it came to

357

a stop and the doors opened. No one was around. She walked into the parking garage and could see the light in the distance. Her fear welled up in her, but she went on anyway.

The first brilliant tongue of sunlight struck her arm and she flinched, but held her ground. There was no pain. Slowly, she walked completely into the sunlight.

Dani could not believe the sensations filtering through her system. Instead of taking her life, the sun *gave* her life. Every cell in her body felt energized. She understood why Immortals would suffer anything for this, and why those in Parliament considered themselves gods. The feelings were intoxicating. If this was possible, anything was possible.

It did not last. She knew it wouldn't. The gift of the Ancients was within her, but it was *once removed*. After standing in the light for ten minutes, Dani began to feel uncomfortable. Her instincts told her that her inhuman physiology could take no more of the delicious light.

She turned and went back inside. Downstairs, James asked her to describe what it had been like. She kissed him, and delivered the sensations into his mind. Then she pulled away and went down the corridor, to her mother's room.

Sam had been expecting her. Dani climbed into bed behind her mother and slid her arms around the woman, holding her from behind as they immediately fell into a deep, impenetrable slumber.

Dani was snapped from her reverie by a sound from the microwave transmission PC installed in the van's dashboard. A message from the other car flashed across the screen and was instantly processed by the machine's voice emulator:

"WE'VE GOT THEM. LET'S GO." The toneless, computer-generated voice unnerved Dani slightly, but she said nothing. They had been two blocks from the hotel and casino. James pulled into traffic, following the directions dictated by the machine. Somewhere ahead, Quest and Liam kept the Tylers' vehicle within visual range. Communications were maintained strictly through the closed computer link. The Tylers would be scanning for other Immortals. Quest and Liam were shielded, but they would not remain that way if they used their powers.

Sam typed in, IS PETER WITH THEM?

After a pause of no more than two seconds, the machine voice said, "YES."

Angel had been transformed once again. She had not attempted to hide that she was an Immortal. Her new persona had been one that would compliment Lily's accepted life-style. Angel was Kelsey Garris, a shy Southern belle who Lily had discovered on her trip to the Carolinas the year before. According to the story they'd created, Kelsey had been an Initiate who used her abilities to seduce men of true breeding and wealth, with the goal of gradually ascending in the ranks of society and perhaps finding a man who was decent enough to marry and father her children. It had been after she had missed two periods that she had gone to a gynecologist and learned that she was not pregnant and would never be able to bear children. The news had devastated her. Lily had come upon the woman by chance, and they had quickly become lovers. The secrets of their race had been revealed to Kelsey, who had been afraid to embrace her blood heritage.

Lily had returned to her job at the Net, and had nearly forgotten Kelsey, until a letter arrived a week ago. Arrangements had been made for the young woman to stay with Lily. Kelsey had arrived two nights earlier, and Lily had turned her. The Southerner was bright, inquisitive, and thoroughly dazzled by the various glamours of the city. She could charm anyone, human or Immortal, and did not need her powers to achieve this.

The red-haired Immortal had used her expertise at manipulating the various databases of the Net to enter information backing up their claims. USAir's computer showed Kelsey's departure and arrival. Even Kelsey's luggage had been "ticketed" and accounted for. An airport spotter in the underground had been ordered to claim that he had picked Kelsey up and brought her to Lily. Several of Lily's friends would back up the story.

Angel had also been physically disguised. She looked like a soft, brunette beauty queen, and wore an elegant floral print dress combining teal and purple on a black background, tightly belted with a large, pretty, C-shaped silver buckle. Her panty hose and formal shoes were driving her insane, but she hid that information along with her true identity.

Lily had set her hair, pulling it back and styling it so that it was fashionable and not the least bit severe. She wore a blazing red, double-breasted V top with gold-tone buttons that ended at her waist, and a matching crimson skirt.

This time, Angel's attire was entirely appropriate. Tonight, the casino would welcome Devin Tyler for the first time, and a reception was scheduled for after the show. Christian De Santo had already arrived. Angel and Lily went into the hotel lobby and phoned his room. De Santo told them he would meet them downstairs. Security was tight after the bombings, and there was no reason to risk putting the women through difficult mental screenings until there was no other choice.

As they waited for De Santo to appear, Angel thought of Lily's dreams. She had gone to Lily's room and watched over the Immortal as she had slept. Angel had the blood of the Ancients, and she had just fed. Her body did not force sleep upon her, as that of a lesser Immortal might. She remained still and rested, but did not allow sleep to claim her. The nightmares would have been terrible, in any case. They always were, directly after making a kill.

It was preferable to watch Lily's dreams unfold.

The red-haired Immortal endured nightmarish visions of a dark, shadowy figure — a man who had violated her in unimaginable ways. Angel wondered who this man had been, but she could not make out his identity. Lily's potential to be anything more than a frightened instrument of others had been destroyed by this creature. Feeling pity for Lily was not within Angel's capacity, but she felt she would have enjoyed meeting the woman before she had been attacked. They would have had much in common.

They waited near a hall that contained six elevators, three on each side. Suddenly, one of the elevators reached the lobby and Angel was struck by the urgent need to get away. She wasn't easily given to panic, and so she respected these feelings of apprehension and acted upon them when they came around. Angel took Lily's hand and dragged her back, lashing out with her power to force a small group of humans to start embracing them and speaking warmly to them, as if they were relatives or close friends.

The reason for Angel's concern soon became apparent. Two men left the elevator and walked past Lily and Angel as if they weren't there. Angel recognized them instantly. She had spent time with them the previous day, at Dorothea Odakota's home.

They were Allen Henkle and Ted Lewis, the other two members of Parliament whose Advocates had been allowed to enter the competition to fill the organization's two open slots. Both men were dressed in expensive designer suits.

After Henkle and Lewis had gone down the corridor, presumably headed for the casino, Angel released her hold on the humans and sank against the wall. Maintaining a shielded persona and utilizing their power for other purposes was a painfully difficult art to master. Dani had known instinctively how to perform this task. Angel had labored for sixteen years before she had been successful at it.

"What the hell are *they* doing here?" Angel hissed.

"They probably heard that Christian and Alyana were coming to pay their respects to the Ancients. If you were them, would you allow yourselves to be outdone?"

"Yeah, I guess those sons of bitches never miss an opportunity to kiss ass."

"I'm sure they didn't notice us. Relax."

"That's not the only problem," Angel said. "Think."

Lily's features grew tight as comprehension washed over her. If Henkle and Lewis were here, their Advocates, who also wanted Danielle and Samantha Walthers, might also be in Vegas. Fortunately, Lily had accessed the files on Henkle and Lewis's Advocates and either woman would recognize them if they suddenly appeared.

The thought brought only a slight degree of comfort to Angel as another elevator opened and Christian De Santo immediately walked in their direction. He greeted them warmly, kissing the hands of both women, and did not seem to recognize Angel. Knowing her disguise was effective enough to deceive a man who had been in her mind and uncovered her secrets made Angel feel a little better. It was possible they would pull this off after all.

Lily explained that Henkle and Lewis were in the hotel.

"I know," De Santo said. "I ran into them upstairs. I wouldn't worry about it. They made reservations weeks ago, the moment they knew the Ancients would be attending."

"When do I talk to the Ancients?" Lily asked.

"Direct," Christian said, utterly delighted. "Good."

Angel restrained a smile. She had told Lily to take this tack with him.

"Alyana is attempting to schedule a private meeting before Devin's performance," Christian said. "If she fails, there's always the reception afterwards. This is a matter best handled discreetly, and a crowded ballroom is not my preference. But if it comes to it, we'll have to make do."

Angel wondered why in the hell she felt so reluctant to reveal herself to De Santo. Suddenly, she recognized the look in Christian De Santo's eyes, the excitement she had only seen on rare occasions. He was making a play of his own, she realized.

"Do you think they'll need time to think it over?" Lily asked, oblivious to Angel's mounting concern.

"You've never been in the presence of the Ancients before," Christian said. "They do everything very quickly. In fact, I'll tell you this. If we're still alive after the proposal is made, we may take *that* as their answer."

Chapter Thirty-two

Devin Tyler was sitting alone in his dressing room when a knock came at his door.

Fuck, he thought, hoping it wasn't that *bitch* from *Entertainment Tonight* again. If it was her, he was going to twist her fucking legs behind her back and break them off. Screw the million-dollar insurance policy she had on those legs. To hell with the Ancients' prohibition on harming media figures who had made their "A-list." The whore had been following him around all day, shoving her goddamned microphone in his face like she wanted to diddle him with it. He had wished to spend a quiet day with his boys before they set off with the Indian to nail the Walthers sluts. With any luck, Clint and Jeremy would skin those cunts and be back at the casino by tomorrow night. But the Walthers sluts had proven to be fairly resourceful in the past, and the hunt could take a while.

He had told his sons to at least wait until after the show. The Ancients were here, and he wanted his boys to pay their respects before they took off. Henkle and Lewis were going to have their dogs with them to lick in between the fucking toes of the three old men.

Clint and Jeremy didn't seem impressed by that.

Goddamned kids, he loved them more than anything except his own skin, but sometimes he wanted to beat some fucking sense into them. Hell, even when he did exactly that it didn't seem to help.

The knock came again.

"Fuckin' Christ," he whispered as he got up and went to the door. He pulled it open, ready to slam his power into the newswoman he had come to loathe over the last twelve hours. Several possibilities for punishment had gone through his mind. He might make her frigid, or a complete slut. Yeah, that would be good. Make her want to *fuck* twenty-four hours a day. She would screw anything that moved. Even charge for it, just for kicks. Sooner or later, what she was doing would get out, and she would be bounced off the air. Then he could come back for her, get all he wanted off her himself, then eat her fucking soul.

Or maybe he'd just give her a cocaine habit. It depended on what excuse she gave for bothering him this time. He recoiled when he saw the face of Caiphas, one of the Ancients. The man was even shorter than Devin. The Ancient had been born in 76 A.D., and humans, as a whole, were shorter in those days. For all their power, the fathers of the Immortals could not inspire a growth spurt within themselves. It was a subject those with an ounce of sense did not bring up when in the presence of the diminutive gods. One of Devin's people, a rhythm guitarist, had been stupid enough to allow the Randy Newman song, "Short People" to go through his mind when an Ancient had come visiting. The musician had disappeared before the show that night, and had been mailed back to Devin, one piece at a time. Devin had made it a point never to employ humans again. Only those who understood their place with respect to the Ancients would work for Devin Tyler.

The Ancient's flesh seemed to burn with a limitless inner fire, as if it were nothing but a colorless, gossamer veil hastily thrown over a wellspring of unimaginable power waiting to explode. Only those who had partaken of the Ancients' blood could see them this way. Humans and the uninitiated would see the man

365

as robust, with downy white hair and proud Roman features. He wore a charcoal gray designer-original suit with a matching shirt and white silk tie. His expensive watch gleamed and the rings he wore sparkled.

"Sheee-ittt, buddy," Tyler said. "You should have given me some warnin'. I'd a slipped my fuckin' shades on."

"It's good to see you," Caiphas said. "I trust everything's going well?"

Devin decided not to mention the bitch from *Entertainment Tonight*. "Fine, right fuckin' fine, you bet."

The hawklike nose of the Ancient wrinkled, his nostrils flaring. "Those *are* Vamp jeans, aren't they?"

"Hey, you know it. Can't you tell from your own product line?"

The Ancient smiled. "Every pair on the market looks the same to me. The only difference is the ad campaign."

"I know that, but we got us a bunch of ads that's workin', and that's what really matters. The bottom line, thet's all you can count on, right?"

"That is what we respect most, yes. That's why you and yours have always been my favorites. You help to secure that *bottom line.*"

"Well," Tyler said, the word coming out as *way-ellll*, "I sure hope it comes down to more than that between us."

"Of course," the Ancient said genially.

Devin Tyler grinned. He knew that was a goddamned lie, but he didn't say anything and he allowed no trace of distrust to flicker across his conscious mind. "Don't get me wrong, it's not that I ain't happy to see you and all, but I was wonderin' what brought you back here. I wasn't expectin' to see you and your partners until the reception, later on."

It had become common practice to refer to the triumvirate of Ancients as "partners" rather than as brothers. In truth, they were the sons of Antonius,

366

the first of their race whom they had killed. Though the doctrines of Antonius were widely held as the accepted beliefs of the Immortals, the Ancients wished to stand on their own, instead of allowing themselves to be diminished by their father's memory.

"I was hoping to see Clint and Jeremy before they set off on their expedition," Caiphas said in his melodius theatrical voice.

Take away some hair and he'd be the spitting fucking image of Jean-Luc Picard from *Star Trek Lite* or whatever it was called, Devin thought, managing to bury the comparison deep in his mind before the Ancient could hear it.

Devin swallowed hard. "They—uh—they wanted to pay their respects, they shoarly did, but you know how it is when you're young and the thrill of the hunt's in front of you. And it would have been pretty late by the time they could have gotten away from the party. You know, they only have the one-day advantage before Ted and Al get to release their Advocates, and—"

"The boys have already left?"

"They have, sir. Yes." He said it as *yay-assss*.

"I'm not offended. I admire their enthusiasm. How long ago did they leave?"

"Not long at all. We just figured, y'know, that y'all would be busy an' such, and that you wouldn't want to be bothered before the reception."

"Do you think they've reached the airport yet?"

"I doubt it."

"They took the limousine?"

"Yeah." A moment later, Devin understood the Ancient's meaning. As he relaxed, his accent became even more pronounced. "Hey, surely now, thet's a wonderful idea, it shoarly is. I'll just dial them up and they can say a right howdy-do, how would that be?"

"Fine."

Devin picked up his phone and punched a number

on the speed-dial. The phone was answered on the second ring.

"Adrien Cassir."

Devin had sent his personal manager along with the boys to make sure they kept out of trouble. "Hey, you butt-lickin' slime-screwin' bag of shit, how the hell are you?"

"Fine, Mister Tyler," Cassir said.

Christ, he sounded *just* like a fucking lawyer, Devin thought.

"I take it you wish to speak to the boys?"

Devin laughed. "I don't, but I got someone right important here who does. Put them wonderful little snots on the line, why don't you?"

Suddenly, another knock at the door. A furious pounding.

"*Jesus,*" Devin snarled. "Do you fuckin' believe that? Don't these fuckin' pinheads realize thet yoah in here and this should be treated as a place of some fuckin' respect?"

"My people are outside that door," the Ancient said. "It must be important."

Devin blanched. "I'm shoar."

Clint came on the line. "Hey, you miserable, piss-drinking, son of a snake! Your dick fall off yet?"

"Hold on," Devin said, in no mood to continue the game he had started. His sons had obviously been scanning Cassir's mind. The manager was only an Initiate, after all, hardly powerful enough to ward off inquiries from two young men with the blood of the Ancients in them.

Clint quieted instantly.

Rising, Devin went to the door and practically ripped it from its hinges as he tore it open. As the Ancient had predicted, one of the old man's people stood in the doorway. Caiphas's assistant, who, to Devin Tyler, looked like just another *GQ* pretty boy in a suit he couldn't afford, nodded and said, "We have someone here you should speak with, Mr. Tyler. He says that he has important information regarding the incident last night."

A thin, blond-haired young man in an ill-fitting black tuxedo was ushered into the room. An Initiate. Twenty at the most. The assistant to the Ancient pulled the door shut behind him, leaving the young man sealed in the dressing room with Devin Tyler and the Ancient. The young man looked at Caiphas and was terrified to make a sound.

"Let's start with yoah name, you little shit, an' why this was so all fired up important that you had to pick this minute to fuckin' bother us."

The Initiate shuddered. His gaze darted between the two older men. The young Initiate's lips trembled, but he did not speak.

"Maybe I'm not making myself clear," Devin said. "Open your fuckin' hole and make somethin' god-damned good come out or I'm gonna peel your fuckin' *mind!*"

The Initiate managed to overcome his fear long enough to mewl, "David Farmer. My name's David Farmer. I'm a baiter. I saw something last night. My boss, Leo Grisham, they killed him because they thought it was him, but it wasn't. It was his user-ID, but I was the one making the request. They got him. Do you understand what that *means?*"

Devin Tyler closed on him. "I don't have a fuckin' clue. Why don't you try enlightening me, or else I'm just gonna wash that information right out a thet rat's nest yew call yoah hair, and when I do it, you ain't gonna have right fuckin' nothin' at all between those fuckin' ears of yours. . . ."

Chapter Thirty-three

Devin Tyler glared at David Farmer. The Initiate was paralyzed, unable to speak. Tyler would have taken the Initiate's secrets the moment the young man had been ushered into the room, but the Ancients deplored acts of violence in their presence. He had hoped to scare the little shit into talking, but that wasn't working. In the background, he could hear his sons talking to Adrien Cassir in their limousine. The line was still open. It was reasonable to assume that they could also hear everything that transpired inside the dressing room.

"Talk, you little bastid," Devin Tyler snarled. "I'm running right the fuck out of patience with you."

David turned and looked at the Ancient, whispering, "Ah — ah — my lord, um, I beg your pardon, but, ah, Mr. Constantine said it would be okay."

"Hey!" Tyler screamed. The Initiate's gaze snapped back to the singer. "He wasn't fuckin' talkin' to you. *I* was fuckin' talkin' to you. Don't you fuckin' disrespect me now."

Farmer bit his lip and looked back to the Ancient. "Um, shit, ah — "

"Thet's it, that's just too fuckin' much," Devin screamed. Images of his sons missing this opportunity to make things right with the Ancients flooded into Tyler. He pictured them disconnecting the line as they arrived at the airport and headed off for fuck knows where.

Farmer's gaze darted back and forth between Tyler and the Ancient. The dressing room was not very large. Tyler had the Initiate against a wall in seconds. A rack of sequined costumes stood beside the young man.

Tyler cursed inwardly. The little son of a bitch wasn't going to say anything of any value and he didn't have any more time to waste. Ignoring the Ancient, Tyler lashed out with his power.

Clint and Jeremy had each done three lines of cocaine, taken barbiturates, downed a bottle of whiskey, and smoked a joint. Their inhuman metabolisms absorbed and dealt with the drugs so quickly that the pleasure they received from the high was no better than a human might get from a cigarette, but the light buzz was appreciated. To get themselves "fucked up right and proper," they would have needed to take several overdoses. That was not necessary tonight. They were on a natural high. The operatives they had hired to follow their prey had reported success. According to their intelligence, the Walthers women and their protector had returned to Los Angeles and were busy attempting to dig in and set up a trap for the Tylers.

It had not occurred to the Tylers that their operatives had been misled. They had no idea that Alyana had anticipated their duplicity and had sent high-powered Initiates to impersonate Angel and the Walthers women, leading the Tylers' people astray.

At the moment, they were completely full of themselves. They were certain that they were going to hop on a plane, go to the killing ground, do their business, and come home to be inducted into the Parliament. When the phone had rung and Adrien Cassir had given the line to Clint, both brothers had been overtaken by the giggles. After all, they would soon be able to grab some prime Immortal ass. Danielle Walthers and Olander were gorgeous. They couldn't wait to fuck them and make them scream. Maybe they had that backwards, who could say?

Then their father had told them to wait, and they had heard some kind of disturbance on the line. Clint popped the receiver into his lap and settled back in the limousine. Adrien Cassir ignored them. He showed no more interest in their words than the glassy-eyed Native American who sat across from them.

"Who do you think it is?" Jeremy asked with a mild degree of caution.

"Probably that fuckin' feeb from MCA who wants to sign us. Let him put in a bid like everyone else."

"You know, we probably should have stayed to see Daddy perform."

"Seen it, done it, been there."

"Yeah, but this is a special night."

"For who? Daddy? He don't give a fuckin' rat's ass. He's gonna lose money on this deal. He just said yes to make the fuckin' old farts happy."

"The Ancients wouldn't like being called that."

"Fuck the Ancients. They won't live forever. Hell, maybe when we get in Parliament, we can fuckin' make sure of that."

"Clint!"

"Well, sheee-ittt. Don't get all wet and juicy on me now. Christ, sometimes you're such a fuckin' pussy, I swear to Christ and the Devil—may he pee down my throat—you *are!*"

Jeremy sat back and crossed his arms over his chest. "Maybe you're right."

"Damn straight I am," Clint said. "Damn fuckin' straight."

David Farmer gasped as Devin Tyler transformed. He had known that Tyler was an Immortal and a major player with the Ancients, but he had bought three of the man's recordings anyway. There had been something soothing in the man's music. His voice had a majesty that had nothing to do with his powers. Stripped to its essence, Tyler's music had true beauty and artistry.

That could not have come from the twisted soul of a true Immortal. Somehow, Tyler was different, David had decided. A man who knew the true meaning of compassion. That was why he had chosen to seek out Tyler when getting an audience with the assistants to the Ancients had proved impossible. The appearance of the old man and his entourage had nearly frightened David off. Then one of the Ancient's men had come for David, reached into his mind, and decided to allow David the pleasure of passing on his information in person.

When he had seen Devin Tyler in the room, David had known that all his preconceptions of the singer had been without foundation. Tyler was a monster. The Ancient, however, did not seem so formidable. The older man had a calming air, a sense of perfect serenity that was so utterly seductive, David wanted to rush into the man's arms and be embraced.

Devin Tyler was not going to allow that to happen. The singer had transformed — something else David had never been able to picture — and he was thrusting his talons into David's chest with blinding speed. Pain exploded in David's brain. He was certain that his soul was being ripped from him as his flesh was being savaged.

He had no time to scream. Death was upon him in a heartbeat.

Angel and Lily reluctantly followed Christian De Santo to the casino. Lily raised an objection before Angel was forced to do it herself.

"Henkle and Lewis came this way," the red-haired Immortal said. "We're running a risk every time we run into them."

"The casino is the best place to keep yourselves concealed for the moment. Your disguises will turn away the attention of any spotters, and I'm sure you're both strong enough to resist the temptations that wait inside."

Angel was rattled. If De Santo actually believed her created persona, he would never think she was strong enough to resist the incredible forces within the casino. Dani had the blood of the Ancients, once removed, and it overwhelmed her.

Perhaps that was the point. "Kelsey" would have no reason to resist the clouds of fear and desire in the room. Lily was supposed to be showing her new charge all the decadent wonders the city had to offer.

To make this work, Angel would have to submerge herself even farther into her character, which would again help in her disguise. Dani's attack on the Tylers was a simple, straightforward matter, the psychic equivalent of a drive-by shooting. Not that something couldn't go wrong. God knows, it always did. She would just have to stay alert.

Angel followed the others to the casino.

"Come on, you fuckin' pussy. You're not dead."

David Farmer was stunned to find himself alive. He looked down at his chest, expecting to find a gory, bloodstained mass, and instead learned that he had not been touched.

Tyler had done it all with his mind. He had made David believe that he was being murdered, when, in fact, nothing was happening to him.

"You fucking bastard!" David screamed, launching himself at the singer.

Tyler caught him easily and drove him face forward into his makeup table. A sharp crack echoed in the room, and David fell back, clutching his skull.

"Well," Tyler said, his drawl transforming the word into *way-ellll*, "at least you can form sentences now. So how about you go ahead and let us in on this little secret of yours?"

David rose to a sitting position and glared at him.

"Shit, if you're gonna fuckin' *pout* now, I'm gonna fuckin' kill ya for real."

Those were brave words, Tyler realized, but the kid didn't know the difference. Tyler had wanted to strip Farmer's secrets from him, but they were protected. Some impenetrable psychic shell encased them. Constantine had probably placed it there. Tyler could kill the boy easily enough, but he could not get to Farmer's information. Therefore, he had decided to scare Farmer. Even that was not working. They were losing too much fucking time!

Managing to climb to his feet, David waited for the throbbing in his head to go away. It didn't. All the while, the Ancient had been watching with a patient smile that David now found thoroughly patronizing.

He had come here with information that had increased geometrically in importance with the death of that scumbag, Leo Grisham. David had realized that it wasn't Grisham the killers had been looking for, it had been *him*. He might have considered the possibility that the killing had nothing to do with David's exploration in the database the night before, but Grisham's killers had dispatched the man in the exact same manner that seven others had been killed in the past year. Grisham had been shot through both eyes, then his head had been cut off, his body burned in a bathtub. The underground's assassins took their victims in this way. He had decided that the golden-eyed vampire with the blood of Ancients had been involved with the underground's attack on the casino the previous evening. If they had killed Leo, there could be only one reason.

In retrospect, he was grateful that his own doubts and then Leo had stopped him from putting in an alert the night before, with his name attached. The information would have been squelched at the Net, where the underground had infiltrated, and *he* would have been killed instead of Leo.

In David's mind, the conclusions had been obvious: The underground was inside the Net. The golden-eyed vampire belonged to the underground. A member of Parliament had given her the blood of the Ancients. It followed that a member of Parliament was involved with the underground, and the key to learning his identity was the golden-eyed Immortal.

True, he had not decided to inform on the underground for altruistic reasons. Safeguarding the structure of their society only mattered to him if it meant providing himself with a better position in the hierarchy. What he had been shown since he had walked into Devin Tyler's dressing room had been a total disregard for his worth as an individual. Even if he imparted his knowledge, he would be nothing more than a means to an end. The Immortals would probably kill him so that he could not accidentlly reveal what he had learned to others of their society.

Leo had been right. He should have just let it go. Now he was a dead man walking, and he had no way out of this situation. If he refused to give up what he had learned, they would rip his secrets from his mind, then kill him afterwards. Tell them and they would dispose of him as they would any other loose end.

This was it. He was dead.

David wondered how one of Stephen King's villains would have reacted in this situation. Though he was about to be killed unfairly, he could still not bring himself to once again project himself into the company of King's stable of sympathetic monsters. He knew that he would probably do the same to the other two men in the room, if their positions were reversed. "Go fuck yourself," David said.

"Shit," Tyler said. "Now I'm really pissed." The singer turned to the Ancient. "I've really taken all I can from this hunk of shit. You have any problem with me shutting him right the fuck down?"

The Ancient nodded. "As a matter of fact, I do."

Angel found herself drifting away in a haze of indescribable pleasure. She had almost forgotten how wonderful it was simply to feed, to live for no other reason than to satiate her own hungers.

The casino was packed. Immortals had driven the humans into a frenzy that was even more intense than the one Angel had experienced the night before. Angel lapped at the fear and desire radiating in sumptuous waves from the humans. A part of her worried that she might become so enraptured by the cloud of ecstasy engulfing her that Angelique Marie Olander might suddenly cease to exist.

Gamblers drifted past. Lily and De Santo were beside her, pleasantly chatting about the casino, her work at the Net — basic conversational bullshit. Angel monitored their words, missing a few here and there, not really worrying about it.

Her consciousness was on the verge of tumbling into a delightful abyss when she saw Christian De Santo and Alyana Du Prey enter the casino.

Impossible, she realized. De Santo stood beside her. She turned to Lily and her employer, saw the momentary panic flicker over their faces, and realized that she had fallen into a trap.

Caiphas watched the cowering human. The poor miscreant actually believed he had been issued a reprieve. The Farmer boy had no idea that the Ancient had already taken his secrets and had decided not to share them with Devin Tyler. The shielding Tyler had found in David's mind had been placed there by the Ancient. The old man's senses had always been remarkably acute, even before Antonius, his father, had turned him into an Immortal. The phone line had still been open and he had heard every word that had been spoken by Jeremy and Clint Tyler in their father's limousine. The ungrateful little shits *deserved* to be killed by the Walthers child. He would do nothing to alert them.

Later, at the party, he would tell Ted Lewis and Allen Henkle to inform their Advocates that the Walthers women were here in Las Vegas. Henkle and Lewis might have been surpassed in grosses by Tyler, De Santo, and Du Prey, but they had more loyalty than Devin Tyler or his spawn would ever display. Also, *their* Advocates showed incentive. The Tyler boys had been handed a glorious honor, and they had spat upon it. Caiphas no longer wanted their kind in the Parliament, and this was a good way of seeing them destroyed.

He wondered how Walthers planned to kill Tyler's wretched children, and fantasized about Walthers rigging the Tylers' plane to explode. That would be perfection. The brats would die while their father was on stage. Devin would miss a few engagements, certainly, but the public outpouring of sympathy for his loss would provide increased awareness and sales for his releases, and might even inspire some interesting lyrics from the self-absorbed Tyler. After all, there was no such thing as bad publicity.

Caiphas was happy with that. All in all, it was a win-win situation. If the Walthers child hadn't considered blowing up the plane, or was unable to kill the Tylers in some other way, Caiphas himself would make the arrangements, then blame their deaths on the underground. As to her involvement with the underground, he surmised that the attack on the casino last night had been a failed attempt by Walthers. If she'd had knowledge of the underground, it would have been a wise move to blame her actions on the movement. She had, in fact, succeeded in deflecting suspicion from herself.

The Net would be scoured, though Caiphas considered it doubtful that any of his people had been turned. In truth, he didn't believe there actually *was* an underground. The screening procedures and other safeguards were tight enough to prohibit any such infiltration. He recalled that Samantha Walthers had a friend in Los Angeles who specialized in breaking into world-class computer nets. It had probably been this man.

That implied, of course, that Walthers had killed Leo Grisham. Not likely, from what he knew of the child and even her adoptive mother. But Angelique Olander, De Santo's Advocate, was with Walthers, and she was one of the most ruthless little bitches he had ever encountered.

Whatever. He would find out the truth soon enough. For now, the boy had to be destroyed. At least he would be more merciful about it than Tyler would have been.

Caiphas opened his arms and drew the boy close. He made certain that David Farmer was overwhelmed by a sense of happiness and belonging when the Ancient struck, shutting down the boy's consciousness and extinguishing his life with the ease of one who had been performing this task for nearly two thousand years.

Farmer's body dropped to the floor. Devin Tyler stared at the Ancient in open disbelief.

"I don't understand," Tyler said slowly, cursing himself inwardly for bringing the matter up at all. He had no business questioning an Ancient.

"Call it a whim," Caiphas said. "Or an old man's prerogative. Besides, I was hungry. And you know as well as I that those of our kind make the tastiest meals. Now, are your sons still on the line?"

Devin said that they were.

Smiling warmly, the Ancient said, "Let me talk to them."

The singer touched the button for the speaker phone.

"Boys!" Caiphas said. He had no intention whatsoever of revealing the information that might have saved their lives. "You're embarking on an adventure. I merely wanted to extend my warmest wishes and bid you a *very* fond farewell."

Chapter Thirty-four

Liam and Quest followed the Tylers' limousine. The tall, handsome Scot had changed T-shirts. He had debated on wearing either his "Will work for sex" shirt or the one he had on, but he knew this one would drive his partner crazy, and so he had gone with "Yeah, but what did that cow ever do to *you?*"

Though they no longer required human food for sustenance, many Immortals had never lost the taste for such pleasures. Liam was not really a devout vegetarian. He enjoyed consuming animal flesh, and occasionally ran to a steak house when Quest was otherwise engaged. They had been partners and close friends for three years. They had gone to see *The Cook, the Thief, His Wife, and Her Lover* together, and the denouement — Helen Hunt forcing her husband to eat the flesh of her lover, whom he had ordered killed in a particularly gruesome fashion, and crying "Cannibal!" as she shot him — had been a running gag with them for almost a week.

One night, they had stopped at a Burger King and the line had come up. Liam had ordered from the salad bar, and said that meat-eaters of any kind were cannibals, Quest the worst of all. The Scot would have dropped the matter and moved on, but it had inspired a startling reaction: Quest had become truly pissed off. It turned out that when he had been a human, in the pioneering days of the "Old West," he had struggled to maintain a cattle herd, and even now owned stock in livestock and meat-distribution companies. He had strenuously argued in favor of the cattle industry, and had gone on to rail about the government's seeming inability to help the American farmer during these terrible times.

Liam had liked Quest far too much to let any of this slide. They were not lovers—in fact, Quest wanted no part of Liam's "escapades" with male humans and Immortals alike—but that issue had not stopped them from becoming the closest of friends. Not that Liam would have wanted to take Quest as a lover. It would add layers of tension to their working relationship and might even spoil their friendship. Better to limit getting his rocks off to the good-natured little annoyances he knew were acceptable to Quest.

The T-shirt had set Quest off, just as Liam knew it would. Quest was in the middle of a tirade that was beginning to get a bit old, and so Liam, who had been driving, cut a quick glance to the street and said, "Well, isn't that something? A revival theater showing *Blacula*."

"I told you, I don't look anything fucking like William Marshall," Quest snarled. "Do you think I would look *attractive* in sideburns and a mustache? Is that it? You beat off picturing me in a fuckin' cape or something?"

"Ah, my secret's out," Liam said, winking and blowing his partner a kiss.

They stopped at a light in the middle of the strip. Liam allowed another car to get between their white 'Vette and the Tylers' stretch limousine.

"I'm surprised they're paying attention to the lights," Liam said. "They've got the blood of the Ancients. Why bother?"

"Don't want to look too anxious, I guess. The Ancients are in town. Other Advocates could see them."

Another limousine pulled up beside them. The

381

windows were rolled down to allow a view of the occupants.

Quest suddenly became animated. "Shit! Look at that."

"What is it, my black friend?"

"Come on, don't start with that shit now. This is important."

"I'll bite," Liam said. "So to speak."

Quest was in a good enough mood to ignore his partner's inane pun. "I've never seen them up close before."

Liam looked over, and was surprised to see Siegfried and Roy in the car, waving to other motorists and people on the street who stopped suddenly to take pictures. A sudden white flash went off and Liam heard a terrible roar. Suddenly, the duo's famous Albino tiger leaned into view. An image raced up from Liam's childhood, startling him with its ferocity, slicing open a tear in the carefully maintained veil of his memories:

He had been fourteen years old, on a safari with his father. Rolland McVicar was not an experienced hunter. The stories of Rudyard Kipling had inspired the man and he had saved for ten years to go on a true African safari. He had not been prepared for the sweltering heat, the bugs, and the exhaustion that had wracked him. His dream vacation was becoming a nightmarish test of endurance.

In one startling moment, the hunters had become the prey. A lion they had been stalking suddenly attacked the small party, heading directly for his father, savaging the man. Rolland McVicar's arm was torn off before their guide could squeeze off a shot. The lion had spun at the last possible second, its jaws now clamped on Rolland McVicar's side. The creature thrust Liam's father directly into the line of fire as the rifle went off. The bullet shattered Rolland's spine. The explosion had been enough to startle the lion into releasing the man, and it had raced into the brush, escaping a volley of shots another of their guides loosed with his weapon.

Liam had no idea what he was doing. One moment he was screaming his father's name, the next he was racing into the jungle, following the animal that had nearly killed the man. The guide went after him, while the rest of the hunting party stayed to help Mc-Vicar. Miraculously, despite the loss of blood and the trauma he had endured, the man would live and even prosper, an inspiration to others who had faced such horrifying tragedies. Liam was unaware of this when he chased the animal. He was only conscious of his exploding heart and the feelings of rage and need coursing through him.

The boy had wanted to destroy this creature for what it had done to his father. He had wanted to immerse himself in its blood, to make it feel the terrible fear it had inspired in his own breast.

The guide grabbed Liam just as he caught a glimpse of the animal ahead. He struggled in the man's arms, angered beyond belief that the man was keeping him from his vengeance. As the lion disappeared from view, Liam focused all of his energies on the guide, releasing a fiery torrent of hatred into the man's mind. The guide stiffened as his was burned away, then fell back, releasing Liam. The boy scrambled away, unaware of what he had done, and went on with the chase.

Liam was found two days later. He had not found the lion, and madness had given way to fear that he would die alone in the jungle. The guide's body was found. The lion had doubled back and killed the human. No one except Liam knew that the guide was already dead, his mind nothing but a memory, his body remaining to serve no better purpose than food for an animal.

"What the fuck was that!?" Quest screamed.

Liam was shocked from his reverie. He suddenly found himself back behind the wheel of the 'Vette, staring at the white tiger in the car opposite. Traffic had started to move and suddenly the limousine streaked away. An explosion of car horns sounded from behind the 'Vette, and Liam changed gears and eased back into traffic.

"I asked you a question," Quest said urgently.

"Nothing," Liam said, severely shaken.

"I felt it through my fucking shields," Quest said, "and if I picked it up, you can be goddamned sure that the Tylers caught it too. That and God only knows how much else."

Quest reached for the computer console sitting before him. He wanted to type a warning onto the screen. Before he could manage that task, he felt a searing bolt of psychic energy slam against his own shields. They held. Beside him, Liam suddenly stiffened and floored the accelerator.

It was already too late.

Clint and Jeremy had fused their minds and their power. They had lashed out at the driver of the pursuing car, burning his mind to a crisp, then taking control of his body. They knew they should have taken his memories first, but they were goddamned pissed to have someone following them. The attempt at the casino by the underground had not been appreciated. The ones following them were certainly in league with the underground. They deserved whatever they got. Anyway, as the Tylers were often heard saying, the fucking facts usually just got in the way, so why bother with them?

Traffic had been tight on the strip. They were approaching the intersection of Las Vegas South and Dunes Road. Caesar's Palace, Bally's, the Barbary Coast, and the Dunes were situated at opposing corners. The white Corvette was two car lengths behind the limousine. Clint and Jeremy used their power to control the other drivers and the man they had destroyed, engineering an accident that would kill the occupants of the 'Vette and remove any evidence of their existence.

The light ahead was green. The limousine passed through the intersection. Then they ordered the driver of the 'Vette to leap around the car that had separated it from the limousine and blast into the crossroads. The driver beside the 'Vette, also southbound, was commanded to give him room. Four drivers who had been stopped in the east-west Dunes Road, waiting for the light to change, suddenly floored their vehicles and charged forward.

In the 'Vette, Quest tried desperately to wrest control of Liam's body from the Tylers, but his efforts failed. Liam pulled out of their lane, into an opening to their right which had "miraculously" opened wide, and sped into the killing ground of the intersection. Quest transformed his hands into talons, raked open the seat belts that had held him into place, and threw himself forward, against the glass, as the first of the four cars slammed into Liam's side of the vehicle.

Sam, Dani, and James had left the strip, cutting across Spring Road, sailing down Paradise to Tropicana, then reentering 604 from the northbound lane. Dani had used her power to circumvent traffic, taking control of human drivers to allow them to race through the crowded streets and ignore any lights. They passed a traffic officer and Dani gave him the compulsion to pull into the nearest casino and gamble away whatever money he had in his pockets.

The plan had been to approach the Tylers' limousine from the opposite lane of traffic and strike at the twins before they had any warning. According to the information Quest had provided, the Tylers were traveling with one other man. Their entourage of bodyguards had been left behind. Again, this made sense. They would not want to look like cowards who

385

had to depend on others to protect them from a trio of stinking *females*.

Dani had decided that she was going to enjoy this.

Ahead, she could see that something had gone wrong. The Tylers' limousine had passed the intersection and Liam's white 'Vette had charged after it. Suddenly, two cars from each of the crossbound lanes had rocketed at the car. One car had slammed directly into each side, crushing the 'Vette. Quest was thrown through the glass, his body tumbling to the ground, then rising up into the air as the third car, which had been traveling westbound with no interference, had struck the shattered 'Vette's front end.

The problem had come with the fourth car.

The Tylers, in their mild drug-induced haze, had forgotten to stop the cars coming northbound. If they had, they might have touched James's mind and realized the trap into which they were driving. Their error, however, was twofold. The most pressing effect of their mistake was the rush of oncoming northbound traffic on the strip. The fourth vehicle was a gray Mercedes-Benz driven by a couple dressed in cowboy gear. They had been heading for Devin Tyler's appearance at the Buccaneer. The Tylers had glimpsed this in their minds and found it hilarious. That would not have been the case had they known the impact that car was about to have on their lives.

The Mercedes pulled into traffic just behind the blue Acura Legend that had slammed into the driver's side of Liam's 'Vette and crushed the Immortal's physical shell. But the Acura had been able to pierce a small hollow in the oncoming lane of traffic. The Mercedes-Benz had not been so fortunate. It was struck by an oncoming vehicle with such force that it had jackknifed. The force of impact had caused the car that had struck the Mercedes, a British Sterling, to spiral up and then get struck by another car, a Saab, and get sent into the southbound lane of traffic, landing on the rear of the Tylers' limousine. Their driver had lost control of the limousine and they had collided with four other cars, the front end of a Mitsubishi collapsing their doors and tearing open the upholstery beside them.

From the borrowed van, James watched the crash in surprise, then cut the wheel sharply to the left, hopping the divider and jamming the front end of the van before the Tylers' limousine. A white station wagon collided with them, driving the van sideways, into the front end of the Tylers' limousine.

Dani had grabbed hold of her mother, protecting her from the shock of impact.

"Go! Go!" Sam commanded, and her daughter released her, then unbuckled her seat belt, kicked out the van's passenger side door, and leaped into the darkness and confusion as James burst through the glass of the driver's side window and followed her.

Chapter Thirty-five

Angel allowed her anger to overtake her. The fires of her rage burned away the seductive embrace of the elegant and wondrous sensations she had been consuming seconds earlier. Without hesitation, she discarded all vestiges of her assumed psychic persona. Kelsey Garris was dead.

"The time has come to do away with masks, I see," the Spanish man beside her whispered.

He was not Christian De Santo, Angel had realized. Her employer had entered the casino with Alyana Du Prey, his partner. For an instant, there had been two Christian De Santos. The look the new man gave when he noticed Angel, seeing past her disguise without difficulty, had told her which man had been De Santo and which had been the imposter. The features of the man beside Angel had lost their solidity. They blurred and changed. The moment they reconfigured, Angel recognized him. She had seen his dark, Italian features the night before, at Dorothea Odakota's house, and then again a few minutes ago, near the elevator.

Allen Henkle smiled, the tiny lines at the corners of his eyes crinkling slightly. He ran his hand through his curly black hair. His sexy mustache seemed to rise as he smiled sheepishly. The phoenix ring he always wore sparkled, despite the dim lighting within the casino.

Angel lashed out with her power. She did not care

that murdering one of her own was a crime punishable by death. Henkle and countless others of their kind had committed this act and had blamed it on the "underground." She would be more direct.

The curly-haired bodybuilder recoiled from her psychic lash, but caught her attack easily and turned it back against Angel. Incredible pain seared her consciousness, causing her to stumble back. Fortunately, she had been weakened when she had attacked Henkle, her power dull and unfocused. When the psychic barrage had been turned upon her, it had lost much of its power.

Her psychic talons had come away with gouts of torn, bloody memories. She had been stunned by what she had uncovered in his mind. The truth of what had been going on was far more labyrinthian and horrible than she had expected. Utilizing all of her will, Angel buried the secrets in the deepest recesses of her own thoughts.

Beside Angel, another transformation was taking place. Lily was dying. Angel turned, expecting the red-haired Immortal's appearance to alter, but it did not. The changes were all taking place in the landscape of Lily's thoughts. The outer edges of the metamorphosis grazed Angel's mind.

The face of the dark man in Lily's dreams was suddenly revealed: It was Allen Henkle. The trauma he had inflicted upon Lily was a matter of fantasy, exactly the same as the memories that made up her existence. Lily was Allen Henkle's Advocate and his lover. It had all been shadows and fog, an illusion.

Like the shattered petals of a delicate flower that had been frozen, then smashed into a thousand ice-cold pieces, the last vestiges of Lily fell away. In their place stood a creature that was completely alien to Angel.

"Nice to meet you," the red-haired vampire said. "My name is Rose."

* * *

Dani had been the first to leave the van. She had been armed with several weapons, but her most formidable tool in the coming fight was her inhuman nature. Finishing this off quickly and with the least amount of risk was her only concern. She prayed that her mother would remain in the relative safety of the van until Peter had been taken from the Tylers' limousine and the threat of the twins had been neutralized.

They had decided it was no longer necessary to *kill* the Tylers. In fact, such an act might seriously harm their position in the new order. If all went according to plan, Lily would soon be delivering the underground's proposal to the Ancients. Before the night was over, the entire society of Immortals would be changed forever.

Dani heard James emerging from the van at the exact same second the driver's side door of the limousine popped open and a tall white-haired man emerged. She could sense that he was an Initiate.

"Do it!" Dani screamed to James. Without hesitation, Dani drew her automatic and fired at the man. At the same moment, she could feel James join his power to hers. Together, they lashed out against the occupants of the car.

The two bullets she had fired ripped neatly through the driver's right shoulder and left hip. He spun and fell to the ground, his body immediately descending into shock from the trauma. She had used her knowledge of human physiology to aim away from the major arteries, ensuring that the man would live.

The combined psychic attack had found its targets. Dani was able to feel the shock and fear rolling off the twins as an explosion of unimaginable intensity seared the unprotected minds of the Tylers. She ran to the car, ripped open one of the doors, and leveled her weapon at the face of the remaining threat, a bald, terrified businessman who was also an Initiate. Peter sat next to him in the back seat. The twins had fallen together, their tongues lolling from their mouths, their eyes rolled up into the back of their skulls.

They were not dead. Their fate was infinitely worse. Dani had not realized the extent of her hatred for these men until her power had grazed their minds and revealed the depths of their depravities. They were exactly the same as Richard Sterling and Bill Yoshino. Worse. Once she had learned their true natures, only one punishment seemed suitable:

Their consciousnesses had been driven deep into the pits of their own inner darkness. They were now experiencing the horror of rape from the point of view of their victims. Fear would be with them in all things, incapacitating them throughout eternity. They would know the true horror of having no control over their bodies or their minds. The Tylers' lives were no longer their own. The violations they had performed over the years would be their only waking reality.

This had been a far more suitable punishment than the mercy of death, Dani had decided. The Tylers had earned every bit of terror they would now experience throughout their lives. They had earned this and more, but for now Dani was satisfied. In ways, she even felt free from the fear that had been a part of her ever since Yoshino had raped her. At long last, she had taken back some vestige of her life.

Inside the limousine, the Initiate said nothing as James flew over the top of the limousine, opened the opposing door, and grabbed Peter's arm. He yanked the man from the vehicle as Dani covered the Initiate.

Dani felt herself start to relax. It was going to work. They would be away from here and no one was going to die. She could feel her own *need* rise up at the scent of the driver's blood, but she could control it. The sound of the van's side door sliding back came

391

to her. Sam was out of the van, helping James load Peter inside.

Suddenly, the Initiate grinned. Dani's instincts told her to empty her gun into the man's face, but she hesitated.

That mistake would cost Danielle Walthers her life.

"I imagine you're considering if you can kill either of us and get away with it," Allen Henkle said. "The truth of the matter is, you can't. If you even *attempt* another little display like the one you just put on, I'll have a dozen Immortals on you. The casino is packed with them, as you know. So behave yourself and you might come out of this not only alive, but in a much better position than you were in before."

Angel stared at the man with open hatred. He had taken on the tone he used in his real-estate infomercials.

Yes, you too can be retired and living well before you're forty! I'll show you how!

Angel looked in Christian De Santo's direction. Alyana was on his arm. They caught her look of distress and sauntered in her direction.

"Play this the right way and you come out ahead," Henkle said. "Remember that."

"I'll be a member of Parliament," Rose whispered. "The first woman since Alyana. I'll have my own Advocates. You can be one of them."

"You're part of the second team," Angel said. "This whole thing has been nothing but bullshit."

"Don't sound so hurt," Henkle said. "Do you honestly believe anyone plays 'fair' in these competitions? What was your first instinct? *Find the loophole in the rules.* That was ours as well."

"Who's the other hunter?" Angel asked.

"Does it matter?" Rose said in a dark, sultry voice. "We have room for you in our stable. Why dwell on—"

"Who is it?"

Henkle smiled broadly. "Let's just say he's with the Walthers right this minute."

James, Angel thought. The other Advocate was James!

Adrien Cassir's hand shot out and slapped at Dani's wrist, shoving her weapon hand out of the way as she fired the automatic. The bullets tore into the roof of the limousine as Cassir's other hand fastened on Dani's throat. Suddenly, Dani's bloodneed became an irresistible force that swallowed her whole. Reason failed her. Whatever reservations she had about the taking of a life fell away. She could no longer deny that she was enjoying this. The incredible fear she sensed within the man flowed into her mind. His terror was a banquet, his blood a red-hot fount in which she needed to immerse herself.

She was perfectly aware of her actions as she allowed her body to transform. Her hands became raking talons and her maw filled with razor-sharp teeth. A scream of triumph and delight issued from her as she gave herself fully to her cravings. Adrien Cassir screamed as Dani descended on him, slashing at his throat with a savage motion that tore open his flesh as if it had been soft wax. Dani opened her mouth wide as she allowed a flow of blood to enter her body. She plunged her talons into his chest, pulled it apart, and tore out his heart, all the while feeding and enjoying an orgasmic fugue state much greater than any she had ever known before.

When it was over, Dani looked down at what she had done and scrambled out of the limousine, falling to the ground as uncontrollable spasms ripped through her. She had made her second kill. Her life as a human was forfeit. For all intents and purposes, Danielle Walthers was dead. An inhuman *thing* had taken her place and would remain there forever.

Behind her, she heard the heart-stopping laughter of a man she had known and trusted.

Christian De Santo and Alyana Du Prey greeted Allen Henkle and his guests as they might any competitor, with respect and a flourish of cheery sentiments that meant absolutely nothing.

"Angel," Christian said. "I'm surprised to see you here. I thought you were staying with friends."

This was the moment, she thought. Dani and Sam were probably dead by now. The Tylers had missed their window of opportunity. That meant Rose and her accomplice would soon become members of Parliament.

Henkle had promised that he could shield Angel's mind from De Santo and Du Prey. She did not have to worry about her thoughts giving her away. He had told her that changing her allegiance might not be a terrible idea. Christian De Santo was no longer in the Parliament, and Alyana was universally hated by her kind.

Of course, Allen Henkle had no idea that Angel had torn his darkest secrets loose. She knew that everything he told her was a lie. He was attempting to ease her concerns as he shepherded both Angel and Christian De Santo to their executions.

Christian De Santo reached out and Angel clasped his hand. The moment their flesh connected, Angel hurled a searing bolt of power at her employer's mind. She felt it snake through the openings in the psychic "net" Allen Henkle had constructed to snare any attempts by Angel to warn De Santo. The web of protection he had spun had been relatively weak. He had not expected Angel to reject his "generous" offer.

De Santo shuddered as the burst of information Angel had sent exploded in his mind. At once he understood the nature of the betrayal he faced. There was time only to decide on a course of action he had contemplated for hundreds of years. Already he could sense the gathering of power within his enemies that was the opening movement in the symphony of destruction they had planned.

Without releasing Angel's hand, Christian De Santo took the first step in his long-awaited walk into the light. When the attack came, he was ready for it.

Dani turned and saw the black vampire, Quest. James was at the van, staring blankly into space. Samantha lay at his feet. Dani could sense that her mother was still alive.

Quest came forward as Dani struggled to rise. He raised his heavy, leather boot and planted a kick that sent her sprawling to the ground. "Don't bother, honey. You're mine."

Dani had no idea of the events transpiring at the casino. If she had, she would have been able to tell Angel that she had been wrong. The second Advocate was Quest, not James.

"See, part of the rules said you had to make a second kill." Quest laughed again. "You had to become one of us before the three days had elapsed. Well, we've done that, now haven't we? I mean, just look at you. One hell of a mess, girl, you're one *hell* of a mess covered in all that blood. I bet you feel like such shit that you probably wish you were dead. Well, don't let *me* stop you."

The black vampire loosed a psychic lash against Dani. She tried to shield herself, but she was unable to focus her power. A torrent of nightmares flooded into her mind, and in the midst of them lay the truth.

Dani was stunned by the maelstrom of knowledge flooding into her mind. The "underground" had been a lie, a fiction created by murderous Parliament members to cover their own crimes. Lily, better known as Rose, and Quest comprised the second team of Advocates sent to kill Dani and Sam. They had succeeded where the Tylers had not, managing to follow their opponents to Las Vegas. On the way to the gambling mecca, Lily had devised a plan. Technically, they were not allowed to kill the Walthers women until forty-eight hours had elapsed. However, there was no clause in the rules of the contest to prevent them from befriending the fugitives, taking them to a safe place, and sequestering them until the Tylers were out of the way and the two-day lead Dani and Sam had been given was nothing but a memory.

They had devised a grand conspiracy, utilizing the fictitious "underground" in a manner that would appeal to Dani and Sam's "us against them" leanings. As Advocates, they had access to the Net, and were able to intercept Leo Grisham's inquiries. They also had it in their power to construct dummy files that showed the Advocates of Henkle and Lewis to be Immortals other than Rose and Quest.

James Yuwai had been a natural lure for Dani. As Lily had put it, he was "Bill Yoshino with a fucking tomahawk." They took the hotel spotter and programmed him to believe that he had known the fictitious "Lily" for years, and had been a crusading member of the underground. Liam McVicar had received similar treatment.

Dani shrugged off the brutal psychic attack Quest had included with the knowledge and propped herself up against the car. He had wanted her to die knowing the full extent of his triumph against her. He had even forced her to make her second kill and become an Immortal, a state she loathed, to truly damn her before her death.

"So you're gonna be more of a challenge than I thought," Quest said.

Dani nodded. Incredibly, she felt no different. The

loss of emotions that she had feared had not occurred. She could feel everything she felt before, including her love for her mother. If she were to live long enough, she would learn that none of her race had ever been strong enough to resist the demons of their blood, to actually conquer them as had Dani.

Quest grinned. "I'm supposed to wait for the forty-eight hours to be up. The deal had been to help you get Peter away, get you to another safe house, and keep you there until the two days was up. But I don't have that kind of patience any more. So with apologies to the Chili Peppers, sweetie, your mind was made to *suck my kiss!*"

Dani screamed as Quest turned the full extent of his powers upon her.

Chapter Thirty-six

Angel knew that she would die.

Her mind flashed back to *the moment,* two years earlier, at the warehouse she had shared with Bill Yoshino and Isabella. She had been stunned when she had gone outside to secure prey and instead had come across Samantha Walthers, sleeping in her car. The quickest of scans had revealed that Walthers had rigged the warehouse to explode. The human had held in her hand an instrument that could have ended the lives of the vampires with the touch of a button.

During her time as an Immortal, Angel had not given much thought to the possibility of death. She had been given the kiss of eternity, she would live forever.

Fat fucking chance, she had come to realize that night. Her recklessness had nearly gotten her killed. The only way she was going to survive was if she smartened up fast. Walthers had taught her that lesson, and in return, Angel had broken all ties with her adopted "family" and allowed Walthers to live.

Samantha Walthers had also earned the one thing Angel had never given anyone before:

Her respect.

Angel had no intention of actually telling Walthers that, of course. The woman was supposed to be a detective. Let her figure it out for herself.

As the attack came, Angel hoped that Walthers

would live long enough to solve the mystery of Angel's deferential treatment of the human. It sure as hell didn't look as if Angel would survive to give her any more clues.

Peter Red Cloud had ceased to exist. His mind had been shut down the moment the strangers had broken into his home and attacked him. The two long-haired blond ones had done things to his mind. He was aware of this. If they hadn't, he would not be in the process of bending down and removing Samantha Walthers's fully loaded Beretta from her waist clip. He watched in horror as his body performed tasks he would never wish them to execute. His finger slid the safety off the Beretta and his steady hand aimed the weapon at Samantha's temple. The man's heart rate did not fluctuate as his finger closed over the trigger, despite the agonized cries he issued within his mind.

He loved this woman. When he had told her that he would die for her, the words had not been idle ones. If he could somehow put the gun to his own temple, override the program that was running in his brain to its horrible climax, he would do it. Gladly.

But his finger curled over the trigger and began to bear down.

Somehow he managed to close his eyes as the gun went off.

The information Angel had imparted to Christian De Santo had taken the man completely by surprise. After he had solved the mystery of his son's death and paid off Bobby's debt to Danielle Walthers by arranging for a contest in which she would have a true chance for survival, Christian had been ready to immerse himself in the cleansing flames. He had gone to Alyana, his partner, and told her of his plans. There had been a chance that she would want to join him in the comforting arms of oblivion, he had reasoned. It would do no harm to ask if she wanted to burn with him. They were both very old, he had reasoned, and she might well have also tired of this existence.

Alyana had been extremely disquieted by Christian's plans. She startled him by offering him a reason to live:

Michael.

She had spoken to the Ancients about the disposition of Samantha Walthers's son, and they had given her leave to raise the child herself, provided she chose a male partner in this endeavor. They wanted to ensure that Michael would be raised in a "suitable environment." In other words, they wanted him to grow up to be another sexist bastard like themselves, or at least, to be able to function properly in the Immortals' male-dominated society.

Christian had been stunned by the offer. He'd decided at once to accept. This time, he would not make the mistakes he had made with Bobby. He would raise Michael to be *decent* by any standards. Alyana had agreed with him.

Christian had wanted to see the child immediately, and Alyana had complied, taking him to the home of the Initiates she had enlisted to care for the baby temporarily. He had fallen hard for the infant, staring into his sky-blue eyes for nearly an hour before summoning the strength to speak.

Alyana told him that she thought it would be a good idea for him to accompany her to Devin's premiere in Vegas. The Ancients would be there, and it would be advisable to reestablish ties with them.

Christian had come along. He had seen no reason to distrust Alyana. Their relationship was as close to that of humans in love as was possible for their kind. They had even gone to bed together, and it had been wonderful.

400

Now he saw that her actions had been a matter of convenience, nothing more.

The psychic assault was a joint effort. Allen Henkle had loosed a killing blow intended to burn away De Santo's soul.

Alyana Du Prey had joined him.

Dani did not hear the shot. Her consciousness had retreated and she was unaware of the insanity going on around her in the outside world. The golden-eyed young woman's perceptions had been driven inward as Quest attempted to take her life. All she perceived was the incredible, seemingly endless onslaught of psychic energies the Advocate was hurling against her.

It wasn't enough.

Mentally scarred and burned, Dani stood against the Immortal's attack. Nevertheless, she knew that she did not have the strength to maintain her defensive position forever. One of them would have to break first. Dani or Quest. The loser would die.

Dani considered the weapons she could use against the vampire, if she could only drop her shields long enough to employ them. Dozens of humans had been racing around in the streets, driven mad by the torrents of fear that were being loosed by the Immortals. She could seize a few of them. One could take a weapon from the van and burn Quest.

No, he would be thinking about that. He would be expecting it. Trying to override his command of James was another likely tack. She was surprised that he had not used his fellow Immortal against her.

Quest was in the same position she was, Dani suddenly realized. He could have attacked her physically, or used a surrogate against her, but he couldn't risk letting down his own guard to do so.

Dani grinned inwardly. There was something she

could utilize without being quite so obvious. It was a terrible risk — she would have to let Quest in past her defenses, if only for a fraction of a second, but she could see no other option.

Praying that she would survive this desperate gamble, Dani lowered her shields and lashed out with her power.

Angel could feel Christian De Santo's agony as his mind was seared into nothingness. She had wanted to help him, and had prayed that the information she had given would help him to prepare for the assault. Without his help, she would not survive. Also, he had made her his Advocate when no other member of Parliament would consider her. She owed the man. Nevertheless, she had been drained by her exertions, and Rose was beside her, coiling her power, preparing to strike Angel down. Angel transformed, her hands becoming talons, her ever-widening mouth filling with a collection of razor-sharp teeth, her eyes blazing.

Without hesitation, Angel launched herself at the woman she now hated above all others, Alyana Du Prey. Hell, she thought as she attacked the dark woman, she would be willing to climb into bed with Devin Tyler before she could ever forgive Alyana her trespasses. The woman had meant to kill Angel. She had plotted Angel's death with a cool, businesslike efficiency.

Angel's only desire was to tear the woman's head off before Alyana was finished with Christian De Santo, and before Rose could stop her.

Suddenly, Angel felt an incredible outpouring of power flood into her mind. It permeated her soul with its intensity. She felt as if she were being burned alive by the most vigorous flames that had ever come into existence, and strangely, the sensation was not unpleasant.

So this is what it's like to die, Angel thought, surprised once again that the agony she had anticipated had not yet materialized.

Give it time, a dark voice within her said with a laugh. *It will.*

The voice was wrong. Instead of feeling any kind of pain, Angel felt a strength unlike any she had ever known. She no longer believed that killing Alyana Du Prey was a *remote possibility.* It was a certainty. With the power flooding into her body, Angel felt that she could even slay one of the Ancients, if they were to stand in her way.

She lashed out at Alyana, unaware of the source of her new, godlike power. It didn't matter to her. Nothing mattered except ending the life of the *bitch* who had tried to kill her. Alyana had treated Angel as if she were beneath contempt. The woman was going to pay for that.

Angel had no idea that beside her, Rose had suddenly stiffened, her life snuffed out a fraction of an instant before she could stop the platinum-blond vampire's attack on Alyana. The Immortal did not see Christian De Santo slowly fall backwards, his body nothing more than a lifeless husk. She was uncaring as Allen Henkle, who had helped to deliver Christian De Santo's death blow, recoiled in horror, too late to avoid the fate he would now share with Alyana.

The dark woman raised one hand, suddenly aware of what was about to happen. Alyana could not ward off Angel's psychic attack. The young Immortal had been empowered to a nearly impossible degree. Talons slashing, Angel sliced Alyana's hand off at the wrist, then tore open the woman's throat. Opening her mouth wide, Angel consumed Alyana's blood as the force of her mind pressed forward, ripping open Alyana's thoughts and effortlessly shredding her incredible mental defenses.

Angel could not manage to restrain a giggle as she ate Alyana's soul.

Samantha Walthers had been shocked into awareness by the deafening roar of a gunshot. She turned over, looked up, and saw Peter fall upon her. Catching his limp body, Sam became aware of the smoking gun in his hand. A terrible grief surged through her. Before she could give voice to her feeling of loss, she heard her daughter scream, and snapped her gaze sharply in the direction of Dani and the black Immortal, who seemed to be engaged in some incredible death duel, though neither was physically making a move toward the other. She brought Peter's gun arm around, closed her fingers over his, and aimed the Beretta at Quest.

Before she could fire, James, who had been standing next to the van, paralyzed, suddenly sprang into motion. Tearing the gun from Peter's hand, James transformed. His talons arced downward, in the direction of Samantha's throat.

It was over. Angel was the only one left standing. She was covered in blood. The incredible surge of power she had enjoyed had vanished. Dozens of Immortals were racing toward her. The humans who had witnessed the killings had been dealt with by the high-powered Initiates working the room, their memories of the bloodshed edited as they were ushered out of the casino.

Angel stood before the bodies of Alyana Du Prey, Christian De Santo, Allen Henkle, and the Advocate, Rose. She had no idea what had just happened. It now occurred to her that it would be the absolute shits to be killed by the horde of Immortals in the casino without ever learning why she had been able to kill a woman who had been infinitely more powerful than her.

Suddenly, the crowd of Immortals parted, and a man she had never expected to see came into view.

"Yew know what I hate?" Devin Tyler asked. "I fuckin' hate duplicitous, two-timin' assholes, thet's what!"

"You helped me," Angel said, thoroughly shocked. She wasn't exactly certain how Tyler had aided her, but she knew that she owed her existence to this man.

"Yeah, well, don't get all fuckin' weepy on me over it. The truth is, I'm really not such a bad guy, once you get to know me. . . ."

The shattered minds of Clint and Jeremy Tyler opened to Dani, who had been the creator of their current, hellish state. She drew out their fear, and with it, their *power.* But it was too late. Quest was inside her, about to deliver the killing blow. Dani was unaware that in the physical world, she was already screaming in agony.

Quest suddenly stopped, as if something had distracted him. Dani had no idea that the black Immortal had been forced to call James into his service to stop Samantha Walthers from firing on him. He had reasoned that the human knew enough about their kind to empty the weapon into his head, which might have either killed him, or sent him so deeply into shock that Dani would have destroyed him on their psychic battlefield.

Dani didn't know that James Yuwai was about to tear Sam's head from her shoulders. She had a killing blow of her own to deliver. Drawing out a measure of the Tylers' life essences, Dani redoubled her attack on Quest. The vampire's mind burst into flames under her concentrated assault. She tore his soul from his body, then extinguished it before she could give in to the temptation of consuming his essence, and making him a part of her forever. Moments earlier, she had taken Adrien Cassir's life, but she had not eaten his soul either. Perhaps, she would later reason, that had contributed to her ability to remain, in her heart, the child Samantha Walthers had raised and risked her life to protect.

Dani's vision cleared, and she saw James Yuwai's talon rip across her mother's throat. The Immortal's hand had already torn a gash in Sam's flesh when James suddenly pulled back, saving the woman's life. Dani was about to lash out with her power to force James away from Sam, but he turned to her, his face set in unimaginable grief, tears of blood streaming down his face.

Sam's hand went to her throat and she fell back, gasping. Dani ran to her, moving past James. The Immortal whose soul had mingled with hers raised his hands nervously, allowing them to lightly brush Dani's back. The gesture—one he had learned from her—was entirely human.

Dani dragged Peter Red Cloud's body from Sam, then took her mother in an embrace. Sam held her daughter, then Dani pulled back and said, "He's alive."

Turning their attentions to Peter, they saw that he had not shot himself after all. But his breathing was shallow, and his consciousness had plummeted into the deepest recesses of his mind.

"An Azrael Block," James said. "They must have put an Azrael Block into his head so he would fulfill his mission and shoot Sam at the first chance he had. He either followed his programming or he died."

Dani nodded, and finally saw the depression in the ground where Peter's bullet had struck. His love for Samantha Walthers had been so all-encompassing that he had been willing to sacrifice himself to save her. The Azrael Block was now eating away at his mind, and would soon destroy his body for his treasonous act.

"Can you do anything?" Sam asked, her concern blazing in her dark eyes.

Dani shuddered and whispered, "I'll try."

She reached out with her power and followed Peter Red Cloud into the hiding place he had found in his own mind.

followers than a number of Proclamatus was involved

Epilogue

"Hell no," Devin Tyler said. "Mary Elise had no idea what I was. She died in childbirth, with the twins. If I had known then how things were gonna turn out, I woulda gladly traded her life for theirs. I mean, you've heard my music, right? There's some real loss in there. I cared about that woman. At least, I cared about her as much as I could, all things considered."

"I understand," Angel said. Love was impossible for *almost* all members of their race. Dani had proved that there were exceptions to even this rule.

They stood together on the balcony of Tyler's suite, looking out at the sunrise.

"Ah, I shoulda worn a fuckin' rubber. Saved us all a lot of fuckin' grief. I mean, shit, the Ancients sure have warmed to you and your girlfriends. They warned me not to go lookin' for revenge. Shit, they could have saved themselves some air in their sorry goddamned lungs. Once I found out how my boys had insulted their betters, I knew there was no hope for them. They wasn't ready for Parliament, never would've been neither. I shoulda seen that. Instead, I was too caught up in the idea that these was my boys, my flesh and blood. Y'know, they were the first and only recorded births of twin males among our kind. Everyone thought it was somethin' special. Now I

409

see it was nothing more than a fuckin' fluke. Shit."

Angel nodded. She thought about what Devin had said. The Ancients had been extremely generous to her and the Walthers women.

Peter had lived.

Sam and James had loaded both Dani and Peter into the van and left the area before the police and other Immortals had arrived. James had used his power to blanket the perceptions of the crowd, blurring their memories of the night's events. As they rode off, Dani had unraveled the complicated web of commands the Tylers had placed in Peter's mind and saved the man's life. Had Dani killed the Tylers in the first place, the compulsion in Peter's head would have died with them.

The van was stopped by an army of vampires on the edge of the city. The small group had prepared to play out the final scene of *Butch Cassidy and the Sundance Kid,* but the Ancients knew what was happening by then and Caiphus himself had gone to them and made them believe that they had nothing to fear.

Before Angel had said her final farewell to Sam and Dani, she had given the young, golden-eyed Immortal a gift: Angel had taken Alyana's soul and her *secrets.* Alyana had kept many startling facts to herself. The key to the woman's entire existence had been her ability to play Machiavellian games and to keep certain matters extremely private. Alyana was older than Christian De Santo. She was older than any Immortal, save the Ancients.

Alyana Du Prey had been the daughter of Seratus, one of the three ruling Ancients. Antonius, the first of the vampires and Seratus's father, had wanted Alyana destroyed. Instead, Seratus had slain his father to protect Alyana. But it was not in the best interests of the Ancients to reveal that a female of practically equal power existed, and so they had allowed Alyana

410

to live and to prosper throughout the ages, provided she did not reveal her connection to them.

The dark woman became involved with the Parliament out of her growing dissatisfaction with the manner in which women were perceived by the Immortals. She wanted to enact a change within the vampire society, and to do that, she would have to begin to integrate females into the Parliament. Isabella, her adopted daughter, would have been the first. But Dani had been forced to kill Isabella. At first, Alyana had chosen to forgive Dani her trespasses and allow Dani, Sam, and the infant, Michael, to escape. For six months, however, she thought about her actions, and decided that she had made a mistake. Dani would be suitable for Parliament, if she could only free herself of her human ties. Even more importantly, Michael, Sam's son, could be raised by Alyana to be the perfect tool to help the dark woman in her plans. Her father and uncles told Alyana that she would have to perform the task of rearing Michael with a male Immortal. Once, she would have seriously considered Christian De Santo, but he had been losing touch with reality. They had a lucrative business together. Alyana could not risk losing all she had worked to achieve because of De Santo's suicidal tendencies.

Christian had surprised her when he came to her with talk of his imminent self-immolation. She was not ready for his demise. To temporarily placate him, she offered De Santo the chance to be Michael's surrogate father. Then she went to Allen Henkle and offered him the chance to merge his business with hers, and acquire half of De Santo's assets. All he would have to do was help her to kill De Santo.

The story would have been that Christian had gone insane. He had planned to kill himself and take as many of the Ancients with him as he could. He loathed his own kind. It seemed perfectly in character

411

for him. Angel would be killed while attempting to help Alyana, Henkle, and Rose stop the assassin. Alyana and Henkle had attempted to manipulate events so that Lily and Dani would occupy the two remaining seats in Parliament. They knew Quest would not prove powerful enough to kill Dani, and Angel was too volatile to be trusted.

Days earlier, Alyana had also gone into Angel's mind and placed the Immortal under a compulsion. She had forced Angel to manipulate events in the bar in Albuquerque so that it would appear to both Dani and Angel that the golden-eyed Immortal had indeed engineered "Tabitha's" gang rape. When Alyana later turned Dani, the dark woman had planted the second, false set of memories concerning Elizabeth Altsoba.

Dani had not harmed Elizabeth. She had granted the dying woman her final wish and had delivered a great mercy upon her.

The Ancients had been grateful to Dani for disposing of Alyana and revealing the unmistakable fact that the underground was a lie. The Parliament would need to be closely screened, perhaps even restructured. Murder and war among their own kind was a slap in the face to the ruling Immortals, and they would not allow it to continue.

Angel had saved the most important fact for last: As Dani had been turned by Alyana, she now possessed the blood of the Ancients. Dani was as powerful as any member of Parliament, and like them, she could exist for all time without ever making another kill.

Dani had cried at hearing this. Angel had shook her head, cursed, and gotten the hell out of there before the outpouring of human emotion from Dani became too much for the platinum-haired Immortal.

"So what are yew gonna do now?" Devin asked, snapping Angel from her reverie.

"I don't know."

"The Ancients are willing to give you anything."

"Almost anything," Angel said darkly.

Devin nodded. The Ancients would not pass on their gift to Angel. They had just relieved themselves of the "burden" of one female in the Parliament. It would be a long time before they were willing to accept another.

"Still, there's the holdings left behind by De Santo, Du Prey, and Henkle," Devin said. They are all up for grabs. Your friends wanted no part of them."

Angel nodded. She stared at the sunset for a long time. "Kind of a shame about the underground, isn't it?"

Devin looked at her sharply. "What do you mean?"

"I dunno. But like you said, the whole system is run by two-timing, scheming shits who would do in anyone just to get ahead. You wanted the loyalty only blood brings. You got involved in my fight and killed Rose because you were sick of all the bullshit."

Tyler had explained that De Santo had given himself to death, transforming the energies Alyana and Henkle had loosed against her into a force that Angel could use and turn back upon its creators, just as Henkle had turned her own attack on her earlier.

The singer now shrugged. "Yeah, so?"

"It's just that, sometimes, when an idea comes up and it turns out that no one's actually doing it, then maybe it falls to someone to try and get the ball rolling. I mean, our society might need a little shaking up. At least a return to the old ways would mean putting some honor back in the name of the Immortals. Who knows, maybe there wouldn't be any more of this skulking around and living like fucking *parasites*. Just a thought."

Devin considered it for a moment. "Yeah, yew know what? It *is* kind of a shame about the underground, isn't it?"

Angel grinned. The intense sunlight was captured in her beautiful, sparkling eyes. "Yeah. Isn't it, though?"

Dani stood inside the airport. Her mother carried Michael, whom neither had been willing to allow out of their sight for the past day, since the child had been returned to them. James had not come. He could not exist in the sunlight, and it was too early for Dani to try and impart the blood of the Ancients to him. She was having a difficult enough time adjusting to her new life as an Immortal.

Peter waited near the gates leading to their flight. Boarding had already begun. He was going back with Sam to Los Angeles. Her life was there, and Peter's life was at her side. Dani had been in Peter's mind, and she knew the extent of his love for Sam.

Sam knew it too.

Dani had chosen not to follow Sam, Peter, and Michael. Not yet, anyway. James had no intention of staying at the casino. He would go with Dani, anywhere she wished to go. Her flight was booked for late that evening. A red-eye to Florida.

"You're going through with this?" Sam asked, still slightly uncomfortable in her daughter's presence. That had been Dani's other deciding factor. Though Dani was not the same as the other Immortals, she had, to a degree, renounced her humanity, and she could sense that everything would now be different between her and her mother. It would be best for them to spend some time apart.

"It was something Angel mentioned. She said that I have the ability to do things other Immortals spend decades learning. For me it comes without thinking. That means I have some pretty powerful blood in me. I'd like to know where it came from."

Sam nodded, recalling the first moment she had

414

seen Dani, abandoned in a garbage dumpster in Tampa, twenty years ago.

Dani noticed that Peter was motioning. The last passengers were boarding. She held her mother and whispered, "I don't know who my father was, but I can say that this: I love you, Mom. I always will. I'm just tired of having this question hanging over me."

"I've thought about it too," Sam said, starting to cry. "Just, for God's sake, be careful. And if you need me, call."

"I will." Dani was crying too. Her tears were clear, *human* tears, despite her condition. She nodded in Peter's direction. "Don't let him give you any bullshit about how he lost the middle finger. He was mowing the lawn one time and had an accident. That's it."

Sam laughed, despite herself. "I love you, sweetie."

"I love you too, Mom."

Kissing her daughter one last time, Sam broke from Dani and rushed to the gates. Peter waved, and in seconds, both of them disappeared down the hallway leading to the plane.

Dani stood at the window, reveling in the incredible warmth of the sun, and waited until her mother's plane had departed before she turned and walked away.

**HAUTALA'S HORROR—HOLD ON
TO YOUR HEAD!**

MOONDEATH   (1844-4, $3.95/$4.95)
Cooper Falls is a small, quiet New Hampshire town, the
kind you'd miss if you blinked an eye. But when darkness
falls and the full moon rises, an uneasy feeling filters
through the air; an unnerving foreboding that causes the
skin to prickle and the body to tense.

NIGHT STONE   (3030-4, $4.50/$5.50)
Their new house was a place of darkness and shadows, but
with her secret doll, Beth was no longer afraid. For as she
stared into the eyes of the wooden doll, she heard it call to
her and felt the force of its evil power. And she knew it
would tell her what she had to do.

MOON WALKER   (2598-X, $4.50/$5.50)
No one in Dyer, Maine ever questioned the strange disap-
pearances that plagued their town. And they never discussed the eerie figures seen harvesting the potato fields by
day . . . the slow, lumbering hulks with expressionless features and a blood-chilling deadness behind their eyes.

LITTLE BROTHERS   (2276-X, $3.95/$4.95)
It has been five years since Kip saw his mother horribly
murdered by a blur of "little brown things." But the "little
brothers" are about to emerge once again from their underground lair. Only this time there will be no escape for the
young boy who witnessed their last feast!

*Available wherever paperbacks are sold, or order direct from the
Publisher. Send cover price plus 50¢ per copy for mailing and
handling to Zebra Books, Dept. 3995, 475 Park Avenue South,
New York, N.Y. 10016. Residents of New York and Tennessee
must include sales tax. DO NOT SEND CASH. For a free Zebra/
Pinnacle catalog please write to the above address.*